Tongue Tied

A novel dedicated to my mother Katie,

and my father Will,

who is seated at the right

of the cover photo.

He poses with four of his five siblings.

Sadly, all those mentioned here

have passed away.

Tongue Tied

PETER GRIFFITHS

dinas

First impression: 2009
Fourth impression: 2010

Cover design: Y Lolfa

ISBN: 9781847710970

Printed on acid-free and partly recycled paper
and published and bound in Wales by
Y Lolfa Cyf., Talybont, Ceredigion SY24 5HE
e-mail ylolfa@ylolfa.com
website www.ylolfa.com
tel 01970 832 304
fax 832 782

Thanks to:

Anna, Andrew and Kim, who, whether they knew it not, encouraged… and crucially.

Marilyn, who not only encouraged but also indispensably assisted, with diligence and without demur, throughout the writing of this book.

Several friends, who read the first proof, and who on the whole responded with more enthusiasm than I could have hoped.

Thanks to Elin Lewis who edited with rigour, but with respect and generosity as well.

And Yvonne, who gave no less than love.

A diolch o galon hefyd i Lefi o'r Lolfa.

1   Capel Celyn   6   Borth y Gest

2   Arenig Fawr   7   Mynydd Sylen

3   Berwyn   8   Cynheidre

4   Tonypandy   9   Gower

5   Llwynypia   10   Liverpool

Author's notes

This book was written to entertain, naturally, but also to glorify Wales, its people and its language, Welsh.

All characters in the novel are fictional, and though most scenes are set in real places, most of them too have been fictionalised to some degree.

Much of the story is set in a valley which is now largely under water. Most of its inhabitants were displaced to accommodate a reservoir which was officially opened in 1965. 35 out of 36 Welsh Members of Parliament voted against the project (the other did not vote), but to no avail. Their ineffectiveness in this matter gave fresh impetus to Welsh devolution.

The red dragon, which pervades the book, is probably Wales' most recognisable symbol, and is featured on the Welsh flag.

The word 'bach' appears frequently in the book. The Welsh word means 'little' but is used as a term of affection. 'Peter bach' means 'dear Peter'. When applied to a female, however, the word mutates and gives rise to 'Enid fach' for example.

On the next page you'll find two family trees in embryo. I encourage you to develop them as you read *Tounge Tied*.

Also, at the back there is a pronounciation aid.

Below, you'll find two family trees in embryo.
I encourage you to develop them as you read *Tounge Tied*.

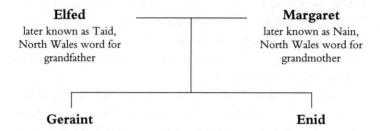

Elfed
later known as Taid,
North Wales word for
grandfather
——————————
Margaret
later known as Nain,
North Wales word for
grandmother

Geraint

Enid

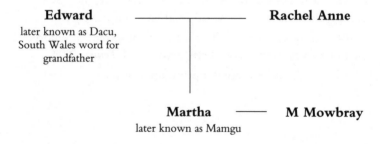

Edward
later known as Dacu,
South Wales word for
grandfather
——————————
Rachel Anne

Martha —— **M Mowbray**
later known as Mamgu

One

IT WAS AN exquisitely beautiful evening in late May, and normally he would have been very excited. Normally, the anticipation of the meeting would have consumed him, but not so this evening, for he was nervous about the decision that he had taken and troubled by the effect it would have on his friend. He was following a trail alongside the Afon Celyn as it bobbed busily down towards Capel Celyn, a little hamlet that was named after both the river and the Calvinistic Methodist chapel that sustained the community in almost every way. He lived in a cottage, a little way upriver, with his parents and younger sister, who was now jumping up and down as she waved at him one last time before he disappeared over a brow. As he always did at this spot, he turned to acknowledge her. Normally, his wave would have been warm and enthusiastic, but this evening it lacked conviction, and he wondered if she'd noticed. The sun was still quite high in a sky that was virtually cloudless as he left the river and then crossed it on an unassuming bridge, which ferried the rough road from Bala to Ffestiniog and which locally linked the hamlet to the chapel up a little hill. He entered the chapel and was cheered by the evening light dancing on what seemed like a sea of rich, highly polished wood, but only to be saddened again as he was reminded of his fondness for this place. He glanced briefly at the notices for the month of May 1876 before slumping on the rearmost pew. Ordinarily, he would have meditated with ease, shifting his mind to a higher, purer plane, but this evening material matters held the upper hand. There was a clock above the pulpit, which he checked and checked again, and when it neared five to seven, he rose surprisingly briskly and left, and then rejoined the river trail below the bridge.

He walked purposefully now. Not many were seen to walk this trail; there would not have been a trail at all, the locals joked, were it not for phantoms fishing, invariably at night. In less than half a mile, the Afon Celyn would merge with another, the Tryweryn, so the valley here was wide. On the valley's other side towered Arenig Fawr. Its summit wasn't visible from where he strode, but the shoulder that faced him was impressive all the same. It pleased him that the trail was unusually firm and forgiving: the confluence was often extremely marshy, but this year an unusually dry spring had taken care of that.

Rounding a tract of hazel trees, he suddenly saw his friend, crouching and gazing into the Tryweryn just above the confluence. How brilliant, he thought, that they always got it right. Normally, this would have triggered an infusion of warmth and well-being, but this evening guilt got in the way. He feared his friend would be floored by his news. Still, he was determined to put a good face on things, and so when they acknowledged each other across the rivers, his warmth appeared to match his friend's. Without a word, both took off their boots and socks, rolled up their trousers and stepped into a river, he to the Celyn and his friend the Tryweryn. With their boots and socks in their left hands, they stepped slowly and silently towards the confluence, where eventually they met. There, they shook hands firmly, looked each other in the eye and stepped out of the river together on the far side. They then donned their socks and boots, and after one glance at each other, walked vigorously up an embankment in the direction of Arenig Fawr. All this they did without a word.

All this they had done, without a word, many times before. Three years earlier, they had determined on this ritual to regularly reaffirm their friendship, and hadn't spoken of it to anyone since. Grown-ups had rituals so why shouldn't they, they'd reasoned. Naturally self-conscious at first, by now they really didn't care who saw them in the rivers. They were firm friends with fine imaginations… that's all. One lived up the Afon Celyn and the other up the Tryweryn, and five times a year they would meet, in a repeat of what their rivers did every minute of every day. All farmers had access to an almanac, so for their meetings each year, they had agreed on five successive full moons, with the first in the month of May. On this arrangement they had agreed, come rain or shine. After their ritual in the rivers, they would scramble to the summit of Arenig Fawr, aiming to be there half an hour before sunset. Once again their almanacs came in handy, for with the sunset thus determined and the time of ascent fixed by experience, the moment of rendezvous in the rivers could be calculated by each independently. As for the times of departure from their homes, the friend from Tryweryn could put his faith in the family clock, but alas, nothing tick-tocked in the home of the one from Celyn. So on these special occasions he always left home in plenty of time and synchronised in the chapel. Remarkably, neither had ever missed a moon nor a moment of river rendezvous.

So, for the sixteenth time together in this way, they scrambled up the embankment, crossed the railway line and hiked energetically for twenty minutes more before dropping down to a lake at the foot of a sheer face. Here they stopped, and as their breathing quietened, they seemed to ponder on the secrets of this lake in shadow. Over the last three years, their affirmations of affection and respect had gradually gained a sweet, spiritual side. This evening, however, one of the two would have felt a good deal more spiritual had he there and then revealed what was on his mind.

Off they went again, fast paced, around the lake and up a ridge towards the shoulder way above. As the ridge flattened out, they emerged from the shadow of the shoulder into the evening sunlight and cast long, lagging shadows of their own. Here they took a detour off the direct route to the summit and aimed for the shoulder where they soon stood, side by side, simply gazing.

In appearance, they were worlds apart. Elfed Evans of Tryweryn was short, stocky, chubby-faced, dark-haired and brown-eyed, while Edward Jones of Celyn, in complete contrast, was much taller, generally lean, fair, with eyes of blue. What particularly set the two apart, was Edward Jones's very light ginger freckles. 'Twas they that caught the eye, and when Edward was ill at ease, they darkened and appeared slightly raised, as they did then, tinging his gentle countenance with mystery. So in appearance, worlds apart, yet in outlook, like two peas in a pod; like two nineteen year-old sons of two farmers working two unyielding valleys just above their confluence; like two spirited members of the same Methodist chapel, inculcated with identical value systems and brought up in the same somewhat narrow, but nevertheless rich, culture. The chapel was the centre of their universe, serving not only as a moral compass but as a school, a cultural catalyst and a community centre. Of its effectiveness in these material terms there was no doubt, but spiritually it had somehow missed the mark with these two. In this ritualistic celebration of their mutual affection was their spirituality lit. How could it fail? Already warmed with generous feelings and elated by physical exertion, they were now treated to a touching, aerial vista of their valleys; all this on an exquisitely beautiful evening. How could it fail, indeed, but this time fail it did with one of them. Edward Jones's freckles remained slightly raised.

Still without a word, off they went again, fast paced as before, and this time for the summit. The ridge they hiked afforded unfettered views to the north and west, where Snowdonia unfolded, as the sun sunk in the sky and reddened slightly. When they reached the top, they shook hands as they always did, a gesture that released them from their silence. For an hour and a half, Edward Jones had restrained himself, but now that his moment had arrived, he didn't know how to begin. Untypically anxious, he flirted with the idea of changing his mind, till the facts regrouped to scotch it. In an attempt to compose himself, he went through the motions of surveying the panorama from the top. Arenig Fawr is relatively isolated, set apart from most other peaks, so its vistas of north Wales are vast. Normally, he would have taken pride in them, but this evening they merely passed him by. He settled on a familiar flat rock and, to his discomfort, was soon joined enthusiastically by his friend. There they sat, next to each other, with their knees to their chins, gazing westward, and as the sun got bigger and redder, Edward Jones felt smaller and smaller. Out of the blue, he started with a stutter.

"Elfed, I... I can't... heck, Elfed, I can't believe I'm up here telling you this," and he stopped and took a very deep breath. He spoke in Welsh: neither could speak English very well.

"A couple of days ago, Watkin Wyn really got to me."

He glanced nervously at his friend whose expression already reflected concern and confusion.

"You... you know Dad has worked on his farm for thirty years, and fair play, Watkin's been pretty good to him overall, but he's never treated me right," with an emphasis on the word 'me', "He's always pushed me to the limit, right from the very start."

Edward Jones's father had been a farmhand all his working life, and so had Edward. He'd had no choice. In a crunch, they had no recourse but to kowtow to Watkin Wyn, their employer. Elfed on the other hand, was a tenant farmer's son. True, the land was owned by the local squire, but at least the tenant ran his own concern and was accountable to no one but himself, as long as the rent was paid... and he voted for his landlord at election time!

"Anyway, the day before yesterday, he really went too far. I refused to do some silly thing, and he started swearing at me. I still didn't pay any attention, so what d'you think? The buffoon started running towards me waving his arms. Goodness knows what would have happened if Dad hadn't stepped in. As it was, I didn't lay a finger on the fool, but he knew all right I would have if… "

"Get to the point, Edward. Just tell me what's on your mind, will you, and get it over and done with."

So sharp an interruption from a normally tolerant Elfed really shook Edward; in fact, it shook him out of his mild funk. He realised that he'd been uncharacteristically unforthright with his friend, and now revitalised, he turned exaggeratedly to make amends.

"Elfed, I'm sorry I'm beating about the bush, but this isn't easy for me, you know. Look, the thing is, Watkin Wyn will be looking for the slightest excuse to get rid of me now, so I won't have work for long, believe me… and what do I do then? Your father will always take care of you, but I've got to take care of myself."

Elfed frowned and nodded. It was a good sign and Edward took heart.

"You know, don't you Elfed, that Wyn Williams was home for a week recently. I knew him quite well, you know, before he went off to the South a couple of years ago. Well, when we met the other day, he went out of his way to try and persuade me to go back to the Rhondda with him."

Elfed's already dark complexion darkened further. The Rhondda in south-east Wales was synonymous with the massive population shift within Wales that was transforming the counties of Glamorgan and Monmouthshire from relatively underdeveloped regions into one of the world's greatest industrial sites. First, iron was king, and then it was coal, whose tell-tale tailings took their toll. Eventually, immigration into the region became dominated by the English. While Welshness largely succeeded in assimilating them, the Welsh language did not, and as a result, English-only speakers proliferated. In any case, in Elfed's mind, the mere mention of the Rhondda had meant that his friend need say no more, but Edward desperately sought to justify himself.

"Honestly, I didn't give it a second thought until this business with Watkin Wyn, but Elfed, I've decided I've just got to do it. There's no other way out, Elfed. I've got no option but to go to south Wales."

Elfed stared westward, lips tight, brow furrowed, head nodding feebly as the worst of his fears were confirmed. Edward gazed at his friend with alternating expressions, offering friendship and begging forgiveness. At the same time, the sun grazed the distant Rhinogau on its way into the sea. As the light softened, Elfed remained sullen but Edward came to life. During the two and a half minutes it took the sun to set, a lot was said.

"Elfed! Why don't you come with me? What's to keep you here? You know your older brother will end up with the farm. Wyn Williams said that he makes four times as much money down there as he ever made here, and he said the place is bubbling... all kinds of different things to do."

Elfed shook his head firmly.

"You know I can't, Edward. I can't let my Dad down like that. Anyway, wouldn't you miss your way of life here? And what about Welsh? You can't speak English very well, so how would you get along?"

Edward had all the answers to all the questions but for one that had not as yet occurred to Elfed.

"Everything would be just the same down there, Elfed. It's still Wales, you know; just another part, that's all. Most people still speak Welsh in the Rhondda, and they go to chapel and do all the things we do here. The difference is there's work down there, Elfed, and people get paid for it... not like here."

In the light from a sliver of unset sun, Elfed's dark complexion betrayed a mild interest, but he soon returned to his former stance.

"No, Edward, I couldn't let my father down," but Edward knew what really gnawed at Elfed's mind. Normally Edward would have pressed the issue because their friendship would have demanded it, but this evening he thought better of reruffling feathers. He changed the subject.

"Elfed," he began cautiously, "The sun has just gone down and I'd like us to carry on with our ritual as if nothing has happened. I know you're not happy but would you do that for me?"

Elfed, dejected, reluctantly agreed and would have shuffled off the summit had the moon not caught his eye.

"Look, Edward, look at that! Isn't she breathtaking?"

At a stroke, it seemed Elfed was transformed. "And d'you know, we've never had such a perfect day for this since we started, have we? Suddenly, I have this very strange feeling, Edward, that something important is happening."

Edward's emotions were at sixes and sevens; he'd steeled himself for everything bar a rollercoaster ride. Meanwhile, Arenig Fawr remained unmoved; or did she? Certainly, the dramatically moving atmosphere at her summit belied the obvious, and anyway, how could she be without feelings when she'd inspired so many for millennia?

Elfed continued.

"I think we're being blessed at this very moment, Edward. In fact, I'm sure of it. What that means to me is that whatever you, or I for that matter, decide to do, it'll be for the best. Just look at the moon, Edward."

She was rising majestically from behind the Berwyn, still only half a moon, but obviously destined to be full. As she rose, her cold, clear light lent the sun's red residual glow a mystique that, Edward had to admit, seemed to give credence to Elfed's grand assertions. At that moving moment, there certainly was no question but that their ritual should go on. After all, they had always agreed that the jog to the bottom was the best part. So they trotted off the summit in their inappropriate boots, revelling in this place called home, in harmony with their roots. Sure-footed and confident of their mountain, they loped and leapt their way down Arenig Fawr towards the confluence. Edward, unable to shake the feeling that he had betrayed Elfed, sought a gesture that would underline his affection for his friend, and just below the shoulder, hit on one. Later, as they stood in the confluence shaking hands, Edward could hardly wait.

"Elfed, you'll be at the fair tomorrow, won't you? Your Dad has some business to do there, I'm sure."

"Yes, I'm pretty sure I'll be there. Why?"

"I'd like us to do something special, so bring some money with you, OK?"

"All right, Edward, and by the way, you shouldn't feel badly about what you've decided to do. Obviously, I wish you weren't leaving, but I know we were blessed up there. You may think I'm being foolish, but I know… everything… will be… all right! All right?"

"Thanks, Elfed," from Edward, nodding his head very slowly and very gratefully.

With boots and socks in hand, they each backed a bit up their respective rivers: Edward, the man of action, up the Celyn, and Elfed, the man with depth of feeling, up the Tryweryn. Then, out they hopped, donned their socks and boots, and walked to their homes, instinctively aware of every tump and turn. Aware too, of the moon, and by now Venus brightly mirroring her in the western sky; still unaware, however, of the question that Elfed had never thought to ask.

Two

A T THE BALA fair, bills were paid and bulls displayed and business mixed with pleasure. It was a big event. Much of the dealing took place in the open air, and what cover there was consisted mainly of open-sided structures. There were a few enclosed tents and of these, two stood out: a blue one where fortunes were told, and a red one, which Edward and Elfed now approached. They had expected the red tent to be popular, so they were surprised that there was no queue. What's more, the red flap was up, which they had been told meant that Madam was ready for her next customer. They had also been told that Madam was something special, and she did not disappoint them. Madam was an Amazon dressed in nothing, as far as they could tell, but a long, tailored leather coat. It was sleeveless, and on both her biceps Tarzans were tattooed. They swung on vines, which the boys could tell were connected across Madam's ample chest. No, they weren't disappointed at all!

"Sorry boys. I can only take you one at a time. I may be good, but not that good. Sorry, but one of you has to leave."

Edward shrugged his shoulders and grimaced.

"Oh! I see. You don't understand English very well," and she repeated herself in broken Welsh. A Welsh-speaking piece of work seemed incongruous, and amused the boys highly. Edward, repressing his chuckles, managed a reply.

"But we want you to do exactly the same thing to both of us, and we'd both like to be here to make sure you do it right. D'you see?" and from his trouser pocket he pulled a card and showed it to her.

"Mmmm. That's interesting. You boys must be really big

mates, yes? I think I can do that. All right! Pull that flap down behind you, will you, and tie it up. Let's get on with it then, but first my fee... hee, hee, heeee! Come over here, freckles!"

They handed over the cash and weren't at all surprised where she put it.

Later, when the flap went up and they emerged from the red tent, there was a short queue outside. It seemed that they had timed it just right. They appeared quite pleased with themselves, and hadn't gone far before Edward turned to his friend excitedly and blurted out, "Elfed, I've just got to see it one more time before I leave."

Elfed shook his head and smiled as if to say, "I don't know," while unbuttoning his shirt, slipping it off his left arm and revealing a petite, bright red Welsh dragon, tattooed just above his shoulder blade. So, out of sadness had sprung a joyful act of camaraderie, consecrated by the pre-eminent symbol of Welshness; an innocent and brotherly contract with consequences they couldn't possibly have anticipated.

"Does it look just like the picture, Edward?"

"It's perfect. She did a really good job. Who'd have thought by looking at her?"

While his friend rebuttoned his shirt, Edward continued.

"I'm glad we did it, Elfed... aren't you?"

"Yes, yes... I am. Of course, to make it really meaningful, we should each promise to persuade one of our sons to do the same. Then, the connection might go on forever."

Elfed beamed, while Edward shook his head in wonder and admiration, slapping his friend playfully on the shoulder.

"You always see into things much more deeply than me; a daughter won't do?" with a grin.

"You can disfigure your daughter if you like, but I'm not going to!"

Serious once again, Edward fixed his friend with a gaze, shook his hand and said, "I promise; do you?"

Elfed nodded slowly, clearly enjoying Edward's approval. As they embraced, rather awkwardly, not too far from the tent where they'd been twinned by tattoos of dragons in red, Edward said slowly, "I'm going to miss you Elfed, I really am.

Then, as they walked side by side a few moments later, he continued, "There's Dad. I better go, I suppose. I... I hope I'll see you again, Elfed."

Edward's tone was full of sadness and guilt; in contrast, his friend seemed to be taking their parting in his stride. Perhaps Elfed's equanimity could be attributed to his conviction that they were both blessed on the summit of Arenig Fawr last evening. Still, it was surprising.

Suddenly, "Are you absolutely certain you don't want to come with me, Elfed?"

"Oh! Let's not go over that again. When are you leaving, by the way?"

"Tomorrow! I told you that."

"I know it's tomorrow, but what time?"

"Oh! Well, I thought the earlier the better. I'm less likely to be found out that way, aren't I? There's a train from here at half past six in the morning. I suppose I better leave home at four to make sure I catch it."

"So, have you bought your ticket already?"

"Heck, no. That would give the game away, wouldn't it? There's Dad waving. I better go. D'you think we'll ever see each other again, Elfed?"

Perhaps Edward hadn't expected an answer, for with little delay, he turned away towards his father. Had he lingered a little longer, he might have heard Elfed whisper, "It certainly looks like it... at the moment, anyway."

Three

WELL BEFORE DAWN the following morning, Edward followed the trail that led from his home to the hamlet of Capel Celyn. Despite the moonlight, he walked with the same uncertainty that surprisingly stalked his mind. Unusually reflective, he worried that this may not be such a good idea after all. He felt his roots entangle his body, while his heritage raced through his head. Even the brook… his brook… reminded him at every step of what he'd loved, and now would leave behind. If only Elfed was coming with him. No, no! He knew deep down that would only have made matters worse. Elfed had more to lose than he, was much closer to his family, and was sensitive to boot. It was hard enough dealing with his own misgivings let alone his friend's as well. No, as much as he liked him, he felt sure that Elfed would have been a liability.

These were his thoughts as he approached the bridge, which explains why all he could say when Elfed barred his way, was "Well! What a surprise!"

Elfed was very close to his mother, as close to her as he was to Edward. When, on Arenig Fawr, Elfed had dismissed Edward's invitation to accompany him to south Wales because of his duty to his father, Edward and Elfed both knew what really gnawed Elfed's mind. They both knew it was Elfed's extraordinarily close relationship with his mother.

Elfed's mother, or Mam as he called her, was in her late forties and had suffered for years from rheumatoid arthritis. She could still take care of herself, but was becoming increasingly immobile. Her illness was referred to in hushed tones as a progressive disease, and everyone knew what that meant. Elfed gave her attention and affection, and as she grew less mobile, so his role grew. Elfed's presence gave his Mam much joy; to her it was the icing on the cake. She had always been an optimistic person and confident of her faith, so that her outlook on life during her illness was positive; Elfed had found her attitude towards her progressive disease inspirational, and his admiration of her had grown in reflection of this. She was, too, a wise woman whose good judgement was only occasionally marred by a strong will. Elfed looked up to her, and also looked to her for daily advice. Ironically, he was more emotionally dependent on her than she on him.

Despite Elfed's closeness to Edward, it would have been no surprise then, had the idea of running away to south Wales with his friend been brushed aside; and so it would have been, but for his revelation of sorts on the summit of Arenig Fawr. The magic of that moment on their mountain had moved Elfed immeasurably. Inexplicably, he'd become convinced that whatever their decision regarding south Wales, all would be well. This had given him the confidence to consider an offer that his dependency on his mother would have otherwise forced him to dismiss. However, with confidence came uncertainty: on the one hand, his mother, on the other, his friend. It was a toss-up, pure and simple. Yet, in his uncertainty he remained calm, for he knew... he was convinced... that whichever way he tipped, it would turn out equally well.

Such was Elfed's frame of mind as he, with rucksack in hand, awaited his friend at the bridge on the moonlit night that followed their act of bonding at the Bala fair. It appeared that Edward was the victor in Elfed's tug of war. Really, he'd won by default, for Elfed's mother had not been given the chance to state her case. Since that moment on the mountain, Elfed had managed in the main to avoid his mother, and in particular evade those knowing glances from her glowing eyes.

As the question had not been aired fully in his mind, he was uncharacteristically drifting into a decision. As a result, he still felt uncertainty, which he reassured himself would surely be swept away by Edward's arrival.

Far from it! When they met, all Edward could say was, "Well! What a surprise!" Nothing as reassuring as "How wonderful! I couldn't have asked for more," or "I'm so happy you've changed your mind." Nothing like that at all; just a cool, unenthusiastic "Well! What a surprise!" Elfed's face fell so hard that even in mere moonlight, Edward noticed.

"I thought you'd be really excited to see me, but you don't seem to care at all."

Such disappointment in one soon led to shame in the other. Edward though, was a man of action; feeling foolish was not his forte. He grasped Elfed by the arms, and set about to make amends.

"Elfed, you know I'm glad to see you. You know how hard I've tried to persuade you to come with me. Mind you, I never thought you would, but I couldn't be happier that you've changed your mind."

That was better. Edward was beginning to strike the perfect chords.

"You gave me a shock, Elfed... that's all. I was so deep in thought that I almost walked right into you."

"So, what was on your mind?"

Edward caught himself just in time. Rather than reveal his misgivings, he concocted imaginary concerns relating to how little money he had, how few clothes he carried, and so forth. Ironically, by now his previous uncertainty had been quelled, banished by the task of reassuring Elfed and the excitement he truly felt at the thought of them emigrating together.

"As you can imagine," from Elfed, much mollified, "I'm feeling quite anxious."

"But you've told me that you're convinced that everything will be all right."

"I know, I know, but still… "

A few more friendly squeezes of the arm from Edward and they parted company with the brook, unafraid of the future. Elfed's emotions weren't given a completely free ride, however. Each familiar landmark they passed that moonlit night cast a shadow in their path. Their symbolism, which was given short shrift by Edward's cheerleading, did not go completely unnoticed by Elfed. Fortunately, dawn soon broke, the shadows turned to grey and gradually went away. Consequently, they were both in good sprits when they arrived in Bala at six on a clear May morning. Loitering in the station would have attracted attention, so rather than raise questions sooner than was necessary, they walked the length of the High Street and back as nonchalantly as one could at six in the morning.

At twenty past six they entered the station. The train was full of energy, watering at the trough, spitting out its stabs of steam, getting ready to be off. They approached the ticket window. Unfortunately, the stationmaster was also the ticketmaster that morning, and he knew everyone within ten miles of Bala, including Edward and Elfed.

"Well, well. Where are you boys off to?" in Welsh of course.

Edward was ready with his story, although he had hoped not to have had to deal with Peter Parry.

"Good morning, Mr Parry. Two singles to Tonypandy, please."

"So are you boys going to tell me what this is all about, then?"

"You know Wyn Williams, don't you, Mr Parry? Well, we're just going down to have a bit of fun with him for a few

24

days, that's all," and to prove the point, he effortlessly raised his little case as if it were filled with straw.

Edward knew quite well that Peter Parry hadn't believed a word of it, but he had to say something, and in any case, they'd be on the train in a few minutes.

"Shouldn't you boys be buying returns, then, if you're coming back in a few days?"

Elfed didn't say a word, because Edward had spent the last couple of days thinking these very things through.

"Well, you see Mr Parry, we don't have enough money to buy returns, but Wyn Williams told us that if we went down to see him, he'd give us the money for the trip back. Mr Parry, don't you think we should hurry up? The train is leaving in a few minutes, isn't it?"

Peter Parry smiled condescendingly, because he knew better.

"No, there's no rush at all, boys. The train has a minor mechanical problem, and Goronwy is working on it as we speak. It's nothing serious, so I wouldn't be surprised if she's out of here by quarter to seven."

A delay of only a quarter of an hour, but, to Elfed, it loomed like a lifetime. At the mere thought of delay, even a perfectly routine one, all the uncertainties that had beset him earlier in the night rushed to the surface again, and this time with a little less of the calm. In contrast, Edward and Peter Parry comfortably continued their charade.

"So if we leave at quarter to seven, Mr Parry, will we arrive in Tonypandy at the same time?"

"Oh, yes. You won't miss your connection. You'll be in Tonypandy on time, don't worry. Tonypandy! Yes, it has a lovely ring to it, doesn't it? Still, I'm really glad you boys aren't thinking of moving there," and quite innocently, it seemed, he answered the question that Elfed had never thought to ask,

"Because, as you probably know, the working conditions in those mines down there are terrible. Just terrible! From what I hear, that's the only word for them."

Edward was taken aback a bit, but outwardly didn't flinch an inch. Elfed though, already uncomfortable due to the delay, did a double take. The conditions are terrible? He'd never thought of that, but now that Peter Parry had mentioned it, why wouldn't they be? Half a mile or more underground in all that filth, how could one have thought otherwise? He tried hard to convince himself that it didn't matter, but he could not lay the dust nor the depth nor the darkness to rest. Yet, he'd made his commitment to Edward. How could he let his friend down now? And hadn't he been convinced that whatever his decision, all would be well? Yes, perhaps, but… working conditions! He felt so foolish that he'd never thought of that. Had Edward he wondered? He decided that Edward must have, otherwise he wouldn't be taking it in his stride.

When Edward returned though from the ticket window with two singles to Tonypandy, his freckles weren't relaxed. Thankfully, Elfed didn't notice: he was too anxious to get the business of working conditions off his chest.

"Are they really that terrible, Edward?"

The simplest of questions at the most awkward of times.

"Oh, don't worry, Elfed. That kind of attitude is typical among people like him around here. They don't like to think that men half their age with a little bit of guts can make four times as much as them and get on in the world as well. I've heard it all before, Elfed. Haven't you?"

He wished he'd had. That would have made it much easier for him to convince himself that Edward wasn't dealing in little white lies. Standing next to his tattooed twin on Platform One at Bala Station, Elfed's conviction that all would be well, regardless, was being put to the test. Edward's eagerness to emigrate ensured against his derailment by a chance remark, but what would insulate Elfed, who'd been uncertain from the start? Baring his soul began to do the trick.

"I don't know, Edward. I must admit that I've got a dose of cold feet. I keep on reminding myself that everything is going to be all right, and my conviction is beginning to come back, but honestly, it's not very easy."

Earlier than expected, the train came puffing to the platform, spitting too much steam, and finality, reality, erased, replaced what till then had been a dream.

"Chin up, Elfed. Listen! I know it's much harder for you, but believe me, it's going to be great. You don't realise how… "

He was interrupted by Peter Parry, whose head and burly shoulders seemed jammed in the ticket window.

"Elfed. Come over here a minute, will you?"

Elfed glanced quizzically at Edward, shrugged his shoulders and with his rucksack tucked under his arm, ran urgently to the ticket office. Clearly, he'd thought there was no time to waste. He'd thought wrong.

"What's the matter, Mr Parry? Why did you call me over here like… Crikey Moses! What are you doing here, Dad?"

Standing next to Peter Parry in the office, and facing Elfed through the ticket window was his father. Elfed was flabbergasted, taken completely by surprise. Millions of charged particles in his brain scattered in all directions, befuddled by hopelessly mixed signals. Then, something remarkable happened. They quietened, and aligned themselves uniformly. Elfed had realised that he might be off the hook. His dilemma regarding the Rhondda and its terrible working conditions looked as if it had been dehorned by his father. In his huge relief, however, he did not overlook appearances. He had his own face to save, and more importantly, his best friend's sensitivity to consider.

"Elfed, I think this whole thing is a very bad idea. You should change your mind and come home with me now. If you do, Peter Parry has agreed to give you back your money, haven't you Mr Parry?"

While Peter Parry nodded a shade too magnanimously, Elfed replied without hesitation, when perhaps a shade might have lent credibility.

"No, Dad. I can't change my mind now. I've made a commitment to myself and Edward, and I've got to stick to it. I'm sorry, but I've got to go through with this."

Elfed took a deep breath, and waited. He noticed Edward's slightly raised freckles moving along the platform towards him. His father still didn't say a word, but looked at the floor reflectively, nodding his head slowly. Elfed took another deep breath, as he felt the return of the dilemma's horn in his chest. He worried that he'd overdone it, but he needn't have feared, for his father was as worried as he. As Edward arrived at the window, Elfed's father played his trump card.

"Your Mam doesn't think you should go either, Elfed. She's the one who sent me, you know. I haven't seen her cry before, and I never want to see her cry again. It broke my heart, I can tell you."

Elfed was completely off the hook! His ploy had worked! Yet this time, millions of charged particles failed to settle down: Elfed's emotions had been churned by the news of his mother, and would be further by the unrestrained farewell he granted his great friend Edward. Gone were the nagging uncertainties of the last day and a half. Gone were the niggling questions concerning terrible working conditions. Gone for a moment, too, was the guilt he felt over his mother. Elfed's emotions were free to focus on the sadness of a fractured friendship. He was unrestrained, and could not have been more sincere.

The train that took Edward Jones to Tonypandy left Bala ten minutes late. Elfed watched sadly from the platform, and although Edward waved and waved, 'twas his freckles that caught the eye. They were a very light ginger, and when raised, as they now were, they tinged his face in mystery. There was no mystery, however, to the fork that clove their lives, as it would tens of thousands of others.

Four

As Elfed Evans trundled home in his father's horse and cart to their farm in the upper middle reaches of the Afon Tryweryn, relief and sadness were his companions. His father certainly wasn't much of one. He hardly said a word and seemed uncharacteristically awkward. When they arrived home, Elfed found out why. He was shocked to discover that his mother had known nothing of her son's intentions. In fact, she'd had no inkling that her husband had been involved in anything that morning other than his normal chores. She hadn't been upset, nor had she wept. Elfed's father had made the whole thing up. Elfed's anger didn't last long though. His calmness returned and once again he was convinced that whatever the decision he took in response to Edward's determination to leave, it would be for the best; he proved to be right.

It is unlikely that his Mam would have lived for another four years without Elfed's encouragement and affection. Without question, her quality of life during this period was greatly enhanced by his presence, and she took pleasure in showing her gratitude. His generosity towards his Mam, and her regular recognition of it, worked wonders for his self-esteem. As wise as she was, she quietly forced a reversal of roles between them, gradually weaning Elfed away from his former emotional dependence on her. As a result, by the time of his mother's death, Elfed had added to his innate generosity of spirit, wisdom and confidence in his own judgement. His decision to stay at home rather than accompany his friend Edward to south Wales may have been taken partly by default, but no one could deny that he was making the most of it.

Elfed and Edward may or may not have been blessed on the summit of Arenig Fawr, but for Elfed, certainly, blessings ensued, although one of them decidedly mixed. About two years after Edward's departure for south Wales, Elfed's older brother Edgar married Margaret. She was from Capel Celyn and had known Edgar, and Elfed as well, all her life. In accepting Edgar as her husband, she had also implicitly accepted the responsibility of taking care of his Mam, who was becoming less and less capable of taking care of herself. Margaret was level-headed and lovely, and her mother-in-law adored her. So much greater, then, the tragedy for Mam when Edgar was killed by a horse two months to the day after his wedding. Hard enough for an ailing mother to swallow the loss of a son, but harder still the loss of a daughter as well, for it would have been perfectly acceptable under the circumstances for the widowed Margaret to have left Tryweryn and returned to her own family in Capel Celyn. Yet, it seemed to have never crossed her mind, and Margaret, once merely adored by Mam, now became the object of her undying love and loyalty.

Now, the farm would be Elfed's one day. His future was assured, but little did it alleviate the shock of his brother's death. Ironically, Margaret would take care of that. Inevitably, she and Elfed spent much time together, working the farm, supporting the community, and tending to Mam. Margaret kept Mam's body clean, and Elfed her spirits high. Poignancy often leads to tenderness, and for them it certainly did. Mam encouraged their affection for she saw them both as her protégés, and the love that grew gave her joy. Soon after Mam's passing, they were married, and despite the sensitive circumstances, few in the community considered the marriage inappropriate.

As time went by in the shadow of the shoulder of Arenig Fawr, Elfed thought of Edward less and less. Yet, his petite, bright red Welsh dragon kept their flame alive. No one had seen his tattoo until his wedding night. When Margaret had asked about it, he'd told her the whole story, and it had given him pleasure. Margaret in turn had been touched, and then she'd touched it.

Five

THE SAME RED tent stood out at the far end of the same fairground. Its flap was down, but there was no one waiting outside. Nearby, the Afon Tryweryn took its time, making the most of its independence. Soon it would be lost in the River Dee and railroaded forty miles to Chester and the Irish Sea. Rhiannon Roberts ambled towards the tent with a book in hand; ambled that is, until she noticed two men approaching it from her left. Suddenly, it seemed very important to her to get there first, but without making it obvious of course, if she could possibly help it. Her amble stepped up into a fast walk, but clearly this wasn't going to work either. She quickly decided that achieving her objective was much more important than keeping appearances. A trot got her to the tent just before the men, who couldn't disguise their surprise. Far from being embarrassed, Rhiannon Roberts turned to them, smiled apologetically and spoke in Welsh.

"I'm sorry about that, but it did seem silly to settle for third in a queue when I could be first. Don't you agree?"

The men, one young and the other middle-aged, took the question to be rhetorical and remained silent, but the younger of the two thought to himself, "God, she's absolutely ruthless, but at the same time nice about it. What an unusual combination: reassuring ruthlessness."

He smiled at her with amusement, but all the older man could do was gaze in slight bewilderment. Rhiannon seemed satisfied with their reaction, and idly fingered the flap of the tent. This was the last spring fair of the nineteenth century in Bala. That's how Rhiannon saw it anyway. She just could not understand how the authorities could possibly pretend that the nineteenth century had ended on the last day of 1899. It was all so clear to her. Who would deny that the first year of our Lord ended on the last day of AD 1? Similarly then, the first decade ended on the last day of AD 10; the first century on the last day of AD 100; the first millennium on the last day of AD 1000; and therefore, the nineteenth century would end on the last day of AD 1900. It was so obvious to her, but not so to officialdom. She turned and smiled at the two men again and wondered in which century they thought she had jumped the queue on this day in the month of May 1900.

Rhiannon abruptly turned her attention to the Tryweryn, slipping slowly towards the Dee. The wind must have changed direction, for she had become aware of the river, and as usual was not indifferent to it. To her, the Tryweryn represented an injustice that had dominated her upbringing, and which privately, she had assumed the role of redressing.

Rhiannon was far from plain, and also far from shapeless. She wasn't very tall, but telling was her presence none the less. Her wavy, rich red hair, short of shoulder length, was striking. Her understated glamour glowed. She had confidence and it showed. All in all, she was a cool cat, who was soon to throw herself amongst the pigeons.

In that same month of May, at the farm on the upper middle reaches of the Tryweryn, Elfed and Margaret continued to toil on their land, just as they had done for the near twenty years of their married life. For most of this time, the economics of farming had changed for the worse, but they had taken comfort from those things that hadn't changed at all… their culture, Arenig Fawr and their faith. Culture, centered on the community and the chapel, though traditional, was rich, and supported their spirits and massaged their minds. Arenig Fawr remained unmoved throughout the market cycles and lent reassuring continuity to their physical activities. Faith sustained their soul and helped them make sense of it all. In recent years, the terms of agricultural trade had swung their way, and now, at long last, their perseverance was paying off.

Elfed's father had passed away in 1890, happy knowing that his bloodline would live on. Now, in May of 1900, his grandson Geraint was nineteen years of age, a year to the day older than his sister Enid. The pair had been brought up to mirror their parents' values, and saw no reason to resist or rebel, for as much as they could see, they could do worse than follow perfectly in their parents' footsteps. Why even contemplate confronting a system that seemed to work so well? Mind you, the remoteness of their community and its homogeneity had sheltered them from any form of alien influence. No cool cat had yet been thrown amongst their calm, complacent pigeons.

In those early years following Edward's emigration to Tonypandy, Elfed couldn't look at Arenig Fawr without thinking of his friend. By now though, Edward rarely crossed his mind, so he was taken completely by surprise when Margaret, late one night in that month of May, fingered his red dragon rather more thoughtfully than usual and asked, "Elfed, do you ever wonder what became of your friend Edward?"

After a moment's hesitation, he replied.

"You know Margaret, I really don't any more. I used to of course, all the time, but a lot of water has passed along the Tryweryn since then. The important thing I think is that I've never regretted my decision not to leave with him. I wouldn't have married you then, would I?"

He nudged his wife gently, and continued.

"I'm sure things have gone well for him too, despite those terrible working conditions. I still, to this day, can't get over not taking them into consideration. I must have been so wet behind the ears."

She put out the candle with her spare hand. The other continued to finger his red dragon, he noticed.

Untrue to form, it took Edward but one day to cross Elfed's mind again. Late in the evening of the following day, Elfed was returning home, crook in hand after checking on a few late-lambing ewes when he noticed the moon rising. It was near full but still subdued, for the sun hadn't set yet. At the very same time, Margaret's question literally came over him, and there, a few fields above his farmhouse, he really, truly did wonder, with warmth and concern, what had become of his very good friend Edward. Working conditions, indeed! He wondered too whether poor Edward at that very moment was labouring half a mile underground, bent like a sickle and beaded with sweat, while he, Elfed, lent on his crook, choked with emotion at the natural beauty that cloaked him. This he wondered while willing his friend to be well. There and then, he knew there was something he had to do.

The next day, the following conversation took place.

"Everything's going all right, is it?"

"Yes, Dad... why?"

"Oh, nothing... well... that's not exactly true. There is one small thing."

Geraint was confused. It wasn't like his father to beat around the bush like this.

"What is it, Dad?" impatiently.

"I'd like you to climb the Arenig with me. Would you mind missing your meeting at the chapel for once."

"But the meeting's not until tonight, Dad. We'll be back by then."

"No. You see, that's when I want us to climb it, so that we can be at the top just as the sun is setting. What do you think?"

"It's fine with me, Dad, but what will Mam think?"

"Oh, she'll understand, all right. I'm telling you, it's going to be a gorgeous evening," and was he ever right.

Elfed could have climbed the Arenig Fawr a hundred times without coming as close as he did that evening to replicating his experience with Edward twenty-four years earlier. It didn't seem appropriate to drag his son through the ritual in the rivers, so they took a short cut to the lake, a route which bypassed the confluence. However, the sky was as cloudless, the light as alluring and the views quite as lovely as Elfed remembered them with Edward. The whole ritual was evolving into as spiritual an experience as before, and it thrilled him that Geraint sensed the mood and was respectful. When, at the top, the full moon's light met the sun's afterglow, Elfed once again felt blessed. As before, he felt he could do no wrong, and there and then he knew there was something else he just had to do.

"Geraint. What do you think about both you and I going to Bala tomorrow? After all, there won't be another spring fair in the nineteenth century."

"Oh! So you agree with me at last about that, do you, Dad?" with a chuckle.

A bit of banter on the subject followed, and Geraint agreed that he thought the fair sounded like a grand idea.

As they rode to Bala the next day in their horse and trap with Geraint at the reins, Elfed told his son the story of his now slightly faded, red Welsh dragon. Geraint had been aware of the tattoo, but unaware of its significance.

"So, will you have one done in exactly the same place, Geraint? I've thought so little about Edward for such a long time that I feel I owe him something, and this would do the trick. You don't have to do it, mind. You know that, don't you, but at the same time I have to tell you it would give me great pleasure."

Geraint took one of the easiest and most pleasurable decisions of his life, but added, "What will Mam think, though?"

"Oh, she'll understand, all right."

As they approached the red tent, Geraint was surprised at how his father went on about the "piece of work" who had taken care of his and Edward's tattoos twenty-four years earlier; went on, that is, until a young red-headed girl, who was far from plain and also far from shapeless, ruthlessly ran from the right and pipped them to the red flap.

Six

A T THAT VERY moment, Edward Jones was indeed half a mile underground; bent like a sickle, beaded with sweat and labouring under terrible conditions. Yet, he'd rarely regretted his move to the Rhondda. He'd heard that his friend Elfed had prospered, but for certain he'd have stumbled had he stuck it out in Celyn. Without doubt, he was much better off here, and touch wood, his health had held so far. His friend Wyn Williams, though, hadn't been so lucky, and had been licked by the coal dust that had lined his lungs. How painful to watch your best friend fading, and how disconcerting to be reminded daily by him of the fate that might await you in the end. Still, in that regard, so far, so good; if only the same could be said for his domestic life.

Within months of arriving in Rhondda, Edward had met Rachel Anne. He'd married her that November and settled in Llwynypia, and true to form as a man of action, had immediately fathered Martha May Jones. Rachel Anne was soon pregnant again, but tragically had miscarried at five months. Shaken by this experience, they had reluctantly settled for an only child, rationalising that now at least they could focus their limited resources on Martha. She had grown to be a lovely young lady; not especially pretty, but swift and vivacious, and bilingual too, but Welsh-speaking at home, as you'd expect. As was common among the working classes, she'd left school at fifteen, only to return immediately as a canteen worker. Within a year, Martha had been appointed a teacher's helper. Her future was bright and her parents were proud and at peace. Then, in January 1895, she'd met Michael Mowbray; she was only seventeen.

When Martha had met him, Michael Mowbray was nineteen years of age and had just arrived in Llwynypia from Bristol. She'd fallen head over heels in love and got badly bruised in the process. From the start, older and wiser heads, and her parents' in particular, had sought to dissuade her and persuade her, if not to end the alliance, then at least to slow down its progress. Their exhortations had intensified as Michael Mowbray's sinister character could no longer be masked by his glossy exterior. They had even appealed to her Welshness, which was daily derided and bashed by her beau. It had been clear to all but Martha that Michael Mowbray was neither a fan of Wales nor a friend of the Welsh.

Not so wise the heads that had preached, perhaps, for the more they mentioned Mowbray's name, the more stubborn the girl became. They had married exactly six months after they'd met, and the saddest part of all was that even Martha had known on her wedding day that she was marrying an angry, selfish, incommunicative man, and a Cambriaphobe to boot. Alas, she'd dug in her heels and sadly was stuck in a mucky situation of her own making.

Just before the wedding Edward and Rachel Anne had moved from their narrow, terraced home into a bungalow, and that's where Michael Mowbray and his wife had spent the first night of their marriage. During the months leading up to the wedding, the strain of being at odds with her family and friends had crimped Martha's vivacity, and now that she was Mrs Mowbray, her emotions and nerves had been given no relief. For better or for worse Martha had seen the light, but much too late, and the shame she'd felt over her folly had crushed her confidence. She'd known only too well that she had blundered and she'd wondered if her judgement could ever get things right again. As a result, she'd become slavishly subservient to her husband, pampering and pandering to a pitiful degree. What's more, all three Welsh speakers in the home had made a conscious effort, which transcended all politeness, never to speak Welsh in his presence. In these ways were Michael Mobray's ego stroked and his Cambriaphobia largely unprovoked, and a tolerable peace maintained... that is, at any rate, until a freckled Jane Myfanwy had come along.

Jane had been conceived on the 17th of January 1896. Martha had remembered this date because it was the day after the humiliation in Newport, south-east Wales, of one D. Lloyd George, and the only day during her married life that she'd remembered her husband being warm to her. Raised and wrought and rooted in Llanystumdwy in Dwyfor in north-west Wales, David Lloyd George would serve as prime minister of the United Kingdom from December 1916 to 1922, and would bring to the First World War the same driving force that Churchill would bring to the second. Before he became prime minister, David Lloyd George achieved much for the Welsh, but when it came to the greatest gift of all, self-government, he fumbled. At least he gave it a go which is more than can be said for most of his contemporaries. To that end, on the 16th of January 1896, David Lloyd George gave a speech in Newport which he hoped would unify the Welsh under the banner of Home Rule. Earlier, he had taken a nationalistic group called Cymru Fydd by the scruff of the neck and had gained for it the support of much of north Wales's political establishment. Now he was in Newport to secure the south. However, he'd overreached, he was made unwelcome and he left that evening with his nose bloodied. The majority of his nemeses were Welshmen who couldn't speak Welsh but who felt themselves to be just as Welsh as he; Welshmen who resented being lectured by someone that they considered to be an archetype of that Welsh-speaking elite which they felt had marginalised those like themselves who could not speak Welsh. Pity to see the language in Wales divisive in this way; particularly at a time when solidarity might have led to self-government. Michael Mowbray had been at that meeting.

He'd seen Lloyd George's defeat as an expression of his own antipathy for Welshness, and he'd loved it. He'd revelled in the rejection of David Lloyd George, who incidentally went on to become one of the most influential statesmen of the twentieth century. Never mind all that. Michael Mowbray had loved it, and the reveling had made his day. The euphoria he felt had survived the night and when he'd returned home to Llwynypia the following afternoon, Martha had been taken aback by his affability. She'd adjusted with difficulty, but adjust she did, so that Jane Myfanwy, the child of a very troubled marriage, had been conceived during a rare moment when her parents were at near peace.

Jane had been born at home in the bungalow late in the afternoon of the 27th of October 1896, after thirty-six hours of labour. All was well in the end and so overwhelming had been their relief, so uninhibited their joy, that the grandparents, mother and midwife cooed and aahed and admired the babe... in Welsh: yes, in Welsh, despite Michael Mowbray's glare and glower.

"Oh, mae'n gariad fach... mae'n bert ofnadwy."

"Mae hi'n gwmws fel ei thad."

"Llygaid Edward yw nw, cofia," and so on, until Jane's sullen father had left the room slowly, deliberately, and without a word.

"What have we gone and done now," in a Welsh whisper from Edward, but soon the cooing had continued and the canoodling as well.

Michael Mowbray had not come home that night, setting a sad pattern for the future. His absence would have been a great relief had they only known he wouldn't be back. He had reappeared the following morning, worse for wear and smelling stale of beer. The inhabitants of the bungalow had resigned themselves to the likelihood that another volatile ingredient had been added to his already volatile brew. Michael Mowbray had dawdled till Martha and he were alone, and only then he exploded.

"No Welsh. Do you hear me? No Welsh. She's my daughter, you know, as well as yours and I won't have you telling her things that I can't understand. Is that clear? No Welsh, and that applies to your bloody parents as well," and out he'd gone again.

While carrying Jane, Martha's sense of purpose had gradually returned, and with it a measure of confidence. This recovery had been reinforced by the birth, so that Martha didn't pander as before, didn't pamper as in the past, wasn't cowed as was her wont and certainly didn't intend to suckle her new born babe in English. Politeness between adults was one thing, but maternal instinct was another. However, Mowbray would not yield. The confrontations had escalated, as did his tirades and his threats, and had climaxed with, "One more time, that's all. If I catch you speaking Welsh to her one more time, I'll beat your bloody brains out, I swear it."

An empty threat maybe, and indeed he never had hurt her physically, but at that point all three Welsh speakers in the bungalow had agreed that Martha's personal safety took precedence over principle. What good would having a Welsh-speaking Jane be without her mother around to raise her? So, as unnatural as it was, Jane was raised in English. That's how seriously had Michael Mowbray's threats and tirades been taken. If the atmosphere in the bungalow had been strained before, now, with Martha generally unsubservient, it was intolerable. Edward had been approached several times by a group of "respectable" locals who were prepared to "knock some sense" into Michael Mowbray, or even to send him packing back to Bristol. All Edward had to do was give the word, but so far he hadn't. He couldn't quite reconcile himself to vigilante law, and in any case, he hadn't given up hope of coping with the problem on his own.

Over time, the situation had gone from bad to worse. There had been respites during which the others held their breaths, but they needn't have bothered for the trend was relentless. Mowbray's selfishness had hardened Martha's heart and she had compensated for her impotence in dealing with him by becoming more strident in her dealings with others. Just as sadly, Mowbray's anger had gnawed at Rachel Anne's nerves so much that they had frayed to a frazzle. On a happier note, Mowbray's lack of interest in the family had allowed Edward to spend more time with Jane, shielding, nurturing and educating... largely in English though.

Half a mile underground and cloaked in coal dust, Edward prepared for the end of his shift; no freckles in view to reveal his frame of mind. As it happened, he was musing on the language issue. To his mind, Martha was overly upset that with her daughter Jane she'd broken a Welsh-speaking chain, as she put it. He should talk to her about it again; and remind her more forcefully this time that Jane had picked up quite a bit of Welsh at school, so with luck, if she married a Welsh speaker, the chain could be repaired. Soon, he surfaced and thankfully was relieved once again of that tension he always felt below. Homebound, he noticed a Welsh flag flapping. Its red dragon reminded him of an old friend. He would have been touched if told that at that very moment, Elfed was keeping a promise, a promise he himself could not keep, for he'd never had a son.

Seven

A T THE RED tent, Elfed had become uneasy. It was especially disturbing that his unease was coming on the heels of the finest of feelings experienced on Arenig Fawr the night before. He'd felt then that he could do no wrong. He'd felt a calm confidence in the future, which now strangely had been dented. In search of a reason, he looked no further than the young lady with the striking, wavy, rich red hair. She was still now, and yet there was a strange aggression about her that unsettled him, even though he had to admit that her manner earlier had been quite disarming. For some reason, he wished she wasn't there, that she would go away, that the red flap would go up, or something; but the more he wished, the more he knew 'twas wishful. Eventually, she turned towards him and Geraint with a natural but provocative smile.

"Wouldn't you have thought that the fair would be busier than this? After all, this is the last spring fair of the century, isn't it?"

Elfed sighed to himself. He couldn't understand why she made him feel so defensive. She couldn't have said anything to better grab his son's attention. Geraint's face lit up as his father's lights went out.

"What do you think of that, Dad? There happens to be others who see it the way I do," and turning to Rhiannon, continued, "Where did you learn about all that kind of stuff?"

"Oh, I read a little bit, you know," waving her book, and adding, "so, you're farmers, are you?"

Elfed's crook was a dead giveaway.

"Yes, but is it that obvious?" from Geraint.

As she glanced playfully at the crook, Geraint smiled as a young man would, and Elfed because he thought he should.

"So, where do you farm, then?"

To Geraint, this was a perfectly natural follow-up question, but to Elfed, an impertinence. It seemed to him that she was asking all the wrong questions.

"Up the Tryweryn... near Capel Celyn. Do you have an idea where I mean?"

Little did Geraint and Elfed know that the noticeable start she gave at the answer had been a lifetime in the making.

Rhiannon changed tack abruptly.

"So, are you going to tell me what your tattoo will be," and then much more slowly and teasingly, "Or is it just that little bit too personal?"

"Of course I'll tell you. It's not that personal."

Elfed began to feel as if he wasn't there, as if this was all happening around him, as if he was a spectator.

"It's going to be a little red dragon, just above my left shoulder blade. What do you think?"

She didn't think, because she couldn't contain herself.

"You're joking! This is incredible. I'm going to have a little red dragon done too. I just can't believe this... so... just above your left shoulder blade, you said? That sounds pretty specific. Is there a special reason for having it done there?"

Elfed braced himself. Surely Geraint wasn't going to tell her everything! As a matter of fact, he thought this whole business was very personal. Experiences don't come much more personal than their last evening. Geraint was normally so careful, even cautious, but she clearly had charmed him completely.

"Well, yes... actually there is. Dad... "

Elfed interrupted. He could be a spectator no longer.

"Do you have a special reason for choosing a red dragon?"

Unruffled, and without a second thought, she replied.

"Yes. I think it's special, anyway. I thought perhaps it might make my father happy."

"Hmm! That's very nice. Who is he, by the way… your father?"

"His name is Rowland Roberts. He works on the railway."

Elfed wasn't sure that he'd ever met him, but everyone had heard the name. He was glad he'd asked, even though the answer hadn't made him any less uncomfortable.

"Where will you have your tattoo done?" asked Geraint out of the blue.

"Geraint, be quiet. Don't be so rude."

"No, Dad. I really would like to know," and addressing Rhiannon, asked, "I'm not being rude am I?"

"Well, I… I don't think so, but… " and she became beautifully bashful, and briefly glanced at her bosom. Then, still irresistibly shy, she coyly came up with the unforgettable line, "… perhaps we can compare them sometime… our little red dragons."

Unforgettable as far as Geraint was concerned, anyway.

"What a hussy," thought Elfed, and none too soon, but far too late, the red flap went up.

Now that he had time to think, Elfed fared no better. The young lady's tattoo posed a threat somehow, and quite irrationally, he wondered whether those little red dragons were such a good idea after all. Suddenly, after twenty-four years, he had a funny feeling that they might come back to haunt him and his family. He couldn't do much about his. Neither did he think that he could persuade Geraint to change his mind, and he was right. Geraint was already looking forward to comparing his with another… an unforgettable another.

Eight

RHIANNON'S GRANDFATHER WAS an established tenant farmer along the lower Tryweryn in 1859, when his right to vote had got the better of him. He had determined he would no longer squirm to the squire's command and voted against his candidate in the General Election. Voted against the squire? Against the squire? Yes, John Roberts had exercised his right, and fully felt his oats. The voting at that election was public, so it was not long before everyone, including the squire, had heard of the tenant's independent act. The squire wasn't a bad sort, but he'd responded to this insubordination by firing John Roberts and a few more who had followed suit. Rhiannon's grandfather had moved his family down the Tryweryn from the tenant farm to the town of Bala. He had carried with him a grievance, which did his health no good, but his independent act had not been in vain. The squire's candidate had narrowly won his parliamentary seat, but the firing of the "renegades" backfired badly. The incident had proved to have legs, and while little comfort came John Roberts's way, the ensuing backlash helped stoke a movement, which led to significant changes. Within fifteen years, voting had become a secret act, the right to vote had been widened significantly and the political power of landowners was already in decline. Alas, John Roberts had not survived to savour these victories. While his spirit was willing, his body was not. His son Rowland, however, had suffered from no such handicap.

Rowland Richard Roberts was only fourteen when his family had been tossed from the Tryweryn, and eighteen when his father had passed away, and by then he was all fired up over the injustice of it all. In fact, he was all fired up over a lot of things; he was a radical. His view of the Tryweryn incident was simple. In his opinion, it would never have happened had Wales not been run for the English, but rather, for the Welsh, and for Wales to be run for the Welsh, Wales had to be run by the Welsh. Rowland Roberts was a nationalist, too.

Rowland had formed a society in which he and his supporters peacefully promoted their objectives, which were: to raise the awareness of England's continuing role as a thorn in Welsh flesh; to push for Home Rule for Wales; and to uphold and encourage the Welsh language. Individually, these objectives were not undeserving of support, but as a trio they were troublesome in one respect. When taken together, other than in the most sensitive, generous and far-sighted of hands, they couldn't help but be divisive. They couldn't help but marginalise Welshmen who could only speak English. The emphasis on the Welsh language, especially when accompanied by an anti-English slant, inevitably, if unwittingly, suggested a subsidiary role in an independent Wales for those who couldn't speak the mother tongue; and as they represented half the population of Wales, this inevitable, if unwitting, divisiveness should have been given much more consideration.

The political concessions that had flowed from his father's act of defiance had given Rowland hope, but it was cruelly false. Each shift in Welsh political power, from Tory landowners to Liberal industrialists to Nonconformists, had bypassed Rowland's ideal of self-government. He'd been particularly disappointed with the Nonconformists. This religious movement had gradually become a unifying symbol for most Welsh-speaking, God-fearing Welsh people, and had evolved into a national institution with political power. Rowland though, had resented what he considered to be indifference on the part of Nonconformists towards Home Rule, and had spent much of his energy attempting to expose the anomalies in their policies as the assumed leaders of the Welsh. It was no surprise then that he had refused to enter any chapel, which, on Sundays in particular, set him apart from the community. All these disappointments had a deep effect, but the straw that had broken the camel's back was Mr Lloyd George's rejection in Newport on 16th January 1896. On that day, Rowland Roberts had lost heart, and blinded by bitterness, had also lost his way... completely. You might say that the English had got the better of him, but in his tired, bitter mind, it wasn't just the English, but also the English-speaking Welshmen of the south, confirming to him that they were not fit to lead in an independent Wales. What had, up until then, been no more than a feeling, became a fact as far as he was concerned. Defeated, disappointed, Rowland had unjustly and unjustifiably blamed his loss on the Welsh in the south. Wales's failure to achieve independence is a complicated subject, but Rowland would have been closer to the mark had he laid the blame squarely on a millennium or more of English interference and oppression.

Rhiannon had been brought up in this contentious atmosphere, and not surprisingly had been indoctrinated by regular attendance at meetings of her father's society. Her views were completely in sync with his, but she had decided, though, that life-long frustration was for the birds, and above all, results were the thing, even if it meant lowering one's sights a rung or two. She would assuage her father's anger at its source. She decided ... more than that, she determined... that she would redress the injustice that had befallen her family by reinstating its representative, Rhiannon Roberts, in the Tryweryn valley. She had determined this and would pursue it with reassuring ruthlessness. She wouldn't have long to wait.

Geraint and Rhiannon would be one of the last couples to be married in Bala in the nineteenth century. That's how they saw it anyway. By traditional standards their courtship was short. Rhiannon saw to that. She loved her Geraint and looked forward to being his wife, but the real driver was her family's reinstatement in Tryweryn. To Geraint's family and their community, there was no reason to rush, so Rhiannon's haste raised eyebrows. Her pretext could not have been loftier: it was no less than the fact that the nineteenth century was quickly drawing to a close! After all, hadn't she and Geraint first fancied each other when they had clicked on the date of its closure? Wouldn't it be nice and appropriate, then, for them to wed before the century ended? And if it was at all possible, shouldn't the effort be made? Yes, yes and yes were her confident answers, but not all were in agreement. Some still failed to see the merit in rushing to marriage, based on a conclusion that was clearly incorrect.

"Would you deny that the first year of our Lord ended..." was Rhiannon's initial reaction to this scepticism, but she immediately thought better of it, for the doubters were experts on the Lord and were unlikely to be convinced by her of anything to do with Him. In the end, her disarming demeanour won the doubters round, and given a glimmer of green light, she ran with it, and made quite sure that the momentum never flagged.

For six months, in public, she was all reassurance, and never seen as ruthless. She was near faultless, and just as well, for she had a family history. Most in the valley were Methodists and a few knew her father's views, particularly the ones critical of the Nonconformists. They would have been only too happy to settle a score with him by exposing and rejecting his daughter, but Rhiannon didn't give them a chance: she was brilliant. Rumblings of her background in Bala were overwhelmed by the favourable press she was creating for herself in Tryweryn.

With Elfed too, she had a mountain to climb. Rhiannon wasn't aware of the discomfort that he'd experienced outside the red flap. The thought of that incident still unsettled Elfed now and then, as did the nagging feeling that he might live to regret the little red dragons. As Rhiannon had been integral to the incident, she would find him harder to win round than expected. In the end though, her charm did win through, and her intimacies, which earlier when aimed at others he'd considered brazen, now, when aimed at him, he'd allowed to tickle his fancy.

In comparison, Enid and Margaret were relative pushovers. Rhiannon could sense that Enid had adored her from the very start, but to play safe, had invited her to be her only bridesmaid. Rhiannon's three sisters would be upset, but she was a dabhand at dealing with them. As for Margaret, Rhiannon gained her respect straightforwardly with a willingness to work whenever she visited the valley. Her affection was gained rather more subtly. Margaret loved lavender, so was touched by the little fragrant gifts that Rhiannon often brought on her weekly visits. Still, she couldn't quite get comfortable with Rhiannon's reluctance to visit them on the Sabbath. She would always come on Saturdays, but never on a Sunday. Lavender or not, Margaret found that odd.

This was an exciting time for Geraint. Before Rhiannon, his life had been happy enough, but humdrum. Now it was on fire. No moment was unmeaningful, each minute seemed to matter. His love was electric, crackling with intrigue, for Rhiannon had decided to tell Geraint all. Rhiannon wasn't everybody's soothing cup of tea. She was complicated, and to most, inconsistent, but to those on her wavelength, her verve and her nerve were a virtual narcotic. Geraint, for certain, was hooked, and so sure was she of her hold over him that she took a risk of rejection. She told him of the appeal of Tryweryn to her, but why should he worry about that when he knew that she adored him? She told him of her politics, but she was sure he wouldn't want her not to be true to herself. She told him of her difficulty with chapels and Sundays, and how she would need his support on that. And she told him that all this would be certain to distance his parents from them, but would surely strengthen their own relationship and make it even more special than it already was. All this she told Geraint in a gentle, reassuring manner over time, drawing him carefully, step by step, into their own wonderful web of intrigue. Naturally, parts of this bothered Geraint, but not for long, for this was heady stuff which excited him. He idolised Rhiannon and glowed with pride that she would want to share so much with him. He was flattered, he was honoured, he was hers. Rhiannon had known that she knew her man.

Ironically, Geraint's family proved to be less of a problem to Rhiannon than her own, and her father in particular. Rowland Roberts would rather die than be seen in a chapel, and though Rhiannon felt the same way, she was quite capable of feeling otherwise when her family's reinstatement in Tryweryn was on the line.

"Principles are all very well, Dad, but d'you want to feel sorry for yourself for the rest of your life? I'm doing this partly for my family, you know... for you; so that you can hold your head high. Surely, that's worth a few, admittedly painful, minutes in a chapel?"

This trade-off was hammered out repeatedly in her father's face until eventually he reluctantly agreed to give her away... and yes, in a chapel. Later, he would say a few words at the reception and none of them gave Rowland Roberts more pleasure than the concluding ones.

"Now, Rhiannon is moving to Tryweryn, moving back, I venture to say, to where everyone knows she belongs."

Elfed, till then in reverie, was vexed by that remark. He was aware of the Roberts' family history, and perhaps could understand a bitter man's need to parade it at this time... but he hoped there was no more to it than that. He really wished

Rowland Roberts hadn't brought it up. It was a great pity, because Elfed truly had thought that the wedding was going quite well.

Elfed's family, larger now by one, arrived home at their Tryweryn farm just before dark. At the front door, the beaming bridegroom gallantly lifted the bride in his arms and calmly carried her over the doorstep. Once inside and on her feet, Rhiannon tiptoed exaggeratedly into the parlour, spread herself dramatically on an easy chair and gazed around and around the busily appointed room, massed with momentos and crammed with culture. Then, and only then, did she turn to Geraint, invite his embrace and affirm her affection for him in front of her in-laws. She then faced them with a satisfied smile, as if to say, "Well, here I am."

Following on her father's contentious remarks, Rhiannon's mild triumphalism bothered Elfed. In view of the occasion, he yearned to approve of all she did, and yet her attitude irked him. But soon she hugged him too, and of course that helped. Yet, for the rest of the evening, he looked back on the day with some misgiving. Geraint looked back as well, but to Rhiannon's unforgettable, "Perhaps we can compare them sometime...our little red dragons," knowing at last, that "sometime" would be soon.

Nine

THE WEDDING HAD taken place on a Saturday, and it took less than a day for Rhiannon to ruffle and rattle the pigeons. It was half past nine, and the weather was fine on that Sunday. It hadn't been light for long, but the sheep had already been fed, and of course, no breakfast in bed for the newlyweds.

The three ladies threaded around each other in the kitchen, peeling and slicing and washing vegetables, preparing for the meal of the week, the Sunday lunch. They had also kneaded dough, which usually rose by the grace of God while the family worshipped Him. Enid was thrilled by Rhiannon's presence and expected now to have not only more spare time, but also a dear friend with whom to share it. Enid realised that she didn't really know Rhiannon all that well, but nevertheless, felt suprisingly close to her. Enid adored Rhiannon, and was optimistic about their future together. Enid was only eighteen. Margaret, the matriarch, spoke.

"I think we better stop now, Rhiannon. It usually takes us half an hour to get ready for chapel, and we have to leave here at ten to get there on time."

After eighteen years, Enid knew the ropes, and had already started to tidy up. As her mother spoke, she glanced over at Rhiannon and was a bit surprised at the reaction. Rather than respond wholeheartedly, Rhiannon nodded her head reassuringly, half-smiled and continued peeling her parsnips. And there she stood, head down, whittling away, when Enid left the kitchen with her mother.

"Oh, well," Enid thought, "It takes all kinds, and I admit... I really don't know Rhiannon all that well."

As she changed into her Sunday best, Enid listened for signs of Rhiannon's response; listened in vain, for there were none. At first, she was merely confused, because she couldn't think of an explanation, but soon became worried, for of the explanations that arose, none were comforting. Later, as she went downstairs, she heard her parents speaking in soft tones, and found them huddled around the clock. Their expressions rattled her, for they looked even more worried than she felt. Never before in her life did she remember her parents betraying such anxiety. The show had to go on however, and soon her father took one last look at the clock, shrugged his shoulders, sighed and said, "I suppose they must be unwell after all the excitement yesterday. We'll just have to go without them, that's all."

Enid didn't feel worried anymore. She had quickly moved beyond that emotion. Suddenly, she was sure that Rhiannon was solely responsible for this upset, and felt bitterly let down by her; and why, she wondered, did not her father's words reflect the way she felt? Well, he was practising what to say at chapel, wasn't he? And she wasn't to know that Elfed and Margaret weren't as surprised as she at Rhiannon's behaviour. After all, Elfed's initial instincts concerning Rhiannon had been partly responsible for his unease at the red tent, and hadn't Margaret known all along that somehow Rhiannon and Sundays didn't mix? What's more, Elfed and Margaret had become aware a few months earlier of Rhiannon's father's aversion to chapels. It had never occurred to them at the time that Rhiannon, as amiable and reassuring as she'd been, might have felt the same. Now though, it looked as if she did.

The service was over. A watery, winter's sun still shone as the congregation shuffled through the Capel Celyn chapel door and formed familiar groups beside the graveyard. Elfed had been practising, so he was ready. His best friend Trebor was the first to broach the subject.

"Well, Elfed, you were awfully nice to let them sleep late today, knowing how funny some people are about that kind of thing around here."

The less said the better, so Elfed merely smiled and nodded. Trebor was diplomatic by nature, and to some degree, constrained by the honour of being present at the wedding. No such constraint was felt by Joseph Jones, who hadn't been invited and set about justifying the omission. He was considered one of the more senior members of the chapel, and was known by his detractors, of which there were many, as the Tyrant of Tryweryn. He didn't help himself by rarely addressing anyone by their Christian name alone.

"I heard that there was a wedding in your family yesterday, Elfed Evans," with such an emphasis on the word "heard", that no one chatting outside the chapel could help but hear it.

"You're right, Mr Jones."

"And the happy couple weren't present this morning, were they?"

Elfed was doing his very best to treat that question as rhetorical, knowing full well that none of Joseph Jones's questions ever were. Finally, he shook his head and mouthed, "No."

Trebor came to his friend's assistance and immediately wished he hadn't.

"Mr Jones, I think it would be polite not… "

"Shut up, Trebor Thomas. You keep your nose out of this. This is between Elfed Evans and me, so you either keep quiet or leave."

Trebor decided that keeping quiet would attract the least attention.

"Now then, Elfed Evans. As you were aware, we, as a congregation, were very much looking forward to congratulating Geraint today and welcoming his new bride to our midst. As a denomination, we haven't been able to get on with her father, as you know, so it was gratifying, wasn't it, that his daughter appeared to feel differently about us."

"The little devil," thought Elfed to himself.

The beating around the bush was about to end.

"So, are you going to tell me where they are?"

Elfed had been practising his answer for hours. "Yes. I'll tell you, Joseph Jones. They've been under a lot of pressure preparing for their wedding, as I'm sure you can understand, and it seems it finally caught up with them. Neither of them felt well enough to come with us this morning."

"So next Sunday then?"

"Yes, Joseph Jones," followed by a disclaimer, "with a little help from the Lord," sadly suspecting it might take much, much more than that.

"I'm sorry to intrude on you like this, Mrs Evans."

Joseph Jones touched his hat at Margaret and then turned to Enid.

"Cheer up, Miss Evans. You should be as happy as a lark. You've got a new sister now," but however hard she tried, poor Enid failed to force a smile.

While walking home from Capel Celyn chapel, they often felt on a fine day that they were being treated to the perfect manifestation of those blessings which they had just been assured were a gift from God. In fact, on rare occasions, the landscape, in its permanence and beauty, took the form of God himself. At other less exalted times, their lovely view of the valley, especially from the highpoint of their hike back home, was a spiritual complement to whatever may have moved them in the chapel down below. From their vantage point, both valleys were visible, tumbling together into one, wide at the confluence and then narrowing significantly before dipping out of sight to the east.

Dotting the valley were cottages and farms, many snugly set in trees. The distant backdrop was the Berwyn, and watching over the idyllic dale, rugged yet reassuring, was the massif of Arenig Fawr. Often, they felt warmth at the thought of belonging to this beauty. Often, they felt whole as a part of this picture: often, but not today.

Enid's disappointment deepened and hardened into anger. She seethed in the certainty that Rhiannon deliberately had duped her. She failed to see the upset in any other light. She was as convinced now of Rhiannon's deviousness as earlier she had been of her devotion. To her, there were no two ways about it. Rhiannon had weaseled her way into their family and woe betide them if, as she feared, the damage done so far was no more than the tip of an iceberg. Until this morning, she had never seen her parents quite as worried, and she'd never heard her father tell a lie. Insecurity had ensued, which was not eased by the uncharacteristic edge to her father's voice as he spoke to her mother.

"I just can't understand why they wouldn't have said something to us, instead of leaving us hanging like that."

Margaret's gentle tone was a genuine relief to Enid, but her message was heard with mounting misgiving.

"Well, Elfed, they were probably very nervous, and thought it wouldn't be at all easy to talk to us."

Enid was again relieved that such tolerance was clearly unacceptable to her father as well.

"At the very least, I would have expected Geraint to say something. He's always treated us with such respect."

Gentle tones replied again.

"Oh, Elfed, I don't think this business had much to do with Geraint, do you?"

"Well, he knew about it, didn't he, so why didn't he give us some warning?"

Very gentle tones replied to this.

"Oh, Elfed! How would you have felt, particularly on the very first day of our marriage, if I'd betrayed you? Wouldn't you think less of Geraint now if he hadn't supported Rhiannon through thick and thin once he had made a commitment to her?"

To Enid, this business was an open and shut case. Without question, the blame should be laid right at Rhiannon's feet. Her emotions underwent a U-turn. By now, she was reassured by her father's aggressive stance, and her mother's gentleness and generosity appalled her, but she didn't say anything. She didn't have to, as her father said it for her, reacting quite ungentlemanly to the very gentle tones.

"I feel you're fighting me all the way on this, Margaret. Whatever I say, you take the opposite tack. What they did this morning, and particularly the way they went about it, has knocked me for six; so I really need your support, but all you do is fight me. You know, I am so angry at this moment that I feel I don't want anything more to do with either of them."

Perhaps Margaret should have sensed that it might have been better to back off, but she lacked a frame of reference. Confrontation was so abnormal in their relationship that she innocently continued her gentle and generous counters.

"Oh, come on now, Elfed. I don't think that would be a good… "

Elfed blew his top. He was looking for support, not advice, gentle or otherwise. He turned on Margaret in a way that shocked all three. He towered over her threateningly.

"Shut your mouth, Margaret. You're talking a load of rubbish. What happened this morning was a threat to our way of life, and you're making light of it all. So just shut up, or I'll get really angry."

Margaret recoiled and shrivelled up. What an ugly scene it

was, an unlovely blemish on an otherwise lovely landscape. Elfed was on fire, Margaret in a little ball, and Enid shaken but now sure of Rhiannon's early fall. No question about it, Rhiannon was solely to blame for these traumatics, and Enid was pleased that her father agreed. At the same time, she felt for her tearful mother and yet, under the circumstances, just could not reach out to her. A warm gesture towards her mother at that point may have broken her own downward spiral of spite, but in its absence she became isolated by the ensuing positive resolution of the ugly scene.

Elfed could not tolerate Margaret's distress. His signs of remorse were muted, but sufficient for Margaret nonetheless. Nothing was said, but she sensed that Elfed was prepared to hear her piece. As they approached home, and Arenig Fawr's north shoulder rose in relation to them, Margaret spoke gently and generously, and Elfed listened without interruption.

"As you know, Elfed, whenever I'm not sure how to handle a situation, I ask myself how your mother would have dealt with it, and that's what I'm asking now, because I do realise we're faced with a very tricky situation."

She was striking all the right chords without even trying.

"I think your mother would have said that of all the things in our life, family is the most important…even ahead of godliness, and cleanliness as well."

There was a smile in her voice.

"So it seems to me that we should bend over backwards to stay close to Geraint, even if it means accepting Rhiannon, warts and all. I admit that Rhiannon is probably more different from us than we had imagined, but we have a responsibility now to try and understand her."

She spoke directly to Elfed, who continuously stared towards Arenig Fawr, but better had she glanced at Enid now and then.

"From a practical point of view, of course, we need to be on good terms with Geraint because we depend on him at the farm, but more important by far to me is the integrity of our family."

Wise words and wonderfully said, but ironically, as she thus embraced Rhiannon, so did she isolate Enid beyond repair. Poor Enid! Despite his grim expression, Enid knew all right that her father's stance had softened, but she? Alas, she remained irretrievably trapped by her anger towards Rhiannon, and left high and dry and lonely by her father's change of heart.

Ten

IT STRUCK MARGARET that their farmyard was especially spick and span. It gave her pleasure, until she realised that Geraint must have done it... on a Sunday! She worried that this might make matters worse between him and his father. Glancing at Elfed though, she fancied that the shadow of a shaft of approval flitted across his face. Better had she glanced at Enid, whose tight-lipped mouth remained unmoved. They were greeted in the kitchen by Rhiannon, who Margaret noticed had finished preparing the vegetables, and was now polishing the brass.

"Hello. I really hope you enjoyed the service."

Margaret found her tone and body language encouraging. It conveyed simultaneously an understanding of the pain she had caused, regret at having caused it and the hope that it had been tolerable.

"Yes. It was very nice, thanks, but they did miss you."

"Oh! I'm really sorry about... "

"It's all right. We'll talk about that later. Let's get going with the dinner now, shall we?"

Margaret thought it better not to broach the matter yet.

"Give Elfed time to get used to Rhiannon's presence," she thought to herself, "and the discussion is bound to go more smoothly."

So far, so good! There was at least hope of reconciliation while Elfed was respectful and Rhiannon reassuring. Margaret glanced at him again, but better had she turned her eye on Enid, whose face was wrapped in rejection. Rhiannon noticed though, and smiling sympathetically, approached to embrace her friend.

The explosion caught all three unawares, but none as much as Margaret.

"Don't you dare lay a hand on me!"

Enid spoke with venom.

"You may manage to sweet-talk my parents, but not me. I can see through you, all right. You're the kind of person who'd walk over your own grandmother to get your own way."

"Enid! How dare you talk like that."

"I'll talk anyway I like, Mam. After all, I'm the only one around here with the guts to stand up to her. She's nothing but a selfish so and so," and finally, revealing the source of her inexplicable virulence, "How could I have possibly let her hoodwink me like that?"

Having finished speaking, she simply stood and stared at Rhiannon. Enid was of medium height and slim, but her noticeably erect stance exuded defiance. The other three were in such shock that they neither moved nor said a word, until Enid slumped at the shoulders, burst into tears and fled from the room. Margaret, aware of Enid's pain at last, followed her to the door, but was stopped in her tracks by Elfed's stern voice.

"Now are you satisfied, Rhiannon? Who's next on your list, I wonder?"

Margaret hugged him from behind, and with her head on the nape of his neck, whispered, "I thought we had an understanding, Elfed. Please don't let me down now!"

"All right... all right," and having doused that fire, Margaret ran after Enid, but only in time to see her stepping over a stile at the far end of the farmyard and running raggedly in the direction of the footbridge and the road to Capel Celyn.

Their posh dinner plates had been cleared from the parlour table and replaced by cups and saucers from the same Sunday-best set. Margaret had determined that they should still put on a show, despite the upset and Enid's absence. All had played their part except Elfed, who seemed unable to join in the small talk. On one occasion, Margaret had left the dinner table in search of her daughter, prompting Elfed to speak up, one of the few times he'd done so since arriving home from chapel. He said, "I'm sure you needn't worry, Margaret. She's probably with Mary and enjoying an afternoon chatting with her friends in the village."

Mary was Margaret's only sister, who lived alone in their family home near Capel Celyn chapel. That suggestion, especially coming from Elfed, quietened her mind. Elfed may have said little during dinner, but he'd thought a lot, much of it about Rhiannon. He was still very angry with his daughter-in-law. How could he be otherwise when, and there were no two ways about it, she was threatening their way of life. Still, he kept on reminding himself of Margaret's advice and entreaty. What's more, he reluctantly had to admit to a grudging admiration of Rhiannon. He found her ability to be utterly ruthless this morning and equally reassuring now remarkable. Impressive too, thought Elfed, was the way that Rhiannon made Geraint so happy. His son sat across the table, bemused it seemed by the ease with which his wife diffused their tension.

"So are you two ready now to tell us what happened this morning?"

Geraint shrugged his shoulders and nodded a shade shyly at his wife, who went straight to the point.

"You've probably heard about my father and the fact that he won't set foot in a chapel. What you may not have heard is the reason why. Well, it's just that he believes very strongly that the Nonconformist movement has let Wales down; I do too, so I prefer not to set foot in a chapel either. Now, I admit that

I could have gone with you today, but sooner or later I'd have had to take a stand. Geraint and I decided the sooner the better, that's all."

"But why didn't you tell us this morning?" from Margaret, "It would have been kinder than letting us stew like that."

"Well, as you can imagine, we were very nervous at the thought of telling you. We just took the easy way out, that's all. I'm sorry."

Margaret smiled at Elfed as if to say, "I told you so," while he somehow failed to conjure an image of a nervous Rhiannon. More likely by far, he thought, that Geraint's were the feet that got cold.

"Geraint," continued Margaret, "You must have known of this for quite some time. Why didn't you warn us earlier? It's been quite a shock coming like this straight after the wedding."

Geraint understandably skirted the truth, even though he must have assumed that his parents were well aware of it. Fair play! It would have been hard for him to admit that he'd not revealed Rhiannon's prejudice for fear the wedding would have been called off.

"Well, I must say," he replied tentatively, "I was really torn at times. We are a close family, but I decided that if I was going to commit to Rhiannon, then my first loyalty had to be to her. You wouldn't have wanted it any other way, would you Mam?"

Margaret turned to Elfed once again, more deliberately this time, and smiled. Elfed though, was growing impatient with her self-serving agenda. Why didn't she get to the heart of the matter, he asked himself, as, it turned out, she was about to do just that.

"But how can you say Nonconformists have let us down, when so many people... in fact, so many respectable, well-educated people... believe that Wales would be much worse off without them?"

Self-assuredly, yet politely and logically, Rhiannon reeled off her father's credo: how England had forever been a thorn in Welsh flesh; how the Welsh language was at greater risk than ever before; how both these issues could be addressed if Wales was self-governed; how this goal had recently been thwarted by Nonconformist indifference; and now again by opposition from English speakers in south Wales.

Elfed wasn't sure he agreed with much of what she'd said, but to a large degree he was with her on England and the English. Along with everyone else in the valley, and every other valley in Wales for that matter, he had been brought up on a diet of Welsh history and folklore, which inevitably portrayed his country in constant conflict with the English, and usually subject to them. Most of his heroes... in fact, every Welsh person's heroes... had been either killed or quelled by the English. No wonder then that Elfed had grown up to think of the English very much as "them" and inimical towards "us"; but he had found, too, that this was not only an inherited, historical notion, but a reality in his own life as well. Too many times in his own experience Englishness had been synonymous with authority and superiority. He realised that this feeling had stemmed partly from habitual subservience, a built-in inferiority complex, perhaps, but regardless, it hadn't helped alleviate the divide between "them" and "us". There weren't any English in the valley, but over the years he had met several and enjoyed their company, despite the difficulty in communication. They may have been English, but to him they didn't represent Englishness and the divide hadn't dominated on those occasions. It seemed that it was more like a blur in the background of his mind, which came into focus only at those times when "they" represented authority or exuded superiority, and "we" were reminded of "our" subservience or inferiority. An upper-class English accent never failed in this regard; an upper-class, pukka, la-di-da, or whatever you want to call it, English accent had always got his goat.

So, yes, Elfed agreed with Rhiannon on the English issue, but rather than challenge her on the others, he responded surprisingly generously, partly out of respect for Margaret's entreaty for conciliation. Shaking his head in a mixture of admiration and disbelief, he said, "I don't know about you, Rhiannon; you're something special, all right."

Everyone smiled at that, and he continued.

"I'm happy that we've had this discussion. And you did it all without a single note," and to make sure everyone understood it was a compliment, he burst out laughing, and the others joined him.

Such was the harmony and hilarity when the back door was heard to shut and Enid showed up in the doorway between the kitchen and the parlour. She was greeted by four freshly radiant faces, which then, one by one, fell flat, Margaret's being the first. It was as if Enid had never left the room. Her face was as tearful and as angry as when she'd run away. She needn't have said anything for her face still said it all.

"So you're all big pals, are you? It didn't take her long to sweet-talk you, did it? You're nothing but a selfish bitch, Rhiannon, and it won't take the rest of you long to find out, you mark my words."

Then a pause while she looked at each in turn, followed by, "Oh! I can't stand this," and off she ran again in tears, this time to the room behind the kitchen where she slept. Margaret soon followed, only to find Enid's bedroom already barricaded. She was joined in the kitchen by Geraint and Rhiannon, where all three washed up in silence, knowing that Enid would have heard every word of what they had said.

"And it won't take the rest of you long to find out, you mark my words."

Only a few minutes earlier, Elfed had been jovial, but now, in the parlour all alone, he worried about these warning words of Enid's. He couldn't help but reflect on the unease he'd felt when he'd first met Rhiannon, and his irrational reaction to her tattoo; and he wished he weren't afraid that the dragon's tail would sting one day; and then suddenly, out of the blue, he wished as well that he weren't aware of where Rhiannon's dragon lay.

Eleven

ELFED, MARGARET AND Enid sat alongside each other on a pew halfway back from the pulpit to the main door. Next to Enid, on the inside of the pew, sat her Anti Mary. All four, along with the hundred or so in the Capel Celyn chapel congregation, were dressed in their Sunday best. Rhiannon and Geraint were nowhere to be seen, so it looked as if four weeks after their wedding, they still could not, on principle, support the Nonconformist movement. The congregation sat down after singing the third hymn, and coughed, as it had done hundreds of times before. Then, just as the congregation had expected him to, the secretary read the announcements... in Welsh. Everyone knew that these would be followed by the sermon. So when they weren't, heads turned a little, and several turned a lot, and an anxious murmur spread through the Sunday bests. The fresh-faced visiting preacher had not, as expected, made his way up the stairway to the pulpit, but sat stock still as Joseph Jones pushed himself laboriously to his feet. The congregation murmured more, but one authoritative cough from the Tyrant of Tryweryn put a stop to that. Another cleared his throat.

"My friends," he began, "There is... one more announcement. We, the deacons, held a meeting this last week. There's nothing uncommon about that of course, and normally the proceedings would not be made public. However, I... " and he cleared his throat again, "However we thought that an announcement regarding this recent meeting was appropriate, because it seems there are rumours flying around the region."

The congregation was agog. Joseph Jones may sometimes be overbearing, but never dull.

"I called that meeting," and he emphasised the "I", "to discuss Elfed Evans's position with respect to our chapel."

Most heads respectfully remained faced forward, but a few members turned instinctively towards Elfed before they could catch themselves, and a few more out of mere spite. The latter struck lucky, for Elfed and his family, taken by surprise, betrayed their embarrassment. The three adults were quick to recover their poise, and the heads would soon have turned again towards the pulpit had it not been for Enid. Poor Enid! Rhiannon's betrayal had battered her nerves. She'd thought of nothing else for weeks, but had bottled up her fury. Under this strain, it would have taken far less than a public humiliation to tip her over the edge. She just stared open-mouthed at Joseph Jones, before turning slowly to her father and speaking in a despairing voice so that all could hear, "Dad, she's destroying us… she… she's destroying our family."

Joseph Jones had resumed speaking, but stopped at this outburst, and remained unmoved as Enid, sobbing uncontrollably, was ushered to the aisle by her Anti Mary. There, they were met by the fresh-faced minister, who had rushed to their aid, and who now accompanied them sympathetically to the lobby. The congregation didn't know which way to turn until Joseph Jones showed them. He continued speaking, unrepentant and unruffled.

"As I was saying, I called last week's meeting to discuss Elfed Evans's position with respect to our chapel."

He proceeded to praise Elfed.

"As you all know, no one has worked harder for our cause than Elfed Evans. I understood he was widely expected to be elected a deacon in the near future, and if he were, he could well be the youngest deacon ever at Capel Celyn, even younger than I was when I was elected one. There is no question that his integrity is highly regarded."

Elfed, now on a pedestal, was a patsy for a put down.

"However, as a congregation we not only demand integrity from our deacons but also good judgement. In this latter regard, I believe Elfed Evans has been found wanting. In a close community like ours, one unfortunate marriage can have painful consequences for all of us, and in a close family like his, I would have thought he could have prevented it from happening. In my opinion, the fact that he didn't casts doubt on his suitability to be a deacon. I called the meeting of deacons last week to air my view, but support for Elfed Evans was strong, so for now," and here he paused pointedly, "I have backed down. It is not with pleasure that I have made this statement, but it seems there were so many rumours flying around that I considered it important to set the record straight."

Joseph Jones lowered himself to his seat no less laboriously than he had risen. The visiting minister hurried up the aisle and ascended to the pulpit, just as many ministers had done hundreds of times before. None with as heavy a heart, however, as this good Samaritan, whose topic, much to his discomfort, was Matthew 5: 7. He made sure his eyes stayed as far as possible from Joseph Jones's as he recited the verse.

"Blessed are the merciful, for they shall obtain mercy."

Elfed and Margaret assumed that members of the congregation wouldn't be quite sure what to say to them, and so to avoid awkwardness had decided to leave immediately after the service for Mary's home, which was just down the hill and across the bridge. Trebor Thomas intercepted them to shake his friend's hand, and Elfed was grateful for that, but overall he was desperately downcast. Enid's anger was the last thing he'd needed. He presumed that not only was she angry at her parents for, in her view, bringing this humiliation upon themselves and their family, but also, at herself for making matters so much worse with her outburst. It turned out that Enid couldn't face the thought of home, and as Margaret couldn't leave her daughter so distraught, it was decided that Elfed should journey home alone.

As Elfed set off after lunch, he noticed Enid peering through the window. Throughout her life he had been able to depend on her pretty face for encouragement, but this afternoon her expression seemed to distance him. As he left the village behind, he felt increasingly lonely. On such a lovely day, he would normally have relished returning home alone. He would have identified warmly with the two rivers that ran into one. He would have taken comfort from the redoubtable Arenig Fawr and considered it his own. He would have surrendered to the beauty and serenity that surrounded him, and imagined it to be God's embrace. Not so this time, for on the prettiest of days and on the loveliest spot on earth, he distinctly felt God distancing him, just as Enid had done earlier.

This was not the first time he'd felt rejected by God that day. Earlier, he'd worried that Joseph Jones may have spoken on God's behalf. This was most peculiar, for along with many others he considered Joseph Jones self-serving, and a joke. Naturally, he would not have sought the embarrassment of having his judgement questioned in public, but usually he would have coped confidently with the elder's comments, and would have dismissed them as those of a crank. He would have taken heart from the deacons' acknowledged support and zeroed in on Joseph Jones's scheming. There hadn't been any rumours! If there had, he felt sure that he would have been made aware of them by someone or another. At any other time, he would have realised that he had been put on notice by one, and only one, member of the chapel, and there was no more to it than that. He would have concluded that in truth, Joseph Jones had been thwarted, and his statement that morning had been no more than an unlovely attempt to make something out of a very bad hand indeed. This is how Elfed would normally have reacted, but these weren't normal times for him. For four weeks he had been burdened with a guilty conscience, and so he had become susceptible to hearing the word of God in the most unusual places.

For the last four weeks, Elfed, just like his daughter, Enid, had struggled with his thoughts about Rhiannon... or, to be precise, with thoughts about her little red dragon. Not that often, but too often for comfort, this symbol, once thought of as friendly, had impinged uncomfortably upon Elfed's mind. Usually, he'd managed to suppress these thoughts, but on those occasions when he'd failed, he would imagine Rhiannon's little red dragon tucked into her bosom, bobbing and weaving and tossing and turning as she toed and froed around the house. Then, he would catch himself, and feel quite ashamed; because he couldn't completely control these thoughts, he felt frustration, and because he couldn't share them, he felt lonely.

Such was Elfed's frame of mind as he trudged upwards towards the farmhouse, crossing the two fields that separated his home from the Tryweryn. In the distance to his right, he noticed Geraint waving at him. He waved back, and wondered how his son would react to this morning's rumpus. In the same breath, he wondered too whether he'd tell Rhiannon what had happened. He was bound to bump into her in the house. He unlatched the back door. The silence surprised him, and he surmised that Rhiannon must have accompanied Geraint on his walk. Funny he hadn't seen her, though. Ahead, to his left, the kitchen door was shut. That was funny too. Deep in thought and despondent, Elfed opened it. The room was low-lit for the curtains were drawn. As a voice that was Rhiannon's asked, "Is that you, Geraint?", it hit him. Elfed realised with horror that he had disturbed Rhiannon during her assigned bath time. As he turned in confusion to leave, he discerned her kneeling in the tub with her back to him. Rhiannon was far from shapeless, and as if to prove it, she swivelled to see who was at the door. Confronted with Elfed, she shrieked and clutched her arms defensively to her lathered breasts. As one would have expected, Elfed mumbled an apology and left. He was about to shut the door when his mind took an uncharacteristic turn. Perhaps, he reasoned, a glimpse of Rhiannon's dragon might exorcise it from his thoughts. And what better a time than the present? She was naked and they were alone, and Geraint, he reminded himself with a spasm of guilt, far removed. At this point, reason gave way to a wing and a prayer, for he had no idea how he'd persuade Rhiannon to reveal her tattoo. Deadpan, he approached, and once at the tub, just gazed at her covered breasts. Rhiannon's face expressed confusion and flashes of concern. For an age, it seemed to Elfed, neither moved. The absurdity of his situation suddenly crystallised and he felt extremely foolish. Without doubt, he would have backed off pathetically had Rhiannon not broken the ice. It seemed that she'd sensed his mission, for she relaxed, and smiling most knowingly, dropped her arms and removed every last bit of lather from her breasts with sensuous sweeps of her hands. With her wonder revealed to the full, it was Elfed's turn to betray confusion. Where was the little red dragon? Rhiannon amused, Elfed confused, and no question now as to who held the upper hand. Their eyes met, but as Rhiannon rose so slowly from the tub, she failed to hold his gaze. He could not help but notice another red feature which not even he, in his confusion, could mistake for a little red dragon. Rhiannon swivelled her hips sexily, and there, high on her right buttock, it lay. Elfed's face fell. He'd felt sure that… yet, with this revelation came sudden relief; to him, a dragon on the buttock beggared belief. In fact, Elfed found it quite comical. He laughed and laughed as he left the kitchen, and thanked Rhiannon profusely. He hadn't laughed so much in a long time. In contrast, Rhiannon looked bewildered, standing naked in a tub, in a low-lit, chilly kitchen.

Later, Elfed relished his relief. No longer did he wish he weren't aware of where Rhiannon's dragon lay, and nor did he fear as much that the dragon's tail would sting one day. It seemed in sum that a dragon on a bum lacked the allure of one on a breast, and hence the cure.

To be fair to Elfed, though, there was a little bit more to it than that. A year ago, the uncertainties of his recent past would have been unimaginable. He had been born generous, and to that attribute, wisdom and self-confidence had been added during those tender years spent tending to his mother. His relationship with Margaret had been enviable, and his family was among the most popular in the community and the chapel; at last, after years of farming without return, his husbandry was paying off. That was a year ago, and then at the red tent, he had met Rhiannon, who out of the blue had challenged his composure. Uncharacteristic had been his reaction, and he had no explanation for it. Irrational had been the unease that had sprung from merely knowing that Rhiannon too would have a little red dragon tattoo. Over the summer and autumn, his uneasiness had virtually evaporated, only to resurface four weeks ago, when Rhiannon had re-emerged as his nemesis. Its reappearance had been disappointing, but by now, the catharsis it had finally wrought, cast it as a blessing in disguise. Elfed was essentially whole again, and as before, he had no explanation for the change. He would have liked to think that God had a hand in the matter. He thought it would be nice to have Him on his side once again.

Elfed had no idea how Rhiannon would react to his intrusion. Be it with reassurance or ruthlessness, it mattered little to him, for he was sure the latter posed no threat to him now.

Twelve

TWO MONTHS ON, Elfed worked at his wall. He and Geraint had just finished feeding the sheep and tending to the lambs, and now for an hour before his midday meal he would work at his wall. Dry stone walls crissed and crossed the hills around the valley, as they had done for centuries. Motionless, yet moving away in waves, racing up the ridges, poking and prying into everybody's business, as far as the eye could see. This morning, mist cut their movement short, but they were there. Maintaining them was an art, which for his part Elfed would make sure he handed down to Geraint. Two fields from the farmhouse, a short section had crumbled and that's where Elfed crouched, relishing the remedial work. At that moment, he was clearing the section stone by stone, content with this preparatory work, knowing that the fun part would follow. There was nothing like the sense of achievement he would experience when the rebuilding began: feeling, eyeing, weighing, hewing, satisfaction in renewing.

"Elfed... Elfed! Where are you?"

Margaret could just about be heard, but was nowhere to be seen.

"Over here, Margaret... over here!" he yelled.

"This is odd," he thought, "It's nowhere near dinner time."

"Over here, Margaret," he yelled repeatedly, and in between thought how much he loved her. Would these thoughts have surfaced, he wondered, had he been wrestling a ram or digging a ditch, rather than working his wall? Probably not. So should he feel shame that in general he felt warmly of others only when content with himself? His perverse reaction was to think again of how much he loved his Margaret. That was not to say she didn't have her faults. In his opinion, she was a bit gullible, but amazingly that never seemed to get her into trouble. Sometimes, he felt she was a bit too self-sufficient. At times, he wished she needed him just a little bit more, but that was ridiculous, wasn't it? What was far more important, he would regularly conclude, was that he felt the need to make her happy, and that she seemed happy to let him. Yes, she had her faults, but nothing gave him more pleasure than overlooking them... except for working the wall, perhaps.

He could see her now, waving madly at the far end of the fogbound field.

"Elfed! Come quickly, please. I need you to come now... please!"

Elfed decided not to shout and ask her why. He scrambled over the crumbled wall, and ran and walked, then ran and walked again in the direction of the farmhouse. He caught up with Margaret at the entrance to the farmyard, and she spluttered, "There's someone to see you, Elfed."

"So what's the rush?"

He was so breathless, he could hardly talk.

"He seemed so ill, Elfed. Honestly, I thought he was going to die, and as you're the first-aid expert, I thought... "

She was short of breath too, but recovered to admonish Elfed.

"Oh! Elfed! Don't bother to take your boots off. Just get in the kitchen... please!"

At one end of the table sat Geraint and opposite him, Rhiannon, holding a stranger's hand. With the other, the stranger sipped a cup of tea. His face was pale, and each laboured breath he took accentuated the gauntness of his face. However, the distress in his eyes soon dissipated as they walked in, and his warm, apologetic smile wiped the tension off his face.

"I'm so sorry, Mrs. Evans," he said in Welsh and took a breath, "But... "

"No, no! I'm the one who should be sorry," interrupted Margaret, "I probably panicked a bit but I thought you were..." and her voice trailed off in embarrassment.

"Going to die?"

He finished the sentence for her and then continued, taking short, shallow breaths between phrases. Despite this, he appeared more comfortable than before.

"I thought I was going to die too. No, not really, but I did have a bit of a fright I must admit. I've got a cold on my chest and that always makes things worse."

Elfed had been primed for action, but since arriving he had been winding down, and now he spoke.

"You're over the worse now, are you? You seem to be settling down. Did you come on the train?"

"Yes, Elfed, but I made a mistake: I got off at Arenig station, instead of the Halt," and as he said Elfed's name, his smile widened, and then contracted suddenly as a cloud crossed his face, "I'm really sorry about all this. It's the coal dust, you know. Because of my cold, perhaps I would have been wiser to have stayed at home."

Rhiannon let go of the stranger's hand. As she did so, Elfed thought that the stranger's gaze lingered on her face a little longer than was normal. He couldn't be sure, but...

"It was in the South, was it?" from Rhiannon.

The stranger nodded, as did the cloud over his face.

"But you have a strong trace of a north Walian accent, don't you?"

The cloud lifted noticeably.

"Well, yes, but it's not surprising because I'm from here. Well, from Bala, anyway."

Again, it seemed to Elfed that the stranger gave Rhiannon unnatural attention. What was going on, he wondered? He didn't dwell on the question though, for another matter had intrigued him ever since the stranger had mentioned his name.

"So… you know me, then?"

"I don't think I've ever met you before, but yes, I know you… very well."

Elfed was confused, and it showed.

"Let me give you a clue. I was told that all I'd have to say were the words "little red dragon", and they would give the game away."

All four reacted visibly. The cloud had lifted completely when Elfed said excitedly, "So you must be… you must be… Wyn Williams?"

Elfed strode around the table and shook the stranger's hand too vigorously, and then apologised.

"Oh, I'm sorry. I got excited. Are you all right?"

Wyn Williams nodded, and in response to three confused expressions at the table, Elfed continued enthusiastically, "Wyn Williams is a friend of my very good friend Edward Jones. This is the fellow who persuaded Edward to go South, and to think I almost went with him! In the end I suppose, I got put off by… " and he trailed off, just as Margaret had done earlier, in embarrassment.

As before, Wyn Williams finished the sentence off.

"The working conditions? Is that what you were going to say?" and he started coughing and wheezing, much to Margaret's distress, for it was this combination that had frightened her earlier.

"Don't worry, please," spluttered Wyn Williams, "Just give me time. Perhaps you could tell me your family news. Didn't I hear in Bala that you had a daughter too?"

Elfed nodded proudly, but then hesitated noticeably before speaking.

"Her name is Enid and she's exactly one year younger than Geraint. Now there's precision for you!"

Everyone laughed, and seemed to have forgotten Elfed's momentary hesitation.

"Enid's with Margaret's older sister Mary today. Mary lives over in Capel Celyn and sadly is failing at far too young an age. So she really appreciates Enid helping her out a couple of times a week. Enid is sleeping over there tonight, so I'm afraid you won't meet her this time."

Wyn Williams had asked for a rest, and they obliged, despite Elfed's keenness to catch up on Edward. Throughout dinner, Elfed encouraged the others to join him in discussing farming conditions, describing the families in the valley and so on. He restrained himself from bringing up Edward, but not from pondering a possible connection between Rhiannon and Wyn Williams. The visitor, saying little, mainly ate and listened, and seemed to strengthen considerably.

By early afternoon, the mist had lifted. Geraint had left to look at the lambs, while Margaret and Rhiannon washed up. Two men remained at the table. Elfed too, had work to do, but politeness was paramount, and in any case, he was dying to hear of his friend.

"So Wyn, tell me about dear old Edward, then. Is he well?"

Although Wyn Williams's breathing seemed more settled by now, his speech remained poignantly punctuated by regular gasps for air.

"I can tell you that Edward still has his light ginger freckles. Remember them? How could you not, right? And he hasn't kept them to himself, either. His daughter has them, and his granddaughter as well. It's a family trait, all right! It's quite funny really. Is he well, you asked. Yes, Edward seems all right. He's been a miner for twenty-five years now, I think, and he seems fine. Yes, he really does, and I'm happy for him."

Elfed glanced at Margaret and fancied her eyes were glazed. As for him, the lump in his throat just wouldn't let go.

"But why should Edward be so lucky and... ?"

Wyn Williams interrupted Rhiannon, softly and sadly.

"Don't get me wrong! Edward hasn't escaped the coal dust. It's inevitable, I'm afraid that it's affected him. He just doesn't feel the effects yet, or perhaps they're so slight that he can hide them."

He straightened his body and took as deep a breath as he could before continuing.

"Edward is lucky that he has good genes. His lungs must be more resistant to the dust than mine, that's all," and he smiled for the first time for a while and thanked Margaret for his cup of tea.

"Tell us about his family, Wyn; his children, grandchildren, whatever."

Wyn Williams took several sips of tea, and the warmth seemed to work wonders.

"I said that he was well, but there is sadness too. Edward himself is very happily married to Rachel Anne, and they have one child, Martha May, and this is where the sadness comes in. About five years ago, she married an Englishman."

He stopped to take a deeper breath, allowing Margaret to ask the obvious question.

"Well, what's wrong with that?"

"In itself, nothing of course, but this one's a hooligan, and because he lives with them, they have to put up with him, day in, day out. That's bad enough, but to make matters worse, he hates all things Welsh."

At this, Elfed noticed Rhiannon lifting her head and turning towards Wyn Williams. He continued talking, seemingly unperturbed. As he did, Rhiannon brought a bunch of knives and forks to the table, and dried them. Elfed thought she looked unusually alert.

"And listen to this," Wyn Williams continued, "He threatened to kill Martha if he ever caught her speaking Welsh to their baby. Can you believe that? She's forbidden to speak Welsh in her own home. Edward and Rachel Anne are very upset, and apparently it drives Martha nuts that her daughter can't speak Welsh. She feels she's letting the side down."

"And so she is, Mr Williams" said Rhiannon, in a sharp and serious tone.

Rhiannon's brusque incisiveness was so much at odds with her earlier tender touch, that Elfed felt sure Wyn Williams would have faltered. Far from it, and to further fuel the intrigue, he glanced at Elfed enigmatically before continuing.

"No she's not, Rhiannon. It's not her fault that… "

"Of course it's her fault, Mr Williams. Each mother and each father who can speak Welsh has a responsibility to make sure their children speak Welsh as well, and if they don't, of course it's their fault. There's too much of this trying to shift the blame going on in south Wales."

Rhiannon had shown no restraint, but at least enough respect to refer to him as Mr Williams. Much to Elfed's surprise, Wyn Williams remained unruffled. He responded softly but steadfastly.

"Oh, were it that simple, Rhiannon. By now, English speakers are moving in in such numbers that… "

Rhiannon interrupted again and countered noticeably seamlessly in comparison to Wyn Williams's irregular delivery.

"There you go again, you see: shifting the blame. It's obvious where the blame should be laid, and also what price should be paid. Because of their lax attitude towards the language, south Walians should accept that they aren't as qualified to carry the flame for Wales as the four of us, for example."

Wyn Williams wasn't lulled by Rhiannon's closing lifeline. You too, Mr Williams, may belong to the elite was her arrogant implication. He was far too familiar with visions of his maker to be flannelled in that way. In response, he leant towards her, holding up his hands, indicating that he wouldn't be interrupted this time.

"You sadden me, Rhiannon. Forgive me for saying this, but you're being left behind by events. Most south Walians who don't speak Welsh think of themselves as being just as Welsh as you; and by the way, they're aware of what people like you are saying, and naturally they resent it. Your attitude towards the language is terribly divisive, I can tell you."

Wyn Williams succumbed to a pitiful bout of coughing. Rhiannon was obviously ready to retaliate. This prompted a stern glance from Elfed and a short, sharp shake of his head. Rhiannon seemed to back down, but just in case, Elfed spoke.

"Take it easy, Wyn bach. You'll be all right in a minute. Your train passes through in half an hour, so if we leave in the horse and trap in twenty minutes, you won't have to hang around at the halt for long. How about another cup of tea, Margaret? That'll warm him up for the journey, and perhaps we can send him off on the train with a hot-water bottle. What do you think?

Margaret spoke for the first time for ages.

"That's a grand idea, Elfed. Mr Williams, are you sure you're fit to travel to Bala?"

He nodded, and she continued.

"It's been so nice having you here. I've really enjoyed listening to you. It'll give me something to think about, I know, and you too, Rhiannon… I hope."

Hoping against hope, she soon realized, for Rhiannon responded with a chilling and challenging glare.

"Rhiannon," said Elfed warmly, "do you mind preparing the bottle for Wyn Williams?"

She made it quite clear that she did.

"Well! You have a nerve. So my reward, is it, for suffering such abuse from the three of you is the privilege of preparing Wyn Williams's bottle?"

No more Mr Williams! The gloves were off.

"So yes… I do mind, but I'll do it anyway, and you can be sure that I won't be such a pushover next time, which incidentally may not be that long in coming."

Wyn Williams smiled at Elfed and winked. What was he to make of that, Elfed wondered.

Thirteen

THEY HAD BARELY clip-clopped out of the farmyard when Elfed turned to Wyn Williams and said earnestly, "Listen Wyn, I'm really sorry about Rhiannon's behaviour. She can be so nice, and yet just as ruthless at times."

"Oh, not to worry, Elfed bach. It's great to see someone her age feel strongly about things."

Elfed held the reins quite casually in his left hand, while his right secured at his neck a couple of sacks that he'd thrown around his shoulders. On his left, Wyn Williams was wrapped in Elfed's long working coat. He hugged a light coloured, earthenware, hot-water bottle to his chest, which was just as well, because even though the mist had lifted completely, a cold wind followed the Tryweryn as it wound around Arenig Fawr, now shrouded to below its shoulder in low cloud. The bone-shaking ride didn't do anything to help Wyn Williams's breathing, but that didn't stop him talking in his now familiar, spasmodic style.

"There's no doubt she has a mind of her own and yet, on these matters, she's undoubtedly parroting her father."

Elfed's head spun smartly to his left.

"So you know Rhiannon's father?"

"Do I know him? Do I ever! I rode his coat-tails, Elfed. I was one of his youngest and most fanatical followers."

All loose ends in Elfed's mind swiftly came together.

"So that explains it all: why you seemed, shall I say, overly interested in Rhiannon, and also why you weren't fazed one bit by any of her arguments."

Another wink and another enigmatic smile.

"Yes, yes, I knew who she was, all right. I'd heard that she'd married Geraint, so I was ready. As I said, I was a Rowland Roberts fan. Fortunately, circumstances forced me to go South…" and the irony of his little gasp for air immediately following the word "fortunately" was not lost on Elfed, "or I too might have been pounding the table with Rhiannon today. As you can imagine, I know her father's credo off by heart. To tell you the truth, I'm sympathetic to most of it, although I doubt my level of conviction matches Rhiannon's. Take self-government, for example. I'd advocate it only if I thought it would benefit the vast majority of the Welsh people, in their pocket and their psyche. The people are the ones that count, right? I wouldn't advocate it just to spite the English, for example, or to benefit a clique in search of a power base. I wouldn't advocate it even to save the Welsh language."

He stopped there, as if implying that this statement was so stunning that it deserved time to sink in.

"All these," he continued, "are secondary to the people. You know what I mean!"

"Slow down now Wyn. You'll wear yourself out at this rate.

Elfed marvelled at Wyn Williams. He loved his enthusiasm, especially in light of his affliction.

"Are you warm enough?" he asked.

"Yes I am, thanks to you, Elfed. I can see what Edward meant now. He talked about you with such affection at times that it made me want to cry, and though he doesn't talk about his little red dragon much, he loves it… I swear to God."

A little weight was lifted right then from Elfed's mind. The remnants of misgivings that Elfed might still have harboured regarding the little red dragons were washed away by this touching reminder of the genuine solidarity that had inspired them. Meanwhile, Wyn Williams was ready to roll again.

"Where Rhiannon is completely wrong is on this south Walian business. At the risk of repeating myself Elfed, let's consider the sequence of events. Iron and coal was found in the south; Welsh speakers moved in from the north, followed by a trickle of English speakers from various places; the trickle soon turned into a tide, and its assimilation with the Welsh language became impossible. Within a generation or two, half the population couldn't speak Welsh; this was an inevitable consequence of industrialization, yet many Welsh speakers... most from outside the south... lay the responsibility on south Walians in general; south Walians naturally resent this, and a division has been created... at a time when any push for self-government is dependent on solidarity. Now, you tell me, Elfed, if there is any blame, where does it lie? Oh! That's enough of that. You're right! I'm wearing myself out."

They could see the halt by now, and faintly hear the train trundling in the distance as it left Arenig station.

"Perfect timing, Elfed. By the way, I'm really sorry I missed Enid. She must be very special."

Elfed debated the dilemma raised by this remark. How much to tell? He hardly knew Wyn Williams, and yet, an instant rapport had been struck. Suddenly, it seemed perfectly natural that he should speak from the heart to Edward's surrogate.

"To tell you the truth, Wyn, she is very special, but she's in Rhiannon's shadow now. Funnily enough, she wouldn't have minded that, but she feels Rhiannon's betrayed her, and it's made her bitter. I understand how she feels because I've been a bit mixed up about Rhiannon myself, at times."

It was almost as if Wyn Williams had anticipated Elfed's answer, because he responded without hesitation.

"Elfed, don't let Rhiannon wear you out. You're a good man, too good for that. She has a quick mind but she's rigid, Elfed, and she's a bully too. You stand up to her. She can't hurt you. It may seem sometimes as if she's succeeded in doing just that, but as long as you remain loyal to those you know to be true, you'll always win through. Don't let her wear you out, Elfed."

Wyn Williams's words could have been taken as patronising, but Elfed embraced them gratefully. No discussion followed, for they had arrived at the railway line and Elfed focused on securing his horse and trap. Elfed helped Wyn Williams across the line to the platform on the other side, and as the train approached, he suddenly felt sad. He felt the train was coming to take his friend away, perhaps far away, and he resented that. Wyn Williams handed Elfed his coat and the hot-water bottle as well.

"I won't need this, Elfed. Thank Margaret for me, won't you? You've all been very nice to me… well, nearly all, anyway."

Elfed smiled a mild reprimand, while the train rattled and squealed and hissed to a halt.

"When do you intend to return to south Wales, Wyn?"

Wyn Williams seemed surprised for a moment, but then his face lit up with understanding.

"That's right! We never talked about that, did we? I'm not going back there, Elfed."

It was Elfed's turn to be taken aback, and he froze with his hand on the handle of the closed compartment door as he was about to open it. He gazed enquiringly at Wyn Williams, who, naturally longing to explain, seemed unaware of the waiting train.

"I've no family down there, you see, but I have brothers and sisters in Bala, and now… I have you."

Elfed filled with emotion, but was determined not to betray it.

The guard had had enough and reminded them quite sharply that he didn't have all day. Elfed hurriedly helped Wyn Williams up the steps, squeezed the window down till open wide and slammed the door shut. More breathless than before, Wyn Williams simply said, "To be honest, Elfed, I've come home to die."

Tears welled in Elfed's eyes and he decided not to bother to try and hide it. The train started spitting stabs of steam, allowing him to partially compose himself.

As Elfed watched Wyn Williams being whisked away, he shouted, "I'll call and see you soon. I promise."

"The sooner the better, Elfed bach," was his friend's reply, but it was drowned in a belch of steam, and just as well. Had Elfed heard it, his tears would have tumbled. Even as it was, he barely held them back as he waved his friend goodbye. With tears still in his eyes, and without a soul in sight, Elfed sat on the platform with his legs dangling over the side. Inevitably, he was reminded of another parting, twenty-five years earlier. Then, too, he had waved a friend goodbye, a friend whose freckles caught the eye. At that moment, he felt very close to Edward, and ashamed of his recent ambivalence towards the little red dragon. He pictured Edward, troubled by his old friend's faithlessness, dispatching an envoy to give him strength. Happily Wyn Williams had succeeded, but sadly it was strength he could ill-afford to give. Humbled by this thought, Elfed begged his Lord forgiveness, and let his tears tumble.

Elfed felt at perfect peace as he clip-clopped home in his horse and trap. Dampness glistened here and there as the clouds atop Arenig Fawr's north shoulder broke up, letting sporadic shafts of sunlight get in on the act. Thanks to Wyn Williams, the little red dragon's bogey had been laid to rest, and for the first time since he'd met Rhiannon, he was confident he could deal with her completely objectively. Enid now would be the rightful object of his attention. In the brouhaha brought about by Rhiannon, he regretted that Enid had been neglected, and he determined, there and then in his horse and trap, to right that wrong with affection. First of all though, he couldn't wait to get home and tell Margaret of his conversation with Mr. Williams, as she had called him. He couldn't wait, but as Rhiannon most likely would be there, he might have to... until he and Margaret and his little red dragon went to bed.

Fourteen

JUST AS RHIANNON had hinted, the next time, as she had so ominously put it, was not long in coming, and as for being a pushover, one needn't even ask.

She waited no later than breakfast time on the day following Wyn Williams's visit to make good on her threat. Her manner, however, betrayed no hint of what lay ahead, for she couldn't have been more pleasant. In fact, ever since Elfed's return from the halt the previous afternoon, Rhiannon had been disconcertingly accommodating and charming. All evening, Elfed had had to restrain himself from not only reminding her of her blatant hostility towards Wyn Williams, but also assuring her that even though she may have already succeeded in forgetting it, he and Margaret certainly had not. So at best, an uneasy peace hung over the breakfast table as Rhiannon prepared to speak. Geraint had yet to return from his rounds, so she addressed only her parents-in-law.

"There's something I've been wanting to talk to you about for a few days now. On this subject, I know I'm speaking for Geraint too, so I don't think it matters that he's not here. Is this a good time to talk about it?"

Margaret, and then Elfed, shrugged their shoulders as if they had no objection, so Rhiannon continued apologetically.

"I'm reluctant to even bring this up, but Geraint assures me that I've got to do it, or I won't be happy. Even though Geraint and I haven't been going to chapel since we got married, I think you know that I've met most of the younger people in the valley, either by chance or at farmers' meetings and things like that. The point is, I seem to have impressed many of them with my ideas on politics, and even religion for that matter."

Elfed wasn't at all surprised to hear that. No doubt about it, Rhiannon could be impressive and persuasive, but he wished she'd hurry up and get her talk over and done with. He was already getting tired of her patronising attitude. He glanced over at Margaret and was disappointed, yet not surprised, that she still seemed to be treating Rhiannon with patience and respect, despite yesterday's drama.

"As a result, several of my new friends are urging me to start a discussion group in the valley, similar to the one my father has run in Bala for a long time. I know this may be hard for you to stomach, but what I wanted to ask you was whether you'd mind if I held the meetings here?"

Elfed didn't move a muscle. He was motionless and betrayed no emotion. Margaret, taken by surprise, admitted as much, but maintained her conciliatory approach.

"Well, Rhiannon, you can imagine that this is a bit of a shock to both of us. We want to do all we can for you and Geraint, of course, but I'm not quite sure how this would look... to our neighbours... and the chapel and all that. What if... "

Elfed wasn't interested in any what ifs. He came straight to the point, but remained polite.

"Excuse me, Margaret. I'm sorry to interrupt you, but let's not beat around the bush here. Rather than answer your question, Rhiannon, let me tell you what the consequences would be if we agreed to your request. I'm sure you know already, I'm sure you've thought them through, but I'll tell you anyway so that you, Margaret and I have no illusions about what will happen."

Elfed fancied that Rhiannon flinched a fraction.

"When the word gets out that we are allowing you to hold such meetings in our home, meetings that are certain to be seen as anti-chapel, you know what's going to happen. A particular elder will struggle to his feet in the chapel," and here Elfed stood up and imitated Joseph Jones's imitable stance to a tee, "And say the following very piously, 'My friends, I have warned you before of Elfed Evans's lack of judgement. You concluded then that that particular matter had been out of his control, and he shouldn't be held responsible for it. Well, you've all heard of his most recent slip-up, I'm sure. In my view, this goes beyond misjudgement. This is collusion with a group that is highly critical of our chapel and all others... et cetera, et cetera.' That's what he'll say, Rhiannon, and this time, reasonable people in the congregation may not be able to stop him disqualifying me as a future deacon. Believe me, that wouldn't be the end of the world, but as you well know, our connection with the chapel is one of the most important pillars of our life, and you are asking us to do something that might well put that at risk. I wanted to be sure that the three of us understood what's at stake here," and he glanced deliberately at Margaret before resuming his emotionless pose.

The silence that followed was interrupted by Geraint with a very little lamb in his arms and a very big smile on his face. Ohs and ahs and age-old terms of affection diffused the tension, but did not divert Margaret for long. She had got the message and was eager to deliver it, and in doing so, show solidarity with her husband.

"Excuse me a minute, Geraint, but Rhiannon... I think Elfed couldn't have put it more clearly."

Geraint was mystified and miffed. He resented being out of the picture, especially so soon after being the centre of it. However, not even her son's sensitivities would divert Margaret now.

"As much as we would like to please you and Geraint, it doesn't make sense for us to risk alienation within our community, does it? Of course, it should be obvious to everyone that we don't agree with all your views, but you know how people are. I think Elfed's analysis is spot on, so we just have to say no, I'm afraid."

It seemed that Margaret, in her refusal, was being typically conciliatory, so no one was prepared for her next remark.

"And I must say, Rhiannon, that I'm a bit surprised that you would have even thought of asking us, knowing as you do our situation in the valley... and the same goes for you too, Geraint."

Geraint was halfway through the door with his bleating newborn lamb when Margaret's softly spoken thunderbolt struck, and he saw no reason not to keep going. Elfed, emotionless no longer, sensed in Rhiannon the onset of another chilling and challenging glare, but this time it was contained. As for himself, he could have jumped over the moon, but only allowed himself a long, thoughtful look at Margaret, as he slowly stroked his stubble in a detached and casual manner. Meanwhile, the heroine rose and moved to follow Geraint and his lamb. Rhiannon, clearly disappointed but disarming as could be, rose as well, and spoke.

"As I told you, I was reluctant to bring it up in the first place. I tried to arrange several other meeting places, but for obvious reasons I suppose, none of them worked out. In any case, I'm sorry to have bothered you. I really understand how you feel, believe me. Geraint of course, will be very disappointed, but he'll get over it, and I'm disappointed too, but that's life; as far as I'm concerned, that's that."

Margaret seemed relieved at Rhiannon's reasonableness. She took her response at face value, but Elfed knew better.

It was late afternoon on the same bright spring day. Elfed stood at the farmyard gate, gazing at a spot in the distance, where Margaret would appear on her way home from her sister's house. She had left much earlier, reassuring herself that even if Enid were unwilling to return home with her, she would at least enjoy a chat with Mary. Elfed continued gazing. It was his way of deferring the decision of which six humdrum chores would be the first. His indecision was resolved by Rhiannon, who called his name as she approached the gate.

"Elfed! I'd like to talk to you for a minute, please. I've been thinking a bit more about our conversation this morning, and I don't think you realize how important this discussion group is to me. I hate to do... "

"Rhiannon. Get to the point, would you? What's on your mind?"

"Well, as I was saying, I really feel strongly about getting this group up and going. As I said this morning, I can't find another place to hold the meetings, so as much as I hate... "

"Rhiannon, please! Don't beat around the bush. Stop patronising me, will you, and just tell me what's on your mind."

Rhiannon seemed wrong-footed by Elfed's aggression. Deprived of her preamble, she appeared slightly uncomfortable as she laid out the terms of her deal.

"It's as simple as this, Elfed. If you don't let me hold the meetings here, I'll tell everyone in the valley that..."

"Let me guess, Rhiannon," in a slow, sarcastic monotone, "You'll tell everyone in the valley that I accidently disturbed you while you were taking a bath, and that I couldn't take my eyes off your beautiful breasts, right?"

"Oh, that's far too harmless, Elfed. I'll tell them that you deliberately disturbed me, and then tried to rape me, and if it hadn't been for my... "

Elfed interrupted matter of factly and as he did so, turned abruptly and opened the gate.

"I'll let you know tomorrow."

That's all he said, and he strode away. Already uncomfortable, and now it appeared rattled by Elfed's calm defiance, Rhiannon lost her composure for the second time in as many days.

"And you know, don't you," she yelled after him frantically, "That when the time comes, anyone who cares to look will find some nasty looking bruises in some very interesting places."

Elfed kept on striding.

Elfed kept on striding until he was out of sight of the farmhouse and Rhiannon. While he strode, his mind was blank, but he slowed once out of sight, so that he could think again. His first thought was that without realizing it, he was on his way to meet Margaret. A happy prospect, made all the happier by the probability of meeting Enid as well. Then his thoughts turned to Rhiannon, and he calmly took stock. He hadn't been at all surprised by her contradictory behaviour, especially after yesterday's scene. He had known better than to expect Rhiannon to take their rejection lying down. It was clear now that a chameleon had come in their midst… reassuring one minute, and ruthless the next. His instincts about her had been right all along. It is true that they'd expressed themselves in disconcerting ways, but they'd been right, and that realization gave him an eerie pleasure.

Rhiannon had presented him with a couple of decisions, one of which he'd already taken. Elfed had decided that if he had to, he would deny Rhiannon's allegations. He would deny all of them. He would deny them to the world and to his friends; he would even deny them to himself, if necessary. This would not ordinarily have been an easy decision for him. He hated lying… he hated lies… the truth was everything to him, but under these circumstances, and at this time, he walked into this netherworld without a second thought. To make it as easy as possible on himself, he clinically chose to limit his lies. He would admit that he had disturbed Rhiannon while she took a bath, but he would insist that it had been accidental. Of course it had been an accident! People knew him better than that! So he would admit that he had disturbed her, but then apologised and left. Yes, as a matter of fact, he had noticed her breasts. Even from the door, even at that angle, it had been hard not to.

Such was Elfed's train of thought as he stopped to admire Arenig Fawr's north shoulder. At that moment, it was lit by the sun, a magnificent monument to God's omnipotence.

"Oh, yes. I'd forgotten about God, hadn't I?" thought Elfed uneasily, "There's no use denying it to him, is there?"

Momentarily, his conviction wavered, but somehow he just knew he was handling this right. He remembered Wyn Williams's advice.

"Elfed, don't let Rhiannon wear you out. You're a good man... too good for that. She's a bully, but you stand up to her. She can't hurt you. Don't let her wear you out, Elfed."

Yes, Elfed was sure that God too would see this his way. To be absolutely sure, he ran through once again his justification for lying. The facts were simple. No question about it, he had done wrong, but he had hurt no one. He hadn't hurt Rhiannon. In fact, she seemed to have enjoyed the incident. Nor had he hurt Margaret. He hadn't done anything to harm their relationship. His lapse had not stemmed from lust, but from a spontaneous attempt at exorcism. It would never happen again, he knew it. Even though he conceded that, in themselves, none of these facts justified lying, when taken together with Rhiannon's threat, he had no doubt that they did. For what he'd done, he did not think he deserved to suffer a lifetime of shame. Nor did he think that Rhiannon deserved the power to inflict it on him. He allowed himself to admit once again that he had done wrong, but Rhiannon's sentence would be out of all proportion to the sin. Whether he liked it or not, he had to lie about this, and as he felt completely justified, he would do so with conviction.

Elfed crossed the little bridge that spanned the Tryweryn without making his customary communion with the waters. Normally, he would have stopped and gazed dreamily at the patterns whipping by, before focusing suddenly on the river bottom and acknowledging a light brown boulder...the very same boulder each time. Today, he gazed instead at the path that wound ahead, up towards the Capel Celyn road. Margaret still was not in sight, and her tardiness surprised him. He looked forward to greeting her with an enthusiasm that reflected not only affection but also inner strength. Before too long, he would arrive at the highpoint of the hike, and surely from there he would see her. In the meantime, another decision was taken. Surprisingly, and especially having steeled himself to lying if necessary, he decided quickly that he would yield to Rhiannon's threat. What was to be gained from defiance, he reasoned? If denied, Rhiannon would almost certainly carry out her threat, forcing him to defend himself to the community. If faced with that, he would rather take his chances with Joseph Jones's inevitable tribunal. And anyway, while he sincerely was prepared to wrestle with Rhiannon in public, why would he put other members of his family through such a spectacle? Why would he even put Rhiannon through it? Despite their differences, they were all going to have to get along together for a long time yet, and a confrontation of this kind would make that all the harder, if not impossible. No, it made no sense to defy, so he would yield. He would agree to the use of his home as the venue for Rhiannon's meetings, but how to explain his change of heart to Margaret? He didn't mind telling her of Rhiannon's threat, because she would believe his story anyway, but why needlessly poison Margaret's opinion of her daughter-in-law? At times, Margaret's naivety in relation to Rhiannon had grated on him, but on the evidence of her remark this morning, she'd struck a beautiful balance. Margaret, he thought to himself, was quite lovely.

"And I must say, Rhiannon," she'd said right out of the blue, "That I'm a bit surprised… "

That had warmed the cockles of his heart; aware yet accommodating, realistic but respectful. From a practical point of view, that expressed a perfect approach to Rhiannon, and he wouldn't want to change that. No, he couldn't tell Margaret all. He'd have to think of something else, and the sooner the better.

He saw her now, with Enid. Margaret looked so much shorter than her daughter, a reflection of her age and Enid's unusually erect stance. They arrived at the highpoint simultaneously and hugged, much to Enid's astonishment, for rarely had she seen her Mam and Dad embrace.

"I'm so happy to see you both," said Elfed, still hugging his wife.

Excitedly, Enid demanded her turn, and hung on in her father's arms while she said her piece.

"Mam tells me that Rhiannon's been up to her antics again, and that you put her in her place. I'm so proud of you, Dad."

This stark reminder of the delicate path he'd have to tread, caught Elfed on the back foot. He held Enid slightly tighter in an attempt to disguise his discomfiture, to which she joked, "I know you're happy to see me, Dad, but… "

Elfed loosened, but only a little. There remained a perceptible tension in his embrace, as he gazed abstractedly down the valley, focusing if anything on the confluence, but peripherally aware of the village and Arenig Fawr. He loved all that lay below, but none nearly as much as the treasure in his arms and her mother smiling proudly at his side. He needed to protect them, above all. He'd have to think of something, and the sooner the better.

Fifteen

As ELFED HAD predicted, Joseph Jones struggled to his feet and proceeded to inform the congregation of a special deacon's meeting that had been held earlier in the week, where Elfed Evans's latest error of judgement had been discussed. So, Elfed had yielded to Rhiannon's threat. He sat in his usual pew, this time though between Enid and Margaret. The three held hands, which was highly unusual. From this show of solidarity, it seemed that Elfed must have done something very right. Joseph Jones continued by reminding the congregation of their previous special meeting, and Elfed Evans's reprieve that time. This time though, there would be none, he pronounced emphatically, for the circumstances, which he was sure he needn't relate, were doubly damning. Not only had Elfed Evans once again demonstrated a pitiful lack of judgement, but also collusion with none other than the forces of the Devil himself. He took no pleasure, he assured the congregation piously, in informing them that he and his colleagues had decided unanimously to disqualify Elfed Evans as a potential deacon at Capel Celyn chapel. With that, he struggled to sit down, but froze in the process. God forbid, but someone was actually shouting from the congregation. Alas, he couldn't raise himself and turn in time to stop Trebor Thomas getting most of what bothered him off his chest.

"I think the congregation should know," Trebor shouted, "that there was nothing unanimous about this decision. I know for a fact that the first vote was in favour of… "

"Shut up, Trebor Thomas."

Joseph Jones, on his feet again, was furious, but Trebor wouldn't give any ground.

"The first vote was in favour of Elfed. In fact, all of the deacons except Joseph Jones and one other were in Elfed's favour, and they only changed their mind when... "

"Trebor Thomas, you are out of order. Sit down and shut up, before I come over and do it for you."

Trebor took his chances, and over Joseph Jones's objections, finished his piece.

"And they only changed their mind when our esteemed member over there threatened to resign from the chapel."

Trebor sat. The chapel was hushed... until the esteemed member spoke again.

"Trebor Thomas had no right to speak. This is not a public forum. I was making an official announcement, which... "

"Mr Joseph Jones?"

Someone spoke from behind his back in a soft but authoritative voice. Joseph Jones wheeled laboriously to find the minister on his feet, smiling benignly. Remarkably, it was the same fresh-faced visiting preacher as before. Joseph Jones was speechless for long enough to allow the minister to continue, and then it was too late to stop him.

"This is a house of the Lord, gentlemen, and it is not appropriate to conduct a slanging match within its sacred walls. Mr Thomas, you were improper to respond as you did," and here Joseph Jones appeared mollified... if only for a moment, "but nevertheless, it was understandable. What would be proper, however, under the circumstances, would be to offer Mr Evans an opportunity to speak, if he wishes."

The fresh, unruffled face was raised quizzically towards Elfed, who seemed to be unprepared for all this. He shuffled his shoulders for a second, and then glanced at Enid and Margaret in turn. Slowly, all three rose, all three still holding hands. Whatever the congregation may have thought of Elfed, these two ladies from Tryweryn were firmly for their man, and they wanted the world to know it. Elfed must have done something very right indeed. All heads to the front of the trio respectfully turned, all but one, for during the minister's reprimand Joseph Jones had settled for a tactical retreat. He had sat down with a struggle, and wasn't about to struggle again. His broad back, bent like a sickle, stuck out in an ocean of expectant faces.

"Thank you, Reverend," began Elfed, with surprising assurance, "And thank you too, Trebor. I'd heard the same story myself, as a matter of fact. My friends, this is the way I see it: it's clear that there is at least one vote against me, and I know for a fact there's at least one for me."

As he finished his sentence, he slowly looked up at the chapel's high ceiling. He looked up, and he kept looking, until there was no doubt in anyone's mind whose vote he was referring to.

"Yes, that's the way I see it. I don't think I need say any more than that, although… if you see fit to censure me, so to speak, you should all know that I won't harbour any hard feelings. This chapel means too much to me for that."

Elfed may be excused perhaps, for laying it on a bit thick, for there was much at stake. There was a risk though that pitting Joseph Jones against God may have been construed as a touch theatrical, and not gone down too well with the more perceptive members of the congregation. They may have questioned too, the sincerity of Elfed's self-righteous declaration of devotion to the chapel. In reality, Elfed wasn't at all certain how he would react to rejection, and to be honest, some of Rhiannon's arguments had made him think twice about blind devotion to any chapel.

He moved as if to sit down, but couldn't. Margaret's hand wouldn't let him. An ocean of faces, relaxed and half-turned to the pulpit, was stopped in its track, and in unison returned to the trio and came alive again. Margaret wanted to speak, and as she was already on her feet, it seemed perfectly natural for her to do so. Any unease left by Elfed's polished performance was swept away by hers. There was no doubt that she was speaking from the heart.

"I'm sorry for imposing on you all like this, but I just think it's important for me to tell you a few things about Elfed. You know him as someone who's respectable and devoted to this cause, but I live with him. I see him day to day as someone who would give his right arm for his family; I see him as someone who is very practical, and not in the least bit bigoted; and I see him too as tolerant, generous and prepared to give credit where credit is due. That's how I see him. I see my husband Elfed as a man this chapel can ill-afford to lose."

Elfed and Enid and Margaret sat down, and the ocean of faces turned in a wave towards the front. Nothing more was said on the matter. Still smiling benignly, the fresh-faced visiting minister climbed to the pulpit, and preached. A few actually listened and found his sermon quite entertaining. The others daydreamt of tolerant and generous husbands and wives. Elfed must have done something very, very right indeed.

Sixteen

Yes, ELFED MUST have done something very right indeed. Well, as a matter of fact, it wasn't so much what he'd done as what he'd said; and to be precise, what he'd said to Margaret, which had then led to her conversation with Rhiannon late in the morning of the day following Rhiannon's threat and outburst in the farmyard. Margaret and Rhiannon had been cooking, while Enid had gone to call her brother and her father, working at the wall. Margaret had glanced through the window at Enid's receding figure and then held her daughter-in-law's arm.

"Rhiannon, while we're alone, I'd like to tell you something. Is that all right?"

Rhiannon had nodded nonchalantly. She was all reassurance, and had been so all day, just as if her outburst had been a part in a play.

"Elfed told me about that time when he walked into the kitchen while you were taking a bath. Apparently, he lingered a little, as he put it. In other words, he didn't avert his eyes as he should have. Men will be men, won't they?"

Margaret had stopped, because Rhiannon wasn't reacting quite as she would have expected. Surprisingly, she'd betrayed confusion, until she suddenly caught herself and smiled appropriately shyly.

"Anyway, he's been too embarrassed about it to apologise himself, so he asked me to do it for him. And by the way, we're both very grateful that you didn't make a fuss, although of course, he didn't mean to make you feel awkward. He was taken by surprise, that's all."

Rhiannon didn't speak, but her expressions implied that she

appreciated the apology, but really there was no need for it at all.

"And another thing, Rhiannon. Elfed and I have been reconsidering our reaction to your request yesterday. I know you understood how we felt at the time, and truly, we still have the same objections, but goodness gracious, if we can't support our own family, there's something wrong somewhere, isn't there?"

Once again, Rhiannon didn't seem quite sure of herself, but Margaret had continued anyway.

"Elfed and I know how strongly you feel about some of these things, and suspect that you'd hold your meetings in a barn or something, rather than give up the idea... and that's no way to carry on, is it? So we wanted to tell you that we've changed our minds. You use your home, because it is your home too, isn't it? You use it for the meetings, if you wish, and we'll take our chances with Joseph Jones and the chapel."

What could Rhiannon say? She'd got her own way, but not quite as she had expected. She'd beamed her appreciation of course, but all she'd said was, "Thanks, Margaret," before carrying on with the cooking.

What had just been said was only part of the talk that Elfed had had with Margaret. As she'd watched her trio trekking home to lunch, she reflected on what she'd carefully left unsaid. Elfed had persuaded her that allowing the meetings to be held at home would enable them to keep an eye on Rhiannon and Geraint and their recruits. You never know with these groups, he had said. They can sometimes get out of hand, and should their ideas become extreme, don't you think it would be a good idea if we knew about it? That's how Elfed had put it, and of course she'd agreed that it would be an excellent idea. Then, he'd suggested that it might also be a bit petty to refuse Rhiannon something that was so important to her, when overall she hadn't been too bad a daughter-in-law, and she obviously made Geraint very happy; and that's when he'd mentioned the bathtub. Those were the things that Elfed had said, which must have been very right indeed.

That one critical conversation between Elfed and Margaret had several long-term favourable consequences for the family. Rhiannon gathered that Elfed would not be pushed around, and like many a bully, backed off. What's more, his generosity and good sense in handling her threat had gained him her respect. Margaret, too, was a beneficiary of his fortitude. Thanks to his foresight, she remained unaware of Rhiannon's darkest side, and happily and quietly cultivated her relationship with her daughter-in-law, with the result that Margaret's sensitivity and reasonableness eventually rubbed off a bit. Obviously, Geraint didn't come out of all this too badly, either. Surprisingly, the family's reputation in the community didn't suffer at all as a result of their maverick in-law. In fact, most people assumed that if Elfed's family could embrace her, then Rhiannon couldn't be too bad. And to cap it all, Elfed became a deacon, after Joseph Jones's death. In a final act of defiance, the esteemed member managed to hold on just long enough to retain the distinction of being the youngest ever deacon of Capel Celyn chapel.

Despite Elfed's wisdom at this time, there was still one flaw in the ointment... Enid. Soon after Elfed's polished performance at the chapel, Enid left home and moved in permanently with her Anti Mary. Many reasons were given, and all of them plausible. Wasn't Mary failing, and wouldn't Enid's company be a welcome tonic and relief? Wasn't it obvious that a young lady like Enid would be much better off in the thick of things, although one would be stretching things to call the hamlet that. Wouldn't Enid's bedroom at Mary's house better befit a young lady than the room behind the kitchen at the farm, a room that Geraint had roughed it in, before his bride's arrival? And how could there possibly be enough for three women to do on the

107

farm? All the possible reasons were given for Enid's move except the real one, which was that she still hated Rhiannon. She just could not make herself overlook Rhiannon's manipulation and treachery. The final decision naturally had fallen to Elfed and Margaret. Enid's departure was the obvious and practical solution to a tricky situation, and she wouldn't be that far away. What's more, Mary would have a companion, and importantly, there would be no question then of Geraint not staying on the farm; so yes, an obvious solution, but so heartwrenching for Elfed and Margaret to recommend. How would they be able to look Enid in the eye? Only by promising to themselves, as they did several times a day for weeks, that whenever possible, they would go out of their way to make her still feel part of the family. Fair play to Enid, she was gracious and understanding: she forgave them, as she had her father for his about-turn on that business of Rhiannon's meetings; and it was respect for her parents that persuaded her not to badmouth Rhiannon and act in public as if nothing was amiss; in itself, quite a remarkable achievement in such a close community.

However, beneath this harmonious surface lurked not only a young lady's repressed hatred for an in-law, whom she couldn't completely avoid, but also, a little red dragon that just wouldn't go away. Ironically, Elfed no longer feared that the dragon's tail would sting one day. In fact, he believed that whatever sting had lain in store had been exhausted now by virtue of Rhiannon's threat. In as much as he himself might not be stung, he was right. . . but wrong in relation to another.

Seventeen

R HIANNON'S PREGNANCY HAD been uneventful, but regardless, the family was on alert. They'd lost too many lambs during apparently normal births to be complacent. However, at the onset of labour, tension was tempered by the relief that comes with action. Margaret took control and Elfed took to the fields alone, advising Geraint to stay at home with Rhiannon. It was a terrible day, the last day of April in 1905. A gusty westerly wind drove persistent rain in frequent, wicked bursts. Low cloud completely obscured Arenig Fawr, and a stranger would have had no idea whereat the valley lay. Despite this violent weather, Elfed came across no crises. A few newborn late lambs had weathered the elements well, and none of the others showed signs of distress. This, thought Elfed, could not be taken other than as a good omen.

Indeed, when he returned to the farmhouse, calm prevailed and Margaret assured him that everything was perfectly normal… and so it was, until that evening, when to Margaret's increasing concern, no progress was being made. It didn't help that Rhiannon fretted. Her pains seemed to be different now, she said, and not at all what she would have expected. Nevertheless, Geraint went to bed at the usual time, at Margaret's insistence, and before long, so did Elfed. The rain had stopped, but the wind still blew, whistling eerily through the farmhouse, and whining with foreboding. Surprisingly, Elfed was enjoying a pleasant dream when a tense Margaret woke him. She whispered that she was very concerned about Rhiannon. She was sure that there was something wrong, but she had no idea what to do. It was four o'clock in the morning, but she urged him to take his horse and trap to Bala to get help. She wasn't sure if he should disturb the doctor, but at the very least a midwife should be brought up the valley as soon as possible. She added that it would be best if he could leave without Rhiannon knowing, because she was worried enough as it was. Within half an hour, he was on the road, clipping and clopping as fast as he thought was wise given the clear but moonless sky and the road's wet, slippery surface.

The journey, naturally, was an extremely worrying time for Elfed, but eventually he was distracted by the reminder of a similar one almost thirty years earlier, when the moon had been nearly full and he'd drifted on the coat-tails of a friend. He thought of Edward, their little red dragons, unspeakable working conditions and how fine are the lines that define our futures. He was reminded as well, and most poignantly, of the last time he'd ridden to Bala, barely a week before, with a heart heavier even than it was now. Wyn Williams, who had become a close friend and an inspiration, had passed away. Many at the funeral had spoken of how their friend had defied the odds, but that had been of little consolation to Elfed, and at the thought, tears filled his eyes as he parallelled the river in his horse and trap to Bala.

Every cloud, and even every funeral, has a silver lining, and at Wyn Williams's, Elfed had briefly met the doctor. So Elfed knew him to be young, Welsh speaking and caring, and in consequence determined to disturb him rather than the midwife. He was immediately justified in his decision, for the doctor, after listening to a breathless, barebones briefing from Elfed, decided he should see Rhiannon as soon as possible. To save time, the young doctor hopped into Elfed's trap, and as dawn developed beyond the Berwyn, off they rode westwards into the relative gloom of Tryweryn; Elfed in his working clothes and the doctor dressed in a long coat, wide-brimmed hat and padded gloves... all in leather, and all as reassuringly well-worn as the leather bag he carried.

For a few minutes, the doctor asked for more information

regarding Rhiannon. Elfed, reminded of Margaret's deep concern, became visibly anxious. Perhaps it was this that prompted the doctor to change the subject.

"I spent quite a lot of time with Wyn Williams over the last few years. What a courageous man he was! He spoke very highly of you, Elfed, and I think it's fair to say that your friendship, as much as anything in his life, helped to sustain him."

Elfed felt the welling come again. He accepted the compliment, even though he knew full well 'twas the doctor who had softened his old friend's living hell. Yes, there was no doubt that this young doctor was a very nice man, and despite the vast difference in their age, education and social status, Elfed felt quite comfortable next to him.

"What do you think of his political views, Elfed?"

A very broad and provocative question, from which the Elfed of old would surely have withdrawn. However, over the last four years his friend Wyn had coached him in such contentious topics. He took the question in his stride.

"Well, I'm sure you'd agree that 'inclusive' was Wyn's big word. By the way, in that regard, he was critical of Rhiannon… and her father too. You probably know him, don't you?"

The young doctor nodded, surprisingly gravely Elfed thought, but didn't say anything, forcing Elfed to continue, a shade uncomfortably by now.

"Yes, 'inclusive' was Wyn's big word, all right, and… "

"Inclusive is all very well, Elfed."

The doctor's rather formal interruption set a sharper tone. He was still polite, but now polemic, taking Elfed by surprise.

"In fact, without it, Home Rule is a sham. But inclusive means accepting the rough along with the smooth. Certainly, it means including on an equal basis all those who think of themselves as Welsh, whether they speak Welsh or not, but it also means including their politics, Elfed. I'm sure you're aware of the gains made by the Labour Party in south Wales. Even Marxists are said to be making an impact. Believe me Elfed, if Wales became independent at this very moment, our government would be more socialistic than anything we've ever experienced."

Elfed was out of his depth. He didn't know what to say, and even if he did, whether to say it in this increasingly charged atmosphere.

"I'll have to think about that," was all he said, and for a long while there was silence. Freed of the need to concentrate, they became aware that they had climbed considerably. A wide, gentle basin beckoned from the distant right, while ahead, a barrier rose proudly in resistance. It was Arenig Fawr. Even in the meagre morning mid-light, its majestic northern ridge was plain to see. So was its distinctive shoulder, but of the sheer cliffs that plunged to the lake below, only a shadowy hint came through. The silence was broken by the doctor, who seemed intent now on focusing on political points on which he knew they would agree. Elfed soon joined in, careful to skirt contention, as if in memory of Wyn Williams and out of respect for the ordeal that almost certainly lay ahead. With the men at ease again, the doctor spread some icing on the cake.

"I heard from Wyn that you're doing very well, Elfed. I understand you've bought your farm from the squire, and that you're adding on to the farmhouse as well. You're becoming a proper old capitalist."

Elfed was rightly proud of his success and didn't mind showing it, to a modest degree.

"That's not all, Doctor. I've bought the farm next door too. I don't know what I'll do with that farmhouse yet, but as I see it, you've got to take your chances when they come up. By the way, Doctor, you've been very generous, not only getting up like this in the middle of the night, but also treating me with kid gloves."

It was quite light by now, and there wasn't far to go. Soon, they would clear a final ridge, and then both valleys, the confluence and Capel Celyn would come to view. It was a glorious day, as glorious as yesterday had been wet and grey. The high plateau on which they travelled remained unlit, but not for long, for even Arenig Fawr's damp, bald north shoulder already glistened in the rising sun. A good omen, thought Elfed, but he was shy to hang his hat on it, after being let down by another the very day before.

The doctor seemed to mull at length his next remark.

"You're a good man, Elfed... you really are. You probably know that Wyn often referred to you as a good man. Who could pay you a greater compliment than that? By the way, you mentioned Rhiannon's father earlier. I'm sure you've heard from Rhiannon that he's been ailing. Well, I was called to see him last night, because suddenly he's much worse, and to be honest, I'm not sure how much longer he'll live. We should keep this from Rhiannon for now, don't you think?"

Elfed nodded.

"Still, this is all the more reason, isn't it," the doctor added with enthusiasm, "why we have to make sure that all ends well up here today."

The sun had beaten them to the farmhouse. As they approached, Geraint stood outside, betraying no sign that the situation within was worse than when Elfed had left. As the doctor doffed his coat and readied to disembark, Elfed spoke.

"Doctor, if you don't need me here, I think I'll take a walk and look at the lambs."

"You go, Elfed. I may need your wife's help, but basically I'm in this on my own. I probably won't be ready to leave for an hour, so take your time."

After Geraint confirmed his reassuring body language with a few remarks, he was introduced by his father to the doctor. Elfed then left to look at his lambs, and in between the looking, did a lot of praying. True, he and Rhiannon still weren't close: they were too little alike to allow themselves to work through their initially rocky relationship, but no more was she his nemesis, and no longer a thorn in his side. In fact, over the years, they'd grown to respect each other's strengths, and with that had come respect. So, Elfed prayed for the mother, and then when he prayed for the child, he prayed for another... himself.

It was a tense, tentative Elfed who returned to the farmhouse to find to his relief rejoicing. It seemed someone's prayers had worked. He returned to the heavenly aroma of bacon frying, to the inexplicable music in a newborn baby's bawling and to three familiar faces broadly smiling: the doctor's at the table, Geraint's at the fireplace and Margaret's in the background gently rocking. No one said a word for no one had to. The young doctor maintained the magic of the moment by rising, and with gestures of relief, embracing Elfed. Still no one said a thing, but now Elfed, a shade mystified and impatient, began to think a word or two were due. As if on cue, the doctor spoke.

"Elfed, it's a boy, but it was... touch and go. Don't worry though, because Rhiannon and the baby are fine now, but I'll tell you, I was worried."

Within a few minutes, three sat at the table with eggs and sizzling bacon, and steaming cups of tea. Margaret, in the background, gently rocked the baby... to little effect.

"Rhiannon's been through the wringer, Elfed. She's asleep now. I gave her a sedative, because she really needs to rest. Now, I don't want to pour cold water on such a happy occasion, but it would be a good idea for Rhiannon to think twice before having another baby. This is no joking matter. Margaret will agree with me, I know; by the way, she was wonderful. I needed her help, I can tell you, and she was terrific."

So much coursed through Elfed's mind...

Who to look at first?
Margaret got the nod,
Next Elfed gazed at Geraint,
And then he praised his God.

Completing his acknowledgements, Elfed put his arm around the doctor, squeezed him quickly and affectionately, and decided it was time to lighten the mood.

"So what are we going to call this crybaby, then?"

Geraint didn't hesitate to reply.

"Rhiannon and I couldn't agree on a girl's name, but a boy was easy. Our son is named Edgar. That's all, just Edgar."

Elfed and Margaret glanced at each other, and the doctor glanced at both.

"That's a lovely thought, Geraint," said Elfed, clearly touched, "It's perfect, actually", and turning to the doctor, said, "My brother was called Edgar," and left it at that.

The doctor responded by repeating "Edgar Evans" a few times, and then addressed Elfed.

"Yes, it does sound nice. So, you're a grandfather for the first time, Elfed. Congratulations! This little fellow won't stop crying though, will he, even after everything he's been through. He's going to be a little terror, if you ask me. It doesn't look as if he's taking after his grandfather."

"He does have another grandfather," ventured Geraint hesitantly.

The three others raised their heads, but none as noticeably as the doctor.

"That reminds me," he said hurriedly, "I better get going. I'll take another look at Rhiannon, and then, may I take the rest of this bacon in a sandwich, Margaret? And are you sure you can take me now, Elfed?"

Yes, yes, yes, a thousand times and more! The young doctor could have asked for anything as far as Elfed was concerned. When he reappeared with a reassuring smile, Elfed helped him with his coat and fetched his hat and gloves.

"Good luck, Edgar Evans," sang the doctor as he left, "and thanks to you all for your kindnesses."

Most of the kindnesses to which the doctor referred were in a basket, and hidden beneath a heavily starched, white napkin. With difficulty, he held this in his right hand. In the other, he clutched a bacon sandwich, while Elfed with childlike pleasure, carried the doctor's well-worn leather bag.

It was still chilly when the trap carried Elfed and the doctor from the sunlit farmyard. Before long, Elfed suddenly felt very tired, and not surprisingly, for even by mid-morning his body, nerves and mind had already been sorely stretched. The doctor must have felt the same, because for most of their return journey, clip-clopping was all that could be heard. Apart from the following brief conversation, the two mostly exchanged warm glances and sympathetic smiles.

"I just wonder, Elfed," said the doctor, "Whether I should consider training someone in the valley who could serve as my nurse and midwife… on a very part-time basis, of course. With someone like that around, Rhiannon probably wouldn't have got into the mess she did. Can you think of anyone?"

"Enid," said Elfed like a shot.

The doctor took a long, thoughtful look at Elfed, and equally thoughtfully, thanked him.

Later, as Elfed helped the doctor step down from the trap, a nurse hurried out from the surgery. Nodding at Elfed to wait, the doctor walked to meet her. She spoke to him in hushed tones for a while, and then at his suggestion, went back indoors carrying his leather hat, coat and gloves. He returned to the trap, and as he took the basket from Elfed, he spoke quietly.

"Rowland, Rhiannon's father, died early this morning; probably around the time that little Edgar was born. Now there's an eerie correspondence for you, Elfed. Forgive me now for what I'm going to say. I told you earlier, half in jest I suppose, that I thought Edgar was going to be a little terror, and didn't seem to be taking after his grandfather at all. Then Geraint, almost apologetically, said the baby does have another grandfather. Yes, indeed, the baby did, on his mother's side of course, and therein lies the rub, which is why... and I hope you don't think what I'm saying is inappropriate... which is why I want to tell you that your influence on little Edgar could make all the difference. Take him under your wing, Elfed... please!"

What was Elfed to think as he travelled the lower reaches of the Tryweryn for the fourth time that morning? He really liked the young doctor, and respected him. His opinions carried weight... alas!

"Take him under your wing, Elfed," he'd said gravely. Elfed intended to, of course. After all, he was Edgar's grandfather and naturally expected not only to contribute significantly to his upbringing, but also to enjoy the experience. The doctor may be clever, he conceded to himself, but he'd gone overboard on this one. All the way home, Elfed tried to rid his mind of the doctor's plea, and all the way home he failed. In this way, the stage was set for the struggle for Edgar's soul.

Eighteen

ALTHOUGH RHIANNON HAD been dead against chapels, she was not averse to God; so when she appreciated how thin the thread that saved her life at Edgar's birth, she gave God the credit, and if He was on her side, she would be on His… in more than equal measure. She not so much as embraced God but suffocated him with her enthusiasm. Ironically, the main beneficiary of her enlightenment was her former nemesis, Capel Celyn chapel. Rhiannon became a member and was not troubled in the slightest by her abrupt U-turn; nor were the other members, except for Enid of course, for the chapel was no stranger to the pendulum in human behavior, although they may not have come across a pendulum quite like this.

Rhiannon soon became the driving force at Capel Celyn. Of course, a woman could never achieve deaconhood nor hope to become an official of the chapel, but that didn't stop her from running the show. Her drive and ruthlessness got things done, and her reassuring empathy helped heal those toes she'd stepped on. In the valley she became a celebrity, whose charisma was matched only by one other… her son.

As a boy, Edgar was short for his age, and this feature accentuated the chubby face which he had acquired, along with his dark complexion, from his father. There were no prizes for guessing from whom he'd inherited his wavy, rich, red hair and remarkable precociousness. During his early childhood, the valley was Edgar's world and the chapel was his stage. It was there he starred on Sundays. Although he performed with ease from an early age, the initial impression he gave on a public platform was incongruity. Somehow, his strong, striking colouring didn't sit quite comfortably on a little boy with a babyface. Audiences would focus on these elements in conflict, until the performance demanded their attention. Three times every Sunday and sometimes in midweek, the world seemed to stop for the Edgar Evans show. Even at the age of seven, he astonished the congregation with long, flawless recitations from memory. He also read confidently from the Bible, and sang with perfect pitch in a typically childlike voice. He was already a star on a par with his mother.

If the other children in the chapel hadn't already felt inferior, they soon would, because when he was eight, it became clear to the valley that Edgar's childlike voice was flowering into a brilliant boy soprano. He now had an instrument to match his self-assurance. Others with this talent had thrilled and thralled the valley in the past; others had sent a thousand shivers down as many spines; others had charmed with their untarnished top notes and warm, uncomplicated cadences; others had impressed with their eerily easy confidence; but of these, few had possessed Edgar's visual appeal. In boy soprano land, little Edgar's babyface, dark complexion and wavy, rich, red hair took some beating.

So it might be said about the chapel that Rhiannon called the tune and her son sang it. Surely, Elfed could not view these developments with anything but satisfaction. Rhiannon's dedication to the chapel, and his grandson's star role in it had benefitted himself and his family. On the face of it, he had every reason to be pleased. So why was it then that he could not rid his mind of the doctor's plea?

"Take him under your wing, Elfed," the doctor had said gravely, many years before.

Elfed had tried to do just that. So many times he'd really tried and so many times he'd failed. Just as the doctor had feared, Edgar had turned out to be a little terror, vocal and self-willed. Perhaps Rhiannon could have mellowed him if she had wished, but in her eyes he was a miracle, a gift from God. In her eyes Edgar could do no wrong, and as Geraint did on most matters, he bowed to Rhiannon on the raising of their child. So remedial work on Edgar was left to his grandparents, who nodded and prodded and pressured in vain. If Edgar's intention was proving to one grandfather that he had another, then he couldn't have done a better job. Still, Arenig Fawr remained unmoved and life went on, but with it, Elfed's frustration mounted. Countless times he'd counselled Rhiannon regarding "Edgar bach", only to be politely rebuffed each time with the same old standard phrases.

"Rhiannon," he would open, "Edgar shows no respect towards anyone, and his stubbornness is unnatural, even for someone of his age. You need to discipline him, Rhiannon, and the sooner the better, if you ask me."

Elfed knew what was coming.

"He's a good boy really, Elfed, and how can you complain when he's doing so well at school?"

"Yes, but at a price, Rhiannon. His tantrums are driving the teachers mad. You know that. How much longer are they going to put up with his nonsense, d'you think?"

"It's their job, Elfed, and anyway, look how well he's doing at the chapel too. He's a star. You should be proud of him."

"He may be a star, Rhiannon, but he's also a spoilt brat, if you don't mind me saying so."

Rhiannon remained polite, bearing this ultimate insult calmly and closing the conversation with the ultimate cliché.

"He's just a child, Elfed. He'll grow out of it, you'll see," and for now, that's what everyone in the valley seemed to think as well. Ironically, Edgar's tantrums seemed to add to his allure. For now, his childish behaviour only underlined his youth, and therefore magnified his accomplishments.

"He'll grow out of it," was a constant refrain in the valley, but he didn't. In time, Elfed's fear became fact, and Edgar's behaviour ceased to be seen as childish, and became bad. He still performed with incomparable panache. He still won competitions, left and right, and he was still admired, but no longer loved.

All was not lost, however. When he was eleven, and sprouting, Edgar left the little school in Capel Celyn and travelled by train to Bala, to the secondary school. Where Elfed had failed, Edgar's fellow students succeeded. Peer pressure penetrated where Elfed had feared to tread. Children can be so cruel, and merciless with spoilt brats. As Edgar was shamed out of his tantrums, he gradually grew reserved and moody. Then one day the inevitable happened: Edgar's voice began to break, and adulation faded. Rhiannon, fair play, had tried to prepare him for this, but who can arm their mind to kissing goodbye to glory, to bid farewell to that fabulous feeling of power over people. The worst part, he told Rhiannon, was not knowing whether his new voice would match the old. Edgar continued to perform. Mainly he recited, and his memory did amaze, but it wasn't the same. The thrill and thrall had gone. Contrary to most expectations though, Edgar seemed to take the loss in his stride. Perhaps he was growing up at last, and even Elfed began to fancy his chances of getting along with his grandson at last. It was at that time, in fact, that Elfed decided to commit Margaret and himself to financing Edgar through college. Admittedly, Elfed, along with most farmers, had done quite well financially during the Great War, but still, it would be a sacrifice, and given his extreme ambivalence towards his grandson in the past, the decision had not been easy. However, it paid off immediately, for Edgar responded warmly, confirming Elfed's feeling that he may soon have a say in his grandson's future.

It was Margaret who first wondered whether Geraint's pains had anything in common with her mother-in-law's affliction. She told Elfed of her concern, but no one else, for fear of worrying them needlessly. Within a year though, it was confirmed that Geraint had rheumatoid arthritis. Elfed had remained close to his doctor friend, and was informed by him that although nothing could be done, remissions were common. The doctor added that it was important for the patient to keep in good spirits. In this regard, Elfed and Margaret went all out, as did Rhiannon despite being floored at first by Geraint's misfortune. Regardless, the unfairness of it all got the better of Geraint, and he became depressed, so not only was he unable to farm his land, he lost interest in it as well. All this, when Edgar was sixteen and gearing up to go away to college.

Elfed was in his sixties and couldn't do much heavy lifting any more. The smooth running of the enlarged farm had depended heavily on Geraint's energy and enthusiasm, and both were now impaired. Repercussions followed fast. All decisions revolved around the farm. The farm was the show, and the show must go on, and it couldn't go on without Edgar. Everyone knew it, including Edgar, but someone had to say it. In the end, it was Elfed who told Rhiannon, and Rhiannon who told her son.

"Edgar, there's something I... "

"Mam, I know what you're going to tell me," sharply from Edgar.

"Please Edgar, don't make this harder on me than it already is."

"Hard on you, Mam?" with an emphasis on "you", "I'm the one who'll suffer, not you."

"I know, but can't you see that... "

"All I see, Mam, is a case of the Lord that giveth with the one hand and taketh away with the other; you know who I mean, and he's a lord I can do without."

No one could be blamed. Elfed had but said what someone had to say, while Edgar, understandably, played the little boy whose toy had been taken away. One moment, he'd been gearing up excitedly for college, and the next, he was stuck for life on the family farm. Elfed had been doing some gearing up of his own, for months preparing optimistically to influence

Edgar's future. That hope was now a dead duck, and Elfed knew it.

Rhiannon's political convictions were still alive and well. Of course, they'd been subjected to a mild amendment when she'd aligned herself with the chapel. Regardless, her weekly meetings at the farm had flourished up until the onset of the Great War, when in the face of a wave of patriotism, she'd pulled in her horns and laid low. The war had now been over for three years, but her responsibilities at the chapel and turmoil at home had interfered with the resurrection of her political group. Yet, her yearning for independence from England, bloody England, as she sometimes referred to it, was as strong as ever. Her love of the language still fired her up, and her irrational disdain for those "traitors" in the south remained unshaken. These vigorous views of Rhiannon's would have vied effectively with Elfed's more moderate ones for Edgar's mind, under any circumstances. As it was, with Elfed already having been given the cold shoulder, Rhiannon had been granted a monopoly. The struggle for Edgar's political soul was over before it began

So with Elfed out in the cold, Geraint simply out of it and Margaret disqualified by association, Rhiannon more than ever became Edgar's mentor. Though her political views were still strong, she didn't go out of her way to inflame Edgar's opinions on this front. He was just ripe for the picking, that's all. Still missing those glorious boy soprano days, unhappy with his present lot in life and resentful of authority, Edgar lapped up Rhiannon's opinions. She, at least, had her interest in the chapel to divert her mind, but he had little but the farm, so he took her views to heart, and really lived them. It angered him that the Welsh were still beholden to the English and that the Welsh language languished. That made no sense to him, a farmer in the shadow of the shoulder of Arenig Fawr. There had to be a villain in the picture. The English were naturals for this role, but no villain would serve this end as well as a villain within. Parroting his mother's prejudice, the English-speaking Welshmen of south Wales became his whipping boys too; once his views were formed, a strong will precluded modification. So Edgar, while still a teenager, became an extreme nationalist, just like his grandfather.

"He does have another grandfather," Geraint had once said.

Edgar had performed in public all his life, so he was a natural on the local political platform. Despite the constraints imposed by his duties at the farm, he became quite a regular on this circuit. Once again, his youth worked in his favour, and once again his strong, striking colouring did as well. When he got worked up, his fairly long, wavy, rich, red hair seemed to catch on fire. Yet, while he certainly was a spectacle on stage, his message was simple, but uncompromising and divisive. Consequently, his supporters idolised him, but many more despaired.

"We have to get the English off our backs," and so on and so forth.

Every time, these were his opening words, usually in Welsh, but sometimes in English, for effect. Yet, the idea of an independent Wales was impractical by now. That window of opportunity had gone, and Edgar was blundering down a blind alley. It is likely he would have kept on going had his voice not revisited him. Much to his delight, the glorious boy soprano metamorphosised into a tenor of true distinction. He found that he thrilled again, and this occupied his mind; so he left south Walian kicking to others. He sang instead of sniping, yet his views remained in place, but they weren't forever shoved in everybody's face. This improvement pleased Elfed, in particular. It had been hard for him to stomach Edgar's strident nationalism day in, day out.

Elfed was sixty-seven. It saddened him that he hadn't made that key connection with his grandson, and never would, but he didn't blame himself. If anyone was to blame, in his opinion it was Rhiannon. After all, it was from her that Edgar had inherited his exaggerated need to have his own way. In truth, Rhiannon had short-changed her son: to get her own way, she'd been ruthless, and to get away with it, reassuring. Poor Edgar had inherited neither of these qualities, so when tantrums couldn't swing it, moodiness moved in.

In any case, the time had come for Elfed to tell his friend that by now he held no hope of taking Edgar under his wing... as if the doctor hadn't known it!

Nineteen

IT WAS NOON in June of 1925 and Elfed, sixty-eight years old, was on the brink of a new experience.

Half an hour earlier, he and Geraint and six bewildered lambs had arrived in Bala in their horse and cart. After dropping his father off in the high street, Geraint had continued to the mart, where the lambs would be sold, with a bit of luck.

Geraint had been feeling better recently. His pain had lessened considerably and his spirits had risen as a result. He'd been more active on the farm and had begun to take an interest in Edgar's progress. He hadn't made much of a dent in his son's workload, but nevertheless, the two had become closer, a development that Elfed had observed with understandably mixed emotions.

On the high street, Elfed had killed time quite pleasurably with a few acquaintances and then had visited the surgery, hoping to catch the doctor as he closed up. His timing had been perfect.

"Hello, Elfed. Come in," in Welsh, of course.

Over the last twenty years, the surgery hadn't changed a bit, but the passage of time had endowed the doctor's appearance with more authority still.

"No, Doctor, I don't want to come in, thanks, but I wonder if you wouldn't mind doing me a favour. Believe it or not, I'd like to go to the Lion for half a pint, but I wouldn't know how to go about it on my own, you see."

He chuckled to himself and then carried on.

"So... would you come with me, Doctor? You know the ropes at the Lion, and I know you don't have another surgery today. Would you come?"

The doctor was amused, but also quite confused.

"What's going on, Elfed? What are you up to?"

"Oh, you'll find out soon enough, and in any case, I want to talk to you. So… will you do it?"

"Yes, of course, but I can't stay long, I'm afraid. I've got a meeting in half an hour."

So within five minutes, Elfed, sixty-eight years old, was walking through the door of a public house for the first time in his life.

"Slow down, Elfed," whispered the doctor, "Not that way. That's the public bar. Come this way. It's much more genteel in here."

"No, no, no," whispered Elfed urgently, "I want to go in there. It's the public bar I want. So… will you go first then?"

The doctor was even more amused at this, but also more confused.

"Elfed bach, you are a case. OK. Let's get on with it. Follow me closely now, so you don't get lost," and he laughed as he opened the door to the public bar. The air was thick with pipe smoke and reeked of stout and ale, and but for the lady behind the bar, the public here was male. The backs along the bar performed Pavlovian turns towards the door, and were about to swivel forward as they'd done a thousand times before, when, sickle-shaped, they stiffened to attention. Not a word was spoke, but the wonder on their faces said it all. The silence was broken by a man behind the door, who Elfed recognised, and whose long, humorous face was lit up by the window light. As Elfed shut the door, the man quipped with a shade of a south Walian accent, "Boys bach, Elfed… what are you doing here? Have you come to convert us, or what? Just joking, Elfed. You're looking well, man. You obviously don't need to be hanging around with the medicine man. Just joking, Doctor. Always joking, boys. Sit down over there by the window, where they can see you from the road. Always joking, you see… just as I said."

But that's exactly where Elfed sat, and there he chatted to the joker as the doctor joined the backs at the bar, and bought a half-pint of beer for Elfed and a wee dram for himself. When Elfed eventually disengaged himself from the wag, he turned his chair emphatically away from him, telegraphing his intention of having a private conversation with his friend, the doctor.

"Elfed, what on earth are you up to? What are we doing here?" asked the doctor in a hushed tone.

While the question was being asked, the answer walked through the door and worked his way through the smoky grey to the line of backs at the bar.

"How's it going then, boys?" was his loud and friendly greeting.

Cold shoulders on sickle-shaped backs provoked a further question.

"What's the matter, boys? Am I missing something?"

The barmaid's nodding was barely perceptible and her eye movements even less so, but Geraint got the message. As he turned his face, it fell… and froze in a quizzical expression, relieved only by his father's friendly beckoning to the table. The doctor greeted him with, "What would you like to drink, Geraint?"

Understandably, Geraint seemed not at all sure how to react, but after glancing puzzledly at his father and surveying the drinks on the table, he ventured, "Half a pint of beer, please," and off the doctor went, winking at the wag.

Geraint just had to say something.

"Crikey Moses, Dad… you gave me a shock then. I must say, I expected you to be angry with me. You will promise, won't you, not to mention a word to Rhiannon?"

"Oh, Geraint bach, come on! Don't you think she realises? If I had an inkling, you can be certain she does too."

The question mark on Geraint's face posed the obvious question.

"She's got a head on her shoulders, Geraint. She's not making a fuss because she knows what you're going through. Now, I am a bit surprised though, that you've taken to this kind of thing. What's come over you?"

Geraint glanced around the room unobtrusively, before leaning forward and speaking quietly but earnestly to his father.

"As you know, Dad, I've been feeling better lately. Well, this sounds silly, but I'm sure the beer has a lot to do with it. Anyway, it's a nice change, isn't it, from the same old routine back home?"

Elfed had very mixed feelings about that.

"I don't know, Geraint. Anyway, here comes the doctor. Tell him what you just told me."

The doctor responded by savouring a sip of his dram in an overly drawn-out fashion, obviously buying himself some time. Then, most tactfully, he focused entirely on the words "nice change".

Silence followed until Geraint rose suddenly and shook the doctor's hand warmly. Moving around the table, he bent over to wrap his arm around his father's shoulder.

"Thanks for being understanding, Dad," he said, "you are a pal," and off he went with his half a pint to join the silent sickles at the bar. Elfed would have cried into his very first beer had the presence of the wag not pushed him to marshal his pride. As the banter resumed at the bar, the doctor took another sip of his dram, followed by the same drawn-out ritual. Elfed's beer had barely been touched.

"You were very kind to come here with me, Doctor, and I know you have to go soon, but there is one thing I'd like to get off my chest. Edgar's bad attitude really upsets me. I mean,

Rhiannon is nice in comparison to him. Perhaps I'm too close to the whole thing, but… "

On this topic, the doctor had no need to buy himself some time.

"Your Edgar Evans is angry, Elfed… that's all: just like his grandfather Rowland Roberts was before him. Fortunately, Rhiannon hasn't followed suit, probably because Geraint has made her happy. Anyway, back to Rowland! Among other things, he was angry because the window of opportunity, which had opened up for self-government during his lifetime, had been wasted."

Here the doctor paused, to drain his glass of its dram. Elfed too took a draught of the Devil's brew, just as Geraint rejoined them.

"Edgar is angry because now there is no window. He has no hope, Elfed; at least his grandfather had hope. So, when you have no hope, what do you do? You say goodbye to the mainstream, and soon you go to the extreme."

Geraint had appeared unusually attentive.

"So, are you saying, Doctor, that Rowland and Edgar's political positions can't be justified?"

"Yes and no, Geraint. I can justify their dream of an independent Wales, but their irresponsible position on south Walians? Not at all! Gosh, I really must go."

Over a blaring bout of laughter from the bar, the doctor said, "I hope I'm not overcomplicating these issues. In the end, you know, nearly everything comes down to the same thing… our language, our lovely, lyrical language."

The language, the language, the language. It was impossible to touch on Welsh affairs without the lovely, lyrical language raising its head… the same language in which they bade goodbye to the backs at the bar as Elfed left a public house for the first, and the last time, in his life.

Twenty

I T WAS A week later. The hill had been steeper than he remembered, and the bag had been a burden he could have done without. He was badly out of breath, although he needn't have been, because he could have driven his car to where he now stood, at one those most special spots on earth. Instead he'd left it in the hamlet, a quarter of a mile down the hill. Now and then he needed to visit a few elderly patients there, and it was this that had made it convenient for the doctor to surprise Elfed and Geraint at this spot this morning. Surely one of them would travel to town today; if both, so much the better. Last week at the pub, he'd spoken to them of Rowland Roberts's dream of self-government; today he intended to justify that dream against this beautiful backdrop.

He'd decided to leave the car in the hamlet because he hadn't been sure where he would have found a place to turn around higher up the road. He had also thought that perhaps the walk would have got him into the spirit of things, but all it had done was wind him. Breathing quickly and deeply, he was barely aware of the breathtaking vista as he was hit by the frightening thought that he'd better get fit, or else! Still, he couldn't have asked for a nicer day in June. It was quite early, not even nine yet, but the sun at this time of the year was already high in the sky.

"God, I'm absolutely puffed, but still, this beats a pint in any old pub!"

Thus the doctor managed to humour himself as he sucked on fresh Welsh air and gradually regained his composure. The road hugged a hill to the north, but in every other direction, views of Wales were sensational. Arenig Fawr dominated the west and shortened the depth of vision there, but to the south and east, the views seemed to go on and on. The south in particular was awesome. Here, gently tiered, receding slopes seemed to whisk the viewer downwards to the valley of the Dee, beyond which a long, stepped ridge relentlessly worked its way to the peak of Aran Benllyn. Distant, just south of east, the Berwyn barred the way. How could one not be a nationalist, thought the doctor, if one saw this scene each day? How could one not identify with one's country if it moves one in this way? And that was without any of the mind-moulding myths and heart-tugging heroics that go hand in hand with the territory.

He heard the trundling of a horse and cart and the urgent bleating of lambs.

"Thank goodness! Here they come. Heck! There are three. Edgar must be with them too! What do I do now? I can't possibly say these things to his face."

The doctor waved, but only two waved back.

Once within earshot, Geraint shouted, "What a lovely surprise, but where's your car? You haven't walked from Bala, have you?"

"This little hill was quite enough for me," thought the doctor, and then shouted back, "I've left it lower down. You can help me crank it later."

Even when the horse and cart had rattled to a halt, they had to raise their voices to be heard over all the lambs in a lather. There were ten for sale today. Geraint spoke first. Elfed as usual was subdued in his grandson's presence.

"So, what are you doing here, Doctor?"

"Well, I had a few patients to see up here, and it's so lovely, I thought I'd surprise you," and then a little white lie, "And it's good to see you, Edgar."

"Edgar is with us today, Doctor," beamed Geraint, "because

we want to show him off after his victory at Porthmadog the day before yesterday. There was a big eisteddfod there, you know, and what d'you think? Edgar won not only the tenor solo but the Blue Riband as well. He's on his way, Doctor, believe you me."

Even Elfed seemed comfortable enough to reflect his grandson's glory. As for the star himself, he continued securing the netting that kept the lambs in line. The doctor now decided he had better take the initiative.

"Edgar, I was hoping to give your father and grandfather a ride in my car. Would you mind taking the lambs to town on your own?"

Edgar bridled as if to say, "Why do you want me out of the way?"

'Twas awkward for the doctor till Geraint intervened chirpily, "Come on, Edgar! You wouldn't deprive your Dad of his moment in the sun, would you?"

No humour in response, but the right result achieved.

"We'll walk with Doctor to the car, Edgar, so we'll see you at the mart, OK?"

Off Edgar went, reflecting little glory. The cart bobbed up and down a bit with the horse's stilted movement. To the three that were left behind, this wave motion seemed to pit a mass of white lamb's wool against a single, red head of hair. It was no contest.

"What are you really doing here, Doctor?" from Elfed with the stress on the "really".

"Before we go to the car," from the doctor, smiling playfully, "Come over here. I've brought a flask. Let's have a cup of tea. D'you mind doing the honours, Geraint?" and he passed the bag, the burden he could have done without. Then he swept his hand in a grand flowing gesture from the Berwyn to Arenig, and added, "This is what all the fuss is about, gentlemen: this, and hundreds of similarly special spots in Wales that make us proud, that move Welsh people everyday, as they have done for centuries."

Geraint thought of his favourite fishing hole on a shady bend in the Tryweryn, and Elfed naturally thought of the top of Arenig Fawr.

"I just felt I needed to wrap up the chat we had about Rowland Roberts last week. It won't take long. Is that all right?"

Nods all round, so, "Geraint wondered whether we could possibly justify Rowland's position, and I said yes, when it came to his dream of self-government. Thanks," as Geraint passed him a cup of tea.

"Now, just imagine Rowland at this very spot at about the time he knew his family would be kicked out of Tryweryn. He was fourteen, let's say. Now, if the squire's action in itself hadn't made a nationalist of him, then surely this beauty would have done the trick, and if that wasn't enough, then throw in the history and myths, and his fate would have been sealed for certain. He'd have gazed at the Berwyn over there, where Owain Gwynedd whipped the English in 1165, and then beyond the Aran to Machynlleth where Owain Glyndŵr held the first Welsh Parliament in 1404. Anyway, you get the idea. How could he not have become a nationalist? How could anyone with his background not have? So, case closed; his dream of independence justified."

The doctor, in his excitement, slurped his sip of tea.

"Next, imagine Rowland in Bala in his forties, ecstatic at the thought of self-government in his lifetime. That's when it all went wrong for him and those like him. They made their first mistake in what might have proved to be the final stretch in their drive for independence. Rather than focus on any number of unifying factors, such as a well-defined homeland with clear-cut borders or that indefinable feeling of belonging, they focused on the language instead. Now, a language is a powerful and wonderful thing, so you can't blame them really. Still, the move proved to be divisive, for by then, the majority of Welshmen couldn't speak the language and were suspicious of the motives of those who could. It's so sad, actually."

Sadness and silence are sisters, and so for a while all was quiet, but for the distant bleating of mother and child, stonechats and pipits and hawks in the wild, and the restrained sipping of tea.

"Then to make matters worse, another mistake! Rather than admit their tactical error and accept responsibility for their failure, they placed the blame on those who they themselves had alienated. There's twisted logic for you. That's why I can't justify Rowland's stance on south Walians... nor Edgar's either. Shall we start walking?"

The doctor had come across as all business, as one intent on making his point. Yet, he'd been aware that Geraint had become subdued, so he silently sought and successfully obtained Elfed's permission to continue. All three drained their cups, and two took another look at their country at its best, before quickly losing altitude.

"The final irrational twist to this tale was Rowland's third mistake. He reasoned that if those he alienated were to blame for his failure, then the alienation was justified in the first place; in other words, emphasising the language had not been a mistake at all, implying of course that you're truly Welsh only if you're a Welsh speaker. As far as I can see, that's Rhiannon's position, and it certainly is Edgar's. It's wrong, unfair and unjustifiable."

The doctor wrapped his arm around Geraint's shoulder, and hugged him. Geraint smiled shyly as if to say, "What you said does hurt a bit, but thanks anyway."

"As I said, it's all very sad, and as usual in Welsh affairs, the language was in the thick of it. Look at that beautiful car! Isn't she gorgeous?"

The next half an hour was characterised by banter... banter about cranking and running out of water, and pushing and wishing the doctor hadn't brought her. Geraint seemed himself again.

"Your car doesn't smell like a horse, Doctor, but she certainly sounds like one sometimes."

"Are you sure you don't want us to get out and push?"

"There's a horse and cart about to pass us, Doctor."

As they drove along the high street in Bala, the car attracted more and more attention. Elfed rose to the occasion and raised his hand regally, much like he imagined George V would have done. In the general excitement, the banter petered out. For half an hour, it had been incessant, conducted as usual in their lovely, lyrical language, an ancient language that had survived against all odds, a language with nine lives.

The Romans weren't good news for ancient languages. Few survived the imperial juggernaut, but Welsh, a language it seemed with nine lives, is one that did. Its survival is a story of successive threats followed by relief, presumably unintended, when often it came from the source of the threat itself.

Its next threat was the Normans. They rolled over England in 1066, one of the most famous dates in history, and kept on rolling till they pocketed the most fertile parts of Wales as well. Even in those days, ethnic cleansing was all the rage, and Welsh people were ruthlessly evicted from certain parts of their own country to make way for colonies of English and Flemish speakers. Further waves of forced English immigration occurred after 1282, the year in which Llywelyn, the last Welsh prince, was killed while battling Edward I of England. The Norman bigwigs ran Wales in French, and true to the bandwagon effect, it wasn't long before "beaucoup de bonjour et merci" were tossed around in Welsh accents. None of this bade well for Welsh, but it seemed to take this challenge in its stride, and for very good reason. As a threat to Welsh, French was not too serious. The other was the tongue to watch, but ironically, the Normans for now had the English language on the defensive, for in their England French was the official language.

One life down, eight to go,
Long live their lovely lingo,
And live it might for quite a bit
For almost all still speak it.

The next threat surfaced when the English language regained its poise in the early 1400s. Gradually, it became the language of councils and courts in Wales. Welsh gentry found it difficult not to bend with this linguistic wind, and by 1500, English had become the dominant medium for official life in their country. Roles had been reversed... now Welsh was on the ropes. It was about this time, in 1536, that Henry VIII, with a quill in his quarrelsome hand, decreed that the Welsh people had ceased to exist. How could their language survive for long without them? Ironically, its future was assured when the same quill in the same old quarrelsome hand told the Pope to take a hike. Henry had petitioned the Pope to grant him a divorce from the first of his six wives, Catherine. The Pope, sensing perhaps that it might become a habit, refused, prompting Henry essentially to break away from Rome, form his own Church with himself at its head and give himself permission to marry the Anne of his dreams. So bold a stroke of a quill was this, that religious conformity hogged the front burner of English politics for a century and a half. But how could the people of Wales be coaxed to conform to this new Church when most of them spoke no English? So crucial was conformity considered that Parliament passed an Act in 1563 requiring translations of the Bible and the Prayer

Book into Welsh. Into Welsh? What a turn up for the books! One minute, Henry tells the Welsh they don't exist, and the next, his daughter Elizabeth glorifies their language with a Bible. Much more than that in fact: she legitimises it, for at the time, Welsh was the only non-state language in Europe to be blessed with a Bible, and what a Bible it was! Translated in 1588 by William Morgan, vicar of, if you can believe it, Llanrhaeadr-ym-Mochnant, the new Bible exposed the Welsh people on a regular basis to their language at its brilliant best, and ensured its survival for at least another century.

Two lives down, seven to go,
Long live their lovely lingo,
And live it might for quite a bit
For nine in ten still speak it.

Throughout the 1600s, an acceleration took place in the Welsh gentry's unpretty scurrying towards the English language. Traditionally, they had been the sponsors of cultural activities in Welsh, but as fewer were fluent in the language, so fewer sponsored poets to magnify it. As a result, the standardised Welsh language that the poets had zealously defended for centuries became in danger of becoming fractured. It was the same old story, really. English was perceived to be the medium of advancement, so why even bother with Welsh. Yes, the same old threat, yet, offset once again by the same old relief, religion. First of all, Griffith Jones, a Church of England rector in Llanddowror, near Carmarthen, founded what became to be known as circulatory schools. During the quiet winter months on farms, instructors would travel, teach people how to read, then travel on wherever else they felt there was a need. Their aim was to enable Welsh people to read the Bible, but as the lessons were of necessity taught in Welsh, they had the serendipitous side effect of making the Welsh people one of the most literate nations in the world... and in their mother tongue. Next came the Dissenters, or Nonconformists, those sects who disapproved of state religions and their trappings. During the late 1700s, itinerant preachers pushed the Dissenter's cause, and they had to do it in Welsh; had they not, no one but a few could have followed them. In a way, they took over where the poets had left off. They became celebrities, saving souls as they should, but unwittingly celebrating and preserving the beauty of the Welsh language every time they spoke. In support of these orators, hundreds of hymns were penned, so stylish and sentimental that they soon became the folk songs of Wales. When these religious movements became respectable, and hundreds of chapels built, the Sunday School took over as the guardian of literacy for children and adults alike... all this too, in Welsh, of course. These developments helped sustain the Welsh language for another century or more.

Three lives down, six to go,
Long live their lovely lingo,
And live it might for quite a bit
For eight in ten still speak it.

On April Fool's Day, 1847, three young English barristers, who couldn't speak a word of Welsh, presented the British Government with a report on the educational system of the Welsh people, over half of whom couldn't speak a word of English. Most of its 1252 pages arrogantly and routinely exaggerated the undeniable weaknesses in Welsh education. Eight inexplicable pages, however, reported that the Welsh were unrestrained when it came to sex, and insinuated that such wanton behaviour was a natural by-product of the emotion, even hysteria, whipped up in the mainly Welsh-speaking chapels. Both criticisms touched a very raw nerve among, not only Welsh patriots, but also the Nonconformist leadership, which scrambled to prove the report wrong by, in many ways, making the Welsh... wait for it... more like the English! Partial capitulation in that quarter, it seemed. As a result, sadly, English-medium schools became the norm. Ironically, the Welsh language was sustained during this period by the well-established, Welsh-speaking Sunday School system, which many moons before had been instigated by the Nonconformists themselves. It didn't take the authorities long to realise that monoglot Welsh-speaking children weren't learning much in English, but it took them long enough to do something about it. Eventually, at the turn of the century, a concession came. Welsh could now be used in primary schools, but only to help Welsh children learn English, mind you. Whatever works! The vital point was, however, that the language had finally gained a foothold in the state educational system.

Four lives down, five to go,
Long live their lovely lingo,
But will it live when many quit,
Just five in ten now speak it.

As Edgar and his lambs had bobbed their way to Bala mart that morning, he'd worried about the Welsh language. Not a line of thought one would have wished on a healthy youth on such a lovely summer's morning, but worry he did... four lives down, five to go. He'd wondered where the language's next life would come from, for it looked as if it might be needed very soon. The census of 1921 had showed that barely a third of Welsh people could speak their mother tongue. In Edgar's opinion, too many people in the past had done too much for him to sit aside and watch the most precious of national treasures slip away… slip away and join a lengthening list of languages that had expired since the Romans had held sway.

An immensely noble sentiment, but alas, in his case, twinned with another equally ignoble one.

Twenty-one

IN EDGAR, A star was born all over again. For the second time in his short life, he became the voice to beat in regional competitions, or eisteddfodau as they are known. His tone as a tenor was clear, and yet without an edge. There was a natural warmth and depth to his voice, and technique was increasingly evident. Edgar had been taking lessons. The tutor though had been wise enough to largely leave his voice alone; rather, he'd focused on control and deportment. These days on stage, Edgar was quite the toff. The colours that he wore were chosen carefully to complement his fairly long, wavy, rich red hair and his naturally dark complexion. The tutor had even choreographed his body language and defined his personality while on stage. Elfed had been astounded by the warm, exuberant Edgar he'd seen perform. Unfortunately, off the stage there was little it seemed the tutor could do. In real life, it was the same old Edgar, the same selfish, moody, intolerant Edgar as before. When things were going well, he was occasionally charming, but the slightest hiccup upset him. Then, he would withdraw, and his petulance would take no account of others. Their feelings were subordinate, it seemed, to the free rein he felt his emotions were due. In this frame of mind, moody was he mainly, and fortunately, not often openly angry or violent.

The tenor from Tryweryn was making a name for himself around the region, but nowhere as resoundingly as in Porthmadog and its vicinity. Edgar had followed his first grand victory there with a series of others, but mostly in minor eisteddfodau. Elfed wondered why he bothered. For experience, for experience, was the standard explanation, but Elfed couldn't quite shake his suspicion of an ulterior motive. It even crossed his mind that romance may be the reason, but that preposterous idea was promptly dismissed: after all, why would anyone fall for Edgar? Yet, someone had, and it wasn't too long before Elfed knew her name.

Myfanwy Morris had been born into a maritime family and lived in Borth-y-gest, a village one half-mile outside Porthmadog. Her father had been a sea captain, and had retired ten years earlier at the age of forty-one. Twenty years at sea on an ocean-going clipper had been quite enough for him. Her grandfather, too, had been a captain. He'd survived on a sailing ship for thirty years, but her great grandfather hadn't been so lucky. One day he'd left for Newfoundland, and had never arrived. Yet, according to Myfanwy, her family had fared well compared to others in the village.

Elfed assumed that the pair had met on either a stage or political platform. It was with relief he learnt it had been the former: at an eisteddfod, where King Edgar starred and stole Myfanwy's heart, and fancied her as his queen. Warmth was not Edgar's strong point, but perversely, it seems he considered it a prerequisite in a lady friend. In this regard Myfanwy was matchless. Her voice was warm, her face was warm, and particularly so, her manner. Myfanwy competed as a contralto, but to Edgar's ear she was closer to a mezzo. It is true that her voice had the depth and lovely caress typical of a contralto, but a surprising lightness too that often exuded excitement. The important thing, though, was that she wasn't a soprano. In Edgar's opinion, most soprano voices were much too thin. Contraltos, above all, sounded warm, and that was essential.

They couldn't have met much before May, but by September 1925, Edgar had decided that she would be his wife. He took Myfanwy's acceptance for granted, but untypically, there was no such presumption when it came to either family. Announcing his intentions to his parents, Edgar was adamant that no official proposal would be made to Myfanwy until his family had visited Borth-y-gest and met her and her family. He insisted too that they, in turn, must view Tryweryn. Elfed just hoped that when they did, it would be a fine day, that's all.

Such was definitely not the case, early one misty late September morning, when four from their farm boarded the train for Ffestiniog. Geraint was tired and would stay at home, and had arranged for Enid to visit him. The family accepted that she was loath to come near the place when Rhiannon was around. Edgar, too, was anathema to her. Enid saw too much of his mother in him, and much too little of Geraint. She realised that her parents, and her mother in particular, had accepted Rhiannon, but still, as far as she was concerned, the family was torn in two: our side, as she called them, and the other, Rhiannon and her son. The divide had been exacerbated at Anti Mary's death by Rhiannon's rumblings regarding Enid as her aunt's sole beneficiary. She had wondered out loud, in her reassuring way, whether her husband should share in the spoils, but when it had become clear that no one else, not even Geraint, did, she had backed down, but the damage had been done.

So now, Enid lived alone in her aunt's cottage near Capel Celyn chapel and supported herself by delivering the post twice a week, and babies whenever the occasion arose. Indeed, the doctor had taken Elfed's recommendation long ago and Enid, to her credit, had not let either down. This morning though, she would deliver the post, and as usual on her route, she would tramp the familiar trail towards her family home, but today she would not leave it as soon as she crossed the Tryweryn. Today, she would cross the river and keep on walking towards her father's farmhouse; keep on walking right by the wooden mailbox that Elfed had nailed to a tree for her comfort and convenience. She would walk by it with a slightly quickening heartbeat, and slowly cross two fields to the farmhouse where she'd been born and raised in a secure setting. She and her brother had been contented and close like peas in a pod. She couldn't have been happier then, but out of the blue a redhead named Rhiannon had ruined it all. She had known she couldn't forgive, but for years had tried to forget... and failed. By now though, she didn't want to forget a thing. In fact, she delighted in the certainty that one day revenge would come her way. But along with the delight came a dilemma too, for she dreaded the thought of hurting her brother. So after crossing two fields, she would stand at the door she knew so well with extremely mixed emotions.

Emotions were mixed on the train as well. There, familiar roles were assumed: Margaret and Rhiannon comfortably chatting, Edgar as ever aloof, and Elfed subdued in his presence. Margaret and Rhiannon were formally dressed in their Sunday best. The train puffed so deliberately away from the halt. Especially for the older three, it was fun to be on a train again: it was fun, but they all felt apprehension in relation to their mission, and the weather didn't help either. The train's rhythm steadily quickened, only to be surpressed again as it approached Arenig station. After that it was plain puffing, and as the engines picked up steam, the clouds dipped lower still and the mist turned to rain. As the train rounded Arenig Fawr, it would have been nice for the four from the farm to have seen the valley form a bowl, as the Tryweryn radiated into its upper tributaries. As the train approached the top, it would have been nice if they'd seen the sun dancing on the bleak, black lake that is the source of the river. As the train crossed the divide, it would have been nice if they'd seen pristine Cwm Prysor in endless shades of green. It would have been nice if they'd enjoyed the views from the viaduct, as well as from the cut that carried the train so high above the river Prysor. It would have been nice, but the low clouds cramped their spirits all the way to Ffestiniog.

They knew they'd be met at the station, but the car was a big surprise. A friend of Captain Morris had agreed to meet them, but the Captain himself had stayed at home so that his guests could ride in comfort. Margaret in particular was excited. Rhiannon too, revelled in the novelty, but Elfed kept his cool, wrily reminding the ladies that as a friend of the doctor, this was old hat to him. In any case, all four perked up noticeably, and even more when the rain stopped. As they dipped into the Dwyryd valley, the clouds broke up, and by the time they reached the estuary and a distant sight of the sea, the sky was partly blue.

"See... there's Borth-y-gest over there," they were informed by their driver, "but first we have to cross the Cob."

The Cob carved the estuary in two. To the left, towards the sea, were sandbanks, taken over by the tide twice daily; to the right, recovered land, courtesy of the Cob. Over they nosed, and once through a gate, they entered Porthmadog, a centre for slate; then, over a hill to beautiful Borth-y-gest.

After twenty years at sea, Captain Morris had turned his back on it. His terraced house faced the other way. It faced Moel y Gest, a hill that appeared to dominate, until one climbed it and marvelled at the mountains of Snowdonia, massive to the north and east. After introductions and a chat, in Welsh of course, a simple lunch was served in the front room. Elfed noticed that its window seemed to be filled by Moel y Gest. He noticed too the hill's twin peaks... there wasn't much he didn't notice. He noticed that Margaret seemed shyer than Rhiannon. His uncharitable Pavlovian response to this was to convince himself that, regardless, his wife's superior character filtered through. Myfanwy Morris reminded him a lot of Margaret, and that pleased him. A few mental frames later, he envisaged his first great-grandson thankfully taking after Myfanwy, and thinking a lot like Margaret. Perhaps he could relate to someone like that, which would be especially nice after missing out with Edgar. It was clear for all to see why Edgar had fallen for Myfanwy. Blue-eyed, fine-featured, with the widest of smiles, her face attracted attention. Without doubt, she was the prettiest of the Captain's three young daughters. The youngest, Mary, was present as well, and obviously doted on Myfanwy. To Elfed, that told all. The eldest, whose wedding picture took pride of place on the mantlepiece, lived with her husband in south Wales. Yes, Myfanwy's appeal was obvious, and now over lunch Elfed could see at last why Edgar appealed to her. No question about it, he was striking, and his voice could move and melt a million hearts, but Elfed had still doubted that any woman, starstruck or not, would tolerate his selfish character. Now, all became clear. Elfed could see that Edgar had assumed his stage personality. Since their arrival, he'd exuded exuberance and warmth. Suddenly, Elfed was certain that Myfanwy and her family hadn't seen Edgar Evans in any other light. In their company, he was, and had been, constantly on stage. All this Elfed noticed, and he hoped and prayed that Myfanwy was as strong as she was pretty.

Despite Elfed's foreboding, the visit had been a huge success. As a result, their journey home was relaxed. Even the weather played along, reflecting and reinforcing their happy frames of mind. The sky was clear, particularly to the west. In the setting sun, Cwm Prysor was a fairyland of long, long shadows and shifting shafts of light. In this magical mood, Edgar seemed to have forgotten that he was once again offstage, encouraging Elfed to be rather more at ease in his presence than normally was the case. As the train climbed confidently along the cut above the valley and traversed the classic viaduct in style, the ladies chipped and chirped, repeatedly approving of the charming Myfanwy and her family who couldn't have done more to please. The mood was mellow. Then to everyone's surprise, Edgar rose as they approached the divide, and began to make a speech.

"Ladies and gentlemen," as he opened the window of the

carriage, "At this divide, two watersheds meet. The one we are about to enter, feeds the Dee, and this one here, the Dwyryd. Now, every little raindrop that falls here will wind its way to the west, and be safe from the English."

At this point, Elfed raised his eyebrows in an exaggerated fashion at Margaret, and shook his head in disbelief. Edgar unaware, continued.

"Wait! Here we are crossing the divide now; so every raindrop that falls this side will flow to the east and can be conveniently confiscated by them."

Here he stopped. He couldn't help noticing Margaret gently nudging Rhiannon. Edgar was clearly disconcerted by this, so when he continued, it was hesitantly.

"Don't you think it would be nice if... "

"Edgar, let's just enjoy the ride, shall we?"

Rhiannon had interrupted, and though she'd done so gently, Edgar reacted petulantly, slapping his cap on his knee and retreating angrily to a corner seat.

"There," thought Elfed, "normal service has been resumed. Fair play to Rhiannon though: she's changed. I think it's a lot to do with her respect for Margaret. She's much more even-handed than she used to be, and Edgar obviously can't take it."

Still labouring over the divide, they were soon to leave the lake behind and gain momentum into the gloaming that was Tryweryn.

As they approached their halt, it was nearly dark. Neither the dusk nor Edgar seemed to have dampened the ladies' good humour. It took something else to do that.

"That's funny," exclaimed Margaret, "That doesn't look like Geraint. Wait a minute! It's Enid, isn't it?"

Surely this meant something was amiss. All but Edgar hurried off the train, to be greeted with reassurance.

"Don't worry, Mam. It's nothing very serious."

She then embraced her parents rather emotionally, and nodded reluctantly at Rhiannon, and that was all. Edgar, in the background, was singularly snubbed. As Margaret was assisted to her seat, Enid expanded.

"Geraint told me that he hasn't felt very well for a few days now. You've probably noticed, haven't you? Anyway, he said he wasn't surprised when his pain worsened noticeably today."

They were leaving the station now, without Edgar. He'd declined the lift.

"He said he suddenly felt very weak and tired," continued Enid, "And a bit depressed too, but he's not too bad, really. Still, I thought I should stay with him, just in case."

Elfed wanted to say that he wished so much that Enid would get involved more often, but all he said was, "I'm so glad you did," which to everyone in the cart, amounted to saying the very same thing. Enid had been right. When they arrived home, Geraint was not so bad as not to be happy to see them. He was comforted by all and embraced at length by Rhiannon.

Surprisingly, Enid agreed to stay and have a cup of tea, and then Elfed insisted on walking her home. She wouldn't hear of it, of course, so compromise ensued. He would take her across the river and up to the Bala road, and no further. Had they both not been so keen to talk of family, the firmament may well have been their topic. This was a rare, cloudless night and the stars were simply awesome.

"Dad, thanks for walking with me, really. It's always so nice to see you and Mam. Anyway, I heard what you told Geraint about your trip, but... did it really go that well?"

"Now, now, Enid! Are you questioning my sincerity?"

"No, of course not, Dad, but... "

"I'm just teasing, Enid, you know that. Anyway, as I said before, our meeting couldn't have gone better. Myfanwy's relatives are first-class people, and Myfanwy herself is a gem. She reminds me so much of your mother: it's uncanny."

"But why would she fall for Edgar, though? He's such an ogre."

Elfed could see where this would lead, and tonight he didn't feel up to it, so he skirted the issue.

"Well, Enid, you should have seen Edgar. He was lively and attentive. She obviously makes him very happy."

If he thought he was off the hook, he was mistaken.

"Come off it, Dad; you of all people. I know you still feel the pain that Rhiannon inflicted on all of us. You wouldn't wish the same on Myfanwy and her family, would you?"

Over the years, Elfed had become very close to his daughter. He had kept little back from her, but he wanted her to stop now.

"From what I know of her, Myfanwy doesn't deserve this, Dad, so are you going to tell her… "

They stopped on the bridge and listened to the babbling. From Enid's intonation, Elfed assumed that she'd finished and was ready with his reply.

"… Or am I?" she added.

This really took the wind out of Elfed's sails. Before, he'd known what to say, but now he had no idea. He wasn't angry with Enid. He knew how she felt about Rhiannon, and Edgar for that matter, and he couldn't blame her, really. But in the past, she'd been so responsible in her hatred, so restrained, and now it seemed she was ready to go on the offensive. He leant on the bridge and listened. He just couldn't speak, but his body language spoke it all. Enid understood, and accepting that she'd gone too far, regretted. She wound her arm in her father's and leant on the bridge as well, and simply said, "Dad, I'm so sorry. I do love you," and then together, they listened.

After a long while, they left and aimed for the Bala road.

"Thanks, Enid, for understanding. We've weathered this storm together for so long now, that it seems to me a pity to rock the boat now."

"Dad, I know... I know... but you do realise, don't you, that if Myfanwy is so nice, it doesn't make matters any easier for me."

Moments of such closeness will disarm, and Enid was actually toying with telling her Dad of her deepening dilemma... telling him of how hard it was to reconcile her hunger for revenge with her strong protective feelings for her brother... and now this Myfanwy, this very nice Myfanwy, was going to come along and likely deepen her dilemma further. With all this she toyed, but in the end she didn't tell.

"What did you say, Enid?" urgently from Elfed.

It seemed she'd said too much already. She panicked slightly, and all she felt for a moment was a need to divert her Dad, so she kept on talking.

"Myfanwy is a gem, you said, so if she moves into the valley, she will deserve my respect. She could even become my friend, and God knows I could do with a few, but it wouldn't be fair, Dad."

Most of this she'd said without thinking. It had tumbled forth and perhaps had done more harm than good, but suddenly, she wasn't concerned any more. She'd recovered her poise and had already decided how to extricate herself.

Enid's fears were well founded. Elfed wasn't sure what he was hearing, but he knew he didn't like it.

"What are you getting at, Enid? What exactly do you mean by not being fair? What's on your mind?"

Enid was ready.

"Well, Dad, you know. You know! If I'm nice to Myfanwy and we become friends, that would put her in a very difficult position at home, don't you think, and probably expose her to a barrage of propaganda from you know who. I really think it's best that I stay away from her, don't you? I won't be rude, I promise… just distant. Don't you think it would be for the best?"

She couldn't tell if her father's mind was eased, so she followed with a sentimental tactic.

"Dad, I'm sorry for upsetting you back at the bridge, but you know how hard this whole business has been for me over the years. It's not always easy for me to see things straight. It's not always easy to be generous."

"Oh!" she thought, "Perhaps I shouldn't have said that, even. I just can't be sure I've convinced him."

No, she couldn't, but she got a hug from her loving, understanding Dad, and that was reassuring. As it happened, Enid's perfectly reasonable response had assuaged but far from settled Elfed's unease.

On his way home, had Elfed not dwelt on their powwow, the Plough might have caught his eye.

Twenty-two

IN DECEMBER 1925, only seven months after they'd met, Myfanwy and Edgar married.

Earlier, in mid-October, Myfanwy and her family had indeed visited the valley as Edgar had insisted, and as Elfed had hoped, the weather had been made to order. For a week, off and on, it had rained, but on that day, sunshine revitalised hillsides of heather together with gorse, framing Tryweryn as it strained in its course.

There were two episodes that had ruffled the calm veneer that otherwise had prevailed.

"I'm very sorry that Enid isn't here," Myfanwy had said to Margaret and Rhiannon, "I was really looking forward to meeting her."

Elfed had overheard this remark and had wondered how Margaret would deal with it.

"Oh, and she was looking forward to meeting you as well," but this was from Rhiannon as cool as can be. "Something must have happened. There are several babies due at the moment, I know. She's a very busy lady."

Elfed had been impressed. He had to admit that over the years, Margaret's good sense had rubbed off on Rhiannon. What a pity he couldn't compliment his daughter-in-law without sharing the credit with Margaret! Still, his relationship with Rhiannon was much more giving than one could possibly have imagined when she, as a cat, had thrown herself among his pigeons.

Later that fine day, Edgar had made another of his speeches.

"He seems incapable of conveying information in the course of a normal conversation," Elfed had said to himself, "But there, he's on stage, isn't he?"

"Ladies and gentlemen," Edgar had commenced, after all those present had been ushered outside to the front of the house, "I haven't asked Myfanwy to marry me yet, but if I do and she happens to accept, I want to tell you where we're going to live."

That remark in itself had created a stir. Everyone naturally had assumed that they'd live in the farmhouse. After all, there was plenty of room.

"Myfanwy and I will live over there," and he had pointed dramatically across a shallow depression at the farmhouse that Elfed had acquired with the land that he'd bought twenty years before.

"I haven't spoken to Dad or Taid about it, but I'm sure they won't object. I have spoken to the renters though, and they won't mind leaving in a month. It's been kept in a good state, and after I've finished with it, it'll be the envy of the valley; and then I'll rename it Hendre!"

Elfed's mind had raced in reaction to this.

"No, he damn well hasn't spoken to Taid about it, but I can't make a scene now, can I? And as for the renters, they're my friends, and they probably think I've agreed to all this. And it's been kept in a good state, he says. Who does he think is responsible for that? Taid, that's who! God, he's got a nerve! Hendre... really!"

Keeping up the pressure, Edgar had then immediately suggested that Myfanwy and her family should see his future home. Captain Morris it seemed had sensed a rift, because he had turned to Elfed, seeking his approval of Edgar's proposal. What could Elfed have done, under the circumstances, but encourage the expedition?

On their return, all the Morrises had been genuinely excited, and to cap it all, Myfanwy had actually run to Elfed and had thanked him with such unaffected enthusiasm that he could hardly bear it. Nevertheless, he had smiled appropriately coyly for the crowd.

Later, after they'd left, Elfed had taken a walk. The day as a whole had thoroughly dismayed him. In the situation that was unfolding, so much had been left unsaid that he had been certain it would have imploded by now. Yet sadly, it had seemed today that the liaison was surviving the lie. Particularly poignant had been Myfanwy's moment of genuine gratitude. Would she ever forgive him, he had wondered, for not shielding her charming innocence from Edgar's massive manipulation. Would she forgive him? On his walk, he had felt the need to air these self-recriminations, and he'd decided that Margaret would be the one to listen to him, even though Enid was often more in sync with his sense of things, but the unease with which his daughter had left him feeling, a month back at the bridge and beyond, had lingered. She'd held something back that night, he was certain. His instincts may have been awry, and in time he could be sorry, but as things were, how could he have committed to candour with Enid when he sensed that she would almost certainly find it impossible to reciprocate?

The wedding wasn't white, but quite special all the same. The service took place at midday in a Congregational chapel situated on a steep hill that led up from the bay at Borth-y-gest. Elfed thought that Edgar looked annoyingly irresistible, and Myfanwy unnaturally serene.

"The lie lives on," he mused, and the harder he tried to suppress the thought, the more frequently it seemed to recur... during the ceremony, at least. Once outside on the hill, diversions did the trick.

"There you are, Trebor! I wondered what had happened to you. Very nice, wasn't it?"

Trebor Thomas had travelled with the family on the train.

"Elfed, I just don't know how you boys do it! First Rhiannon, and now Myfanwy. Such good lookers, both of them, and not to forget Margaret, of course. It can't hurt, can it, to grow old surrounded by these beauties."

"Come off it, Trebor," was all he said, when he could have said much more… but Trebor wasn't that good a friend.

Elfed's mind's eye travelled down the hill to the bay, and beyond to the estuary, then down the Dwyryd, over the bar and into the sea. Here it was called Cardigan Bay, and through it, for years, there was rarely a day when a ship hadn't left this area. The sea's link with the Morris family was unravelling, though, but the Captain didn't seem to care. Personally, he'd had enough, and anyway, as far as this part of the world was concerned, the shipping game was over. In the same thought, Elfed couldn't help but wonder about the sorry state of his own game. Farming once again was a struggle, with no relief in sight.

The wedding service was followed by lunch at the terraced house that had turned its back on the sea. Elfed had to admit that the mood was quite convivial. Edgar, of course, made another one of his speeches: he was on stage, wasn't he? As for Myfanwy, she graced the gathering with gentleness and calm. Her long neck and smooth, effortless movements reminded Elfed of a heron in unhurried flight. Remarkably, she was the centre of attraction, yet above the hullaballoo, just like a queen.

Later, members of both families ganged up on the bride and groom, and demanded a duet. As far as the song was concerned, the couple had only to glance at each other before smiling and nodding. Queen Myfanwy, smiling widely and warmly, moved magically through the crowd towards Margaret, who looked up in surprise, and pointing at herself, said "Me?" Eventually, they arrived back at the table by the window, which framed Moel y Gest. Suddenly, Margaret started beating a rhythm on the table. Rest, two, three, FOUR, five, six, rest, two, three, FOUR, five, six, and so on, with the emphasis each time on the four. After eight bars, Edgar and Myfanwy burst into Schubert's "Ave Maria". Together, they stretched the "A" in "Ave", tripped over the next two syllables, before milking the "ri" in Maria. More of the same in the second line, but Myfanwy sang the third and fourth on her own. God, she was good! Her rich contralto voice caressed the sadness out of the tune, till Elfed could literally feel the pain. Then, together in the next two lines, they diffused the tension without sacrificing a scrap of emotion. All the while, Margaret beat the rhythm, doing her very best to adjust to the couple's improvisational phrasing. Edgar then, in his crystal clear and wonderfully warm tenor voice, lightly skipped through the next two lines, to be joined by Myfanwy for arguably the most emotional phrase of the whole verse. Elfed swore that nowhere 'neath the sun had so many Adam's apples moved as one. What a perfect pair they seemed, so happy side by side: how could anyone see their marriage as set against the tide? In fact, during those harmonious moments, Elfed felt quite ungenerous dwelling on his fears for Myfanwy's future. Yet, he could not help feeling particularly protective of her when she was on a pedestal like this, for as they say, the higher they climb, the harder... yes, yes, enough of that! He then worried that he wouldn't be there to catch her. He needn't have, for his conscience would see to that.

As it happened, the disintegration of Myfanwy's life in Tryweryn wasn't as devastating as Elfed had feared. For one thing, Edgar, as ogreish as he could often be, appeared to be not totally indifferent to her feelings. Certainly, it took Edgar no time at all to reveal his true colours, and true to form, he did so as if it shouldn't have been a surprise. Yet, surprisingly, at times, he did seem sensitive to Myfanwy's disappointment, and did make sporadic gestures of appeasement. Still, the let down came, as Elfed knew it would, but at least she was being let down lightly. Helpful as well to Myfanwy's transition was Edgar's general absence from the farmhouse. Despite his moody personality, or perhaps because of it, he was assiduous at all his tasks. He worked extremely hard on the farm, continued to compete energetically, and in his little remaining spare time, strove to improve his future home. Although he regularly worked at it well into the dark evenings, it was a slow process. In any case, there were two felicitous fallouts from Edgar's franticness in those winter months: the surprisingly little time that Myfanwy spent with him, and the correspondingly vast amounts she spent with Elfed and Margaret. They doted on her and revelled in her company, which was fortuitous for Myfanwy, because their support in those early days was crucial.

During those premarital months… in which Elfed had fretted over Myfanwy's future, but had done nothing to alert her… during those months, Margaret had been vital in maintaining some perspective.

"How can you be so certain that their marriage is doomed?" she had asked.

"Anyway, I'd say it's none of your business."

"Let them decide for themselves," she had counselled, so on her advice, he had done what he probably would have done anyway: nothing, but at least he'd done it with the comfort of knowing that he wasn't alone.

Anyway, late on a day in early March, a few months after the wedding, Elfed and Margaret had just gone up to bed. It was Elfed who started the conversation.

"Margaret, aren't you surprised at how well Myfanwy is coping? She must know by now that Edgar isn't at all the man she thought she was marrying. Aren't you just a bit surprised?"

They were in bed by now, but contrary to custom, their candle continued to flicker. Margaret hadn't snuffed it tonight, as if this conversation called for all their senses. She spoke in a whisper.

"Well, yes, Elfed, I am a bit surprised, of course, but not as much as you, I don't think. Myfanwy looks so lovely and acts so ladylike that it's easy to think of her as vulnerable, but she's tough, Elfed, and very practical, too."

Elfed agreed that he'd underestimated Myfanwy, but her stoicism still surprised him.

"I even wonder sometimes," he whispered, "whether she knew exactly what she was getting into, so Edgar's behaviour is no surprise to her at all."

"Oh no, Elfed, she feels let down, and confused. But, as I said, she's tough. Look how warm and radiant she is despite her disappointments. She makes people feel good, doesn't she? And people love her for it. You know that everyone at the chapel adores her. We'd do anything for her, wouldn't we? Even Rhiannon is under her spell."

Elfed was already feeling sleepy, but through the fog that weighed so sweetly on his mind, it did occur to him that he had been surprised at Rhiannon's deference towards Myfanwy. So, perhaps Margaret was right. Perhaps Myfanwy did indeed possess an inner strength, which would have been instantly apparent to a bully like Rhiannon, who tended to trade on people's vulnerabilities. He thought all this as the fog fell further still.

"I wouldn't be surprised," continued Margaret, "if deep down, Myfanwy hasn't convinced herself that in the end, Edgar, just like his mother, will come round. That would explain a lot, wouldn't it?"

Elfed was really nodding off now, and would have fallen asleep agreeing… agreeing… agreeing, had Margaret not whispered a whopper.

"And there is actually one more little fact that keeps her going. She happens to be pregnant."

At that moment, on the brink of sleep, Elfed couldn't quite decide whether to be pleased or not at what he thought he'd heard. He roused himself sufficiently to say, "Well done, Margaret fach, but aren't you a bit old for that sort of thing?"

What had been a whisper, now became a hiss.

"Not me, silly! It's Myfanwy that's pregnant."

At this urgent hiss, bye bye to bliss, and with this his mind got moving.

"So are you saying she was pregnant before they got married? Now, that would explain a lot, wouldn't it, and I wouldn't put it past Edgar, one little bit!"

"No Elfed Evans, you're grasping at straws. When Myfanwy told me the news yesterday, she was concerned that people might jump to that very conclusion, although I doubt she had you in mind. You should be ashamed of yourself. She said she knows for a fact that the baby was conceived during their first night together, and she wanted to be sure that I believed her… and I do. So, there!"

Still, Elfed's mind was moving, but he kept quiet.

"Your little red dragon just won't go away, will it, Elfed?" whispered Margaret, fingering it fondly, "Have you given up by now on the idea of persuading Edgar to get one?"

"Well, yes, I suppose I have, but to be honest, I'm not sure now how I feel about Edgar wearing one. Still, I suppose I really should try and overcome my prejudice, shouldn't I, for Edward's sake."

"But, there," Margaret countered, "even if Edgar's persuaded, there's little guarantee that he'd keep the tradition going. Perhaps we better wait until the baby's born."

"I'd thought of that, Margaret, but what if it's a girl? No, no! Now that you've brought it up, I'm thinking there's much to be said for planting that dragon on Edgar's shoulder, but honestly, what's the point of me even thinking about it? He'd never listen to me."

"No, he might not listen to you, it's true, but... let me see what I can do," and with that, his thinning hair was fluffed, and the flickering candle snuffed, and the dragon re-entered the picture.

Twenty-three

I T WAS A morning in May, 1926. Edward Jones sat at the little front window of his bungalow in Llwynypia in south Wales, his freckled face a picture. His daughter Martha fussed around the kitchen. On any other day, he would have subconsciously tuned in to her vibes because he couldn't help worrying about her. Today though, there were no worries: he was bursting with pride and awash in good will. He had just been told the good news. It was very good news: brilliant news in fact, and it couldn't have come at a better time. He'd been slightly depressed recently. The same familiar factors had finally got him down. He still missed Rachel Anne, even though five years had elapsed since she'd passed away. His granddaughter Jane and her husband Jon had helped fill the void; having them at home had been a fillip, but Martha's resentful attitude had taken much of the gloss off that. She'd been a huge damper, but he couldn't blame her: she'd been through such a lot. It didn't help that his health had deteriorated over the last few years, but gosh, he shouldn't really complain about that either. Just think, he'd already lived twenty years longer than his poor friend, Wyn Williams. To top things off, he'd retired from the coalmine just after Rachel Anne had died, so he'd had time on his hands... time to think. No doubt about it, Jane's good news couldn't have been more timely. Just this morning, she and Jon had told him that by late summer, he'd be a great-grandfather. As he'd tried to jump for joy, he'd prayed this time it would be a boy.

Jonathan Devereux, now known as Jon, had been born on 2nd March 1901 in a little village just outside Harrogate, Yorkshire. He was the youngest child of four born to a harsh father and neurotic mother. He was intelligent, but intellectually uncurious, so he'd left school at the age of sixteen. He'd continued to live at home while working as a junior accountant for a medium-sized bakery. On his eighteenth birthday, he'd left home for Tonypandy in the Rhondda. There, he'd got an identical job almost immediately upon arrival.

Right from the word go, Jon Devereux had loved Wales. He'd loved the warmth of the people, their classlessness, their light, lilting accents, and their solid sense of community. And he'd loved one other thing as well. Yorkshire people felt the same antipathy, the same resentment toward the establishment based in south-east England as the Welsh did. With respect to Yorkshire, however, the sentiment could too easily be marginalised as pettiness on the periphery of power, but in Wales it embedded itself into Welshness itself, and became more real. Jon Devereux had loved that. Yes, to his surprise, he had found that Wales was definitely not England, and he had revelled in it.

So, in the spring of 1919, Jon Devereux had fallen in love with Wales and had become a Welshman. In the spring of 1920, he'd fallen in love.

Jane Myfanwy Mowbray was four years older than him. They had met at the bakery shop where he'd kept the books and where she'd sold bread with a twinkle in her blue eyes and very light ginger freckles on her face. Inexplicably, his consumption of bread suddenly had taken a leap, which of course had necessitated a daily visit to the shop's counter. Sometimes on a quiet day he'd catch Jane deep in thought and clearly troubled, and that's when it seemed her freckles would darken a touch, appear slightly raised and tinge her gentle countenance in mystery. It had pleased him that she always lightened up when he arrived, and the freckles seemed to settle down once more. Even though it was plain that she was older, his banter had became bolder by the day, and she seemed to like it. On a morning in June, when he had laid all the groundwork that he thought he could, he'd challenged the age barrier and asked her if he could walk her home after work. To his surprise she'd nodded confidently. Her lips had brimmed with pleasure and her light ginger freckles had stayed quite still. Later, she told him that she'd always fancied his fair and curly hair, but what had made him irresistible was his open, gentle, round face and easy-going manner.

When they met outside the shop at five past five, she'd told him that she lived in Llwynypia, just a mile or so up the Rhondda Valley. He'd smiled in a way that told her he already knew. The second thing she said, though, had taken the wind out of his nineteen-year-old sails.

"Before we spend any time together, I'm sorry but I just have to tell you that my father is a bugger. He's got a huge chip on his shoulder. He treats my mother like dirt, you know, and so far he hasn't taken much of a liking to any of my boyfriends."

Jon Devereux's instinctive reaction had been to hide his shock with a nervous laugh.

"No, don't laugh, I'm serious. When you asked to walk me home today, I must admit I wasn't at all surprised, but I really haven't thought it through as far as my father is concerned. I wanted to accept your invitation because I want you to know I really like you, but honestly, I've no idea how much time I can spend with you. My father drinks a lot, you know and as I said, he can be a real bugger. I'm really sorry I have to tell you all this."

Jon was recovering from his shock.

"Listen, my father's a bugger too, so I know exactly how you feel, but don't worry about it. Let's just take things as they come, and it'll all work out, you'll see."

He must have said just the right thing because she'd slowly clasped his right hand in her left and had looked him closely in the eye, an appreciative smile on her face and her head nodding very slowly, as if to say, "I knew I was right to like you."

He had said it would work out and work out it did. Within six months her father had died. Not even his constitution could withstand a continuous bombardment of alcohol, cigarette smoke and coal dust. The end hadn't been pretty and no one mourned his passing, but he'd left a sad legacy. He'd left a mother-in-law so drawn and drained from the strain of dealing with him daily that she too passed away within three months of his death. He'd left a widow, Martha, withered within and so withdrawn in habitual self-preservation that she was virtually incapable of warmth. Jane had fared better. Her grandparents had made sure of that, and the pride Edward Jones felt over his role in her upbringing helped him deal with the shame of never having truly been able to tackle the problem that was her father.

Jon and Jane had been married in the spring of 1921. So Michael Mowbray's place in the bungalow had been almost immediately taken by Jon. Jane had been deliriously happy and Edward, laid low by the loss of his wife, had been consoled. Martha, though, hadn't been able to cope. She'd needed time to lick her wounds. She'd needed space in which to rest and then to grow. She'd needed Edward and Jane's undivided attention, and she'd needed time to revive her relationships with them without distraction and without threat. Sadly, this delicate process had not been able to assimilate Jon Devereux, whose arrival unwittingly nipped it in the bud. As a result, Martha's unsoothed, raw resentments had quickly coalesced into envy towards Jane. Her own marriage throughout had been an albatross around her neck, and here was Jane ecstatic with her Jon, and it appeared, on a par with him in their relationship. It was quite unfair and far too much to bear. Her resentment had expressed itself in antagonism towards her daughter and indifference towards Jon. She had been pained by her own ungenerous behaviour, but couldn't snap the cycle that controlled it. In sum, she had failed to find that peace of mind that had beckoned briefly at Michael Mowbray's death.

For five years, Jon and Jane were childless, but they almost hadn't noticed, so happy they were. Others had seemed much more concerned and it became a standing joke among Jon's pals.

"What's the secret, Jon? You could make a fortune, you know!" was a familiar refrain, or "Get Martha out of there, Jon bach. She's enough to scare the devil away," or "Don't tell me I didn't warn you about the age difference, Jon," and so on, until the spring of 1926 when it became obvious to everyone that a baby was well on its way.

Edward still sat at the window, savouring the news, but reality was setting in, and there was a worry now. Jane, herself a non-Welsh speaker, had married another, so the chances were their child wouldn't speak Welsh either. This didn't matter to Edward: Welsh speaking or not, his great-grandson would be as Welsh as they come. Martha though, would feel responsible; would continue to live with the guilt she'd felt at failing to bring her daughter up in Welsh. So, yes, there was a worry, but more important to Edward by far was that this baby should be a boy. He couldn't say that he'd lost sleep over not being able to keep his promise to his friend Elfed, but he knew that he'd feel good at finally being able to hand down the dragon in his family. He wondered whether Elfed had, unaware that at that moment, Elfed too was occupied by both the dragon and the birth of his first great-grandchild.

Twenty-four

THOSE DAYS IN Capel Celyn, the announcement of a pregnancy portended a visit from Enid. As much as she strove to avoid her father's farmhouse, Enid had known that sooner or later this call would have to be made... but so soon? She wasn't at all prepared for this or, she'd find out, for Myfanwy either.

During their first meeting, Elfed observed the ladies with nervous interest. He knew that Enid would rather not have come, though her reasons, to his slight chagrin, were not entirely clear. He also knew that she'd keep her word, that she'd be polite at all times, if distant! Yet, apart from Edgar, no one he knew had managed to keep their distance from Myfanwy, and soon he saw that Enid would be no exception. Myfanwy Evans, he could tell, had taken a liking to her.

"Poor Enid," he thought, "Myfanwy's attention will make you glow against your will. She'll elicit admiration when you'd much prefer disdain. You'd rather stay away, but you'll visit her again."

Contrary to Enid's plan, but in line with Elfed's prediction, the two ladies grew to really like each other. Enid gradually became Myfanwy's confidante and helped fill the void left by an increasingly inattentive Edgar. To Myfanwy, Enid was security, a mother figure and her baby's guardian angel. Enid herself was no less fulfilled by the relationship. Everyone liked Myfanwy, so Enid couldn't help but be flattered by her very special attention. To Enid, Myfanwy was excitement, and to some degree the daughter that she'd never had; and while she could, and sometimes did, take pleasure from the discomfort their liaison must lay on Rhiannon and Edgar, out of respect for her new-found friend, she tried really hard not to think about that.

Early on, Myfanwy had asked Enid why it was she rarely came to the farm.

"Rhiannon and I just don't see eye to eye."

"But why, Enid? She's not that bad with me."

Enid paused, debating on how much to tell.

"I must admit, Myfanwy, that she's mellowed with time, mainly because of Mam, I think, but she hasn't changed. People don't change much, you know, and anyway, she and I can never be friends. Let's leave it at that, all right?"

No talk of reassurance, nor ruthlessness nor strife that wrecked a happy family and wrung their way of life. Myfanwy acceded to Enid's request. She wasn't yet in the know, but knew enough to think better of fussing over Enid at chapel on Sundays. Instead, she started accompanying her on parts of her postal round. Twice a week, she would appear nonchalant as she waited near the farmhouse for Enid's figure to emerge from the trees, quite far beyond the river; twice a week, she would arrive excitedly at the postbox nailed to a tree by the bridge, and meet Enid there or beyond. Usually, she would arrive home three-quarters of an hour later with the post, if there happened to be any, nonchalant once again.

Myfanwy's friendship was a wonderful tonic for Enid. It heightened her senses and lightened her heart. She wouldn't trade this friendship for the world, and yet, she hadn't sought it because with it would come a dilemma. She already had a plot to avenge Rhiannon's betrayal, a plot that, sooner or later, she knew would clash with her friendship with Myfanwy. At the moment though, both were too precious to drop, so rather than rein one in, she rode the two, though she had no clue how the conflict would be resolved.

It was mid-May, a mere week before the Bala fair. As Margaret had feared, she hadn't had much luck planting the notion of a little red dragon in Edgar's in-growing mind. In fact, she hadn't been able to set up a situation where the subject could even be broached. The previous evening, hoping against hope, she'd mentioned the matter to Myfanwy, who by now was nearly five months pregnant. Margaret had related Edward and Elfed's story, and also how Geraint and Rhiannon had met, and then, how much Elfed would love to keep the tradition of the dragon going. So Edgar was obviously the key, but to Elfed, antagonistic he. Did Myfanwy think that she could possibly swing it? Myfanwy made the mistake of not saying no, so Margaret took her opening.

"May I suggest a few things, Myfanwy? For goodness sake, keep Elfed out of it. If ever Edgar thought he was doing it for his Taid, all bets would be off. One way of getting the whole thing going would be to ask... well, Geraint, I suppose... how he and Rhiannon met and then... "

"Geraint, may I ask you how you and Rhiannon met?"

Of the six that sat at the solid wooden table eating supper, four laughed. It was early evening, two days before the fair. Myfanwy liked Geraint, or Mr Evans as she had called him until very recently. For some reason, it had always been Rhiannon from the very start, and Elfed and Margaret as well.

Six sat, but only four laughed, and three thought, "Oh dear, that's not a very good start."

"Myfanwy! I'm surprised you haven't heard. It's quite funny really, isn't it Rhiannon? I was standing in a queue outside a tent at the fair, waiting to be tattooed, when this redhead barged in front of... "

"Really, Geraint, it wasn't at all like that," from Rhiannon, very warmly.

Geraint was wallowing in his wife's affection.

"Yes it was. You can ask Dad. He… "

Myfanwy interrupted so naturally that the only one surprised was she.

"So that was Rhiannon, was it? What was she doing there?"

"Well, she wanted a tattoo as well, didn't she? But the funniest thing was that we both wanted the same thing… a little red dragon. I just couldn't believe it. Could you, Rhiannon?"

"No, it was quite a shock to me too, and I think Elfed felt…"

"I think it's quite lovely, and the most romantic thing I've ever heard. Did you know all this, Edgar?"

Perfect timing from Myfanwy once again.

Edgar's manner conveyed to Myfanwy that he was being put out by this question, but he answered it, and with humour.

"Oh, I may have, but I think it's a bit silly, myself. I don't suppose it ever occurred to them that I might have been born with a little red dragon as well."

"Very funny, but that's a great idea, Edgar. Yes! You should have one too, in recognition of this wonderfully romantic coincidence that eventually led to you."

Edgar was ready to put an end to this nonsense.

"I am disappointed in you, Myfanwy Evans. You know that you can't possibly talk me into something like that. All you're doing is making me angry. So just drop it, will you?"

"Oh, come on, Edgar," exclaimed Rhiannon, "I think it's a great idea too. Don't you agree, Geraint?"

Six sat, five were firmly in favour, and two thought, "There's no chance. He's digging his heels in."

Myfanwy was not one of them. She refused to interpret Edgar's words as an outright "no", and readied herself for theatrics. She lent to her right and whispered to Margaret, who looked surprised, and pointing to herself, said, "Me?" Myfanwy nodded, and as the rhythm was rapped on the table, she stood. Rest, two, three, FOUR, five, six, rest, two, three, FOUR, five, six.

"I can't believe it," thought Elfed, "She's going to sing "Ave Maria". She's going to evoke the memory of the exuberant Edgar that she once knew. You've got to hand it to her… she's tough. Margaret was right there."

Elfed's heart quickened further as he noticed Edgar's head drop in desperation, and then rise again, shaking in angry disbelief. He appeared poised to leave the table, and as the rhythm rapped relentlessly, Myfanwy strove to pin him with her stare. Rest, two, three, FOUR, five, six, rest, two, three, FOUR, five, six. Of the six at the table, two glanced around nervously as the rhythm was rapped, but Myfanwy just stared, and wouldn't let him go.

To himself, Elfed begged and begged Myfanwy to sing, before Edgar broke her grip. After sixteen bars, she did, to Schubert's haunting tune. That surprised no one by now, but the first few syllables did. Immediately, they were spellbound.

"I haven't asked for much… "

Sadly, sweetly, and still gazing. She dwelt on the "I", essentially giving herself to him, and then milked the "asked" poignantly, before skipping over the next line.

"… Not for your touch or company… "

"… You know I could now be so dejected,

Neglected so by the one that I wed… "

Thus, she bared her disappointment, stretching the long vowels in "know" and "ject" and "lect" for maximum emotional impact, and packing her down notes in particular with the pathos of her contralto voice. Next, she countered with her commitment to him, and an unequivocal statement of her constancy.

"… But I have made my commitment to you,

I'll be faithful for life."

As she, still gazing at Edgar's now bowed head, went down the scale into "life", each note progressively radiated throughout the kitchen and bombarded every heartstring in sight. Elfed had never seen anything like this in his life: Myfanwy was magnificent.

She tripped lightly over the next two lines, as if sensing the mood was in need of a lift.

"… Your fam'ly has been so supportive,

My friends round here have been wonderf'lly kind… "

Myfanwy may have meant to lift the mood, but the first line in particular had the opposite effect. Her deft inflections and the excitement created by a light, lilting contralto voice proved devastating. Tears came to Margaret's eyes, but she kept on rapping. Elfed nearly choked on the biggest Adam's apple he'd ever experienced. Rhiannon took Geraint's hand, and the object of this whole exercise raised his head and returned Myfanwy's gaze, just in time for

"… But now and then I need your affection

Or I… will surely go out of my mind."

She would have loved to have played on the word "your" but the rhythm of the line led her beyond it. Still, every possible emotion went into "affection", other than mirth, which it seems she had reserved for the delightful little curl in which she wrapped the "I".

To finish, she repeated her first line, but this time straightforwardly and in a whisper.

"I haven't asked for much."

As soon as Margaret stopped drumming, she burst into tears. Myfanwy remained on her feet, limp now, but still gazing at Edgar.

"Absolutely brilliant," thought Elfed, "She's told him

everything that's on her mind, at a time when he had to listen, and in a language that he understands. What a virtuoso performance."

Elfed really had no idea how Edgar would react. He appeared unmoved, and everyone knew how difficult it would be for him to apologise, directly anyway. In the end, he was at least as nice as he had to be, and possibly as nice as he could be, without becoming personal.

"Myfanwy, that was truly incredible. I mean it. I know it'll be hard, but would you sing it again, please? Would you... please? Don't you worry, Nain... I'll provide the rhythm."

Yes, it would be hard, indeed, yet this was a breakthrough of sorts, so she had to make herself do it. At that instant, she felt drained of emotion. It was a relief, really, because she'd rather not perform as before, but she found she couldn't do it any other way.

"I haven't asked for much,

Not for your touch or company.

You know I could now be so dejected,

Neglected so by the one that I wed,

But I have made my commitment to you,

I'll be faithful for life.

Your fam'ly has been so supportive,

My friends round here have been wonderf'lly kind,

But now and then I need your affection,

Or I... will surely go out of my mind.

I haven't asked for much."

Now it was Myfanwy's turn to cry, and Margaret was quick to comfort her. Eventually, in between sobs, Myfanwy took everyone aback with, "So Edgar, will you have the tattoo done, then?"

Elfed had completely forgotten about the little red dragon that had inspired Myfanwy's theatrics. From his reaction, Edgar had too, but what could he say but, "OK... OK!"

Once over that hump though, he jumped into the spirit of things.

"Right, then," taking everyone by surprise, "A little red dragon it'll be, but where I wonder? I know where Dad's is, but Mam, what about yours?"

"The less you know about mine, the better, Edgar bach. You follow your father's example."

"Come on, Mam. Show it to us. We'd all like to see it, wouldn't we?"

Elfed, for one, would rather not, and he felt himself blush a bit.

"You follow your father's example, Edgar. That's all I have to say. Why don't you go with him to the fair, Geraint, just like Elfed did with you... "

Myfanwy was just as quick to intercede as she'd been the time before

"No, no, I'd like to go with Edgar. You needn't bother, Geraint. Can I come with you, Edgar?"

Her diversion worked, but for some reason, he answered, "No, I'd prefer to go on my own."

Given the magic of those moments, one would have thought that Edgar would have jumped at Myfanwy's offer. What a pity he should sully their spirit of communion, just like that! Within minutes, a breakthrough of sorts had been compromised by his rejection... but there was even more to it than that. Completely unintentionally, Myfanwy had given Edgar the opportunity of immunising himself against the sting in the dragon's tail. The future rests on choices, unless one believes in fate, and thrice had Edgar chosen, and now it was too late. The little red dragon had been back in the picture since Elfed and Margaret's chat in early March, and there was nothing that Edgar could have done about that. Yet, he needn't have chosen to be tattooed, although to be fair, Myfanwy's emotional appeal had given him little choice. He needn't have chosen his mother's advice on where to put it, although to be fair again, she had made it hard for him not to. However, he certainly needn't have chosen to reject Myfanwy's offer to accompany him. Indeed, under such touching circumstances, he'd had every reason not to, but he did.

Yes, thrice had Edgar chosen, and now it was too late.

Twenty-five

ELFED WOULDN'T HAVE been a bit surprised had Edgar already changed his mind about the dragon. Yet, to be honest, somewhat encouraging was his demeanour. There he stood with Rhiannon outside the stable at half past eight on the morning of the day of the fair, securing a dozen lambs in his slightly dilapidated cart. Ever since Myfanwy's remarkably emotional appeal, he had behaved a shade more politely and warmly to all. This morning, even, he had agreed without demur to let Myfanwy accompany him part of the way, to the ridge above the farm. As the couple left along the rutted track, they bobbed comically like marionettes. Elfed allowed himself the luxury of imagining their relationship in a better light. Perhaps Myfanwy's masterful performance the other night had done the trick, but he doubted it. She now turned and waved warmly, but Edgar's broad back didn't budge.

Rhiannon returned indoors but Elfed watched the marionettes till they bobbed out of sight. Shortly, they appeared on the road higher up. Before long they stopped, just below the ridge. Myfanwy appeared reluctant to step down, and when she did, Edgar continued on his way rather abruptly, it seemed. All the while, Elfed heard the receding bleating of lambs, protesting of course, but who knows, perhaps lamenting Edgar's decision to reject Myfanwy's offer to accompany him to the fair.

Myfanwy glanced a few times at her husband's unresponsive back gradually disappearing over the ridge and onto the high plateau, and then she scrambled cautiously to a vantage point just off the road. As she sat very carefully on a wide, flattish stone, she was at last under no illusions. She felt a huge relief and a lightness of spirit, and a suprisingly intense pleasure from her baby's kicking.

She surveyed the scene around her. At first, she had missed her childhood estuary and the sea, but they were gradually being replaced in her affections by these lovely mountain vistas. As a matter of fact, she'd recently visited her parents to show off her baby bulge. She'd enjoyed being in Borth-y-gest, but on the return trip it had struck her, for the first time really, that this valley was her home now... and Edgar's too, worse luck! Myfanwy had been bewildered by Edgar's metamorphosis. Had the change been delayed, she'd have accepted it, she was sure; and it wasn't that he'd switched to black from white without warning overnight. It had just gradually become clear that Edgar had empathy for no one but himself. The realisation had shocked her and she'd been hurt, but she'd never lost heart, or the hope that perhaps she could change him. Elfed and Margaret had been crucial in their support as she struggled to regroup. Surprisingly during this time, she'd rarely felt angry... just foolish.

"What came over me?" she had regularly asked herself, and then she'd reel off the mitigating circumstances.

"Well, he is attractive, isn't he, and he certainly put on a good show for all of us. Every girl fancied him, so naturally I felt chuffed to be the one... and he's a star, so why should anyone be surprised that I fell for him? My parents were impressed as well and encouraged me, and of course his family were really, really nice. Even Rhiannon, who I know now can be difficult, was unusually warm to me. In a way, I was marrying the family, I suppose."

There! She'd exonerated herself... for a few moments, till self-recrimination had struck again.

"I should have given myself more time to decide... that's all there is to it. So why didn't I? I have to come back to bad judgement, I suppose."

Myfanwy shouldn't have been so hard on herself. Had her idea of marriage been a purely romantic one, then perhaps alarm bells would have rung rather than wedding ones. But Myfanwy's idea of marriage had always been more down to earth than that. No immersion or submission or dependency for her. What she'd sought in marriage were children, a dependable partner to help support them, and a companion. Well, she'd got her child all right. Naturally, she hoped her baby would inherit Edgar's many talents. If, by any chance, a few of his undesirable behavioural traits managed to wriggle through as well, she was confident that they would be ironed out by her nurturing. As for a dependable partner? Well, if Edgar had anything, it was a sense of duty. On that front, she felt reasonably secure, but forget about companionship. This was where her judgement had really let her down. Happily, her bouts of self-recrimination had been striking less frequently, and now she had a feeling that they would strike no more.

She'd been foolish, and yet, no longer would she fret. A man, and a woman in a postman's hat, by noon today will have seen to that. As the man, at that moment, ushered a dozen disorientated lambs from his slightly dilapidated cart, Myfanwy saw the woman emerging from a house in the village, and then approach the bridge. No one could have identified her from that distance, but to Myfanwy her jizz was unmistakable, as was her postman's hat.

When earlier, Edgar and Myfanwy had stopped just short of the ridge, she had begged him to change his mind and let her go with him to the fair.

"Please, Edgar, please let me go with you!"

She had begged, because out of the blue she had defined this moment as a point of no return in their relationship. She had decided that if Edgar, despite her emotional plea two nights earlier, could not agree to such a simple request of companionship, then her attitude towards him would be allowed to harden forever.

She realised that she had sung of her commitment and constancy, and in a narrow sense, those vows would still be honoured; but a wider and deeper commitment depended on Edgar's response right then.

"Please, Edgar, please let me go with you!"

She had begged and begged. As it was, she had been not so much denied as dismissed, which of course had made her decision that much easier. At that moment, she gave up on him. Emotionally, she had divorced him, and with it had experienced release, and somehow had felt less foolish. The incident had come close to wiping her slate clean. The completion of the task would be left to a lady in a postman's hat.

Myfanwy watched Enid disappear round a bend in the River Celyn, and for half an hour thought mostly of her baby and the love she would lavish on him. Him? If she was sure of anything, she was sure of that. Every now and then her mind was hijacked by little shadows flitting across the valley and the hills, and the sun's rays dancing on the rivers. They reminded her of how lucky she felt to be part of this special scene. Growing up in Borth-y-gest, she'd been sheltered from the community by her middle-class family, so this was the first time that she had experienced a communal camaraderie... and she loved it. She'd found that not only had she married Edgar and his family, but a system of support as well. In bringing her here, Edgar had sowed the seeds of his own dispensability.

Enid reappeared on the other bank, snapping Myfanwy's reverie, at the very same moment that Edgar approached the red tent, alone... but only from choice. Myfanwy's decision to divorce her emotions from Edgar had been made much easier by the confidence she drew from her friendship with Enid. Enid gave her strength without seeking submission in return. Myfanwy couldn't wait to tell her tale. Enid knew a little bit about her Schubertian drama and the third generation red dragon, but nothing at all of her emotional break with Edgar. Never had she had so much to say to her friend, and yet she forced herself to be patient. Even allowing for the baby on board, it would take Myfanwy no more than ten minutes to reach the bridge where she invariably met her friend. Today it seemed particularly important that they both arrive at exactly the same time. So Myfanwy waited and watched excitedly as Enid descended the Celyn and skirted Arenig Fach along the main road. When the time came, Myfanwy had to restrain herself from running.

As Myfanwy approached the bridge and her friend, Edgar was far from her mind. He happened to be leaving the red tent at that moment, still alone, with a little red dragon on his shoulder blade. He strode across the fairground, shaking his head in wonder at the way he'd been talked into such a foolish act, and unaware that he'd live to regret not being talked into allowing Myfanwy to be with him.

"Enid, I've got so much to tell you."

Myfanwy spoke with enthusiasm, but it was forced. There was something amiss, she knew it, but she couldn't immediately bring herself to abandon the excitement she'd felt on the ridge. Even as she'd approached the bridge, Myfanwy had known there was something wrong. Normally Enid would have waved her postman's hat playfully and behaved in a way that belied her years... but not today.

"Enid," repeated Myfanwy, now in a tone that reflected reality, but she got no further.

"Stop, Myfanwy, for a moment, please."

Enid laid her postbag beside the bridge, and in a sudden show of frustration, jerked her head and clenched fists downwards so violently that her hat fell off. She swiped at it with her foot, but missed, and then just stared at the ground as she spoke.

"Before you say another word, Myfanwy, there's something I've just got to get off my chest... and I'm not sure I can look you straight in the eye as I tell you this, so let's lean on the bridge, all right?"

Myfanwy obeyed in a daze. She felt a crucial rug being pulled from under her feet. It was devastating.

"What an earth is going on?" she wondered, "Have I got Enid all wrong as well?" and at the thought, her chest tightened, and suddenly she felt very lonely.

Meanwhile, as Enid's troubled gaze met the Tryweryn, she was reminded vividly of a conversation she'd had with her father at this very spot six months earlier, a conversation that had foreseen the dilemma on which she now felt torn. The memory, however, injected a measure of perspective, which calmed her slightly, so she turned to face her friend.

"Myfanwy, I'm so sorry for upsetting you like this. Believe me, I could see how excited you were just now and I hated the thought of bursting your bubble, but after weeks of dithering around, I had finally plucked up the courage to talk to you about something, and not even your excitement could make me change my mind."

Only to a slight degree was Myfanwy consoled; she was still confused and fearful. It showed, unnerving Enid who turned to face the river again.

"Listen, Myfanwy... what I'm going to say is no reflection on you one bit, all right? It's all to do with me... with me and my problems."

Myfanwy was heartened by Enid's tone. Perhaps things weren't quite as bad as she'd feared.

"Just after my father met you, I remember him talking to me about you in such glowing terms. He went as far as to say that you reminded him of my mother. I told him then that it seemed to me that you could really complicate my life. I remember saying to Dad that he shouldn't worry, though. I promised him I wouldn't be rude to you, just distant."

Myfanwy was totally confused, and once again an awful loneliness gripped her.

"Then we met, and we became friends, and in a way we're soulmates, aren't we?"

Myfanwy moved towards her friend and touched her arm, only to be rebuffed.

"Don't touch me now, Myfanwy… please! Let me finish, all right?"

Myfanwy's emotions were churning. The rejection confused her further.

"Myfanwy, I shouldn't have allowed us to become close. It was a mistake, and all along I knew it. I should have distanced myself from you, but I couldn't make myself do it, and as you became more and more important in my life, it became harder and harder still. I just… don't seem… to be able to do anything right."

Resorting to self-pity cracked her resolve. She sighed deeply, and then suddenly started sobbing and crying in pathetic little bursts. Myfanwy, herself in turmoil, was surprised by her friend's distress, and at first was reluctant to approach her. When in the end she did, to her relief she was not rebuffed. Enid accepted her embrace and comfort. For many minutes, they were still, silent and soothed by the Tryweryn and each other; in that position they remained as Enid continued her story. After a good cry, and with Myfanwy's arm around her, she was much, much calmer than before.

"Myfanwy, I said we were soulmates, but we're not, you know, because I've been living a lie. I've been keeping something from you and it's been eating at me. Every time I see you or even think of you, it pops up and reminds me of what a fraud I am. I couldn't stand it any more, which is why I have to clear the air."

Myfanwy was none the wiser, but she, too, was calmer,

despite her confusion. She was a comforter now, and that quietened her mind.

"What is it, Enid? What are you talking about?" and she encouraged her friend with a squeeze of her hand.

"Myfanwy, it all comes back to Rhiannon. You may have heard bits of this story, so be patient. During those months before her wedding to Geraint, she pulled the wool over our eyes. She really did, and clinically too. When we realised this, and it became clear that the real Rhiannon had no qualms about ruining our way of life, we were all terribly hurt. Yes, Mam and Dad too, but no one as hurt as me. In my mind, I had put Rhiannon on a pedestal and was in awe of her. I would have trusted her with anything. I was broken when I knew I'd been fooled. I couldn't get over it, and I'm telling you, it ruined my life. I lost my self-confidence and was torn away from my family. It was awful."

They still stood side by side, facing downriver, Myfanwy's arm across Enid's back and her hand quite firm on her shoulder. Enid had completely settled down by now, and continued unemotionally.

"For years I tried to forgive her, and failed. For goodness sake, I couldn't even forgive myself for being so naive. I was down on myself for ages and only turned the corner when I decided to seek my revenge. I honestly don't think of myself as a bad person, but in this instance it seems important for me to know that I'll get my own back one day, because that's the only way it seems I can feel good about myself."

Concentrating on her caring role, and only gradually becoming aware of the significance of Enid's words, Myfanwy was taken aback when Enid gently shook off her arm, turned to face her and with a sad, resigned expression said, "And that's why we can't be friends, Myfanwy."

When Myfanwy had grasped the full implication of what Enid had said, the loneliness returned, this time laced with panic.

"Now wait a minute," she said to herself, "just take it easy. This isn't like you at all," and she forced herself to speak.

"Oh, Enid," she started in an awkward, off-hand manner, "I don't care that much for Rhiannon either, so if you hurt her, that's no skin off my nose."

Enid couldn't quite decide if Myfanwy was being naive, but just in case, she played along.

"Now think about it, Myfanwy. It might happen that I'll get at Rhiannon through her son… your husband, Myfanwy… remember?"

"Oh, Enid, that's what I've been dying to tell you. This morning I washed my hands… "

"Come on Myfanwy, think this through, will you? When I succeed in shaming your husband, it'll reflect on the whole family. It'll reflect on your children and it'll reflect on you. How can you possibly be my friend when I'm plotting against you, even if it is indirectly? Come on, Myfanwy!"

The more they sparred this way, the more assured was Myfanwy's approach. Somehow, she now knew it wouldn't be anywhere near as bad as she'd feared. Suddenly, it made no sense at all that she and Enid couldn't be the best of friends. There had to be a way out of it. Convinced of this, her tone strengthened, and she became more animated.

"So you're prepared to hurt your Mam and Dad, are you?"

It was Enid's turn now to be on the defensive.

"No," she stuttered, "I wouldn't do anything while Mam and Dad are living."

"That could be years then," said Myfanwy excitedly, "And what about Geraint?"

"No… not while he's alive either."

Relief is always relative, and Myfanwy's was intense,

a reflection of the fright she'd felt with their friendship in suspense.

"Well, Enid fach! What are we worrying about, then? You know that the doctor visited your brother only a fortnight ago. He thinks Geraint could easily live another ten years. That's what he said, anyway. So let's not worry about what might happen, Enid. Let's enjoy our friendship now. Let's enjoy it day by day."

Myfanwy moved towards her friend, but Enid quickly backed away. She almost tripped on her hat, and as she stooped to retrieve it, she shook her head and spoke dejectedly.

"You're being hopelessly unrealistic, Myfanwy. How can we be comfortable as friends, when every moment of every day I'll be, in a sense, plotting to hurt you?"

Following her decisive break with Edgar that morning, Myfanwy had hung her hat on her friendship with Enid, so the prospect of losing it had devastated her. Now that she could feel it in her grasp again, she determined to make whatever mental adjustments were necessary to keep it. Enid could not so easily be as flexible. True, she'd got things off her chest, and her friend had remained supportive, but even if Myfanwy could live with her dilemma, how possibly could she?

Myfanwy moved to mould the other's mind, and spoke perhaps too forcefully.

"Enid, I know you love me, and wouldn't want to hurt me or my children. Now, I understand how important it is for you to get your own back on Rhiannon, and perhaps in the process I'd be affected too, but I could live with that. In any case, that could be ten years from now... or more! Let's not worry about that! Isn't our friendship more important?"

Enid was dying for a way out of her dilemma, but she couldn't possibly square that circle. A commitment to both Myfanwy and an act of revenge that would almost certainly hurt her were clearly incompatible. She'd give anything to reconcile her conflict, but it was hopeless. She felt extremely dejected, and it showed.

Myfanwy fell back on a tack that had worked before. She took Enid's arm firmly, and once again they lent on the bridge together, Myfanwy's arm across Enid's back and her hand quite firm on her shoulder. They gazed at the running river, and were soothed by the Tryweryn and each other. Myfanwy's eyes were carried downstream by the boisterous current, until she snapped them back for the movement to be repeated all over again. For once, her gaze penetrated the surface of the water and focused on the river floor.

"My goodness," she thought, "what a pretty boulder. It really stands out."

It was no bigger than most of the others, but its light sandy colour caught her eye. She turned to Enid and pointed it out.

"That's funny," said Enid, surprised, "I was looking at it too."

The ladies laughed and then, for the first time that morning, looked at each other and smiled. Their eyes returned to the river and the light sandy boulder on the bottom. Myfanwy spoke much more softly now.

"What keeps on coming back to me, Enid, is that nothing would make sense if we weren't friends, so there's got to be a way out of this. The obvious answer is for you to give up on revenge, isn't it, but from what you say, the idea has been part of your make-up for twenty years. It's so much a part of you that you probably hadn't even considered giving it up, had you?"

Myfanwy glanced at Enid, who was shaking her head, but looking a little brighter on the brow, she thought.

"I can understand how you thought you needed the notion of revenge to preserve your sanity," and here she turned to her friend and raised her voice a bit, "But you've got me now, Enid.

186

You've got our friendship to sustain you. Don't you think the revenge thing will naturally become less and less important as you grow to be able to depend on me?"

Was Enid nodding slightly? Myfanwy couldn't tell. Enid continued to gaze at the river as Myfanwy made her case.

"Even though it hadn't occurred to you, don't you think that's what will happen, really? It won't happen overnight but I think you know it will in the end. Don't you, Enid?"

The movements of Enid's mouth expressed an inkling of agreement.

"And knowing it'll happen in the end, won't that allow you in the meantime to be completely comfortable with our friendship? Won't you try, Enid? And we can talk about it now and then to make sure that there's absolutely nothing coming between us. What do you think, Enid? Will you give it a try... for me?"

Enid turned towards Myfanwy and smiled reassuringly, gratefully and lovingly. It was a beautiful smile, made all the more beautiful in Myfanwy's eyes by what might have been. As Enid hugged her friend on the bridge, all she said was, "Thanks, Myfanwy." Without another word she picked up the bag that was on the ground, secured her hat with a little pat and off she went on her postal round. She walked tall, though she was only of medium height. That unmistakable jizz was momentarily disturbed as Enid turned and waved her hat, behaving in a way that belied her years. It was then that Myfanwy realised that she'd told nothing of her news to her friend. Yet another reason, she thought, to look forward to their next meeting. She realised too that she hadn't thought of her baby once during her forty-five minute conversation with Enid. Surely, that was a record? Was she guilty of neglect, she wondered with amusement.

When Enid had disappeared, Myfanwy returned to lean against the bridge. Yes, she knew she'd been foolish, and yet, she also knew no longer would she fret: she'd rid her emotional space of Edgar, and happily she now knew that Enid would move in. Her gaze penetrated the boisterous current until she found the sandy coloured boulder, and she thanked it. As she did, she felt wonderfully connected to Enid and yet completely free, which is more than could be said at that moment for Edgar and the little red dragon on his shoulder blade.

Twenty-six

A S HE LEAVES the red tent, Edgar is alone... very much from choice. He meets Gareth Griffiths, an acquaintance from the eisteddfod circuit, who has little difficulty persuading him to drop in at the Lion for a quick one. On the way there, they stop off at Michael Meredith's, the smartest of the clothes shops in Bala.

Behind the counter, Michael Meredith stiffens as they enter his shop. His welcome is polite but no more.

Edgar explains, in Welsh, that he'd like to buy a shirt, in the same colours as before, but looser this time. As Mr Meredith turns towards the back room, the bell on the door clangs, and a very well dressed lady enters, followed by a toff, whose similarly chinless face suggests that he's her son. The silver knob on his walking stick glistens.

"Well, how very nice it is to see you again, Lady Ben-Bowen," from Mr Meredith as he rushes past Edgar and Gareth, "And you too, Bertie. It's been a very long time... far too long, if I may say so."

The lady replies in very far back English.

"Well you see, poor old Sir Basil has been so awfully busy in the City that we've neglected our friends, the Ponsobys, something awful. Between you and me, they consider our neglect inexcusable. And what a lovely home they have. I believe you're all very fortunate that they've settled in your county."

Bertie Ben-Bowen looks bored, and Edgar and Gareth look agitated, presumably on account of their being ignored because of the Ben-Bowens' presence.

"Well, madam, what can I do for you today?"

"I must admit I took a fancy to a little something in your window. Now, there's a blouse just… "

"Ah! You must mean the light blue one. Let me get it for you so that you can try it on."

Edgar expresses his indignation to Gareth in Welsh. The shopkeeper hears, but continues to promote the blouse. Edgar, visibly upset, remarks on the toff's stick, and rudely recommends where the gentleman should stuff it. Gareth and he guffaw.

"Don't you agree, Bertie," reacts the lady, "that it's frightfully uncouth of that fellow to insist on conversing in that vulgar tongue. They're quite likely to be ribbing us, you know, which makes the whole situation perfectly intolerable, don't you think? Would you be a poppet, Bertie, and ask them not to be so awfully rude?"

"Oh, mother dear, don't let such provincial antics bother you. What on earth do you expect, anyway, coming in here, rubbing shoulders with the working classes?"

Bertie's expression is one of heroic indifference, which soon yields to wounded pride when Gareth apes his chinless arrogance to perfection.

"I say, dear fellow," from Bertie, "That kind of behaviour just isn't on. And by the way…yes, you over there… I do believe an apology is called for, affronting my mother as you did."

Edgar steps forward, exaggeratedly hitching up his trousers.

"Come over here and make me do it, sweetheart," in English from Edgar.

Michael Meredith nervously steps forward, but is pushed aside by Bertie Ben-Bowen, who strides arrogantly towards Edgar and pokes his walking stick firmly into his chest.

"Look here… no farmhand talks to me like that."

Edgar snatches the silver-knobbed stick effortlessly, snaps it in two on his thigh and tosses the pieces over his shoulder.

Bertie Ben-Bowen, now apoplectic, grabs Edgar by the shirt. Edgar lifts his right hob-nailed boot and stamps Bertie Ben-Bowen's fancy left shoe with an enormous thud. The toff shrieks in agony, and his chinless face is raised in pain. Fortunately for all involved, Edgar's raised fist is grabbed by Gareth, who ushers him out of the shop. There is a hush, broken by the bell as the door is pulled shut rather sharply. Bertie slumps on the floor, still in agony.

"Don't just stand there, man," from the lady to the shopkeeper, "I'm holding you totally responsible for this provincial farce. Aren't you going to do something, you ditherer?"

Michael Meredith's eyes dart around the shop. Suddenly, he reaches for his hat and approaches the door, bowing to the Ben-Bowens obsequiously.

"I'm terribly sorry, madam. I'll go and get the doctor. I won't be long at all."

"I should jolly well hope not, and the police had better not be too far behind, either."

Michael Meredith stiffens, looks very surprised, drops his head in thought and then nods. As he leaves, the doorbell hardly jangles at all. The lady sits on a chair, crosses her legs elegantly and smoothes her skirt.

"Poor old Bertie! The things you do for your dear mother!"

Ten minutes later, PC Prosser enters the public bar of the Lion, glances at the backs at the bar and notices Edgar and Gareth by the window and casually sits at their table. He informs them that he's been told of their spot of bother. Edgar does not react well, and is advised by the constable to calm down and use his head. He is reminded that there's a way to handle this that would make it easier for everybody, to which Edgar replies that he's more interested in bringing the matter to a head.

"Edgar, don't be ridiculous," seethes the constable, "you're acting as if you don't have anything to lose. If you push these people too far, they'll come after you, and your property. Now, you may not care about that, but think of your mam and dad and the rest of your family."

Edgar looks at Gareth, who's nodding vigorously, and then back at the constable, who recommends that Edgar accompanies him to the station and allow himself to be locked up for a bit. Edgar jumps forward in his chair and sharply bangs his fist on the table. Droplets of beer fly through the air.

"What do you mean, lock me up? It's that fart, Bertie, you should lock up. Crikey!"

Edgar is promised that if he cooperates, he'll be home in a couple of hours.

"It's all to do with appearances, Edgar. Trust me, OK? I know how to deal with these people."

Edgar thinks quietly, and at his friend's urging, decides to accept the constable's recommendation.

"All right," from the constable, "but one more thing before we go. Don't think I'm getting soft in my old age, all right? My job is still to uphold the law. I just find it a little fuzzy when it comes to things like this, that's all."

All three rise, and leave the Lion.

An hour later, PC Prosser is greeted at the Ponsoby's front door by Captain Ponsoby himself.

"Good afternoon, Constable. I presume you've come to talk about that frightful to-do at Meredith's shop? The Ben-Bowens are resting upstairs... they're awfully cut-up over this miserable business, but I'll get them for you."

The constable asks him not to, and suggests that as he, the captain, better understands the issues involved in this local matter, perhaps the two of them could sort it out quieter and quicker.

"My dear Constable, don't pin your hopes on it. The Ben-Bowens are frightfully miffed and are determined to make that confounded farmhand pay for his uncivilised behaviour."

The constable looks around deliberately, leans towards the Captain, and whispers, "It's all very well for the Ben-Bowens to be on their high horse, because they'll be gone from here in a few days, but you Captain, you live here, and should a backlash… "

"Am I to take that as a threat, Constable? If so, you're treading on very thin ice."

The constable shakes his head in disbelief, and expresses surprise at the captain's reaction.

"You've been sensitive to local issues in the past, so I'm at a loss as to understand why, if I may say so, you've suddenly lost your touch. If it's face-saving you're worried about, then I… "

The captain interrupts with a gesture of hands. His head beckons the constable indoors, and presumably in an attempt to reassert himself, says, "My dear fellow, look at your boots. I'd be much obliged if you left them on the doorstep."

Another hour later, Edgar and Gareth are drinking tea. They seem sombre, and are behind bars, but the cell door is open. PC Prosser appears from the front of the police station to tell them that the captain will arrive any minute, and that Gareth should leave by the back door

"Now Edgar, we understand each other, right? I've done my bit, now you do yours. Don't make me look foolish, all right?"

Edgar nods sourly, and Gareth disappears. PC Prosser locks the cell and returns to the front office, just as Captain Ponsoby strides in impatiently.

"Well, here it is, Constable. I don't mind telling you that I had a deuce of a time persuading Sir Basil to agree to this. Anyway, let's get on with it. This is a dreadful waste of my time."

He brusquely hands a document to the constable.

"Thank you, Captain. I'll take your word for it that this document is exactly as we agreed."

"How awfully magnanimous of you, Constable. Of course, you're not to know are you that in my circle only a bounder would say something like that."

"Would you like to deal with the prisoner, Captain, or shall I?" ignoring the previous remark.

"Good heavens, man, you better not let me near the confounded fellow. I'm not at all sure that I could trust myself not to give him a dressing down."

PC Prosser leaves the room and reappears in Edgar's cell.

"Here it is, Edgar, as promised. I know! I know! But just do it, man, and get yourself out of here. Now, I haven't checked it, and even though the captain boasts that he's a man of his word, you better read what you're signing."

Edgar takes the document and slowly whispers its contents in English.

"I, Edgar Evans, hereby acknowledge that my behaviour this morning at Michael Meredith's shop was inappropriate. I duly apologise to Lady Ben-Bowen for affronting her, and to Bertrand Ben-Bowen for badly bruising his left foot."

Then in Welsh, "Oh! I hate all this. I don't even understand all the words, but I suppose it's all OK, isn't it, Constable? There's another bit here, so hang on a minute."

Continuing in English, "I also apologise to both the Ben-Bowens for conversing in Welsh in their presence."

And now most definitely in Welsh, "What the hell is this, Constable? Are you trying to pull the wool over my eyes? We didn't agree to that, and there's no hope in hell that I will. Good God!"

"What's the matter, Edgar? Just sign it, and get it over and done with."

"Didn't you hear what I just read? They want me to apologise for speaking in Welsh. Didn't you hear that?"

"Hear what? Let me look at it myself."

The document is passed to the constable, who glances at it quickly, and erupts.

"I don't believe this. What a bastard! Just stay there, Edgar. I'll be back in a flash."

As the constable rushes from the cell in a rage, leaving the door ajar, Edgar taunts him angrily.

"Don't make me look foolish, you said. It looks as if you should have been preaching to Ponsoby, not me."

The constable approaches Captain Ponsoby in a fury, waving the document jerkily.

"Ah! You're back already."

"I'm afraid, there is a problem, Captain Ponsoby. Tell me, if a person from your circle who doubts your word is called a bounder, what do you call a person who breaks his word? Or is that acceptable... in your circle?"

"Oh! Be done with the theatrics, Constable. It's high time I left."

The constable waves the document emphatically in front of the captain's face.

"What is this nonsense in here about the Welsh language? We never agreed on that."

"My word, you are an unreasonable fellow. I had a deuce of a struggle persuading the Ben-Bowens to agree to this settlement in the first place, and without that bit about the language, Lady Ben-Bowen just would not budge. You should be grateful for my enterprise, instead of bullying me like this."

"But why didn't you tell me that you'd included another condition?"

"Good God, man, that's hardly a condition. Far too trivial a matter, old boy, to make such a song and dance about. Now, it really is time I left for home."

"He won't sign it," emphatically from the constable, "Yes, that's right... he won't sign it, and I wouldn't either. Here's the pen. Cross out that condition, or he won't sign."

"I couldn't possibly, dear fellow. The Ben-Bowens would lynch me. No, no chance... couldn't possibly do that."

PC Prosser turns and walks away very slowly, speaking as he goes.

"Good day, Captain Ponsoby. I am now going to release Edgar Evans and won't take any further action against him until charges are pressed."

As the constable leaves the room, the captain shuffles to his feet.

"Oh, all right, bring it here. You are a bully. God knows how I'll swing this with the Ben-Bowens. Tiresome business all round. There you are, and I suppose you'll insist, won't you, that I sign by the amendment. There!"

The constable takes the document without a word and leaves the room.

Half an hour later, Edgar is aboard his horse and cart, and leaving the fair field. With him is Gareth, who suggests that they stop at the Lion to finish off their drinks.

"After all, you do have something to celebrate."

"Not a bit of it, Gareth. I am so angry about the whole thing that I feel weak. I just can't believe I was talked into going against my principles, just to make everyone happy, except for myself, of course. At least I dug my heels in over the language bit, which is something, I suppose. Still, what a bloody cheek, they've got, aye... the bloody English! No, there's nothing to celebrate, Gareth. I'm not a bit happy, believe me... just angry as hell."

The horse and cart, Edgar and his little red dragon turn to the right, up the Tryweryn valley.

Twenty-seven

IT WAS JULY 1926, and late afternoon, as Edgar arrived by train at Swansea station. He would change there and arrive at Llanelli half an hour later.

For the last two months, since his run-in with the Ben-Bowens, his anger, and the shame associated with the affair, had nagged him incessantly. Still, during this time, he had farmed, continued to refurbish his future home and competed, just as usual; yet he'd failed to ease his mind. His moodiness had pervaded the farmhouse, and to one degree or another had infected all its occupants, but for Myfanwy who seemed immune to it. So worried were Geraint and Rhiannon by mid-July that the doctor's advice had been sought. His recommendation was a complete change of scenery and a break in routine. Hence Edgar's train journey to Llanelli where he would live for a fortnight with Myfanwy's older sister Mavis and her husband, and compete in a regional eisteddfod there just before returning home. The timing had been deemed perfect, for the farm was seasonally slow, and as for the baby, there were more than two months to go.

Five years earlier, Mavis Morris had married a milkman from Llanelli. Many had joked that she'd chosen David, or Dai as he was known, for his name, because she'd longed to be Mrs Mavis Davies. They had met while Dai was on holiday in Borth-y-gest. She had loved the way he laughed so readily, and he her sense of humour. Perhaps, too, he'd been impressed by her social status, while fortunately she cared not a fig about his. Not so the Captain, however, who let it be known that Mavis had not been pampered in silk to marry a mere milkman. Yet, Mavis protested, and Mavis prevailed, and her judgement had been vindicated. Dai turned out to be no ordinary milkman: by now his business was big, the biggest in Llanelli. He employed four milkmen, owned two vans and was interested, as he put it, in vertical integration. These days, when Dai laughed, it was often all the way to the bank. To top it all, Mavis was going to have a baby, after years of trying, and crying at times.

Dai and Mavis Davies met Edgar at the station in the newer of their two vans. Edgar was clearly impressed, and also polite! Indeed, Edgar was putting his very best foot forward, which surprised and pleased Mavis, because all three were well aware that in the recuperative ointment on offer to Edgar, there was one particularly tricky fly… Dai couldn't speak Welsh; to make matters worse from Edgar's point of view, Dai's father, who lived just down the road, could. The trouble had been his mother, an English-speaking lady from Leominster, who had steadfastly resisted assimilation, and the father had deferred to her. Dai admitted that he had been, and still was, indifferent to this business of his father's mother tongue. Everyone in the family had known that such an attitude wouldn't endear Dai to Edgar, but Mavis had insisted that the visit still take place. After all, she'd quipped, Dai was early to bed, and Dai was early to rise, which made him quite healthy, and certainly wealthy… and with Edgar he'd sworn to be wise.

Mavis's judgement proved to be spot on. Edgar and Dai saw little of each other during that fortnight. Each morning, Edgar got up surprisingly late for a farmer, and chatted while Mavis prepared his breakfast. Edgar's sociability surprised her. It was hard to believe that this was the impossible man her sister had frequently written about. He wasn't at all as cold or morose as she'd been warned to expect. Perhaps the change was already doing him good. Still, at times it was clear that something was eating at him, so she appreciated all the more the effort she knew he must be making. By mid-morning, Edgar was gone, regardless of the weather, and Mavis wouldn't see him then until dinnertime, which was at five. Most evenings, Edgar seemed keen to tell them where he'd been that day. After the first few excursions, though, it was the same old story: it was always Mynydd Sylen. Day after day, Edgar tramped to the top of this hill, and most days he managed to couch the same old story in a new and interesting light.

It was between five and six miles to the top, the first half along the Mynydd Mawr Railway which followed the Afon Lliedi to Horeb, and the second on a country road that climbed consistently from the railway and the river. He walked it the first time on a sultry, sunny day. The sleepers on the railway were, as usual, quite the wrong distance apart, and demanded his attention. Once on the road, however, his mind slipped into what was fast becoming its default mode: a relentless regurgitation of his anger. He dwelt fruitlessly on the Ben-Bowen affair. He just couldn't shake the feeling that he'd let the side down. The sun, shimmering through the late morning haze, beat encouragingly on his back, and the widening vistas begged for his attention, but all his feelings were folded inwards. Change, when it finally came, was no consolation. His mind just switched to his other pet hates. The English were given their regular roasting, until his thoughts finally settled on south Walians. He continued to adhere to his irrational view that they were traitors; as if this was embedded in his genetic make-up, and there was nothing he could do about it.

"Oh yes!" was his reaction to them, "Talk about letting the side down!"

He was aware that the resistance to Anglicisation had been more resolute here in Carmarthenshire than anywhere further east, but he had no doubt that in the end it too would succumb.

"I feel quite queasy," he suddenly thought, "I feel as if I'm in a foreign land."

Poor old Edgar! Dogmatic, and incapable of seeing the world in anything other than black and white: he was never not right, while they who strayed a mere shade, even if not for long, were never not wrong.

Thus Edgar Evans approached the gradual arc that is the summit of Mynydd Sylen. Still bewailing the betrayal he attributed to south Wales, and increasingly uneasy at actually being there, the top was attained without warning. Edgar was stunned by what he saw. At that instant, his spirit exploded from its straitjacket and whisked him away in all directions. The freedom he felt was phenomenal. He lapped up the Loughor, the Gower and the sea, was greeted by the Gwendraeth, and beyond, by Preseli; drawn to the mountain that's not black, though so it's named, and felt welcomed by those valleys that Swansea'd gone and tamed. Diversity in all directions, but this was no foreign land! He identified as readily with the soft surrounds of this modest mountain as he did with the rockiness that ranged around his home. Certainly, this was the South which to him had become anathema, but up here he felt part of it. He started to sing, and his lovely voice reflected the warmth he felt within. At that moment, the world seemed almost a happy place. Two traditional standards, 'Calon Lân' and 'Mi Glywaf Dyner Lais', were followed by the songs he would sing at the eisteddfod. A few of his notes rode the occasional waft of wind to a field quite far below. There, a border collie repeatedly cocked her head towards the mountain, and occasionally, her master did too. The farmer was reminded by these sweet and carefree notes of the routine that ran his life, and he felt a twinge of envy. Alas, to Edgar's disappointment, his spirits fell anew into a familiar trough as he descended Mynydd Sylen. Yet, his experience at the top could not so easily be dismissed. The memory of the magic of the mountain, and the hope therein, encouraged civility in his dealings with Dai and Mavis, and south Wales felt nowhere near as foreign as before.

Each visit to the top of Mynydd Sylen had a cumulatively beneficial effect on Edgar. By the Thursday of the second week, Edgar was almost himself again… self-centred as before, of course, but no longer chronically depressed. The change, and Mynydd Sylen, it seemed had done the trick.

It was on that Thursday he first set eyes on Dorothy. Preliminaries for the eisteddfod were held that evening, and soon after Edgar arrived, she was on stage, preparing to sing her pieces. She was tall and fairly slim, pretty and pensive, and her shoulder-length blonde hair shimmered. She was striking, and Edgar was struck. Whatever it was Edgar felt, was heightened as soon as she sang. He wasn't keen on soprano voices, but Dorothy's was different. He was taken by the sweetness and depth of her every note.

"There's nothing thin about her voice," he thought.

He chose not to restrain whatever it was he felt. Conscience cautioned, but Edgar took no notice.

At the end of her performance, Edgar clapped enthusiastically. Few others did, so he was sure he caught her eye; he most certainly did when his turn came to sing. He sang to her, and her only.

They both qualified easily for the finals the following evening. She didn't seem surprised when Edgar approached her, but was still reserved.

"Hello. You were fantastic," he said in English.

"You too," she replied in Welsh, as a slightly teasing smile lit up her pretty face.

"Oh! You speak Welsh. That's even better."

Her face focused questioningly.

"Oh! What I meant was that however much I like you, I like you even more because you speak Welsh. That happens to be very important to me, that's all."

She bowed her head slightly and nodded. Edgar struggled to retrieve the situation.

"What's your name?"

"Dorothy... Dorothy Darkin."

Her head remained slightly bowed.

"Where do you live, Dorothy?"

"Cynheidre."

"Cynheidre? That's near Horeb, isn't it?"

Only then did her gaze meet his, as she nodded, expectantly he thought.

"So you must know Mynydd Sylen very well then?"

They were outside by now. The sky was darkening, but even in the half-light he thought he could tell he'd struck a chord.

"Well, I grew up with it, so I know it of course. I used to go up there several times a year when I was younger... not to the top, mind you. My mother and I went to pick berries."

Edgar was without inhibition. He was attracted to Dorothy, and the idea of sharing his mountain with her was irresistible.

"Oh! You don't know what you're missing, and right on your own doorstep, too. Why don't you come up there with me tomorrow? I'll meet you in Cynheidre and we can go from there, OK?"

Of course it wasn't OK. He was being presumptuous. Dorothy appeared to fumble for reasons to refuse, when she would have been totally justified in flatly turning him down.

"But I'm not going back to... "

She stopped, presumably realising that she was digging herself a deeper hole.

"What were you going to say, Dorothy?"

It seemed she felt she had no option but to finish her sentence.

"I'm not going home tonight. I'm staying with a friend in Llanelli while the eisteddfod is going on."

Edgar was relentless.

"Well, that's even better, isn't it? I can pick you up in town, and we…"

Dorothy stiffened like a cornered creature, and countered with vigour.

"Stop it, will you? Stop it… please! You're totally out of control. Who do you think you're dealing with? I don't know you from Adam."

Edgar was completely taken aback: he always expected to get his own way. Even now, his instincts egged him on, but he backed off, surprising himself and Dorothy, it seemed. Both stared at the ground for quite a while, and then Edgar, again uncharacteristically, mended fences.

"My name is Edgar Evans and I live in Tryweryn, near Bala. I'm sorry for upsetting you."

His reward was immediate. Dorothy smiled that same slightly teasing smile, which seemed to be saying that she thought he'd been forward, but that she liked him anyway.

"Are you going back to your friend's house now, Dorothy?"

She nodded tentatively.

"So, can I walk with you?"

This time she nodded more confidently.

Their walk was quite short, and mostly they were quiet. Dorothy seemed distinctly unrelaxed, alternately furrowing her brow, biting her lip, massaging her chin, and rubbing her nose, as if she had something on her mind. Edgar certainly did; back and forth he went on how best to broach again the subject of a walk to Mynydd Sylen. He thought he had it subtly phrased, but in the end, at the door of her friend's house, he simply blurted it out.

"So... so... Dorothy, have you thought anymore about the... "

"Yes... yes, I have, actually. What time should I expect you tomorrow, then?"

Edgar managed not to do a double take. He'd prepared for disappointment, and now was so surprised that it never occurred to him to wonder why she'd changed her mind. What's more, he almost forgot to answer her question.

They talked off and on all the way to Horeb. Initially, Edgar had flirted with her, but she'd firmly discouraged that. Remarkably, they both had avoided as yet any reference to personal matters, such as family background, marital status, and such. Still, Edgar must have sensed an intimacy developing, because as soon as they left Horeb, he reached to hold her hand.

"Please don't do that," was Dorothy's civil response. Edgar persisted, prompting her to jerk her hand away angrily.

"Why d'you upset me like this?"

As ever, rejection for Edgar was hard to take. If only he could have considered her feelings, but he was too wrapped up in his own; he reacted as usual by moping. Neither said a word for twenty minutes. Not surprisingly, it was she who made a move to break the ice.

"Edgar, I know you must have noticed my wedding ring. Shouldn't it affect the way you behave towards me?"

Edgar was quick to counter this, as if the subject was fresh in his mind.

"If you want me to treat you like a married woman, then you have to behave like one, which in my book doesn't involve accepting an invitation to go for a walk with me."

"See, I knew it! I was afraid that's what you'd think! I should have refused to come with you for that very reason."

Edgar was stuck behind his mask.

"All right, Edgar... listen to me. Let's start this conversation all over again. I admit that I wasn't totally straight with you just then. To be honest, I did realise what I may be getting into when I accepted your invitation, but because I'm so mixed up, I just have to take everything slowly."

By now, Edgar was responding; he seemed confused. His eyebrows were depressed and he shook his head slightly.

"When you tried to hold my hand earlier, I just didn't feel ready for it, that's all. You must try and understand that this isn't as easy for me."

At last, Edgar looked at Dorothy. His confused expression suggested regret. Then, shaking his head again, he began walking, with his shoulders hunched and his hands dug deep in his pockets. Dorothy ran after him and put her arm through his. Edgar stiffened visibly. It was true he seemed to be getting his way, but it bothered him that this lady's mind was firm, while his was confused. Eventually, Edgar began to relax, and arm in arm they arrived at the top of Mynydd Sylen. In his grand plan, Edgar had envisioned this moment as a beautiful one of sharing and coming together, but he wasn't in the mood anymore. In contrast, she seemed light-hearted until, "Edgar, you can see my home from here. Look! It's over there, right by the water station," at which point, a sadness seemed to stifle her. She spent the next few minutes pacing with her head bowed, again unable to keep her hands still. So distracted was Edgar by this that when she asked, "Will you sing with me... please?", he agreed.

First, 'Calon Lân', heavy with harmony, followed by 'Mi Glywaf Dyner Lais' unimaginably effective in unison, and finally their respective solos. What a treat the farmer had missed. The air was perfectly still, but somewhere, no doubt, his collie was cocking her head. By the time Dorothy led the way from the top of Mynydd Sylen, Edgar was feeling better.

On the descent, she told him stories of the competitors he

should expect at the eisteddfod that evening. She told him that she knew all the local tenors well, and in her opinion he would win in a canter. Suddenly, just before Horeb, her tone tightened, and she asked him a question, almost apologetically.

"I know you told me last night roughly where you're staying in town, but do you mind me asking why you chose that place?"

"It's my sister-in-law's home," matter of factly.

Dorothy paused, and swished her hair with a casual shake of the head.

"It must be really nice for you to spend all this time with your brother. What's his… "

Edgar took the offensive, and as he spoke, stared at her, daring her to castigate him.

"No, no! You've got it wrong, Dorothy. My sister-in-law isn't my brother's wife, but my wife's sister. Yes, Dorothy, I have a wife."

Dorothy betrayed no surprise as she held his eyes with hers. Then, she walked straight into his stare and took his arm, just as she'd done before.

"I just wanted to know, that's all," she whispered, "And how old are your children?"

"I don't have… well, there is one on the way," he replied sullenly.

Not even Edgar's touchy temperament could for long be immune to her obviously sincere reassurances. Eventually emboldened, he ventured to ask, "Dorothy, would you walk with me to the beach tonight… after the eisteddfod?"

She stopped walking and faced him.

"I can't, Edgar. I've promised my friend to be with her tonight."

He'd risked rejection, and had been rebuffed.

"You could walk me home though, just like last night…

"Oh! Thank you… very much!" thought Edgar churlishly.

"… I'm afraid I've promised to be with my friend during the day tomorrow as well… "

Edgar's disappointment showed.

"… I can't help it, Edgar. This was all arranged before we met… "

He should have been encouraged by her tone, but in Edgar's eyes, it was as ever all or nothing, as ever black or white.

"… But you know, we could go to the beach tomorrow night. We could go quite early actually, because I don't need…"

Her lovely voice faded into the confusing cocktail of self-recrimination and relief that was Edgar's mind.

"… To hang around…"

His arm pressured hers, for the very first time.

"… For the closing ceremony. Do you?"

They both won their competitions, so they would be pitted against each other and three more in the Blue Riband on Saturday night. On their way home, Dorothy was jaunty and jocular.

"See, I told you that you'd win, didn't I, Edgar?"

"What about tomorrow night though? Do you predict another famous victory… for me?"

She laughed and moved closer to his side.

"Dorothy? Would you reward me for winning tonight?"

At this point, much to his chagrin, guilt had the gall to appear. It was dismissed with such conviction that it would fail to visit him later at a time when it might have been of assistance.

"Will you reward me with a kiss?" he asked.

"All right then."

She said it matter-of-factly, as if she'd rewarded him in this way a thousand times before.

"We're almost at your street, Dorothy. I think I would prefer to get my reward before we arrive at your friend's doorstep, if that's all right?"

It wasn't what he'd hoped for. She'd held back distinctly, so naturally now, he craved to kiss her again.

The adjudicator was summing up.

"What I'm about to say may not sound generous, but actually, it does stem from admiration, and should be taken in a positive light. I told you earlier, ladies and gentlemen, that you missed a treat this evening. Those of you who were here last night knew exactly what I meant. You will have recognised that our tenor was off form tonight. That happens to all of us occasionally, of course, but from our selfish point of view, it was particularly unfortunate in this case, because as you know, Edgar Evans is not from here, and most of us are unlikely to hear him sing again. I hasten to add though, that even if he had been at his best today, he would have been given a run for his money by our soprano, Dorothy Darkin. Most of you know her, of course. I've heard her sing countless times, and I don't mind telling you that I detected a special quality in her singing this evening. Intangible as it was, may this quality persist, because if it does, we'll all be the beneficiaries. As I said earlier, the other three contestants are inexperienced in comparison, but their time will come. It takes top-class talent to win a solo competition in Llanelli, so the three should take heart from that. Nevertheless, this evening belongs to Dorothy, and on this showing it won't be the last. Please step over here, Dorothy. Ladies and gentlemen, I give you Dorothy Darkin."

Out of the evening light into the shadowy bushes, hand in hand, towards the beach they walked. The competition had been dissected. They'd agreed that Edgar had not been at his best, but neither had pursued an explanation; understandable in his case for he was loath to reveal he'd been distracted on account of their tryst, while presumably she'd been far too wise.

They reemerged from the shadows into a wide-open band of dunes, in places covered with rushes.

"It's still quite light, isn't it?" was Dorothy's only comment.

Their path eventually climbed a sandy ridge. Here they stopped, now arm in arm. Out of the blue, Edgar disengaged, raced back down the ridge and took off into the dunes. He scampered up the first one, and as he tumbled over the top, yelled at her to join him. In the dale beyond the dune, he settled into a depression in the sand, and listened. She was coming! He reassured himself that she wouldn't be holding back tonight. As he did, Dorothy tripped on the tip of a dune, and rolling uncontrollably towards Edgar, came to an abrupt halt more or less at his side. She didn't move, and her face reflected how scared and shaken she felt. Edgar offered his arms and after a moment's hesitation, she turned into them. Blinded by hubris, he misinterpreted her move, so rather than comfort her in her distress, he kissed her eagerly. She mumbled disapproval, but he took no notice. As his focus left her lips for the softness of her thighs, she pleaded in a whisper, "Edgar, please stop now. Please! This doesn't feel right."

Still he took no notice, neither of her plea nor of the anger now on her face. She managed to raise herself on one elbow, and despite an awkward angle, slapped him soundly on the side of his head. She stiffened and stared at him apprehensively, presumably unsure of how he'd respond. Retaliation was written on his face, but his reaction, to her obvious relief, was retreat. He stumbled a short distance, and stood with his head in his hand, while she, with a sigh, flopped back on the sand. The sky was darkening now.

Waves were breaking gently,
And Jupiter jazzed up the sky,
As Dorothy set about healing
Their wounds; and the world wondered why.
Yes, the world wondered!
Why?

"Edgar," she said softly, still on her back.

No reply.

"Edgar, I'm sorry, but you've just got to try and see things from my point of view."

Still no reply.

"It's too light out here, Edgar. I'm sorry but I felt so exposed... as if the world was watching. Is your head all right? Does it hurt much?"

At that, Edgar spoke in a surprisingly quiet tone.

"I don't know where I stand with you, Dorothy. Still, that's no excuse for the way I just behaved."

That's as contrite as Edgar could be, but it apparently sufficed for Dorothy, who was quickly on her feet. She straightened her skirt after shaking the sand from her hair. Quite deliberately, she took Edgar's arm.

... And the world wondered why.

Together they threaded the dunes towards the path. Not a word they spoke as they approached and then entered the bushes. His thoughts dwelt on the train journey back home to Bala tomorrow, and the sad significance it assumed following tonight's fiasco. He'd certainly made a hash of things, so not a word he spoke, and nor did she, which is why they heard the oncoming walkers while they were still some distance away. Dorothy dived for the bushes, taking Edgar with her into the pitch-blackness, where they stood silently, apart, awaiting the voices. They were two boys, obviously happy in each other's company, talking in English about those chores that lay in the week ahead and the thrilling time they seemed to have had the night before. As their voices faded towards the beach, Edgar whispered angrily, "It really irritates me to hear young people like that speaking English in a region that used to be completely Welsh. You probably don't understand how I can feel so strongly about something like that, do you, Dorothy?"

Dorothy took his arm again, squeezed it, put her head on his shoulder, and whispered warmly, "I'm just glad, Edgar, to hear you excited again... about anything. I was afraid for a while that your spirit had gone and left you."

Almost certainly unintentionally, she had skirted a contentious issue. Edgar, meanwhile, felt quite strange. Everything seemed to be happening around him as if he had no control over the situation. Ten minutes earlier, he had been in the driver's seat, focused on seducing her; he'd made such a mess of things, that he deserved to be out in the cold. Now though, it looked again as if he might be getting his own way; if so, it was all too good to be true, to the point of being eerie. It even crossed his mind that perhaps he should be suspicious. A visitation of guilt might have tipped the scales; without it, he couldn't change his fate. Dorothy squeezed his arm tighter still.

...And the world wondered why.
Yes, the world wondered!
Why?

Twenty-eight

DOROTHY HARDING WAS born on 22nd March 1901 in Cynheidre, a village five miles from Llanelli on the Carmarthen road that runs inland through Pontyates. Dorothy, the youngest of three children to Walter and Millie, was Welsh speaking, unlike her parents who were born in Devon and had moved to south-west Wales in search of work.

The semi-detached house in which Dorothy was born was ordinary: as ordinary as she was not. Dorothy was pretty and her long blond hair, in particular, attracted attention. She was bright too, but what soon struck everyone was the joy that Dorothy derived from life. Even as a child she took most things in her stride. The nitty-gritties that niggled normal lives were disallowed from diluting the pleasures of hers. What was also noticeable from an early age was her interest in babies: she seemed unusually attracted to them and wonderfully natural around them.

Right across the road from Dorothy's house ran the railway, which wound around to Horeb and roughly followed the Afon Lliedi to Felin-foel and Llanelli. Beyond the water tank and the railway rose Mynydd Sylen, which dominated the window of her bedroom. As a child she became friends with its gently arching summit, and even when the mountain was enveloped in mist, she could convince herself that it still reached out to her. When she spoke of this to her friends, most would either gawk or giggle. By this, she was puzzled, but never perturbed.

English was the language that she usually spoke at home, yet Dorothy thought in Welsh and spoke it everywhere else: at chapel, at school and at play. Even at home she would chat with her brothers in Welsh if her parents weren't around, but at the mere hint of their presence, a switch was made to English. So the two languages co-existed quite comfortably in her life.

Each school day, the children of Cynheidre would walk the mile and a half to Five Roads primary school. There were one or two in Dorothy's class who were cleverer than her, but none enjoyed learning as much as she. As the girl became a little lady, she grew to appreciate the magic of numbers and to open her mind to the wonder of words. At the age of fourteen, Dorothy's mind was a bud about to bloom. At the age of fourteen, in order to help her mother support the three breadwinners in the family, Dorothy left Five Roads primary school, and at the age of fourteen, she had known for years that she would.

At home she was drawn into the uncertainty which went hand in hand with the danger her family's menfolk faced at work; an uncertainty heightened now by the war in Europe. Her father and brothers were coalminers; so far, they were exempt from the fighting in Flanders, but their workplace was a war zone anyway, where one of their foes was coaldust, both around their frames… and within. Little could be done about the latter, but pity the dust that settled in view. Dorothy joined her mother as a member of a massive support system dedicated to the eradication of blankets of coaldust. She was a dustbuster now! Billions of buckets of water were boiled and millions of tubs were filled, broad backs were brushed, some soon to be crushed by calamitous cave-ins that killed. However hard she brushed her father's back, there was little she could do to alleviate his incipient breathlessness. Dorothy was touched by the helplessness of it all. Eventually though, her spirit managed to rise above the relentless reality of mining life. Her positive attitude did prevail… and the singing didn't hurt either.

Dorothy had sung for as long as she could remember: in Sunday School, like many other children, but in a few competitions as well. Everyone had always told her that she had a nice voice, a soprano by now, but she'd never taken the compliment to be anything more than just that. Dorothy's father belonged to a colliery choir. Even though he hadn't learnt Welsh, he sang it quite happily, and no one felt more Welsh than he. Not too long after Dorothy had left school, her father took her to a concert that his choir was putting on in Pont-henri. She felt pride at his presence on the platform, and the occasional stab of envy too. When Madam Madeira hit the stage though, Dorothy's envy gave way to aspiration. Madam was a former Portuguese opera star who had retired to Carmarthenshire, and was frequently featured as a soloist by male voice choirs. Her voice perhaps had lost its edge, but her presence on stage had not. That night, Walter Harding's daughter dreamt that she sang with Madam Madeira, and the following morning she determined to train her voice. Initially, she sought the advice of acquaintances who'd sung competitively. Then, when her own voice training paid off in victories at local competitions, she was approached by an expert who offered to coach her.

"And what's more," said Madam Madeira, "I'd like to do it for free."

Dorothy was on her way to regional recognition, casting credit on her family and community. Her father in particular was proud of her accomplishments.

"You mark my words, she's going to go a long way," was his standard and frequent prediction.

Sadly these days, standard as well was the ensuing gasp for air. Dorothy appreciated her father's persistent praise, but still, she wished he'd be more discreet about it. She'd always been his favourite, and had never really understood why. As far as she could tell, her brothers deserved the same acclaim as she, and ever since she'd realised that they bore resentment, she'd gone to great lengths to foster her relationships with them. Now, her father's ringing enthusiasm for her singing made that so much the harder. She wished she could confront him on the matter, but she refrained for fear of an upset. That was the last thing she wanted: with her father, in particular, she'd vowed to make the most of every moment... just in case.

During the early twenties, employment became increasingly scarce, especially for women. Dorothy's wish was to work with babies, and she'd investigated various training schemes, despite the educational and financial hurdles she knew that she'd encounter. The idea was reluctantly scotched when she was fortunate – that was the prevailing opinion, anyway –to land a job at Pontyates Post Office. In January 1920, the timing couldn't have been better from a family point of view, for the household income had shrunk. Both Dorothy's brothers had recently married and left to live with their in-laws. Still, their departure might have led to an improvement in the atmosphere at home had Walter Harding's health not slipped into noticeable decline. By now, his shortness of breath was such that the slightest infection on his chest floored him. In fact, he was home, struggling bravely with his breathing, on the morning of the first day that Dorothy left for work. Having to leave him in such a state saddened her. The thought that she was about to walk two miles without an effort, while he, as he was, could barely walk at all, saddened her even more.

At the Post Office, not only was she always on her feet, but forever on her toes: whether peddling a parsnip or selling a stamp, she was in truth a number cruncher. Most of her moves demanded concentration, so naturally by the end of each day she was tired, but never so tired as not to enjoy her two-mile trek back home. Mostly uphill, often in the rain and invariably after dark in those early days, Dorothy didn't care, for those moments were her own. It was on those walks that she was cheered by reflections on the occasional temporary improvement in her father's health. She pondered too on how to further improve her relationship with her mother. Was it impractical though, she wondered, to aim to be as close to one parent as the other?

Was it an impossibility, even? Regardless, in her instance, she knew it would now be tricky. Her earliest memories were of a mother who was often reserved, and a father who openly doted on her. The obvious delight that Dorothy had naturally taken in being with her father seemed to have distanced her mother, and lacking wisdom and sensitivity on his part, the process had just fed on itself. These days, Dorothy deeply regretted she'd not recognised and addressed this drift sooner. She still loved her father to bits, but she could see now that he was caught up in himself and complicated, and for his own obscure reasons had always been possessive of her; and so he'd had no incentive to encourage her relationship with her mother. This realisation helped explain her mother's general sensitivity, and as well, her bouts of indifference towards her husband, often at times when things seemed to be going well. Recently, her father had become noticeably touchier, exacerbating the tension at home. Dorothy was now faced with an unenviable balancing act: continuing to reach out to her mother without unduly hurting her father. On her walks home, there were more prosaic thoughts as well. For example, she used this time to carefully plan her weekends. Surprisingly, she wasn't expected to work on Saturdays, so these extended breaks were devoted to her voice... doing her drills alone, as well as with Madam Madeira.

All in all, 1920 was turning out to be a good year for Dorothy, despite domestic difficulties; and good became great in November, when Donald Darkin, out of beyond the yonder blue, asked her out on a date, exquisitely ruffling her tidy routine. Donald lived with his Welsh-speaking parents just outside the village, down the hill towards Pont-henri. He was an excellent sportsman, of medium build, good-looking and good-natured too, with a complexion less fair than you'd expect of one with such red hair. He'd lived in the village all his life, and like most of the men from there, was a miner. He was six years older than Dorothy. These six years had meant that for most of Dorothy's life, he might as well have been of a different generation. Mind you, this hadn't stopped her, as a young girl, from idolising him… at a distance; nor later from being infatuated with him, admittedly with little expectation. Without knowing it, he'd indelibly coloured her childhood canvas. Yet, as the age gap narrowed relatively, reality had set it. Singing and earning a living had monopolised Dorothy's days, and to no one's surprise, Donald had been taken, by a teacher from Tumble. Now though, after three years, that romance appeared to be in trouble.

"You're probably too busy, Dorothy," he ventured in Welsh, "what with your singing and all, but will you go out on a date with me?"

So polite and so modest, but it made little difference: Dorothy was floored all the same. Childhood fantasies flowed to the fore. Her mind was a maze and she was lost in it; she couldn't think, she couldn't talk.

"I realise that you don't know me very well, Dorothy, but …"

So polite and modest again, but so far off the mark. Dorothy knew him all right, even if it was from a distance. As he paused, he smiled shyly. This surprised her, for she'd never thought of him as shy. It settled her as well; his proposal assumed a more cohesive form. It was still too good to be true, though. Yet, there it was: a dream thought unattainable now lay within her grasp. All she had to do was say, "Yes, Donald, I will. I'd love to."

This she did eventually with weakness in her tummy and wonder in her eyes. Uncharacteristically for one innately optimistic, she allowed a cloud across nirvana: she really, really hoped that Dadi… her complicated Dadi… wouldn't be jealous, that's all.

Poor Walter Harding! He was stewing, stewing in bed in the front room on a Saturday afternoon when he should have been taking a nap. The stairs had become too much of a strain for him, so his sons had moved the bed down a fortnight earlier. They'd appeared matter of fact as they'd wrestled with the monster, insensitive to a transition that Walter had found distressing. He'd fought the change... oh yes, and who could blame him for resisting another nod to the progressive nature of his disease and another reminder that he was dying. In the end, he'd agreed to it on the understanding that it would be... temporary.

"You know full well, Millie," he'd reasoned with his wife, "that my mobility's affected by my state of mind. I'll be in better spirits soon, you'll see, and then I'll be back upstairs again."

This argument would not have been far-fetched had Walter at that moment not felt so low and so devoid of hope. As things stood, it was disingenuous. In any case, poor Walter Harding was stewing in bed in the front room, stewing because it was hard for him to accept the recent shift in Dorothy's relationship with her mother. For several months now, Dorothy had appeared to be going out of her way to reach out to Millie; wait a minute! Why shouldn't she reach out in this way? A surprisingly generous thought from Walter, one that was immediately and inevitably overwhelmed by behavioral patterns in place, patterns he found hard to counter. Walter was an insecure person; it was a problem he'd learnt to live with, but not without consequences. For instance, he'd been overly strict with his two sons; in part, subconsciously taking his shortcomings out on them. They'd understandably sought comfort from their mother, and became closer to her, further fuelling Walter's insecurity. Dorothy's birth had been a godsend; with her, Walter's sunny side was in evidence. He became her favourite, bolstering his confidence, with beneficial consequences for all. So, since Dorothy was a few years old, the family had assumed a better, if still imperfect, balance. Now, to Walter's chagrin, Dorothy was upsetting the apple cart at a time when he in ill health could least tolerate it. Walter sat up in bed and decided that today a nap was out of the question. He rose, and shuffled along a short corridor towards the kitchen. He stopped when he heard voices, and intrigued by their hushed tones, behaved out of character: he listened with his ear to the door. This simple act transformed him: before, he'd been flat and mired in introspection, but now, totally distracted and agog; on edge for fear of being caught behaving badly, and most anxious too regarding what may be overheard. Dorothy, who he assumed had come home early from her singing lesson, immediately justified his unease.

"But, Mami," in a whisper, "I'm afraid he'll take it very badly."

Walter recoiled slightly in reaction. What on earth could she be referring to?

"I don't see why he should," from Millie, "And anyway, aren't you the one who's usually optimistic?"

"But he's so touchy these days, Mami," continued Dorothy, "Every little thing seems to upset him."

"Of course, you of all people should know how he'll react: you're so close to him," followed by a silence which Walter found inexplicable, that is until Millie continued, "So close that I get jealous sometimes. I've felt left out of things, you know. Anyway, back to your father and… "

Dorothy interrupted with, "Oh, Mami fach, oh Mami."

There was nothing inexplicable about this interlude. Walter could picture Dorothy embracing her mother. The improvement that he'd noticed in their relationship was clearly gathering pace. Millie may have been excluded at times in the past, but it was he who felt like a foreigner now. At that moment of vulnerability, it also struck him how she seemed to be gaining in confidence at a time when he was losing his. Sad, wasn't it? He just couldn't stop himself from imagining his special relationship with Dorothy slipping away, slipping away just like his life, and taken together they were almost too much to bear. Yet, he steeled himself into composure.

"Perhaps I shouldn't go through with this, Mami. The last thing I want to do is upset Dadi when he's not well."

"Don't be silly, Dorothy. Just tell him, and do it soon!"

At that moment, Walter, while dying to hear of his daughter's dilemma, felt a need to represent himself. He returned to the front room and coughed persistently as he slowly remade his way to the kitchen.

"You ladies are quiet. What's going on, I wonder?"

Millie blurted out, "Dorothy has something to tell you, Walter."

Dorothy was aghast. Open-mouthed and openly angry, she spun towards her mother.

"You shouldn't have said that, Mami. I've got no choice but to tell Dadi now."

Millie smiled confidently as if to say it was about time too. Walter's face, washed with bemusement, ticked back and fore like a metronome during this exchange.

"Dadi," ventured Dorothy with eyes lowered, "Donald Darkin has asked me out on a date."

Walter had prepared himself for the worst, and remained braced for it. With a "Yes?" he encouraged Dorothy to continue.

"That's all, Dadi," more comfortable now, "He's asked me out on a date; that's all."

Give Walter his due: it took a lot not to reveal how relieved... and foolish... he felt. While Dorothy and Millie saw an ailing elder seemingly gathering his words of wisdom, in truth, Walter's troubled mind was rapidly assessing the implications of this development, as always in the context of his life-long insecurity.

"Don't tell me you turned him down," were the words that soon ensued; words which, judging from Dorothy's uninhibited expressions, were at first considered by her to be most mystifying, but then very soon, just as magical.

"I'm going out with him tonight, Dadi," was her joyful rejoinder.

"We'd like you to bring him in to meet us, wouldn't we Millie?"

Dorothy's enthusiastic embrace of her father implied that she most certainly would.

Remarkably, four weeks later, Walter's bed was on its way upstairs again, and now there was nothing matter of fact about his sons' demeanour. Apart from this time having gravity to contend with, they also resented their subjection to what to them was a mere whim. In fact, behind their father's back, they openly derided the project as nonsensical. As they toiled at their task, Walter would have been forgiven a session of smugness. After all, he'd proven his doubters wrong, and chief among them, to his mind, were his sons. Happiness though has no room for smugness and Walter Harding was as happy as he could be; a man named Darkin had done the trick. So what magic had this Donald wrought? What had these men in common? Of course, both had mined for coal, but Walter, retired by now, drew no pleasure from reminiscing on subterranean exploits. More telling was Donald's membership in Walter's choir and even moreso, his respect as a junior tenor for a very senior one. Walter much appreciated that, as he did Donald's keen interest in sports. He'd been a bit of an athlete himself in his day, and Donald seemed genuinely interested in his achievements, in a way that his sons had never been; in fact, they'd held no interest in sports at all. So in a sense, Donald was the lad that Walter felt he'd never had. Topping all was Donald's personality. Despite his obvious gifts, he remained modest and extremely sensitive to others; in particular, he truly empathised with Walter's physical predicament. So Walter couldn't have been more correct in his snap assessment on the day that Dorothy had so nervously announced her beau. Walter had in that instant inexplicably foreseen that he and Donald would hit it off in a big way, that Dorothy would revel in their company, and that he, as a result, might well be more accepting of Dorothy's overtures to her mother. At times now, he even thought of himself as almost generous, and that felt good; and as his spirits rose to a higher plane, so did his health... as now did his bed as well! Whether he deserved it was debatable, but poor Walter Harding had been given another chance.

"I'm so happy, Dadi."

Dorothy sat close to her father, perched on one of the two high steps that led down from their back door to an immaculate backyard, and beyond to a vegetable garden that Donald only yesterday had turned over. It was an early spring evening, five months on from the reinstatement of Walter's bed upstairs, and the sun was setting very red. Of course Dorothy was happy: how could she be otherwise? To be so beautifully in love was thrilling; to be at ease once again in her relationship with her father was comforting; to be warming to her mother was exciting; to be progressing with her singing was gratifying; and to be contented at a job that kept her on her toes was satisfying. How could she not be happy?

"Am I too happy, Dadi? You know how optimistic I usually am, but it's hard, even for me, not to wonder what could go wrong."

Her father brushed off her concerns with, "You're no happier than you deserve to be, Dorothy fach. Before you know it, you'll be married and having babies. You've always been keen on babies, haven't you?"

Dorothy reflected with discomfort on the timing of that remark. It was only recently that she'd dwelt on the issue of having children. All her life she'd doted on babies, and couldn't foresee anything, not even her singing career, interfering with her yearning to have her own. So she would be devastated should Donald be averse to starting a family. She had no reason to believe that he was, but still, the uncertainty was beginning to unsettle her. She'd bring it up with him soon. So far though, the moment hadn't seemed quite right. Considering the sensitivity of the subject, her response to her father was surprisingly forthright. She wasn't quite sure why, but perhaps subconsciously she'd decided it might help to clear the air.

"That's jumping the gun a bit, Dadi, isn't it? As far as I know, Donald might not even want to have children."

"Don't tell me that you haven't talked to Donald about it?"

She was taken aback by her father's aggressive tone, but was spared the effort of crafting an appropriate reply by the arrival of her beau; Donald appeared around the pine end of the house, open-faced and warm as usual. It was lovely to see him so unexpectedly.

"I've come to check on the garden, if that's all right," he said in English... always in English with Walter around... and then grinning broadly, "But I couldn't help overhearing my name. Talking about me behind my back, are you?"

Again Dorothy was spared, but this time less agreeably, for her father blurted out, "Talking about babies we were, and funnily enough, your name came up."

"Dadi! That's none of your business. That kind of thing is between Donald and me."

Dorothy was visibly upset, but what was one to make of Donald's conflicting signals? His deliberate nodding reflected understanding while his expression conveyed confusion. Now on a roll, Walter latched on to the latter and ignored his daughter's distress. She felt so embarrassed that she heard her father's words with her face in her hands.

"You probably don't know this, Donald, but Dorothy's been very keen on babies all her life. Fair play, she's been too polite to bring this up with you, but it is important for her to know, if you do get married, that you'd agree to have a family."

Donald's face was an open book; a beam replaced bemusement.

"Sounds good to me," he said chirpily, as he laid his hand on Dorothy's shoulder. Hugely relieved at the news but still uncomfortable with what had happened, she now was shy as well as she embraced her boyfriend in front of her father. She'd never done that before.

Twenty-nine

A S SHE WALKED up the aisle with her father, Dorothy glowed. She squeezed his arm and said, "I'm so happy, Dadi," and it showed.

The party afterwards was thrown at their home in Cynheidre. All foods and juices had been prepared in advance; that aspect of the arrangements had been well under control; not so the touchy business of who should... or more to the point, who shouldn't be invited. In the end, rather than risk acrimony in a very close community, all the villagers had been asked. Of those not truly welcome, many, seemingly reflecting the same communal understanding, had respectfully declined. Actually, Walter and Millie had known who they would be; their parsimony precluded the giving of presents. Others among the unwelcome felt no allegiance to that particular quid pro quo, and turned up giftless. Thus the party was peppered with loose cannons. During the brief formalities, one of them impressed the gathering by describing the marriage as one made in heaven; and of course, there was something to that. Donald and Dorothy were especially good-looking and their families well respected; both sets of parents subscribed to similar value systems, and obviously got along very well.

"Made in 'eaven," the unwelcome repeated.

Another brought the house down with, "What do you know about bloody 'eaven?" with a comical emphasis on "you".

Others tossed around the usual clichés. If they had their way, the happy couple's worries would definitely be confined to little ones!

One of the loose cannons made no bones about the fact that

while the couple were wed, he'd been in bed, and then at the pub in Five Roads. Thus fortified, he threatened to throw a spanner in the works with:

"Storks are notoriously fickle... "

"You've studied them all your life, haven't you Dai?" was the heckle that resonated above the others.

Unfazed and confident, the cannon gave it another go, this time with his grubby hand in the air. God knows why, but it worked.

"Storks are notoriously fickle,

Landing many a maid in a pickle,

Yet some ovens they'll shun,

Not a whiff of a bun

Despite fun at the old slap and tickle."

He beamed in response to a reasonably broad ovation. Many glanced nervously at the bride, but she managed not to betray the grey that briefly grazed her glorious state of mind. There was sporadic booing too, and a booming, "Get out of 'ere, mun."

Fat chance of that, for the limerick lad hadn't had his second helping of cake, and the pub wasn't open yet. Walter and Millie sidled over to Dorothy's side.

"Did he upset you, Dorothy?"

"No, no, Mami, not at all."

Her reply was close to the truth. The cannon's remarks were utterly tactless, but the grey only briefly grazed. Heck! She was Dorothy Darkin now: untouchable and unbelievably happy.

"Perhaps we should have done the invitations diff... "

Dorothy interrupted to reassure her mother. That night, in Dorothy's bed, Mr and Mrs Donald Darkin slept together for the very first time, and storks couldn't be further from their minds.

Dorothy descended the stairs very deliberately. At every other step she sniffed exaggeratedly and sobbed. At the foot of the flight, in the passageway, her sobbing intensified, and by the time she reached the sitting room, it was totally out of control. Her parents looked up, alarmed. Without taking his eyes off Dorothy, Walter slowly laid down his newspaper, just in time to be handed a letter by her. She, midst her sobbing, nodded, encouraging her father to read it. Eighteen months had passed since the wedding. Following an extended remission, Walter's disease had begun to progress again, but his more generous outlook on life, wrought by Donald's arrival, had been maintained. Walter glanced at the letter which he noticed was written in English, and then again at Dorothy, who motioned him more vigorously to read.

"Dear Dorothy,

For reasons you know only too well, I've decided that I must leave you for a while. I hate myself for doing this, because I think the world of you. We're so good for each other, and I love you very much. So the last thing I want to do is hurt you, and yet, that's exactly what I'm doing. Please forgive me. I just don't see any other way out of the mess I'm in. I'm sure you'll be under pressure to explain what happened. Please consider my feelings at those times. I know I can trust you to do that. Tell your parents and mine that I'm sorry to shock them too, but I'm sure they'll understand that I couldn't say a word to anybody. I'm going to the Birmingham area. I don't want to be more definite than that because I really need to make a clean break for now. I'm sure I'll get work, and when I do, I'll be sending money to you and my parents. I don't know when yet, but I do intend to come home and see you. I know it looks as if I'm behaving childishly, and you may stop loving me because of it, but I'll forever love you. Donald."

Walter had read this very slowly, without emotion or inflection. Regardless, Millie joined Dorothy in sobbing.

Walter's assessment of the letter, as ever against the background of his insecurity, was suprisingly positive. He did register that his lifeline was adrift: the letter had said that his talisman had left. Yet he couldn't really take it seriously. No, it couldn't possibly be! Millie and he had been aware of minor newly-wed ups and downs, but nothing in the marriage had remotely suggested this. It didn't make sense, and he wouldn't accept it without elaboration from Dorothy. So, his generous side prevailed as he advised his daughter and distracted his wife.

"Sit down, Dorothy fach. Would you make us a cup of tea, Millie?"

He then sat silently next to Dorothy on the settee, with his arm around her shoulders. She calmed, and eventually the time was right to talk.

"This is a shock, isn't it, Dorothy, but what makes it worse is that we didn't have an inkling. How can it be true?"

Dorothy sighed deeply, but responded firmly with head bowed slightly and eyes closed, "Well, that's the first thing we have to accept: it most certainly is true."

That she was so emphatic unsettled Walter. Demons from his troubled past threatened to resurface. It astounded him how little time they'd wasted. He forced himself to focus on the issue at hand while Millie returned with the tea.

"What happened, Dorothy?" was all he asked. So absorbing would her revelations be that Walter would be free of his fears for a while.

"I'll tell you the whole truth," declared Dorothy, weighing on the "you", "Because it's really important to me that you don't misjudge either Donald or me, but you've got to promise that you'll keep most of this to yourself. D'you promise?"

Walter and Millie nodded almost sheepishly, as if cowed by Dorothy's resurgent self-assurance.

"Now, first of all, I love Donald as much as he loves me. It's funny, isn't it? We still love each other… and I know we always will."

She paused to compose herself, but with her head held high now.

"Everything was brilliant for six months. I know we didn't flaunt our feelings in front of you, out of respect, I suppose, but believe me, we were very, very happy. Then babies gradually became an issue. Yes, this is all to do with babies. Remember that stupid poem at the wedding? The one about the storks? Well, it's almost as if that's put a jinx on us. Put yourself in Donald's shoes. He knew how much I wanted a baby, but nothing was happening, and not through lack of trying."

She blushed a shade at that and took another deliberate and deep breath.

"I remember the moment when he told me that he was beginning to feel pressure. And as you know, you were always joking around the house about having babies. As it happened, it didn't help Donald. As time went by, Donald couldn't help but put more and more pressure on himself. In the end, he got so nervous that he couldn't make love to me, and then, he wouldn't even try. That's how bad it got, and even though we talked and talked, there was nothing I could say to reassure him. It didn't help that he's so sensitive to other people's feelings. Anyway, he began to lose some sleep over it, and even lost confidence in himself too; and to make matters worse, this nervousness began to affect other aspects of his life. The worst thing was that he became afraid of being down the mine. Just imagine that: each working day was a nightmare. Claustrophobia, I think they call it. So that's how it all became such a mess, as he called it."

Walter was spellbound, and Millie seemed to be too.

"Remember your promise to me earlier? Don't you agree that we should keep the stuff about the baby to ourselves?"

Again her parents nodded, but more animatedly this time.

"We'd be more comfortable telling people the truth, but we'll omit some of it, that's all. Let's tell people about his fear of being underground. In this mining community, where toughness is taken for granted, they'll understand why Donald would feel so ashamed of his weakness. They'll accept that it would have been hard for him to face his friends at the rugby club, for example."

"But why didn't we have an inkling?" was Millie's plaintive question.

"Don't feel badly, Mami," as Dorothy crossed the room to console her mother, "He kept it... what I should say is that we kept it to ourselves very well. You see, he told me everything, and that helped him handle it all. As for me, it's the same old problem... my eternal optimism. Until recently, I was sure that everything would be fine in the end, so it wasn't hard for me to put a good face on things. And of course, we never quarreled, so it's not surprising that we appeared reasonably normal around you."

Poor Walter Harding once again! Completely against his own will, he was suddenly bothered by how warm she was with her mother. On cue, old fears flowed anew, and he at a loss how to stem 'em. Following several years of contentment, imagine his disappointment. To make matters worse, Dorothy thanked him so sincerely for his understanding at this trying time. He cringed at that, as he did when comparing his cowardice to her courage.

"But in the letter he called this place his home, didn't he," from Millie, "And he says that he will come home to see you, so there is hope."

"I don't know what to expect, Mami. I feel silly that I really, truly didn't see this coming. Anyway, I hope you're right, Mami, because I know that I'll never love anyone else."

This she said with sadness, but soon she was all business again.

"Would you do me a favour, Mami? I know this is asking a lot, but would you go and tell Maggie and Trevor what's happened? As his parents, I think they should be among the first to know. And you'll be careful what you say, won't you?"

Walter's spirits were sinking. He pictured his demons alert and intense, ever at the ready to storm his fragile defense. They'd struck with such little delay that, for now at least, he was on the defensive. All he could hear was Mami this and Mami that; and as Mami left to tell a tale, Walter and Dorothy faced the future, he without his talisman, and she without her man.

Donald kept his promise; he did return for a weekend two months later. Dorothy had received a letter giving notice of his visit, so the family was prepared. Dorothy seemed excited, as did her mother. Walter however, was ambivalent. Indeed, he thought it would be nice to see Donald again, but a twenty-four hour visit would offer no solace at all, and certainly no reversal of the funk that had befallen him immediately following Donald's departure. Since that time, he'd too readily slipped into his default mode: too often ungenerous with his wife, and worse, erratic with his daughter. Against this negative backdrop, his health had rapidly deteriorated: poor Walter Harding! Yet, after lunch on the first day of the visit, he did take pleasure from touring the vegetable patch with Donald and Dorothy; he who'd turned and laid it before his departure, and she, who'd hoed and tended it since. After visiting his parents, Donald took a long walk with Dorothy... towards Mynydd Sylen, they said. They appeared so happy on their return, and Donald made a point of saying how good it felt to be home. Later, they talked about his new job and the sporting activities on offer in Birmingham; in fact, they talked about every topic but one. Walter assumed that the couple slept together, but judging from their body language at breakfast, he couldn't but conclude that nothing had changed. Dorothy was tearful at their parting, and Walter really felt for her, but soon succumbed to a bout of introspection. In contrast, Dorothy appeared to recover, and be content to revert to her routine. Walter viewed her natural optimism with wonder... and a touch of resentment. He could just imagine her saying to herself that the next visit was bound to be better, but it wasn't.

A week after Donald's second visit, on a sunny Saturday evening in September, Walter leant on the garden gate. Several yards away in the garden, Dorothy sat with her back to him on a bench, facing the setting sun, seemingly serene despite everything. Walter envied her courage and once again lamented his cowardice. This comparison had often been the trigger that had tripped him into despondency, and it did so now. He supposed he deserved to be tormented in this way, but wasn't it grief enough for one day that his bed had been moved downstairs again? At least he'd had the grit to insist that his sons be left out of the loop. This time, neighbours had done the heavy lifting. Anyway, it was a sad and broken man that unlatched the gate and shuffled laboriously down the garden path. Breathless, he lowered himself onto the bench next to his daughter. She didn't turn to greet him, piling hurt upon hurt, till he saw the reason why: tears were streaming down her pretty face. Before he could react, she slid towards him, took his thin arm very gently, and with her head on his bony shoulder, carried on crying. Even when looking back, he had no explanation for what happened next. A massive wave of compassion overcame him, and then, many more; each purged his psyche, purged him of all that was not good. A complete release ensued, and a wonderfully refreshing affection for his daughter suffused him. She was his to protect and to nourish... it was as simple as that. Eventually, he relaxed, and found himself instinctively awaiting introspection and despair; he waited and waited and waited... in vain. Perplexed but pleased, his mind returned to his daughter's distress and what could be done to heal her. But first, touching her with his other arm, he pleaded, one might say, pathetically,

"Dorothy, I'm begging you to forgive me. I've been hopeless. I'm begging for forgiveness."

"Oh Dadi," from Dorothy, calmer by now, "You don't need to do that. You've had a lot on your plate."

"Well, that is true, up to a point," in a firmer tone, "When you're dying, it is easy to feel hard done by; it is easy to feel resentment. But still, I have slipped up in a big way, because you see, also when you're dying… "

Walter Harding choked up, and when Dorothy squeezed his arm and said, "Oh Dadi bach, don't you cry now… please," he burst into tears. His daughter then held his thin, blue-veined hands, and as she stroked them, his tears were joined by hers.

The gate's latch clicked, and Walter without turning sobbed, "Is that you, Millie?"

"I'll be… I'll come back in just a minute," she stammered.

"No, no, don't go, Millie," spluttered Walter, "Please come and sit down. I'd like you to hear this too."

He took what was for him a deep breath and composed himself, as Millie sat next to her daughter.

"As I was about to say to Dorothy, when you're dying, there's an obvious opportunity to clear the decks and be perfectly honest about everything. You understand what I'm saying, don't you?"

Both ladies nodded sympathetically.

"Well, I don't need to tell you that I haven't done much of that. Worst of all, I've been very unfair to you, Millie. You've been so good to me and strong too, and I just haven't given you your due."

It looked as if Walter was about to weep again.

"Oh, come on, Walter bach, you're too hard on yourself. Things aren't quite as simple as they… "

"No, Millie! Because of my, shall we say, weaknesses, we've

never really pulled together, have we? And I haven't really supported you, Dorothy; not really, truly, have I? Perhaps I can make up for it, from now... till I die."

Dorothy moved to stroke his blue-veined hands and, in the prevailing spirit of openness, whispered, "I'm going to miss you so much, Dadi."

The four hands were joined by another, well-worn pair.

"... And the same goes for me," they seemed to say.

The thin blue-veined hand which stroked them in response said so many things that he himself had failed to say over thirty years. While he silently thanked his wife for their life together, Walter heaped praise on his daughter for her courage, and then gently enquired of her weeping earlier.

Dorothy exhaled exaggeratedly.

"Yes, well that wasn't being very brave, was it? Talk about eternal optimism! It's not on show at the moment, I can tell you. Today somehow, it really hit me that even though Donald and I love each other so much, it's not going to work. It doesn't make sense, but there it is; and I'm not going to have my baby. If I can't have Donald, I don't want anyone else. So, if he can't sort himself out, I'm stuffed, aren't I?"

Two pairs of distinctly different hands stiffened a touch at such a strong word coming from Dorothy. Then they relaxed as Walter pondered this problem. When he suddenly said, "It'll work out all right, Dorothy. You wait and see," he seemed pleased by the pair of ladylike double takes.

"Come off it, Dadi. That's my line. Fathers aren't supposed to say things like that."

"No, I... I really mean it. I just have this very strong feeling that you won't be disappointed. Somehow, I just know that you'll have a baby," and then ruffled feathers rather with, "Whether it's Donald's or not!"

Dorothy stiffened, but then immediately shook her head with a smile that said, "Dadi, you know better than that."

"And another thing," said Walter, "You're going to love her... very much."

"Hey, you said her? You're even narrowing it down to a girl? You must really mean it."

Nothing more was said. Still holding hands, the three smiled in wonder. The decks had been cleared, and their guards were down; no resentment, no fear, only love allowed here.

For three months, Walter Harding lived each day this way. Each morning brimmed with hope, and he was never to be disappointed. Each day was imbued with joy, and each thought was framed in unconditional love. Naturally, he wondered where he'd been all his life. For the first time he truly understood the universal appeal of religion. How could one knock a concept that gave millions a framework in which to feel the way he felt today? He wasn't religious, mind you, and yet he felt he'd been converted to something and was certainly born again. He enthusiastically shared his experience with those who visited him. They too, he said, could feel the way he felt. A few were moved, but most were just amused. Never mind! During those three short months, he lived a lifetime, beautifully brushing shoulders with his wife and daughter... beautifully brushing shoulders till he died.

Walter died in December. Donald returned home for the funeral, and as before, could only stay for one night. He and Dorothy greeted each other with overt affection and much emotion. Their love for each other was as obvious as their grief; clearly, the circumstances so dwarfed their personal difficulties that they were essentially relieved of them. During a difficult day, Donald was a solid support for Dorothy and an effective distraction too. By bedtime, both were exhausted. Donald was first upstairs, thoughtfully allowing Dorothy and her mother a moment alone. Later, Dorothy found him in the chair in deep sleep, and she chose not to disturb him. At breakfast, the three appeared relaxed.

"It's so nice for me to have the two of you here together," said Millie.

Shy smiles in response, but no development of that theme, and all morning, Dorothy skirted their burning issue, preferring on this occasion to settle for a superficial harmony. Donald played his part as well, fair play, making Dorothy feel special, despite the shadow that surely lurked in the alcove of his mind. At parting, Dorothy felt pleased that on this particular visit they'd papered over the cracks. Yet, the reality was never far from her mind, and she walked home from the bus stop with heaviness in her heart.

The next seven months were trying for Dorothy. Grief subsided, but her fears and frustration mounted. On Donald's next visit, three months later, he was not given the option of sleeping in the chair. She hated to hurt him, but for how much longer could they avoid taking the bull by the horns. Later, in bed, lying side by side, Donald lamented.

"Oh! I just don't know what to tell you, Dorothy. I've said this before, I know, but it's nothing personal. You know that, don't you?"

Dorothy stroked and squeezed his hand. Despite her frustration, she adored him, but why did it have to come to this?

"I love being with you," he continued, "but these disappointments set me back. I know they hurt you too, but they absolutely shatter my self-esteem. What I'm getting at is that overall it would be easier for me if I came to see you less often."

After months of searching, yet seeing no solution, Dorothy's optimism was severely challenged. Still, she groped for an answer.

"Donald, let's forget about making love, all right," she offered, "Come home just to be with me. We'll just enjoy being with each other."

It rang hollow, yet apparently it was this above all which induced Donald to come home for a long weekend in July. For two days, an artificial calm prevailed till a carnal call derailed it. Disappointment again, and deeper this time for Dorothy; she, for the first time, even felt despair. Totally discouraged, she took another unrealistic tack.

"Look Donald! Let's forget about the baby. I don't want a baby any more. Just move back home, and let's forget about the baby."

It seemed Donald wouldn't fall for another lifeline that was limp.

"Oh come on, Dorothy; it's easier for you to say that than it is for me to believe it."

She got the impression that he was less defensive than on previous occasions.

"You can't change your feelings about something like that," he continued, "Do you remember your father making sure I knew how much you wanted a baby? D'you remember that? At the time, I thought nothing of it. Just as well, I suppose."

Despite everything, Dorothy was infused with warmth for this man. She loved him, and the thought made her eerily happy. Then he shocked her with an outrageous suggestion.

"Listen Dorothy, why don't you have a baby with somebody else. I urge you, Dorothy… I beg you!"

This was no self-pitying, whining wimp. Donald was animated.

"I know that you love me and won't love anyone else; so I could deal with it. It would be strange for a while; stranger for you than me probably, but it would be worth it, wouldn't it? Then I wouldn't have to worry as I do. I could come home, Dorothy, and spend my life with you. I mean it! Honestly!"

"Don't be so soft, Donald," and that's how they appeared to leave it. She embraced her man, feeling no tension for the first time for a while. It was disconcerting. Don't be so soft, she'd said, but she knew he'd meant it. He was so sensitive to her feelings and wanted to be with her so much. Oh yes, he'd meant it, all right. Still, "Don't be so soft, Donald," she repeated to herself.

'Twas Tuesday, and the following morning, Donald left. Later that evening, Dorothy and Millie sat outside the back door, on the topmost step.

"D'you miss Dadi, Mami?"

"I still do, yes; much more than I would have if he hadn't had his epiphany, as he called it."

"D'you remember the day he saw the light, Mami? Remember him saying that he was certain I'd have a baby?"

Millie's face was suddenly a picture of joy.

"Don't tell me that you and Donald are... "

"No, no, Mami... I wish! No, what I was going to ask you was whether you remember Dadi saying that he was certain I'd have a baby, whether it was Donald's or not? Remember that?"

"Yes, I remember, but don't you think he was just being a bit sensational? Milking the moment, so to speak?"

"No, Mami, I don't. He seemed so sure of himself; as if he knew something, as if he could read the future."

"Don't be so soft, Dorothy!"

Don't be so soft! An emphatic phrase, but doth she protest too much?

On that Wednesday, Dorothy went to bed especially early. She wanted to be as fresh as possible for the preliminaries of the eisteddfod, which would be held at Llanelli the following evening.

Thirty

"GOSH! WHAT ON earth is Donald doing here? So he didn't go back to Birmingham yesterday? That probably means there's something wrong. Oh, dear!"

This was Dorothy's troubled train of thought as she sat in the shadows at the back of the stage, awaiting her turn to sing. At the prelims, there weren't many spectators to distract her, so she couldn't have helped but notice Donald slip inside the hall, far at the back of the building. As lovely as it was to see him, his appearance couldn't have been more untimely. Dorothy now was forced to repel once again a disturbing notion that had teased her off and on over the last twenty-four hours. She fleetingly pictured Donald earnestly urging her to have a baby with another; and with her equally earnest father assuring her of a baby girl, whether she be Donald's or not. The usual revulsion, rejection and admonition followed.

"Don't be so soft, Dorothy."

Each time, this sequence gave her the creeps, which lingered.

"I really wish Donald hadn't brought that up. Look at the mess I'm in now. How can I compete like this? Come on, Dorothy, you've got to try and calm down. But wait a minute! That's not Donald... he just looks like him. Actually, now that he's closer, he doesn't really look like him at all. It's his build that fooled me, wasn't it, and his dark complexion... as well as his red hair, of course. Oh! I suppose that's a relief. Settle down now then. That's better. Now go through your breathing exercises... slowly... and focus... on the opening. There, that's much better."

Surprisingly, in view of her shock, she focused effectively and performed to near perfection. It wasn't until the last several bars of her second song that her concentration wavered, and thoughts were allowed to intrude.

"Crikey! There's that man again. I'd forgotten about him. I don't know why, because his red hair stands out a mile. Gosh, he's smiling as if he knows me. What's the matter with him? And look now, he's getting ready to clap!"

Eventually, she joined the audience in the hall, which by now was filling up, and quite enjoyed regular glances of recognition.

"There's that man with the red hair. So he's a tenor, is he? Hmmm! He doesn't have a bad voice, I must admit. I haven't seen him before, I'm sure. Oh, no! He's looking at me again. Why can't he just get on with his song and leave me alone?"

Instinctively, Dorothy's thoughts turned to Donald, and much to her distress, a flash of his shocking suggestion teased her again. Later on she was approached by the red-headed man. With him she was reticent; uncomfortable with his presumptuousness and in any case, agitated over the recurring and disturbing flashes in her mind.

"He's full of himself, isn't he? He's so cocky."

It was while the man was pressing her to accompany him to Mynydd Sylen that Dorothy thought the unthinkable. Up till then, Donald's proposal in conjunction with her father's assurances had been vague intrusions, disallowed from alighting on her mind. This time though, they were not repulsed; they sat there, settling into a thought which whispered, "Another can father your baby, Dorothy; another can father your baby."

The thought made Dorothy extremely nervous but now it was not dismissed; it gave her the creeps, but they were not repressed. She was startled by this change and she whined to herself.

"I know, I know! Donald begged me to consider it, and in

so many words, my father condoned it, but... this is ridiculous! I can't do something like that."

She glared at the man who persisted in trying to persuade her to walk with him to the top of Mynydd Sylen. She shocked herself by taking the next slippery mental step, "I don't even like him," and to prove it, she spat, "Stop it, will you. Stop it... please! You're totally out of control. I don't know you from Adam."

He apologised; he told her his name was Edgar Evans and that he lived in Tryweryn near Bala. She drifted into agreeing to let him walk her to the home of a family friend where she was staying. The walk was quite short and mostly they were quiet; not surprisingly in her case for she remained very nervous. But what was she nervous about? A mere thought? Yes, and justifiably so, for she found that she couldn't quite distance herself from its appeal, especially when it came to deciding whether to accept this man Edgar Evans's invitation to go up Mynydd Sylen. She'd already refused him, more or less, but he was bound to ask her again.

"Of course I shouldn't go with him. It wouldn't be right. Oh! This is all so silly."

So of course, her instinct was to reject his invitation, and for a moment she felt less nervous. The whole thing was a joke! Yet, a mere thought, and an outrageous one at that, in opposition proved tenacious.

"Another can father your baby, Dorothy, another can father your baby."

Dorothy was all at sea, understandably tossed into turmoil by an outlandish idea she couldn't completely dismiss, and one that was evolving too rapidly for comfort. As torn as she was, she might be forgiven for keeping her options open.

"So... so... Dorothy, have you thought any more about the... "

"Yes... yes, I have actually," she forced herself to reply, "What time should I expect you tomorrow then?"

This too gave her the creeps, which lingered.

Half an hour later, having feigned a headache, Dorothy was free of her family friend, a chatterbox. She lay on her bed, still very nervous, yet with her turmoil in retreat. She'd needed some time to herself, that's all. At her own pace, she retravelled the tracks she'd trod so far. She was struck more than ever by the intensity of Donald's plea and the certainty of her father's remarks.

"Another can father your baby," was the message, and eerily, it seemed to be ordained by the timeliness of the opportunity that had arisen. It was an opportunity, wasn't it? A man who lived far away and who looked a bit like Donald, to say the least?

"No, no, no," was her immediate reaction as usual, "This is ridiculous. I couldn't possibly do it, not with him... not with anyone."

Yet, this time, she reasoned with herself.

"Perhaps not, but isn't it important enough for you to find out whether you can? Remember, you'd be doing this for Donald, the man you love. This would be no selfish gesture but a bold move to save your marriage. In a way, you'd be sacrificing yourself for your future together. Remember too that he predicted it would be stranger for you than for him; so stop worrying about Donald. He's told you with conviction that he'd accept the baby. So you can't use him as an excuse. It comes down really to whether you have the guts to do what's best for both of you."

"But it's sinful! It's wrong."

Resistance, it is true, but perfunctory. She taunted herself.

"Come on, Dorothy! Can't you do better than that? How

can it be sinful when your father condoned it? And even if it is, he forgave you in advance. Well, didn't he?"

Overwhelmingly logical, but the idea still gave her the creeps.

It took twenty minutes of this for Dorothy to arrive at the crux of the matter.

"Well, the only way I could go through with this is to think of myself as a character in a play. I've got to be able to shut myself off completely from my real life. Can I do that? Well, that's what I do each time I perform, isn't it? Yes, but this might last for a couple of days. Can I do it for that long? And am I sure that I could then successfully switch back to reality?"

Most would have shied away, but Dorothy's optimism kept the idea in play. As an optimist, she was less likely to give proper weight to risk in a decision-making process. After all, she had confidence that all would always be well in the end. So doubts in Dorothy's mind were checked, and she found the guts to at least take the next step in finding out if she could make herself have a child with Edgar Evans. She still couldn't believe that she might go through with it. Ironically, this allowed her the composure to lay some ground rules on the assumption that she would. In fact, before she fell asleep, she promised herself three things: her child would not be conceived under a cloud she called the creeps; she certainly would not proceed if they continued to haunt her; nor would if she felt he didn't respect her. Finally, as part of her character in this play, she promised herself not to think of Donald till the final curtain came down. She knew she would call on her father a lot, each time she felt a doubt, but Donald would be divorced for now. Yet, that night she dreamt of him, and it felt good.

On her Sylen walk, there were moments when Dorothy wished for nothing more than to be let off the hook; had she thought this whole thing through, she wondered. It was at those times that the spectre of her father rose to the rescue. Then, at the top of the hill, the sight of her home by the water tank below unsettled her, and she almost thought of Donald. Overall though, she succeeded in relegating her emotions to the need of playing her part in a drama. Ironically in this regard, she found it helped that Edgar Evans was a prickly character.

That afternoon, alone at her lodgings, she accepted that her decision could be deferred no longer. As a result, it was with nervousness that she reviewed what she'd learnt on the walk.

"So I know that he's married, and he can have children. Of course, I can't tell if his child's going to be healthy. As for his personality, he's certainly self-centred, but I think he likes me, and from the way he took a lot of cheek from me today, I'm sure he respects me too; that's the most important thing of all. I may be groping in the dark, but that's one thing I'm firm on: Edgar Evans must respect me."

This she said to herself with the utmost seriousness. How comical that she saw no humour in piously binding herself to such an admirable litmus test as she contemplated an equally outrageous and morally ambiguous venture.

"No respect, no baby!"

The litmus test became her mantra.

"Hold on though! He may like you and respect you, but he still may not be interested."

"Oh, I think I can tell. More to the point is whether I like him. I suppose I have to admit that I wish I liked him more, but there, if I did, I shouldn't... and certainly wouldn't... go any further. There's no room for emotion in this. No! I think we like each other just enough."

So would she take the next, decisive step? The light wavered at amber; would it turn to green? Dorothy reminded herself that she hadn't really touched Edgar Evans yet; in fact, she'd been careful not to. She'd taken his arm at times, and had looked him in the eye, but she hadn't touched. It was then she suddenly became aware of the absence of the creeps; no revulsion at the thought of touching the tenor? Her reaction was excitement which prevailed over apprehension. At that moment, she knew: she just knew she would have a baby. There would be no turning back now; there would be no further pretending that the notion was preposterous. At that moment she accepted her role in the play. She was not at all ruthless by nature, but she saw this as a production: this was business and she would be as disciplined and as clinical as need be.

Soon, at the eisteddfod, her excitement tumbled all over the stage and bubbled throughout the hall. The other sopranos didn't stand a chance.

Edgar, who had also won, walked her home again.

"Gosh, he is in a good mood. That's a relief! I don't want anything to go wrong, now that I've made up my mind at last. Crumbs! He wants to kiss me."

She agreed, but kissed half-heartedly. In playing her part in this drama, she'd found a mental sweet spot, which allowed her to pursue the conception of her baby with comfort yet without emotion. If she was to have her baby, that sweet spot would have to be nurtured, protected, maintained.

Yet, so unconventional and morally dubious was the role that she'd assumed, that not even her determination and excitement could completely insulate her. She was a good person; it was not in her nature to be dismissive of others. During these first moments she'd had to herself since she'd known she would have a baby, it occurred to her that so far her sole focus had been on her own issues; she hadn't considered at all the morality of her decision in relation to Edgar Evans.

"I'm being unfair to him, aren't I? I know I can live with my decision, but what about him?"

Enter her father, m'lady's loyal deluder.

"Dorothy, Dorothy! Who started the ball rolling, anyway? Don't you think he has his own agenda? He's not exactly an innocent in this affair, you know."

"Yes, I know, but he's no idea that I'm planning to use him."

"That is true, but no one's going to get hurt, Dorothy. Edgar Evans will get his thrill, you'll get your baby, and Donald will get his wish. Everybody wins."

"But if the word gets out, Edgar Evans will be ruined."

"Come on Dorothy! Donald will be the only one who knows, and he's not going to tell anybody."

So did her father carry the day. Not even he could help her with her next concern though. She chewed on the fact that as detached as she was determined to be, there would likely be times when Edgar Evans would need encouragement. Dorothy came close to feeling the creeps.

"Perhaps I'll pretend that he is… " and in the nick of time, she repressed the thought of Donald.

Eventually, she convinced herself that, faced with such a challenge, she possessed both the requisite grit and desire to succeed. Thus, she fell asleep excited. Doubts of all shapes had been readily extinguished by the spectre of her father and the pious reassurance supplied by her mantra.

Dorothy's excitement spilled over into Saturday, and riding its wave, she swept the Blue Riband competition as well. Such a notable victory was especially sweet, and a good omen, she thought; everything was going so well. She quietly, confidently, dedicated her success to her daughter.

"Funny, Edgar seemed a bit nervous, didn't he? Still, he can't help but respect me now."

Hand in hand, they were crossing the dunes towards a ridge. Her sweet spot was in the ascendance.

"Yes, I feel just as I hoped I would. It's still a little bit light though, isn't it, but it'll be dark soon, I think. I know everything's going to be all right now."

As if in confirmation, she put her arm through his and squeezed herself against him. That's when he ran away playfully and disappeared over a dune; that's when she followed him expectantly, lost her footing and rolled uncontrollably down beside him; that's when he fondled her vigorously, despite her frightened expression, and for his insensitivity was slapped soundly on the face; and that's when she feared her baby was gone for good.

Yet, he appeared to be sufficiently ashamed not to be at odds with Dorothy's mantra.

"No respect, no baby!" was still her guiding light. As it was, she was encouraged to nurse him out of his pout.

Waves were breaking gently,
And Jupiter jazzed up the sky
As Dorothy set about healing their wounds,
And the world no longer wondered why.

She led him back through the bushes, and into them when voices approached. She glossed over his nationalistic outburst and squeezing his arm with her head on his shoulder, focused instead on the revival of his spirit. Then, pushing her sweet spot to the limit, she kissed him, and told him that she wanted to make love, but not tonight because now she felt too tense. Would tomorrow be OK?

"Will you make love to me tomorrow night, Edgar?" begged Dorothy, "We can come back here after dark, and I know I'll feel better then. So will you, then? Will you make love to me... Edgar?"

"All right, then."

He said it as if he'd answered this question in this way a thousand times before. Hugely relieved, Dorothy hugged him.

Later, lying in bed, Dorothy experienced a peace as never before. Tomorrow's test would be massive, yet she was relaxed and supremely confident. She felt as she imagined a darts player would when throwing doubles on command, or an orator when aware that he held his listeners in the palm of his hand. She felt in complete control of her situation. Yet, just as she had at times in the past, she wondered if all this was too good to be true. Now, as then, her loyal deluder delivered. He reminded her that Edgar Evans was eminently suitable, her creeps had been held at bay, her requirements had been met, and above all, her sweet spot held sway.

As a train rumbled by from east to west, Edgar ventured to take Dorothy's hand in his, even though it wasn't quite dark yet. Almost immediately, he let go of it again, and after dropping his suitcase on the ground, took off his shirt. As he knelt to cram it in his case, Dorothy noticed a little red dragon on his left shoulder blade.

"Oh, that's pretty, Edgar. What does it stand for?"

"What's so pretty? Oh! You mean the red dragon!"

There was an awkward silence, an unwelcome subsidence in his mood, and then no more than a moderate recovery.

"Well, it doesn't stand for anything, really. I was talked into it one day against my better judgement. I just hope to God I don't live to regret it, that's all."

God wasn't showing his hand, but Dorothy's rose to the occasion. Her confident caress of the dragon's tail seemed to drain it, and the moment, of its menace. This time, Edgar took her arm. Under the other, she carried a couple of blankets.

At the spot where Dorothy laid the blankets on the sand, what little residual light remained in the west was blacked out by the ridge of dunes behind her. It was a balmy evening. As she knelt on the blankets, she was completely bare. When he'd undressed, he faced her, on his knees as well. He shuffled forward, so that their knees touched. She sensed his hand rising and she tensed. It brushed against her breast, and she shivered; she even squealed as he titillated and tickled his way around and then across her belly. His hand moved away, but she was sure she could sense it hovering. She felt tension in those shadows where she knew his shameless hand would settle next. Once it did, she sighed, but still, she felt completely in control. Her roving hands did some settling of their own. They grasped what would now be her anchor for the rest of their lovemaking, and she wouldn't…she wouldn't let it go. Even when he laid her on her back, she refused to release it, forcing his body to follow hers closely. Her grip did not yield until she'd fully replaced it with another. Even at this intensely intimate moment, her sweet spot held sway; amazingly, Dorothy remained comfortable and without emotion, and as a professional would, she heightened his excitement by faking expressions of abandon and pleasure. She mirrored the movement of the ocean, and with each wave that broke beyond the dunes, she voiced her fake satisfaction. All that remained now was to turn him over; instinctively, she felt that from now on she needed to be in the driver's seat.

When it was over, she felt omnipotence and total peace. Three days earlier, she'd embarked on a complicated and bizarre project, and had seen it through, systematically and with little anxiety. So good did she feel that she allowed a little warmth for him, and so magnanimous was her mood that she determined to seal her baby's conception with a kiss. Forward she leant, belly on belly, then her breasts on his… "

"You Welsh-speaking girls are all the same."

This stark remark in English, hurled literally from the night, naturally startled Dorothy. She strove to compose herself, but her lover's delayed reaction put a brake on that.

"What did he say?" he spat in Welsh, "What did he say? Did you hear what he said, Dorothy?"

She tried to calm him.

"It's just a prankster, Edgar."

Saying his name for the first time since she laid the blankets on the sand, gave her an eerie feeling. Edgar! The label put some flesh on him somehow.

"You're all the same… you're all sluts."

The shot from the dark had been repeated, with a crucial amendment. Edgar leapt to his feet without consideration for his lover, tossing her off his torso like a little leaf. He shouted angrily in his slightly awkward English.

"Come back here, you bastard! You wouldn't say that to my face, would you, you Wenglish wimp."

He fell back on the blanket in exasperation and pounded the ground with his fist. At that moment, they lay close to each other, but their thoughts were worlds apart. His were grounded on one of the less grey areas in Welsh history. After all, he knew for a fact that those three young English barristers, who could speak not a word of Welsh had said those things. Well, they'd written them down, hadn't they. It was there in black and white. As for Dorothy's thoughts, they were on her baby. Things had been going so well, so why would Edgar have tossed her off so roughly? How could he have been so disrespectful? She had sensed an unpredictability in him, but she hadn't been prepared for roughness, verging on violence. Why did it have to end like this? Would she feel as good about her baby now? Suddenly, it seemed very important to try and patch things up, but the tack she took did nothing but upset him further.

"He was just a child, Edgar, just doing childish things. Don't let a child get to you… please!"

If only she'd left it at that, but she'd been humiliated, and even if she'd had an inkling of the historical significance of those stark remarks she would have found it difficult to be wise. Uninformed, she stumbled into quicksand.

"Edgar, what does that child know about such things, really? You're far too sensitive, you know, about anything to do with the Welsh. Anyway, it's obvious that what he said meant nothing to him."

She noticed that he'd stopped pounding the ground. Encouraged, she was leaning forward to face him, when he leapt to his feet, pushing her backwards roughly in the process, and erupted. He was very angry.

"Exactly! That's the whole point, isn't it? Of course it doesn't mean a thing to him. If that idiot had been brought up properly, brought up as a true Welshman in his mother tongue, he wouldn't have dreamt of saying anything like that."

"You're overreacting this a bit, aren't… "

"Oh, overreacting, am I?" he mimicked, "Listen, someone's got to care about these things. I'm telling you, these bloody south Walians are all the same. None of them are brought up to respect their country, and most of them don't give a damn about their own language; so if you ask me, they're bloody well not fit to be called Welsh in the first place."

"Hey, careful now Edgar, I'm one of those bloody south Wal… "

"Yes, and you're as bad as the rest of them. There's no middle ground on this issue as far as I'm concerned. You're either with me on this or you're not, and it's pretty obvious to me where you stand."

Within a minute and a half, he'd dressed and was gone.

The taller of the two boys was entranced and mesmerised by the lady's expressions of abandon and pleasure. He and his friend had eavesdropped on lovers for weeks, but not until tonight had he not felt like an outsider. It was as if this lady was his, and her expressions of pleasure were for him alone. He longed to stay with her all night, but his friend inexplicably insisted on leaving. Much against his will, he crept to the path. Once there, insults were hurled by his friend, and then both ran like hell. A little later, they ducked into bushes to catch their breath. Within a few minutes, a man was heard approaching from the beach, striding along the path alone, muttering angrily to himself in a language that they recognised but didn't understand.

Dorothy was upset as she drifted across the band of dunes, her blankets underarm; her bubble had been badly burst. She didn't understand fully what had happened. Welshness, and the language in particular, was involved, of course, and there was no question in her mind that at least some of Edgar's principles had hardened into prejudice. Not even she, his lover, would be immune to that. She felt rejection too, but managed to take comfort from the success of the scheme that she'd masterminded.

The pitch blackness in the bushes was her undoing. They crowded her, and suddenly, she felt very alone and frightened. Her emotions got the better of her, and she sobbed intermittently.

"How could he have been so disrespectful? And everything was going so well, for me... and my baby. I mean, there's nothing wrong with someone feeling strongly about his Welshness and his language, but he's turned it into a vendetta. He's just unreasonable, isn't he?"

Later that night, sitting on her bed at her family friend's house, she continued to question Edgar's behaviour. Principles were all very well, she thought, but were often far too convenient a cover for less noble sentiments. She knew she wasn't capable of logically refuting Edgar's assertions, but there was no question that he was wrong in condemning south Walians en masse. She felt as Welsh as he did, and resented his blanket judgement. She resented being belittled, as well.

How sad to see a language and its trappings, which for centuries had been a decisively cohesive force in Wales, at its divisive worst. Admittedly, the union that it had torn apart was not the loveliest; the aspirations that it had sullied were in the main immoral; and the thoughts that it had partly thwarted were, for the most part, calculating; but a step out of spite is a step too far, and once again, the language had been evoked ungenerously. Yet, true to its innate benevolence, it seemed it couldn't help but do some good, thanks this time to the appearance on Dorothy's cloud of her habitual silver lining.

"Imagine if there hadn't been a flare-up," she reasoned with herself, "It wouldn't have been good, Dorothy, believe you me. Your emotions may have become involved. This had to be done clinically. What's more, your part in the play is over now. It's time to return to reality. Don't you think that the flare-up will make it that much easier to put Edgar Evans behind you? Anyway, by far the most important thing is that you have your baby... and you know it!"

In this way, Dorothy rationalised her disappointment. All of a sudden, she felt drained. Her constant concentration during the play over the last few days had caught up with her. It was with difficulty that she gave herself a body wash, but it had to be done. It was an essential physical and symbolic act. She slumped into bed, and only then thought of Donald. All this she had done for him; what irony in this gesture of everlasting love! Later, she dreamt of him too, and it felt so good.

Thirty-one

L ATE IN THE morning of the following day, Mavis Davies received a telegram from her sister's family in Tryweryn. Telegrams were so rare as to invariably stir emotions, and this one would do so in Welsh. Unfortunately, the script was shabby. As a result, Mavis found it impossible to scan, so she read it very slowly.

"A telegram! Oh dear, what's happened now? Who's it from? Rhiannon! Good Lord! 'Peter Morris Evans born yesterday p.m.' Oh! That's very premature, isn't it?"

She glanced anxiously at her own slightly distended tummy.

"I hope the little thing's all right, and what about Myfanwy? '5lbs, 6oz. Both doing well.' Oooh! That's a relief. That's not too small at all, then. Good old Myfanwy! 'Thanks to Enid.'"

This stopped Mavis Davies in her tracks. Rhiannon had actually written 'Thanks to Enid'? Mavis was well aware of the tensions in Tryweryn, so for Rhiannon to write in that way meant that Enid must have done something really special.

"So it was a difficult birth then? Poor Myfanwy! Never mind though: it says they're all right. That's what counts, isn't it? 'Where's Edgar?' Good God! That puts everything in the shade, doesn't it? Where's Edgar? So he didn't arrive home last night? I had a funny feeling about him when he left yesterday. He didn't want a lift to the station, he said. Oh no, he definitely didn't want a lift! It seemed to me then that he was hiding something. So he didn't get home, aye? Perhaps the train broke down. No, no, no! Come on, Mavis! You had a funny feeling, and your instincts are rarely wrong. So it's a fancy woman? But you know, I've never thought of him as a lady's man. Still, I shouldn't say anything to Myfanwy, should I? What's the point? I mean, she wouldn't be able to do anything about it anyway, and things between them are bad enough as it is. No! I think it's best I keep this one under my hat."

She replied, again in Welsh.

"Congratulations little sister. You beat me to it. Edgar's on his way. Mavis."

Later she informed her husband Dai of Peter Morris Evans's birth, but not before she had discretely disposed of the telegram and her reply.

"So did Rhiannon say anything else?" he asked unexpectedly.

"Dai! This was a telegram not a letter."

"No mention of our tenor? Just wondered," he replied, which set Mavis awondering about Edgar again.

Thirty-two

PETER MORRIS EVANS was one day old already! His mother, who had been relieved of him by Rhiannon, was resting in her room and ruminating.

"I wonder what Edgar will think of the name. I mean, it isn't as if he showed much interest, but you never know. He may feel strongly about it, now that it's too late."

Myfanwy marvelled at the change in her tummy. She felt huge relief, of course, but one marred around the margin by regret, which at this time she managed to divert by dwelling on the circumstances of Peter's birth.

"Oh, I did get scared for a while, didn't I? Well, it was a shock! He came so early. And then of course Rhiannon panicked, at the thought of Edgar's difficult birth I suppose. At least she had the sense to get Enid. Anti Enid now!"

Once again, Myfanwy marvelled at her tummy, but this time the regret that tinged her relief was given a freer rein.

"Still, I can't help feeling a bit short-changed. My baby and I were getting along so well. I'm not denying that I feel relieved, but I do have to share my baby now, and more to the point, I have to share him with Edgar."

Her husband's absence had been a happy time for Myfanwy. Had she dwelt on the degree of release she'd felt, she may have been reminded rather too cruelly of the compromise that underlined her life. As it was, she'd merely lived her life on a lighter plane and hardly thought of her husband at all. No longer would she have that option. She remembered that moment on the ridge above their farmhouse, when she had determined on her emotional break with Edgar. She had realised then that the birth of her baby would be the easy part; far trickier would be sharing his upbringing with Edgar. Tricky too would be the ironing out of those undesirable traits of Edgar's, some of which were bound to have wriggled through. What on earth was keeping Edgar, anyway?

A few minutes later, Enid delivered Mavis Davies's telegram.

No one had looked forward to Edgar's departure more eagerly than Enid, but even she was surprised by the lightness that lapped the farmhouse in his absence. His departure seemed to have tripped a domino effect that had drawn Rhiannon closer still to the Evans family fold. At times like these, Enid considered reconciliation, but the hurt had lodged too deeply. That hump proved insurmountable still, despite Rhiannon's extravagant praise for her midwifery skills.

Enid was happy for Myfanwy, of course, but still disappointed at the birth of a boy before his time. How typically Enid to be mired so in conflicting emotions. Since her heart to heart with Myfanwy on the footbridge over the Tryweryn, Enid had been reasonably successful in rationalising their relationship. However, her demons were never far below the surface, and now and then she'd been forced to turn to her friend for encouragement. On one of those occasions, she had admitted to Myfanwy that for years she had opened every letter that she'd delivered to the farmhouse. By now, the practice had become routine; she was that good at it, and sooner or later she was sure she'd come across something personal that could be used against Rhiannon. To Enid's relief, Myfanwy had seemed totally unperturbed. Yet, uneasy was the balance of her patched-up peace of mind, and vulnerable also at the slightest intrusion. Weighing in at under eighty ounces, Peter Morris Evans was as slight as they could be, but still stood as another formidable horn on Enid's dilemma. There he lay, helpless and innocent, and the most poignant yet among those potential casualties of her drive to avenge Rhiannon. Why, she asked, could he not have given her a few more months of peace? Her bleeding heart was worn on her sleeve.

"What's eating at you, Enid?"

"I think you know, Myfanwy."

"Enid fach, come here. It's the shock, that's all. Little Peter took us all by surprise, didn't he? You wait and see. You'll love this little boy as if he was your own, and Anti Enid will be his favourite. There'll be no room for revenge, Enid, with so much affection flying around."

"I know, I know, Myfanwy."

Elfed knocked before entering Myfanwy's bedroom, and smiled warmly at Myfanwy and Enid.

"What a nice man he is," thought Enid, "I'm so lucky to have him for a father. If only I could bare my soul to him, but it would be so selfish of me to upset him at this stage in his life. No, no, Myfanwy will see me through. I'll just do my best to enjoy being Anti Enid in a way that I could never do with Edgar. What on earth is keeping Edgar, anyway? Shouldn't he be here by now?"

Peter Morris Evans. Elfed had to admit there was something stylish about the name, but still, it didn't have that ring, did it, like Edgar Evans, for example; an unfortunate comparison, which alas reminded Elfed of another birth, over twenty years before.

"Take him under your wing, Elfed," the doctor had said gravely, and Elfed had intended to, of course. For years though, he'd fretted over his failure, but he hadn't stood a chance, had he? This time though, he could just feel that the odds were stacked in his favour. He just knew that Peter Morris Evans was destined to be his friend. It was time he buried once and for all his disappointment over Edgar. What on earth was keeping

Edgar, anyway? According to Mavis, he should have been here by now.

Peter Morris Evans was only one day old, still. An hour of daylight remained, and while Margaret tidied up downstairs alone, five adults doted over Peter in Myfanwy's bedroom, and none with more delight than Geraint, who, though constrained by pain, poured affection on his grandson. Everyone agreed with varying degrees of enthusiasm that he'd inherited his fairly dark complexion from his father, but no one could be sure about his hair... it certainly wasn't red, in any case. His widish mouth, without doubt, was his mother's, and so was the suggestion of a slightly long neck. As for his chubby face? Well, most babies were chubby, weren't they?

"Well, hello Edgar. It's nice to have you back. How are you?"

All five heard Margaret's greeting.

"Not bad," was all they heard in reply.

"Well, I'm glad to hear that, Edgar."

Meanwhile, Rhiannon shuffled loyally towards the head of the stairs, to hear Edgar ask, "So, where is everyone?"

"Up here, Edgar," replied his mother, non-comitally, much to Myfanwy's surprise, "We're all up here. Come up and say hello."

He took a while before eventually making his way up the stairs. Now, Edgar must have had something weighing on his mind, for otherwise, he surely would have had an inkling of what lay in store. If he had, he certainly hadn't prepared himself for it, because when he saw the crib, his face fell a shade, and turned a shade to pale. He recovered to smile rather confusedly, Myfanwy thought.

"It's a boy?" he asked softly, and then, "What's his name?"

"Peter Morris Evans," answered Elfed with deliberation. He

was not acknowledged by his grandson, who merely grimaced and gazed abstractedly through the little window at the failing light. Edgar didn't even congratulate his wife, much to her relief.

"Well, I've got a lot of catching up to do tomorrow," he murmured, "I think it would be just as well if I sleep over at Hendre tonight."

He turned towards the stairs, and was followed by Rhiannon.

"I'll come with you part of the way, Edgar."

Two heads of red disappeared down the staircase, leaving palpable relief in their wake. Thus, lines were drawn and the tone set for the first eight years of little Peter's life.

"Surprise, surprise! Well, at least the man's consistent," was Myfanwy's assessment of her husband's homecoming. It was just as well she didn't know that the real surprise was his civility, in light of the anguish he'd suffered over the previous twenty-four hours.

Following his flare-up with Dorothy, Edgar had sensibly aimed for the station. He'd overlooked the slight risk of detection involved, because he'd felt too tired to think. Yet, ironically, that's all he'd done throughout the night, and none of his thoughts had been pretty. Oh, Edgar, why didn't you regret your childish reaction and beg your lover's forgiveness, if *in absentia*? Why didn't you? You might have slept like a baby, then.

As Edgar had trudged into the waiting room at Llanelli station, he wasn't sure of much, but of his reaction in the dunes he was in no doubt. He just wished he could have laid his hands on the buggers, and as for Dorothy, her stance was unforgivable, but not surprising, really.

"These bloody south Walians are all the same!"

Dorothy became the victim of a generalisation. No ground could he give on her, guaranteeing himself a night of joyless introspection; all this in the waiting room of Llanelli station.

A visitation of guilt had been dealt with ruthlessly. He'd convinced himself that his principled stand on Welshness had absolved him of that lack of principle, which with Dorothy, he now acknowledged had been his guide. So guilt put behind him, but fear was soon to come. The fear of being found out had overwhelmed him. What if she was pregnant and came after him? Could she find him? For goodness sake, she knew his name and that he came from around Bala. He was pretty sure that he'd even mentioned Tryweryn, but anyway, how many Edgar Evanses could there be within ten miles, say, of Bala? And she knew that he was a tenor, and a pretty damn good one at that. Oh, yes, she could find him all right, if she wanted to, and she'd only want to if she was pregnant, right? If it came to that, he would deny it all. He'd flat out deny it, and then it would be his word against hers. Oh, no! His mind had come to a screeching halt. He'd remembered that she'd noticed his little red dragon. Oh, God! That could be really tricky. He knew he shouldn't have had it done. He knew it! It was all Myfanwy's fault. The fear of being found out had him in a vice, and he just couldn't crack the uncertainty; an uncertainty which he realised could last for a year, and maybe much, much longer. Oh, God!

All night long, this uncertainty had driven him crazy, and the poor fellow wouldn't even allow himself the compensatory luxury of reliving the indiscretion that was at the root of it all. Dawn had broken deceptively early. He'd become very distressed. Perhaps it was the bench that was to blame, but the uncertainty had persisted even in the train, and if anything at a higher pitch.

Halfway through the train journey, Edgar had had enough. He'd failed to see a light at the end of the tunnel. He just had to do something! With verdant Border valleys as his background, he'd decided to do a deal.

"Please, God," he'd prayed to himself, "Please help me. Please don't let me be found out."

For Edgar, this wasn't such a startling leap of faith. He'd merely fallen back on the familiar. The Sacred Word had pervaded his life, although his soul had never been touched by it. However, now that the chips were on the table, he'd gravitated gratefully towards God. A deal was a natural outcome, but the terms of the trade had proven tricky. He'd often read of characters selling their souls to the devil, but in those deals the terms invariably spoke for themselves. But when it came to dealing with God, Edgar had to struggle with intangible concepts like giving himself to Jesus and opening his heart to the Holy Spirit. What did it all really mean, anyway? In the end, he'd tried to work out a deal on his own terms, terms he could actually understand.

"God," he'd promised, "I'll go to chapel regularly for the rest of my life in exchange for peace of mind. Please help me, God."

Smugly, he'd settled for that, but a recurring unease soon told him it wouldn't be anywhere near enough. Come on, Edgar, you know better than that. God's currency is selflessness and sacrifice. Perhaps a little leap of faith is called for, Edgar. Thus was he cajoled to a concession that might actually work; thus was his mind shifted from the fearful uncertainty of one baby to the very real prospect of another, leading to a genuinely altruistic gesture. Edgar had promised God that he would play second fiddle to Myfanwy when it came to raising their baby. Given their irreconcilable differences, in no other way would the infant stand a chance. There! That feels better, doesn't it? Edgar had received no concrete confirmation that God had agreed to the terms. No Border bush burst forth in flames, no

Gabriel graced the train, but the very commitment lightened his heart, and gave him hope again.

Remarkably, neither throughout the night nor during the day, had Edgar once asked himself point blank what it was he feared. Well, the fear of being found out, of course, he would have said. So what if you were found out, Edgar? What if Dorothy chose to… betray you? What consequences would you suffer if Dorothy spilt the beans? You've never given two hoots about what the chapel thinks, and Myfanwy couldn't think less of you, anyway. On the plus side, you know your mother would never disown you, and a little notoriety wouldn't do your career any harm, would it? Not once had he asked himself the question.

Still, the deal had done the trick. He had met his newborn son with civility. The sight, the sound and even the smell of a baby had been a little disconcerting, to say the least, in light of the uncertainty he'd suffered all day. Yet, he'd steadied himself, and had been civil.

As he slipped into a sleep that only a few hours earlier had seemed impossible, he took solace from his deal with God. What a fortnight it had been! Edgar realised that he hadn't focused for days on the incident that had sent him to Llanelli in the first place. As he slipped further into sleep, he actually gave the doctor credit for his good advice, and even pictured Dorothy's shoulder length blonde hair shimmering on the top of Mynydd Sylen, or was he dreaming already?

He woke the following morning refreshed. He had slept like a baby. Suddenly, he remembered the deal he'd struck, and the obligations it entailed. Then he thought of his son, and that awful uncertainty grabbed him again, until God's side of the bargain began to kick in. Soon, he became reasonably confident that he'd be able to face his son without worrying each time that there may be another, a south Walian half-brother.

Thirty-three

EVERYONE IN THE valley liked Peter Evans. He was quite good at everything he did, but not much better at anything than anyone else. So he threatened no one, and it seemed that in everything he thought, said and did, he was sensitive to the feelings of others. He was nice looking as well. Blue eyes stood out against a fairly dark complexion. In an otherwise fine-featured face was a widish mouth and with it, a broad and infectious smile. His chubbiness at birth had faded in childhood, but that hint of Myfanwy's elegant neck persisted.

If affection be the root of contentment, then Peter Evans was raised in clover. Elfed was his pal right from the beginning; of the ladies, Myfanwy and Margaret were the leaders in ladling out love, but Anti Enid couldn't have been too far behind, because clearly she was his favourite. Even Rhiannon, somewhat handicapped by lines that were drawn at his birth, even she got into the act. However, with affection comes attention, more often than not its nemesis. Peter's great gift, it seemed, was the ability to filter the affection and absorb it, while allowing the attention to flow by.

Until she got used to the idea, it really confused Myfanwy that all was going so well. It made no sense whatsoever that Edgar was yielding the right to raise his son. Ever since she'd divorced herself emotionally from her husband, the most Myfanwy had allowed herself to hope was to be able to tolerate him. Yet, here he was, actually accommodating her. Edgar even slept downstairs behind the kitchen on those nights when he wasn't at Hendre, and to top it all, he'd started going to chapel regularly.

"I really hope he's not doing this to try and win me back,"

was Myfanwy's reaction. She remained perfectly comfortable with her decision to effectively divorce him. Indeed, she was comfortable with life, thanks to Enid, who provided her with companionship, which under her peculiar marital circumstances, she would otherwise have lacked.

Peter completely changed his Anti Enid's life. Myfanwy had set the stage, of course. She'd already coaxed her friend out of her cocoon, but tenacious strands of resentment still strapped Enid to the past; so her doubts persisted, her dilemmas remained. Peter came along and swept all these away. True, the timing was fortuitous, but the charm was uniquely his. As for Peter, Anti Enid was too good to be true. She was as dependable as his mother, but informal and fun in a way a real mother couldn't consistently be. She was that one step removed from the tensions and realities of his family life, and yet always reassuringly close. He found that he could take risks with her: he could tell her secrets and be sure she wouldn't talk; he could ask her favours and be sure she wouldn't balk. She was a mother, she was a friend, and she was his favourite!

Myfanwy took to this arrangement with genuine pleasure. No risk of resentment there. By now, the two ladies couldn't have been more secure in their relationship, nor more in tune with respect to Peter. Myfanwy still met Enid at the bridge and brightened her day for part of the postal round. During the school holidays, Peter would go one better. Barring foul weather, early in the morning he would hop and skip and occasionally trip to Anti Enid's house. True, all they did was deliver the post together, but each time his enthusiasm transformed what was routine into an adventure. What an odd couple they made, though. Enid sedate and as straight as a beanpole, with a postman's hat on her head, and Peter, most of the time, like a little kite in constant and erratic motion. Now and then, he would suddenly stop, and for a short while they'd walk side by side, hand in hand. Usually, he'd go home with his mother after she'd met them at the bridge, but occasionally, a very special occasionally, he'd do the whole round with Anti Enid and stay the night at her house. Just as Myfanwy had predicted, there would be little room for revenge with so much affection flying around. Enid was a new person, and it was there for all the villagers to see. How they would have revelled in what was unrevealed! Foolishly, Enid was persisting in opening selected letters. No longer did her sense of grievance demand it, for her little friend had cleansed her of that. Yet, she persisted. Blame it on the force of habit, but it was an ill wind, which usually blows no good.

As to nomenclature, Geraint suggested that Peter should know him by his Christian name. This way, Elfed could be called Taid by everyone, except for Edgar who somehow managed never to call him anything at all. Rhiannon generously played along with Geraint's idea, so that Margaret could be unequivocally Nain. Peter naturally became the focus of attention in the farmhouse, and in the process, seemed to diffuse the tension that previously had prevailed whenever his father was in the picture. Not that Edgar was around much these days, anyway. Taid marvelled at the way he wove his way through their farmhouse life as if he were a ghost. In those early years after Peter's birth, Taid had worried that Edgar's withdrawal, as convenient as it was for most of the family, would one day backfire on them all, but eventually he came to accept that for some reason, this was the way Edgar was happiest. Taid wondered what Peter made of it all. Although he didn't see that much of his father, Peter always treated him perfectly naturally, as if he understood the situation and accepted that this was how it had to be. Taid found it all so eerie, but it worked, and to his advantage, for he became the man in little Peter's life.

Taid was sixty-nine when his great-grandson was born. Peter brought him to life, and Taid was delighted to reciprocate. He wasn't going to miss this chance for the world! He devoted the rest of his life to the boy, but for one short, sad interruption.

In Peter's second year, Geraint suffered another relapse. For two months, the pain wracked his frame and gradually fried his mind. Rhiannon and Taid assumed the responsibility of caring for him. Initially, one or the other was constantly at his side, but Rhiannon was intolerant of pain, of her own at the thought of life without him, and Geraint's.

"I don't understand," was her regular refrain, "I thought the doctor said that he would live for ten more years."

For "could" she'd heard "would"; she'd misunderstood, perhaps knowingly. Regardless, she was ill-equipped to deal with suffering. Gradually, her place at Geraint's bedside was taken by Nain; so she and Taid assumed the same supporting roles that they had with his mother half a century before. The doctor visited often, but he could do little. As a friend, he did help though, when it was plain for all to see that the pain had broken Geraint. At least the sadness drew Edgar and the family together. Yet, following Geraint's internment, the same old battle lines sadly were redrawn, and now more sharply. At Geraint's death, Rhiannon abruptly reversed the reconciliation she'd fostered with his parents, as if he at her side had been her sole motivation. Perhaps his loss had unhinged her, or perhaps she felt isolated within the farmhouse without him. Regardless, she became more distant, more contentious, and aligned herself noticeably with Edgar. Nain in particular was upset by this. In trying to engage Rhiannon on the matter, she suffered much discomfort and occasional humiliation. In light of Nain's experience, Taid didn't even try. Actually, he was less upset about Rhiannon than he might have been, thanks at first to grief, and after that, to Peter.

However early Peter rose, his Taid was there awaiting. Taid became his great-grandson's intellectual mentor. It was he who kept Peter bubbling with curiosity; it was he who pointed out, questioned and cajoled, and it was he who kept him honest. Often over breakfast, and nearly always on their way together to meet Peter's train to Bala school, Taid gently probed his protégé on the previous day's schoolwork. On the return trip from the train each afternoon, there was none of that: for there were so many natural wonders to uncover that school may have overlooked.

It was the last day of January. The afternoon was crisp and clear as Taid met Peter off the school train. Peter was eight, and was flourishing in every way, much to his Taid's delight. Taid himself was holding up remarkably well, too, although he no longer went anywhere without his stick.

"Taid, a new teacher arrived today. He told us he was English."

"So? You've got other teachers who are English, don't you? What's so special about this one, then?"

"He's not like the others. It was odd, because he made a point of telling us several times that he was English... very English, he said, and that he hoped that all of us would make a special effort to get along well together. He was very nice, though."

"Come here, Peter. Now, what's bothering you?"

"It's hard to explain, Taid. I know that I'm Welsh, and I know lots of other people aren't, because they're English, aren't they, and we make jokes about them, don't we... but... you know what I mean, Taid?"

"I know what you mean, Peter, but try and explain it to me... please!"

"What I'm saying is that I've always sort of known that me and my friends are different from the English people that I've met, but I've never really thought about the differences before today, so that's why I say it's all so odd."

Under pressure, he'd confessed to some confusion, and Taid, gentle as ever, merely took his hand and they walked towards the farmhouse without another word. Just before they arrived,

Taid said, "If it's nice tomorrow when I meet you off the train, we'll go for a short walk, and I'll try and make you actually feel the difference, OK?"

Peter smiled knowingly, and said in an obviously faked and frustrated tone, "Oh, all right, Taid."

The following afternoon was dry and partly cloudy. Peter was lively; he often was in anticipation of Taid's little projects. From the halt, Taid walked with him to that special spot where the doctor had said his piece, almost ten years earlier. Taid leant on his walking stick, but Peter couldn't stand still. He clasped a clump of grass, and tossed it to the breeze; he threw a pebble, and then another, with childhood's carefree ease. Regardless, Taid patiently followed his script.

"So Peter, here's your country, laid right out in front of you. It's Wales, isn't it, but how can you tell? How d'you know, Peter?"

"Taid, really! I can't tell you how I know. I just know, don't I? That's all."

Peter obviously wasn't concentrating, but Taid could always rely on him to say just the right thing. There was something very special between them, somehow. These were exquisite moments, savoured in silence by an old but very happy man. When he spoke, it was with more emotion than usual, and he could tell that Peter noticed. He talked of the Berwyn where Owain Gwynedd had beat the English hollow. But in the end they got him: weight of numbers, Peter bach. He talked of Owain Glyndŵr's rebellion, but in the end they got him too. Peter had settled down by now.

"So you see, Peter, both of them lost, but neither of them failed, because it was the resistance put up by people like them that kept the spirit of the Welsh unbroken. Without their kind, Welshness might not have survived, and I wonder whether you'd be standing here at this special spot, not only speaking

Welsh, and feeling Welsh, but also… as you said… just knowing that this is Wales."

Peter normally challenged and questioned whatever his Taid said, but was now quiet. Taid was sure that he was touched.

"Your teacher, Peter, your very English teacher, could never feel the way that you feel now, sitting at this spot, and there's the difference you were talking about."

Taid was pleased with himself. He felt contented, and so close to Peter that it occurred to him that perhaps this was that special moment he'd been waiting for, to tell Peter the tale of the dragon, and…

"Taid, does Dad know about all this as well?"

The wind was squeezed out of Taid's sails, and the landscape drained of magic and myth. Despite Edgar being the black sheep of their family, Taid had recently made a point of referring to him regularly when talking to Peter, but today, today of all days, he would have preferred to have kept him out of the conversation.

"Oh, yes, he does indeed."

His reply was short, but his discomfort lingered longer; one moment untroubled, the very next deflated. The pair were almost home before Peter grasped his Taid's hand, and nearly healed him.

"Thanks, pal," thought Taid, "As for the dragon? Well, there'll be many more special moments, won't there?"

Dwelling on the dragon led Taid to thoughts of his old friend Edward; with this, the healing process was complete.

Thirty-four

TWO DAYS ON, a boy sat at the little front window of Edward Jones's bungalow in Llwynypia in south Wales. This was Edward's great-grandson David Devereux, eight and a half years old. Sunday was not his favourite day. Sunday often meant going to chapel, and he never looked forward to that, even though he had to admit the sermons were usually fun. He had a funny feeling that if the services were held on Tuesday, say, he wouldn't dread them half as much. Sunday was a reminder that Saturday had come and gone. Sunday was followed by Monday and the thought of another week at school always gave him a sinking feeling. Yet, the thought on a Monday night of going to school on Tuesday didn't seem to bother him at all. No doubt about it, there was definitely something sad about Sunday, and to rub it in, it nearly always rained. No, Sunday was not his favourite day.

This Sunday was different though. There was a march taking place, but not any old march. He'd heard that this one would be the march of the century, and one peep through the little window that poorly lit their parlour confirmed it would be so. It was barely half past eight on this Sunday morning, and yet the street in front of their bungalow was already teeming with marchers.

Most were dressed in their Sunday best,
Marching in formation,
Lively, yet their faces set
With grim determination.

Yes, this Sunday was definitely different. He had been told that there would be no chapel and, better still, no school tomorrow. This was the way Sundays were meant to be. True to form, though, it had rained heavily earlier in the morning, but now the clouds had broken up a bit, underlining this Sunday's special status. There was nothing sad about this Sunday. Not a whiff of a sinking feeling, he thought to himself, but he'd thought too soon.

"I really don't understand why you have to march in the first place, Jane, but if you have to go, why with him? Why don't you march with the other women? You'll look completely out of place."

His grandmother always got up late, but not late enough by half for him today. He liked her, he really liked her; they were the best of friends, but he wished she hadn't spoilt things by being mean to his mother like that. He kept staring out of the window, and it started to rain again. Even as a little boy, he had been renowned for not missing a thing, and now he was aware beyond his years. It didn't take any brains, though, to realise that his grandmother's feelings towards her daughter Jane were not very warm. It was obvious to anyone. To his credit, he had managed to live his life around this problem and still remain close to both of them. Thankfully, tensions were usually kept under wraps, but he had noticed that when they surfaced, it was usually on Sundays. He knew that the problem had something to do with his father, because his grandmother never referred to him by his name, Jon, but always as "him" or "he". Eight and a half years old he was and beginning to grasp the gremlins in his grandmother's mind. All but one of these he sensed to some degree. Of the other he was completely unaware. Only Edward Jones, his Dacu, could fill him in on that in full.

"Let her be, Martha. She knows what she's doing. I'm sure she's thought it through."

Dacu could always be relied on to stick up for Jane. He would go to the end of the earth for his one and only grandchild, even if it meant stepping on his one and only daughter's toes. He spoke from the kitchen, where he sat at their dining table working at a jigsaw puzzle, while Jane washed up at the sink. Dacu was always up early, was rarely idle, and was never caught in his pyjamas. The grandmother, on the other hand, loved to hang around in her dressing gown, and rarely dressed before ten, except on Sundays of course, when she went to chapel. This Sunday was different though. No chapel on account of the march of the century, but no march would stop her now. She pounced on poor Dacu in Welsh. She usually spoke Welsh to him, but did so without fail when intent on irritating her daughter and son-in-law. They couldn't speak Welsh, you see.

"You're always sticking up... "

Where the march of the century had failed, her grandson succeeded and foiled her attack with an interruption.

"Mamgu! Mamgu! I'm going out to see if Dadi's on his way home. OK?"

He spoke instinctively, and it wasn't until halfway through his sentence that he realised the risk of introducing his father into the equation... but it worked! As he spoke, he was careful not to look at anyone, but had he done so, he would have enjoyed the palpable relief on his mother's face and the proud smile on Dacu's. On Mamgu's there was only resignation, which sprung from respect for her grandson. All she said was, "All right, David, but put your mack on, won't you."

He did as she said before stepping outside and pulling the door a little bit harder than usual to remind everyone perhaps that the subject was closed... for now, at least.

Walking through the door from the parlour to the pavement was like entering another world. Gone was the discord and narrowmindedness, to be replaced by an enthusiastic and expectant solidarity. The street was packed with people pulling together, marching en masse, confident in the righteousness of their cause. He looked to his left up the hill, but there was no sign of his father. It didn't matter though, for his mind was on the march. Each marcher of course was bigger than him, but what struck him was the power and the massiveness of the movement as a whole. He was cowed by the force of it all. It wasn't that he was afraid, for he saw the force as a friend, but it did make him feel very small, so that when a few of the marchers smiled and waved at him, it was shyly that he waved back. The distant strain of a brass band was suddenly transformed into a blaring, pressing call to action as its vanguard appeared on the main road at the top of the hill and wheeled right towards him. Wheeling with them was his father, marching exaggeratedly with several others, and smiling… his father was always smiling. The boy thought of waiting for him, but instead decided to let his mother know, so back into the bungalow he ran, and while wiping his feet on the mat, shouted, "Dadi's coming. He's just turned the corner on the main road."

Once the door was shut, he saw to his surprise that all three were now kneeling side by side at the little window. He joined them, just as his Dacu, who'd been on a march or two himself, said with his hand over his mouth and his head shaking slowly, "I really feel sorry for those poor blighters. Nothing will come of this." During that damp Sunday morning, tens of thousands would march past his little window in Llwynypia, disagreeing with him… and they would turn out to be right!

The vanguard of the brass band was wheeling right from the main road down the hill and wheeling with them, marching exaggeratedly, was a smiling Jon Devereux with a packet of bacon in one hand and the *Western Mail* in the other. He spotted his son down the hill and stepped away from the band to wave at him, just as David decided to run back indoors. A minute later, as Jon stepped towards the door of the bungalow, four faces at the window caught his eye. Four generations, four freckled faces, three hugely happy, at ease with their spaces, but the fourth much troubled... her freckles a touch darker and seemingly raised, tingeing her face in mystery.

"Those freckles don't give up very easily," thought Jon to himself, "It's a trait, all right. Just look at the four of them... and come to think of it, they don't give up very easily either. They keep on chugging along while their partners drop away."

Jon pointed a finger at Dacu in a gesture of camaraderie and immediately blew a kiss at Jane. He waved at David and then clenched his fists and ducked his head, assuming a sparring pose; then back to his train of thought.

"He probably doesn't realise how lucky he is to have a mother like Jane. He's got her freckles, all right, and her brains too, but David bach, I'm afraid that you're stuck with my round face and curly hair... fair curly hair, at that. You'll stand out in a crowd, I'll tell you that now."

He admired the four freckled faces one more time. On opening the front door, he was kissed by one of them. Dacu collected his paper and slapped Jon on the back, and David punched his father lightly in his stomach. Mamgu remained at the window with her head at a slight angle, revealing half her freckles which were still slightly raised.

"Come on, Jane fach, let's go. I can't tell you how good it feels out there. There's something powerful at work, I'm telling you. Honestly, it makes me want to be a miner."

Dacu cleared his throat and repeated his assertion, "Oh, I really feel sorry for them, Jon. You wait and see. Nothing will come of it."

On Sunday, the 3rd of February 1935, despite the cold and the wind and the rain, it is estimated that 300,000 Welsh people marched in the various valleys of south-east Wales. Three hundred thousand people! For every seven persons who lived in Wales on that Sunday, one marched. They marched in protest at the Unemployment Act of 1934–5, which ostensibly was created to centralise the granting of unemployment benefits, but in reality was designed to reduce them. That was on Sunday, the 3rd of February 1935. On the Monday, women, many carrying babies, took up the running, but this time there was violence. On the Tuesday, the new Act was put on hold by the House of Commons and would not reappear for eighteen months, and then it would appear in a less offensive form.

So the tens of thousands of men and women who marched past Dacu's little window on that cold, windy and rainy Sunday did not do so in vain. Dacu had been wrong, but he would not be afforded the pleasure of admitting it.

Thirty-five

I T WAS LATE morning and by now noticeably fewer marchers passed the bungalow's little window on their way down the hill to the bridge, where they would turn left and follow the river to the mass meeting in Tonypandy. David rose from the old bedsheet that he had laid out by the window where he had been sandpapering a little robin that his father had carved out of wood. As he lost interest in the march, so the little robin lost its charm. David jogged into the kitchen where Dacu and his jigsaw still locked horns.

"Look, David. I'm gradually getting the better of this puzzle. Don't you think it's funny though that Big Ben shows half past twelve? They could have chosen any time, but why half past twelve?"

David glanced at the half finished jigsaw puzzle, which eerily depicted the Houses of Parliament under construction, and focused on Big Ben.

"It doesn't say half past twelve, Dacu. It's six o'clock it is. You've got the hands mixed up."

Dacu considered David's observation for a moment, because between the two of them he was used to being right.

"I admit David that my eyes aren't what they used to be, but I can still read the time, you know, and I'm telling you, when I can't my time will be up."

David was only eight, but the morbid implication of that innocent remark was not lost on him. It even discouraged him from pursuing an argument he knew he couldn't lose. Knowing David though, he probably wouldn't have shown his Dacu up in any case.

Often, he just knows he's right,
Heck! It's there in black and white,
But he lets it rest
'Cos Dacu knows best
And anyway, he loves him.

Back at the window, David, with the little robin in his grasp again, gazed at the reflections of a watery, midday sun in the puddles on the road and rued not being allowed to accompany his mother and father on the march. Mamgu had put her foot down over that and in truth, till now he hadn't cared, for her prediction of dire weather had proven to be right, but after the sight of the reflected sun, he was sorry to be home, and he almost sulked.

Speaking of the devil, though David himself would never have thought of her like that, Mamgu emerged from her bedroom, their bedroom as a matter of fact, for David slept in a little bed at the foot of his grandmother's. She smiled briefly at her grandson on her way into the kitchen and nodded her head with amusement at Dacu, who was hunched over his jigsaw, and humming. She then settled at the sink to prepare potatoes. Her comments as she peeled and scraped, and Dacu's brief retorts, were reassuring background music to David as he rapidly rubbed the little wooden bird. He couldn't understand the Welsh they spoke, but the tone was so neutral and the flow so natural that he lost himself in thoughts of men and women massed and on the move. He felt content again, until Mamgu mentioned his mother's name. So slight was her change in tone that Dacu's humming never wavered, but to David it resembled a slingshot that hurled "Jane" like a lightning bolt through the kitchen door and across the front room to slap him solidly in the chest. David's instincts were on the mark, because it was all downhill after that. The edge to Mamgu's remarks grew sharper, and the more indifferent Dacu's demeanour, the more strident she became. David turned his back to the kitchen and stared out of the little window, nervously sandpapering the wooden bird while Mamgu repeatedly asked the same question of Dacu, over and over and over again, with increasing urgency. David was braced for the inevitable, but even he was surprised by the ferocity with which Dacu's fragile fist met the table, and also by the anger in Dacu's voice as Big Ben hit the floor. As Dacu hobbled out of the kitchen, shaking his head in disbelief, he spoke to David.

"Let's get out of this place, David. I can't stand Martha nagging me any more. Let's go for a walk, shall we? I'll go and get my boots on. I won't be long," and off he went to his bedroom.

David generally didn't do anything without his Mamgu's approval, but she continued to stand at the kitchen sink with her head in her hands, and he took that to mean that she was leaving this decision to him. She stirred as they left the bungalow, dressed up identically in their fawn raincoats, dark blue caps and black boots. Dacu was already outside on the pavement when she spoke wistfully and, as usual, warmly to David.

"David, your Dacu shouldn't be going out at all, you know. One of these days he's going to kill himself. It's going to rain again any minute and what with his bad heart and tight chest, he's asking for it. Still, after what happened back there, there's no point me talking to him. He just wouldn't listen, so you take care of him, OK? Don't let him go too far, now," and David nodded with greater confidence than he felt in his heart.

Dacu didn't seem quite himself. He stopped regularly, ostensibly to greet the marchers, but in reality to lean on his favourite stick and catch his breath, just as, over the years, thousands of ex-miners had done before him. David was used to this, but today Dacu's breathlessness seemed more pressing and his recoveries less complete. David dwelt on Mamgu's parting words and worried.

"Are you sure you're all right, Dacu? It's going to rain again soon, so we'd be better off at home, don't you think?"

"Just look at your freckles, David bach," from Dacu who choked as he chuckled, "Mine used to darken when I was worried, too, but they don't do it any more. Funny, isn't it? Anyway, the last thing I want to do, David, is go home and have to deal with Mamgu. Look, we're almost at the main road, and then we can sit on the bench around the corner and have a chat. What d'you say?"

David just smiled, only slightly reassured.

Often, he just knows he's right,
Heck! It's there in black and white...

Dacu and David settled on the bench just as thousands of ex-miners had done before them, thousands with little to show for their heroic subterranean exploits but coal-black lungs and shockingly low life expectancies. There on the bench they sat, two freckled faces framed in fawn and black and blue, Dacu puffing and panting and David pretending not to notice. Marchers still trooped by, mostly dressed in their Sunday best, and thankful it was dry.

"Dacu, why was Mamgu so upset in the kitchen? What was she on about?"

"Give me a few minutes David bach to get my breath back," but he couldn't wait to tell his tale, and his story tumbled out, punctured with pauses for panting.

"Your Mamgu has had a rough life, David. I'm not saying that it's not her fault, mind, but in dealing with her, we've all got to try and take account of that. Her husband, your grandfather, was as mean as they come. You never met him and it's just as well."

He paused again, visibly struggling to draw a breath, this time wheezing as he did so. Though Dacu's breathing difficulties had been part and parcel of David's childhood, he'd never got used to the wheezing; it still disconcerted him. As a distraction, he overcame his shyness and waved at the marchers. They couldn't help but notice the freckled faces on the bench and responded enthusiastically. Dacu in turn waved back as he gamely gasped for air.

"Your Mamgu hardened while she was married. She turned to ice. She had to, to survive, but now her husband's gone, she can't seem to shake it off, she can't change, she can't… melt."

Yet another pause for catching breath and waving at the marchers.

"It seems that once anger and resentment takes over a person, something always comes along to feed it…and keep it going. You can see, can't you, that Mamgu is mean to your mother?"

David nodded, quickly and a little sharply.

"And that she basically ignores your father?"

David kept nodding, now patently impatiently, but Dacu chose not to notice. Rather, he stuck to the point he wanted to make, pausing for air increasingly frequently.

"Caught up in her own anger, she's jealous. That's all it is. Of course, she would never admit it. But can you believe it? A mother being jealous of her own daughter and resenting her happiness, and to make matters worse, she hates herself for it. Your Mamgu is not like her husband who was mean through and through and didn't give a damn for anyone. Deep down, she cares. Did you see her in the kitchen with her head in her hands? It's always the same. She was just as angry at herself for upsetting me as she was at me for not agreeing with her."

David had lost his patience, and just a little angry himself, pleaded with his Dacu.

"Why was she angry with you, Dacu? You're not answering

my question. Why was Mamgu so upset?" and then he stopped, suddenly ashamed of himself for raising his voice at Dacu, who could hardly breathe: silence, regret, reflection, recovery.

"That's a bit harder to explain, David bach. You see, there is one more thing that eats at Mamgu. Something that'll surprise you, I'm sure."

He was interrupted by the approach of a small red van which had turned the corner at the top of the hill, and now wove its way deftly through the dwindling line of marchers, and past their bench. On its side, starkly written in white was "Ifor Williams, Baker". Dacu was surprisingly quick to his feet, waving down the van with his blue cap. He had known Ifor Williams for ages, but their friendship had been refreshed in recent years by Ifor's generosity as Jon's employer. They greeted each other in Welsh and marvelled at the march. Dacu then switched to English, smiling at Ifor and glancing at David.

"Are you going over the top, Ifor?"

Ifor nodded, furrowing his brow and flattening his lips.

"I'd like to show David something, so would you mind giving us a lift to the top and picking us up again on your way back from Ferndale?"

David was on his feet and sprinting towards the van before Dacu had finished his question. His disappointment over the interruption of Dacu's tale was forgotten in an acute concern for his well-being.

"Dacu, let's not go…please! Mamgu made me promise we wouldn't go far and if we're not back soon, she'll be worried sick. Please, Dacu."

"Your Mamgu's the least of my worries this morning. I just want to show you something, David. We won't be long… just over an hour… and it'll help you understand what I was going to explain to you before Ifor came along."

This put a slightly different complexion on the matter, but

nowhere near enough to overcome David's concerns. He wasn't at all happy with Dacu's cavalier attitude,

… But he lets it rest
'Cos Dacu knows best…

On the short journey to the top of the ridge that separated Rhondda Fawr from Fach, Dacu's excitement did little to reassure David. While an animated Dacu sparred with Ifor over the potential impact of the march of the century, David fretted over Dacu's breathlessness as coal-black clouds converged on the Rhondda valleys.

"See you in half an hour then, and don't be late, now." It was still dry when Ifor tooted goodbye and slowly trundled out of sight, but that didn't stop David from feeling eerily exposed on the lonely, treeless ridge.

"Cheer up, David bach. You shouldn't worry so much about me. I've never been better," turned out to be one of Dacu's worst-timed remarks, for no sooner had he finished reassuring David than he doubled up in pain and moaned, and moaned again. David rushed to his side with Mamgu's parting words echoing in his head. Dacu lent on him for a few moments, breathing laboriously, and, unbeknownst to David, calmly and deliberately followed a sequence of simple steps to recovery, mind games that in the past he knew had served him well. Then, without announcement, Dacu began inching up the short ridge, stopping after every six, shuffled steps or so for air. With each determined gasp came a rasping wheeze, and a pathetic little squeak. Yet, his face was a picture of concentration, and his spirits were surely buoyed by the control he'd just imposed upon his fragile frame. Even David, so concerned and disconcerted by the wheezing, began to feel that he might enjoy the walk. The path, which to this point had skirted the ridge on its east side, took a sharp left turn and within moments met the ridge at a precipice. There, David's worries were washed away by the awesome view that hit him. Immediately below, the Rhondda Fawr valley snaked from north to south, hugged by endless terraces, torn by tips and guarded by pithead gear. This was nothing new for David, and then he raised his eyes. To the north were countless valleys like fingers feeling their way towards the Brecon Beacons, and to the west and south, rows of ridges tumbling over each other to Swansea Bay, still well-defined despite the coal-black clouds converging on the Rhondda. The view was vast and beautiful, and not a word was said as David, unspoilt and spongy, soaked it up.

"This is what I wanted you to see," Dacu said eventually, "Is it fair to say that you're not angry with me any more?"

David smiled coyly at him, shaking his head in amusement as if to say he could never be angry at Dacu,

... 'Cos Dacu knows best,
And anyway, he loves him.

Dacu was vindicated, but how on earth could he carry on in his state? Pained were his eyes, and so tired and strained his face, but in his favour there was pluck and years of involuntary practice. He fumbled for ages in his mack pocket. The mint he'd sought was placed very slowly in his mouth.

"This is Wales, David. This is what it's all about. There's no sign out there telling us it's Wales, is there? We just know it is, right? As you know, I grew up in a totally different part of the country, but it was just the same there. I'd look around from the tops of different mountains, and I just knew instinctively it was Wales. It felt Welsh, and I felt a part of it. It's funny how that works, isn't it?"

Dacu's breathing was painfully laboured. It seemed he gasped after every word, but he persevered, as if he knew that this tale was one of the last that he would tell. Leaning on his favourite stick, he shifted the mint around his mouth as if it gave him comfort.

"Just imagine, David. Up to about fifty years ago, everyone who had stood here marvelling at this sight had done so in Welsh. That's the way it had been for twenty-five hundred years, one Welsh-speaking generation after another passing down the torch along a human chain, and that's what eats at Mamgu."

David's interest-level took a leap.

"She has never forgiven herself for being the weakest link. She just can't get over not bringing your mother up in Welsh, even though it wasn't her fault. After all, her husband threatened to kill her if she as much as thought about it. No, it wasn't her fault at all, but you try telling her that."

Dacu winced and furrowed his brow as he held his hand to his breast. He sucked deeply on his mint again as if its zest gave his chest relief. Then on he went with his tale... doggedly.

"See, David, when it comes to the fact that fewer people are speaking Welsh these days, it's easy for me to convince myself that I did my bit. Your mother's off the hook of course, but Mamgu is a different kettle of fish. It's harder for her to get over those little niggly, guilty feelings, because who can deny that she's the one who broke the chain. But dammit, David, it wasn't her fault in the least. She had no choice, but will she listen to me? Not on your nellie, but she'd listen to you though. Will you talk to her David and try to make her see some sense? Will you promise?"

David nodded, but at this point he would have promised almost anything to get Dacu to answer his burning question.

"Dacu, you still haven't told me why Mamgu was angry with you. What was she going on about?"

"Oh, David bach, I'd almost forgotten. Well! You see,

what happens is that when Mamgu gets at your mother, her first reaction is often to turn to me for support, and as she can hardly expect me to understand her jealousy, she has to think of something else, right? So what she latches on to is the fact that you, her only grandchild, don't speak Welsh. She says it's your mother's fault for marrying a man who didn't speak Welsh either. She says that once your mother married an Englishman, you didn't stand a chance. She tries to get me to agree with this idea, and when I don't, she pesters me then... and that's what she was going on about this morning... trying to shift the blame from herself, and at the same time trying to find a real reason, if you know what I mean, for feeling badly about your mother... and your father too. Do you understand what I'm saying? In any case, you'll talk to Mamgu, won't you, and try and knock some sense into her? You will, won't you?"

David nodded again, aware that something of importance had been said, but severely disappointed with its content. He had expected so much more. As if to make up for it, Dacu carried on.

"David, there's something else I want to show you," and he set about unbuttoning his fawn raincoat. With difficulty, he strained to pull his left arm out of the sleeve.

"Dacu! What are you doing? You'll catch a cold, you know," but seeing that his great-grandfather was adamant, continued, "Here, let me help you. Tell me what you're doing Dacu."

"I just want to show you something, David. Now pull up my shirt and jersey. Ooooh! Not too sharply, David bach. Just a little bit further now and you should be able see it."

Dacu began to shiver, so David was loath to carry on, but at his great-grandfather's insistence, he gently raised the shirt and jumper further, and suddenly, there it was... a dainty, indistinct, red dragon, faded by now but very Welsh, tattooed just above Dacu's left shoulder blade.

"Can you see it, David?" asked Dacu, still shivering.

"It's beautiful, Dacu. It's lovely. When did you do it? When you were young?" and as David carefully eased down Dacu's shirt and jersey, rebuttoning his fawn raincoat and forgetting to slip his left arm into the sleeve... as David did all this, he was fitfully and emotionally told the outlines of the dragon's tale, a tale of two close friends, of the fork that clove their lives and the promise that they made to each other.

"It amazes me, David," concluded Dacu, "That whenever I think about that story, it still sends shivers down my spine."

Poor Dacu! He was already shivering and the storytelling made it worse. He was struck again by sharp pains in the chest, which this time his mind games could not ease. As he sunk to the ground, visibly shaking and gasping for air, he managed to utter Ifor's name. This snapped David out of shock and down the ridge he went, but soon turned back. The coal-black clouds converging on the Rhondda had run aground atop Dacu's ridge and were suddenly dumping drops of freezing rain. David took off his own fawn raincoat jerkily, laid it over Dacu, mumbled encouragingly, and took off down the ridge again. To David's huge relief, the baker's van was waiting and within minutes, Ifor Williams was striding heroically down the short ridge with his friend, still shaking, in his arms. In the van, Ifor wrapped him in everything he could find, so that on the way home Dacu warmed a little, and just before arriving, his shaking and his wheezing had settled down enough to allow him to remind David that he had promised to try and make Mamgu see sense.

"You will, won't you?" and David nodded, "And thank God you heard the dragon's tale. Funny, but I really thought I had plenty of time."

Dacu smiled wanly, and David squeezed his hand for the last time...

When they reached the bungalow, Mamgu took charge,

relieving David, and in relief's wake came the rushing unwelcome realisation of what was really happening, and with it the greatest sadness he had ever known. While Ifor sped for the doctor, Dacu was tucked in bed with four hot water bottles, but his shaking and his wheezing never stopped. The next bout of chest pains proved too much, and by the time the doctor had arrived, Dacu had died. The undertaker was already in the bungalow when Jane and Jon returned wet through from Tonypandy. They had hurried home enthusiastically to tell Dacu that his scepticism, in this instance anyway, was surely misplaced, but they were too late. Yes, Dacu would be proven wrong over the march of the century, but alas, he would not be afforded the pleasure of admitting it.

Thirty-six

DAVID WAS USUALLY fast asleep by the time Mamgu came to bed, but not tonight. He lay uneasily on his back, for the first time in his life incapable of sleep. Earlier that day, he had attended his first funeral, as Dacu was laid to rest. He'd felt very sad, but to his vague disappointment he hadn't cried. Neither had his Mami nor his Dadi much at all. Mamgu, on the other hand, had cried her eyes out, which he could not understand. He decided that the rules of the crying game were just too confusing. As he lay in bed staring at the faint but familiar fantasies depicted on the ceiling by decades of dampening and drying, the happenings of the day weighed heavily on him. He had missed Dacu from the day he'd died, but the burial represented a finality that had hit him hard. Regarding the pivotal role he had played in Dacu's final hours, he had experienced very mixed emotions, which had intensified since the burial. Now the funeral was over, he was unsettled too by the changes he knew would ensue. Quietly, Mamgu addressed one of them.

"David, you are awake, aren't you?"

"Yes, Mamgu."

"I suppose Mammy has already told you that you'll be sleeping in Dacu's room from now on?"

"Yes"

"What's the matter? Don't you want to?"

"No."

"C'mon David bach, you're going to have to get used to sleeping in a room on your own sooner or later, so you might as well start now, don't you think?"

"I suppose so."

Mamgu let him be for a while before consoling him.

"Dacu was very old, David, and he'd had a wonderful life, thanks to you in large part. You should try and look at it that way and then you won't feel so sad."

David had been waiting for the slightest reassurance before getting one subject in particular off his chest.

"But Mamgu, if I had looked after him properly on Sunday, he wouldn't have died. You told me to take care of him and I still let him go up to the top with Ifor Williams. I really tried to stop him... but he wouldn't listen."

Mamgu took her time to answer: she knew the importance of getting this just right.

"David, no one's to blame for what happened. You see, Dacu did what he had to do and that's all there is to it. I don't know why he wanted to go up to the top on Sunday, but I do know no one could have stopped him... and in any case, if anyone's to blame, it's me. I'm the one who drove him out of the house. I was getting at him, wasn't I, and he couldn't stand it any longer. You know that! He was very old, David, and not at all well, and what I say is, it must have been a great comfort for him to have you with him when it happened, because he thought the world of you."

Though bright enough not to be completely convinced, David was still young enough to be reassured by Mamgu's words. The conversation brought his thoughts back to Dacu's final plea, a subject which had occupied him regularly over the last few days. He had decided he might have difficulty making Mamgu see sense, as Dacu had put it, so instead he had taken another tack and had hit on what he thought was the perfect answer.

"Mamgu?" he half whispered nervously.

"Yes, David bach?"

"I've decided I'd like to learn to speak Welsh."

Mamgu didn't say a word, and suddenly worried that he may

have got things wrong, neither did David. The familiar forms discernible on the ceiling even after dark evolved into sinister shapes, as doubts devoured David's mind.

"That's wonderful news, David. I know I shouldn't say this just after Dacu's funeral, but you've made me very happy. You've no idea."

For a moment only, David felt both foolish and relieved.

"I am so happy… so happy, David. What made you think of it?"

David was still quite nervous but growing in confidence, and slipped surprisingly comfortably into his little white lies, knowing now that they were very white indeed.

"Well, Dacu spoke Welsh and I thought he would have liked it if I sort of took his place. Now that I know it makes you happy, that's good too."

"That's a lovely thought, David. Dacu would be so proud of you. Would you like me to teach you? I don't think Mami would mind, would she?"

"Well, you're the obvious one, Mamgu, and I'm sure Mami would like it a lot if you did."

For Mamgu, his reply was golden, as was the silence that followed. This was a surprisingly happy ending to a sad day and she was keen now to savour it in what was the rare quiet of her mind.

"Don't you think it's time to go to sleep now, David? Nos da, 'te."

No, David didn't think so… not just yet, anyway. Buoyed by Mamgu's enthusiasm and feeling less nervous than expected under cover of darkness, he decided to grasp the nettle that Dacu had described in detail a few hours before he died. He started obliquely.

"Mamgu, you mentioned just now how you upset Dacu last Sunday. Well, when you upset him… or, for that matter, anyone else in the house… you upset me as well. Did you hear me, Mamgu?"

No response, no encouragement, but he came to the point anyway.

"You've always been lovely to me, Mamgu, but every time you upset Mami, you upset me too. I know you don't mean to, but I wish you would try not to."

Still no response for a while, and when it came it confused him. Mamgu was crying and her sobs bubbled out in little bursts. Suddenly he didn't know what to do or say. He felt the situation had got out of control, but just as he wished he hadn't said a word, Mamgu helped him out.

"David, don't be worried. I'm all right, really. It's only that one minute I felt so happy and the next just as guilty. I couldn't control myself, I'm sorry," and here a burst of sobbing briefly threw her off her stride. She continued amidst sniffles and the occasional sigh, "But it's good that you said what you did. I'm sure that from now on, whenever I feel unkindness coming over me, I'll think of what you said, and I know it'll help."

This episode reminded David of Mamgu's prolific weeping at the funeral, and he realised he was beginning to understand the rules of the crying game. Relieved at Mamgu's reaction, he relaxed, and the shapes on the ceiling settled down to more familiar forms.

"Nos da, Mamgu."

"Nos da, David."

Thirty-seven

APPROXIMATELY THREE WEEKS later, Myfanwy and Edgar were waiting to sing at a St David's Day concert in Bala, while an official made a string of announcements. Myfanwy still couldn't believe she was there on stage, and really regretted it now. She felt quite peculiar, and deeply resented what she judged to be Edgar's interference. He was the one who had agreed to perform at this charity concert, but apparently a little bird had told the organisers that she was pretty good as well. Would she please join Edgar for a few songs? They'd only asked her four days ago, so she could easily have made an excuse, but she hadn't. She knew for a fact that Edgar had put them up to it, and had known full well why he would have done so. What's more, she'd been quite aware that if she accepted, there might well be uncomfortable consequences. Despite all this, she'd still agreed to sing. What had come over her, she wondered?

The official milked her moment. Meanwhile, Myfanwy could just imagine Edgar's smug satisfaction at seeing Peter there, sandwiched between his Taid and Anti Enid. She cringed at the thought. While Edgar had sung his solos, Myfanwy had focused on Peter's face from her seat at the back of the stage. For four days, she'd steeled herself for this, but still she'd been hopelessly unprepared for her son's lapdog look: he'd been transfixed by his father's charisma on stage. As Edgar had bowed repeatedly to acknowledge the audience's accolades, pride had painted Peter's darkish face, but did she detect the odd wave of confusion as well? She wasn't surprised that Peter may have wondered why he'd never heard his father sing like this before. She'd found it remarkable too, given the chapel's central role in all their lives, but Edgar never seemed to sing his heart out along with the rest of the congregation in the hymns, nor did he participate in the chapel's small local eisteddfodau. Why would he not want to impress in the chapel, as he did when he competed? Another imponderable, another piece in an enigma that had been Edgar since the birth of their son. As for Peter not having heard his father sing at a major eisteddfod, there was nothing mysterious about that, because she, Myfanwy, had seen to it. It had been part of her plan to distance him from his father's morose and self-centred personality. Now, at what she feared would turn out to be a pivotal point in Peter's life, she worried that she'd erred in shielding him. Yet, she along with her family had felt it had been her duty, and eerily, Edgar had gone along with it.

Myfanwy sensed the official finally winding down. Peter's face was relaxed again as he chatted to Taid and Anti Enid. Yet, his earlier confusion continued to dog Myfanwy, and she began to fret that, at any rate, she shouldn't have shielded her son for so long. Should Peter grow to resent that, all she could tell him was that, for better or for worse, she'd done what she had thought was best. She had to assume that this shift on Edgar's part implied that as a father he'd be passive no longer. In light of this, didn't it make sense that in the future, her protection of Peter would be less ambitious and therefore less intense? For a moment, she actually felt relief at the thought that she'd bend with the wind a bit more. Yet, her mind kept returning to her original interpretation of Edgar's move as a ploy and gross interference, and each time her mind returned to this thought, her resentment grew. She wondered if Rhiannon had anything to do with all this; but if so, wouldn't she be at the concert? In any case, now that Peter had seen his father at his best, and had clearly been impressed... Hey, wait a minute! Two could play at that game. She too would shine and show her son a thing or two.

"Ladies and gentlemen! Now, here's Edgar again, this time with a partner from Tryweryn. Please give a warm welcome to Mr and Mrs Edgar Evans!"

"Mr and Mrs? Really! What a cheek," Myfanwy thought angrily

Suddenly, she felt so combative that it frightened her a bit. She attacked the first duet and grabbed it by the throat. What she lacked in technique, she more than made up with her power and purity of voice. Myfanwy astonished the audience, few of whom had heard her rich contralto voice before. Their applause was thunderous; she knew it was largely hers, and that pleased her. She squeezed her fists in self-congratulation, and repeated her coup in the second duet. Somehow, the second applause was even more satisfying, as it confirmed that the first was no fluke. She scanned the crowd for faces that she knew, and settled on Peter's. She was shocked to find that he was deep in thought; indifferent to her triumph was how she saw it. With horror, she realised that there was something in that particular pose that reminded her of his father.

"He's moping for the first time in his life," she thought, "And that's no coincidence, is it?"

She felt helpless and also sad. The chairwoman rose to announce their third and final song, Schubert's "Ave Maria". Myfanwy saw Taid turn excitedly to Peter, who was roused from his reverie. She could have read Taid's lips, if she'd needed to.

"This was the song your Mam and Dad sang at their wedding," without doubt was what he said. Yet, how trivial, she thought, was that rendering in comparison to the emotional one she'd sung to Edgar at the dinner table. Two days after that, though, she'd been spurned just as before. She shuddered at the thought of his cold indifference, and was fired up again. Her selfish, self-centred husband may have turned the tables on her today, but she would sing this "Ave Maria" with the same passion as she'd sung at the table, just to remind him what their impasse was really all about. Power gave way to pathos. She gave the crowd a heart-rending performance and earned a standing ovation. Well, they'd both earned it, but she knew deep down that though the crowd may have heard two voices, they'd really only listened to one.

She hadn't bargained for this reception, and it overwhelmed her. Again she clenched her fists in triumph, and then waved excitedly, especially at Peter who seemed himself again. His smile was the smile she'd known for years. Broad and infectious, it betrayed no concern. For those few moments, she felt fantastic, but it was fleeting. She'd known for the last few days that this concert would be a revelation to Peter, and soon, that reality again set in. She'd definitely underestimated the effect that all this would have on her. She'd never thought that her husband could get under her skin like this. She hoped, she really hoped she could cope with it. It was a worry, and yet, she was the one who'd agreed to sing.

Peter's bedtime had been delayed by Taid's glowing, drawn-out descriptions of Myfanwy's exploits. By the time Peter scrambled upstairs, it was gone nine, and his room was dark. He struggled into his pyjamas and then knelt by the only window. His shoulders shook as he felt a little chill. As it happened, his mother needn't have worried about him resenting being shielded from his father. It was true that he had wondered why he'd never heard his father sing like that before, but he hadn't dwelt on it. He'd felt no resentment, for as far as he was concerned, his childhood had been happy and complete. He'd accepted that his father's role so far had been minor; it hadn't been a big thing at all, and in his mind, his father's increased role in the future wouldn't be either. Yes, indeed, Peter had been seduced by his dad's charisma in concert and not surprisingly he wished to identify with it.

Actually, as Myfanwy had noticed from the stage, it hadn't been quite as smooth as that. During the performance, Peter had actually considered the consequences of his decision to spend time with his father. In particular, he'd worried about Taid and Anti Enid.

"Will they mind," he'd wondered, "If they don't see quite as much of me? I don't think so, because I'll still want to be with them a lot, and though Mam and Dad don't get along that well, she looks so happy and excited singing with him now, that I'm sure she won't mind either."

As his Dad, and then his Mam, had wowed the crowd in Welsh, these had been the thoughts behind Peter's expressions. His thoughts had mistaken his Mam's enthusiasm for approval of his Dad, and his expressions had been mistaken for indifference by his Mam.

"Here comes Rhiannon," he thought, laughing to himself as he lay in bed. Her step was heavier than the others, heavier even than Taid's, and she always managed somehow to find every squeak on the stairs. Peter knew them all, so he recognised exactly which stair Rhiannon was on. Nain was the easiest of all to spot. She'd just gone to bed, and as usual had played the prettiest rhythm. Nain was getting on a bit, so she took one stair at a time: her right foot up was followed by the left, right foot up was followed by the left. Peter loved that rhythm. He sat up and stepped to the window again.

"I wonder how Anti Enid's would sound?" he asked himself, as he recognised the flickering light in her window, far away across the valley. At last, he was beginning to feel sleepy, but nevertheless he panned across the valley to the right, and settled his gaze on a solitary light.

"I thought Dad might have stayed for dinner tonight. I know he doesn't usually, but I mean... after the concert and all... well... "

He ran out of words, and turned to the safety of the stars. Each clear night for weeks, he'd traced the Big Dipper, and each time he'd pinpointed Polaris, and thought of Taid.

"I wonder what Taid will talk to me about tomorrow afternoon?"

It didn't occur to him that perhaps Taid would want to talk about the changes that might materialise from today's startling event. Why should it have, because it wasn't a big thing, really. Not a big thing? Big enough, he would discover, to tamper with his temperament, shake his self-assurance and complicate his life... that's all!

He flopped into bed, and when he'd settled, he became vaguely aware of voices in the kitchen down below. He was as good with intonations as with patterns on the stairs, but these voices were stifled. As he fell asleep, he was halfway to wondering why Mam and Taid where whispering in this way.

Downstairs, the fire was almost out. In the light of a single candle, Myfanwy was tidying the kitchen the best she could, and Taid hovered. She couldn't believe how he'd gone on about her voluptuous voice, as he'd called it. Poor Taid! He'd meant well, but how was he to know that her memories of the day were at best, bittersweet... and still he hovered.

"You wouldn't mind if I asked you something, would you Taid?"

"Of course not, Myfanwy," as he moved closer and squeezed her hand, "Come and sit down for a minute."

Once at the table, Myfanwy leant forward and continued in a whisper.

"Well, Taid, it's just that I'm very surprised that you don't seem at all upset at what went on today. You saw Peter in awe of his father. I'm afraid nothing will be the same around here anymore, but you seem untroubled. For example, when "Ave Maria" was announced this afternoon, I remember I was so upset, and yet, when you turned to Peter at that moment, you seemed so carefree."

"Oh, Myfanwy fach!" and he squeezed her hand again.

"Please, Taid, keep your voice down..."

After that, he whispered too... at least most of the time.

"Oh, Myfanwy, I'm really sorry, but you know, there is an explanation. You see, I've been getting the feeling from Peter that perhaps shielding him from his father is beginning to do more harm than good, so I've been trying to change and regularly mentioning Edgar in our conversations. I was going to talk to you about it a few days ago, but then you agreed to sing at the concert. It was obvious then that Peter would be there to see his father perform, so I just assumed that you were beginning to feel the same way as me. I remember feeling quite pleased, actually. Oh, Myfanwy! Of course, I feel terrible now."

Myfanwy certainly felt terrible, and couldn't decide if she was justified in feeling a little let down by Taid.

"I don't know what it is, Taid, but I just can't stand the thought of Edgar coming... "

"So why did you agree to sing, then, if you feel like that?" in a distinctly louder voice.

"Well, the trouble is I can't win, can I? I mean, protecting Peter was becoming a strain, and of course, I agree with you really, that going on like this will soon do more harm than good, especially if Edgar is determined to get more involved, and to be honest, I never thought at the time that seeing Peter in awe of his miserable father would get under my skin so much... and that'll happen all the time now. Ugh! The man makes me sick. So you see, I just can't win. I just... I don't... quite... "

Myfanwy so muddled, and uncharacteristically venomous, took Elfed by surprise. He'd never thought of her as anything but strong and sensible, and was reluctant to change his mind.

"She's just tired after the singing, that's all," he rationalised, and the thought of her powerful performance restored Myfanwy to her pedestal in his mind.

"Come on, Myfanwy fach! You'll feel better soon, you'll see. You had to shield your boy, but now you've got to let go a little, I think. To my mind, you've always been very sensible, so I know you'll do this right. Come on! You'll feel fine tomorrow, you'll see."

It was not unreasonable of Elfed to hold this view, but he was wrong... so very wrong!

"And in any case," he continued in the same optimistic vein, "I'll take care of Peter for you."

Myfanwy failed to suppress a sardonic smile. Had he noticed it, Taid just might have linked its irony to his advancing age... but he was tired too.

Myfanwy's venom left her in distress, while the object of it slept like a child. Edgar had even forgotten to snuff his candle out, an oversight that spoke of a quiet mind.

Contrary to Myfanwy's conviction, Edgar had not been the instigator of the day's events. It was the organisers who'd suggested approaching her, but admittedly on this occasion, Edgar hadn't dissuaded them as he had done many times before. The time had come, he'd felt, for Myfanwy to face up to things. For a while now, his mother Rhiannon had nagged him for neglecting his son. He'd had to brush her off, of course, but no longer. Myfanwy had had her own way: for eight years he'd uncomplainingly played her game, so that now in forcing the issue, he'd done so with a clear conscience. The terms of his deal with God were ambiguous. The bit about the chapel was clear enough, but how long was he expected to play second fiddle to Myfanwy when it came to their son? There'd been no mention of a time limit, and by now he felt strongly that he'd done his bit. These days, he had little trouble convincing himself that the terms of the deal had been met. Of course, it didn't hurt that over the years his fear of having fathered an illegitimate child had eroded. In fact by now, he felt sure that he was in the clear, but he would continue to attend the chapel... just in case!

Actually, Myfanwy's acceptance of the invitation to sing hadn't really surprised him. Very early in their marriage, he'd had to accept that she was a much stronger person than he'd bargained for. He was certain that this adjustment would be easy for her. He would be wrong... so very wrong, but why should he care? His conscience was clear, and he slept like a child.

As a beneficiary of it, Enid too was well aware of Myfanwy's inner strength. That evening, she repeatedly sought reassurance from it, and just as often failed. Her candle, too, flickered unusually late into that night. She was haunted by the horror that had settled for an instant on Myfanwy's face that afternoon on stage. It had to have been an emotional day, of course, and yet, Enid had never seen her friend frightened like that before. She worried about it, late into the night, and she was right to do so... so very right!

In the end, Enid fell asleep, even with Myfanwy on her mind.

So, but for Enid, everyone seemed to think that Myfanwy would be fine. Even she herself had thought so, until that moment when Peter's lapdog look had unnerved her. She had never assumed that dealing with a change in Edgar's role would be easy, but she was confident that she could handle it. Otherwise she wouldn't have so readily agreed to sing, but Peter's look... that lapdog look... reflected an admiration that frightened her. It foreshadowed an affinity with his father that put his whole carefully orchestrated childhood at risk, and there was nothing she could do about it now. She felt cornered, and in her hopelessness, she blamed it all on Edgar and felt anger towards him. It was certain that she would now see more of

Edgar than before, and not only in person, but also on Peter's face. The prospect horrified her, but still she felt she could probably bear it, because she'd borne such things before. Peter must never become aware of her feeling, though. It would be unfair to burden him with her pain. Altruism in part, but also pride, because deep down she knew that in this phase of her struggle with Edgar, she did not monopolise the moral high ground as she'd done before. Now, if Peter was to be in the dark, then presumably Taid would be as well, for Taid would talk, simply because he'd feel that it would help. So Enid would be the one: she would be her confidante, as usual. Enid would respect her wishes. She was right... Enid would, whether she questioned her motives or not.

Thus Myfanwy stewed, while Enid was worrying that she would, and while three others slept, quite certain that she wouldn't. Things wouldn't always be this bad. After all, she'd had a shock and was still recovering from it. Her life would go on, but the impact of that lapdog look, and her unfortunate overreaction to it, would affect her in varying degrees forever.

The next day was Myfanwy's birthday. She felt no joy, and the weather reflected her gloom. Still, while Peter was at school, she visited Enid, and during their chat, justified her friend's worst fears. As Myfanwy walked home, she felt a measure of relief, but her surroundings were not encouraging, their portents far from fair. The trees were bare and the clouds low, the river dark and each sheep a show of resignation. Even the footbridge seemed more shaky than usual, but good old Arenig Fawr was still there, although she couldn't be sure of that either. The cloud cover today lay well below its north shoulder.

Thirty-eight

I T WAS FOUR months later; Peter was excited. He stood
tiptoe on a bale of straw at the back of the barn, craning his
neck for a better view. Soon he tired and his body relaxed, but
before long his short-cropped head of dark brown hair popped
up again. Ahead of him stood at least three dozen people, mostly
men, murmuring but often shouting and raising and pumping
their fists. At the front, on another bale, stood his dad. His dad!
It was hard to believe that his dad was the star of this show. He
rarely focused on how his father looked, but here in this exciting
atmosphere, his dad's dark complexion framed by fairly long,
wavy, rich red hair could hardly fail to make an impression on
him. Yes, Peter was excited!

Everyone here seemed to like his dad. At least, they'd
appeared to until he mentioned south Wales. Peter didn't catch
his father's comment, but a lady's voice stood out, questioning.

"Isn't all this stuff about south Walians way off the mark?
And aren't you persisting with it because it's self-serving?"

A few men's voices agreed with her, and then many more
told them quite harshly to shut up and give the speaker a chance,
but the lady wouldn't listen, and then she and her friends were
thrown out of the barn and told to go to hell, and his dad carried
on saying rude things about south Walians to further shouting
and raising and pumping of fists. Peter had the impression that
his dad was saying the same thing over and over and over…

Peter became sleepier and sleepier. It was late for him, and
anyway, it didn't help that he couldn't understand what his dad
was on about. The stuff at the beginning had been all right,
because he and Taid had talked about those things: the language

and feeling Welsh and all that, but this stuff about south Wales was new to him. He wondered why Taid hadn't brought it up. He would ask Taid about it tomorrow on the way to school, or perhaps he'd talk to Mam tonight. Oh! He felt really sleepy now, but he had to stay awake… for Dad. What a horrible feeling it was, obviously horrible enough for one of the ladies just in front of him to notice, and gently help him to the ground before setting his head on the bale. Oh, she felt so nice, and smelt nice too. He would have wished she wouldn't leave had he not fallen straight to sleep.

Peter was laid on the floor at the front of the cart where his father could see him, and was partly covered by a sack. Through the familiar melange of mealy smells came the occasional waft of that lovely lady's scent. It had been half past nine by the time his dad had carried him from the barn, but it was still light. Peter vaguely remembered Taid talking to him recently about the longest day of the year. The cart settled into the horse's rocking action; normally a perfect backdrop for drifting into sleep, but his dad had given a couple of young men a lift up the valley and they talked nonstop. Actually, Peter didn't mind that much, because they were going over the meeting, and he sort of liked to hear little snippets in between waves of sleepiness. They too seemed to be talking a lot about south Walians, and not very nicely either. What was it all about? He really would have to ask Taid the first chance he got, but it was funny, wasn't it, that his dad, the expert, wasn't saying a word on the subject. He hadn't said much on the way to the meeting either, when it had been just the two of them. His dad was strange like that. Well, his dad was strange all round, really, but he didn't mind. He was sure all his friends would die to have a famous dad like him. That was a nice thought to have as another snatch of scent carried him off to sleep.

Taid didn't feel himself the following morning. As he'd got out of bed, he'd had a funny turn, the third in as many weeks. Once again his chest was tight and he felt so exhausted that there was no question of him accompanying Peter to the train. Nor was Taid at the halt to meet him after school. The upshot was that by the time the family met at teatime in the kitchen, the business about south Walians was far from Peter's mind, which is where it stayed. His mam debated whether or not to broach the little matter of last night's meeting: her instinct was to refrain, for she feared that what she'd hear would not please her. As indeed with anything to do with Edgar, her preference was detachment, but in this instance, curiosity won the day. Perhaps it was because she was more on edge than usual, on account of Taid's funny turn.

"Your eyes look really tired, Peter," she began circuitously, so as not to appear curious. Rhiannon next to her, and Taid across the table, were unmoved and carried on chewing their bread and jam. Peter smiled slightly.

"I don't think it's a good idea, you know, to be out so late when you've got school the next day."

The reprimand, of course, was an indirect rap at Edgar. Myfanwy's persistent inability to reconcile herself to what she saw as her husband's interference in their lives had by now nurtured a deep resentment. Usually though, she managed to give unrevealing vent to it with innocent remarks such as that.

"No, Mam, you're right."

"What did you say about being out late, Myfanwy?" from Taid, now aroused, "Oh, yes, of course, Peter! You were with your Dad last night."

At least something was going right! Myfanwy had been betting that Taid would take up the running for her.

"Did you enjoy the meeting?"

"It was all right."

"Come on, Peter! What was the most exciting thing that happened?"

"I don't know, Taid! Well, I suppose a few people did get thrown out of the barn."

That remark caught everyone's attention, and Myfanwy's in particular. She failed to contain her curiosity.

"What d'you mean, Peter," she asked pressingly, "Thrown out? Who got thrown out?"

Peter glanced around the table self-consciously. That which had been far from his mind came tumbling to the fore again. He remembered now how he'd wanted to ask Taid about that business to do with south Walians, but not in front of everyone, like this, and certainly not in front of Rhiannon, because she could get carried away and wasn't always gentle. He tried to divert the question.

"Oh, Mam! I really don't know what happened... honestly!"

But the hounds at the table had hit upon a scent, so the fox had little option, for no way would they relent. Peter rushed through his story, intent only, it seemed, on demonstrating to his mother that he honestly had no idea what it was really all about.

"Good old Edgar," exclaimed Rhiannon several times during the telling, and when it was over, "No one enjoys putting other people down, but with something as important as this, somebody's got to say it. Good old Edgar, that's what I say!"

Peter was perplexed, and his face showed it; Myfanwy's was a mask, as she bit her tongue.

"Mam," said Peter, still seeking to redeem himself, "You can see that I didn't really know what was happening. You can, can't you?"

Myfanwy's rush of maternal warmth was immediately

swamped by a sharp reminder, from deep within, of her general frustration.

"Yes, yes, Peter," she responded gamely, "I believe you, don't worry. It's a complicated matter."

"It's not complicated at all," from Rhiannon like a shot, "It's as simple as ABC. Wales is a small country. You know that, Peter, and there aren't many of us. England is huge in comparison, and has done everything it can to get rid of us and our language. In fact, the only way we've been able to avoid being swamped by the bloody Engli… "

"Watch your language, Rhiannon, please, and in front of the boy and everything. I know how… "

Taid failed to stop his daughter-in-law, but at least she respected his specific request.

"All right, Taid! All right. As I was saying, the only way we've survived this long is by sticking together, standing up for our culture and loving our language… and not all of us are doing that any more. In fact, millions of south Walians have left the language in the lurch, after generations of Welsh heroes have given their lives for it. It's a scandal, and someone has to speak out about it. So you see, Peter, that's what your father was on about, and whoever didn't agree with him deserved to be thrown out of the barn. That's what I say, anyway. Good old Edgar!"

Peter heard every word, and understood most, but was embarrassed by Rhiannon's confrontational tone. He stared at his hands, and consequently didn't notice Taid's jumpy reaction to Myfanwy's little kick under the table; nor her silent but explicit appeal to Taid to counter Rhiannon; nor Taid's dismissal of it. Peter stared at his hands until mercifully Nain appeared and broke the ice. Fresh from her nap, she'd been eager for conversation, and the others, relieved, hastened to oblige. Even Myfanwy played along, despite her anger at Rhiannon, her running resentment of Edgar and her conviction that she'd lost another round.

A little later, Myfanwy contrived to be alone with Peter in the kitchen. Ignoring again her preferred policy of detachment, she had decided to probe Peter further on last evening's meeting. Better if she'd waited for her anger to abate, but she needed a fillip, and took a risk.

"So you had a good time last night, did you?"

"Yes, Mam, it was all right."

She took encouragement from that.

"So what did Dad talk about, Peter?"

"Well, you heard what I said, Mam, about the south Wal..."

"No, no, Peter. What I meant was what did he talk about when you were together in the cart?"

"Not much, Mam. You know Dad doesn't have much to say. He hardly said a word even when those two boys went on and on about his speech. He's strange like that, isn't he?"

Myfanwy began to feel vindicated.

"Well, Dad is strange all round, really, if it comes to that."

She couldn't believe this. It had never occurred to her that Peter might have reservations about Edgar. She'd assumed that his famous lapdog look implied unqualified admiration, but it wasn't so. Perhaps she could live with this situation after all. "Speak on, my son! Confirm this fragile feeling."

"I don't mind though, Mam. It's still nice to do more things with Dad. I bet my friends wish they had a famous dad like me."

Fragile her feeling, indeed. She hated to hear him speak of Edgar so. Her hopes had been raised, but in the end her risk taking had backfired. Resentment resurfaced, and tension returned. Months of pent-up hopelessness threatened to explode.

"Not in front of Peter, Myfanwy," she begged of herself, "This is a cross that I myself must bear."

Heroically, she smiled if only briefly at her son, and then swiftly turned towards the window. She couldn't bear the thought of this for the rest of her life. She felt a desperate need to let off steam. She felt like shouting someone's head off, but not Peter's, please.

Behind her, there was a crash. It made her jump, her nerves jangled, she spun around.

"I'm sorry, Mam," quite calmly from Peter, "It's just one of those old cups. It was cracked al... "

"Just... one of those cups?"

Myfanwy was beside herself.

"Is that what you said? Just... one of those cups? A cup is a cup. They don't grow on trees, you know."

By anyone's standard, Myfanwy was maniacal.

"What's come over you? I'm finding I can't depend on you anymore. Just... one of those cups? Honestly! I'm sure you wouldn't say that if you had to buy a new one out of your own pocket. Now, brush up the pieces and leave me alone!"

Had she been aware of the hurt across Peter's bewildered face, she may have relented, but all she saw was red. There! She'd let off steam! For a few seconds, she'd felt fantastic, but now, already, she felt terrible about her son. Her only consolation was the likelihood that he wouldn't link her outburst to her hatred of his father. It was very important that he'd never have to deal with that.

It was much later that same evening. Rhiannon and Peter had both just gone to bed, and now Nain was on her way as well, playing her pretty rhythm on the stairs. As usual, Taid dallied in the kitchen so as not to rush his wife. He was quietly joined at the table by Myfanwy, now mellower in remorse.

"You're feeling a bit better now, aren't you Taid," she said softly, "It's good that you recover quickly, but don't you think you should talk to Doctor?"

"Oh, I don't think so, Myfanwy; not now, anyway. Lots of people have funny turns, and if mine don't get any worse than this, I can cope."

Myfanwy took his hands, lent forward and whispered.

"Taid, I was surprised that you let Rhiannon get away with that stuff at teatime."

"Well, I didn't feel a hundred percent, did I? I might have tackled her otherwise."

"Yes, yes, of course! That did occur to me, and I'm not saying that she's completely wrong, but nothing like that can possibly be as black and white as she makes it out to be."

"Well, there's Rhiannon for you. There's no grey in her life, is there, nor in Edgar's either, for that matter."

"I suppose really I was hoping that you'd have said something for Peter's sake. Last night he heard his father, a father whom he seems to adore, express extreme views about south Walians, views that are irrational and unfair. Tonight, he heard the very same from Rhiannon, but he hasn't heard the other side, has he? And he needs to!"

Taid nodded his head in understanding.

"I'm sorry, Myfanwy. I just didn't feel up to it. In any case, I've got my own plans for making the opposite case."

Taid rubbed his hands and smiled wickedly, obviously pleased, both with himself and the urgent enquiry on the face across the table. It seemed appropriate for him now to take Myfanwy's hands.

"No, Myfanwy, I can't tell you. Just be patient, all right? Look, I'd better go to bed now, but before I go, I hope you don't mind me telling you that I couldn't help overhearing you shouting at Peter just after teatime. Myfanwy, you mustn't let

Rhiannon get under your skin, nor Edgar either, and if they do, for goodness sake don't take it out on the boy."

Myfanwy wasn't so ashamed of herself as to be incapable of gratitude towards Taid for immediately going to bed.

Meanwhile, Peter lay awake in bed, licking wounds which had lasted longer than any in his life hitherto. Nothing made sense. Mam had never blown up like that before, and anyway, he hadn't done anything that bad. He was confused and upset. Not even Nain's song on the stairs had given him any pleasure. Taid had just gone to bed too, but what a boring song he played. Taid had once said that his climb upstairs to bed was a daily test. As long as he could do it without stopping, he felt pretty sure that he'd wake up the next morning, alive and well. With his life put on the line like that, it wasn't surprising that over the years, Taid had slowed his pace quite a bit, but so far he'd never stopped. Oh dear, Mam was coming up now. Normally her rhythm was quick and decisive, yet very light, but tonight it felt different, as if there was hesitation in her step. Oh no! She was stopping right outside his door. He became alert, for he was unsure of what to expect. He wasn't even sure if he wanted to see her, and then quietly she came in.

Looking back on it all the following morning, he felt shame at having doubted her. He should have known better, he kept on telling himself. He hated himself for having been surprised when she had eased herself onto his bed, with her head next to his, crying in his ear and whispering over and over how sorry she was for blowing up, and how she hated to hurt him, because that was the last thing she wanted to do, but she had a lot on her mind, and he just happened to be around when it all became too much for her, that's all. Yes, he hated himself for doubting her, but he loved thinking about her in his room last night, especially the bit when she'd stopped talking and just held him tight. Come to think of it, he didn't remember Mam leaving his bedroom. A lovely, warm feeling raced up and down his spine as he realised that she must have held him till he'd gone to sleep. He glanced at her across the breakfast table. He decided that perhaps he wouldn't mind his mother blowing up again. It might be worth it, just to have her say that she was sorry. It wasn't too long before his theory was put to the test, and of course, it didn't hold water. Yet, there was no question that what would become his Mam's habitual venting would have been much harder to stomach had she even once not told him that she was sorry.

Thirty-nine

HIS FUNNY TURN had shaken Taid a little bit more than he'd let on. He wished it hadn't happened so soon after the one before. Disappointing too, was his slower rate of recovery, and with inactivity came reflections on mortality but these were not as morbid in his case as they might be, for although he'd cooled on the chapel, his religious convictions were as ardent as ever. Besides, Taid was tough, so it didn't take much of an improvement in his energy level to restore his spirits. By the following Saturday, he was back into his stride and wasted little time in pursuing the fulfillment of his promise to Myfanwy. "Making the opposite case" had become his signature goal. Actually, in Taid's plan for today, not only would Peter be put right on the issue of south Walians, but also entrusted with the responsibility of carrying on the tradition of the little red dragon.

Just after breakfast, Myfanwy glanced through the kitchen window. Taid was in deep discussion with Peter in the farmyard. Then off they went together, only to reappear soon with a horse. Peter led it proudly, and then under Taid's animated direction began to dress it, obviously in preparation for hitching to the cart.

Myfanwy, clearly worried, hurried outside.

"What's going on, Peter?" she demanded.

Peter peered underneath the horse's belly.

"I don't know, Mam. I'm just following Taid's instructions, that's all."

Taid held the bridle loosely while the horse gently bucked its head. He didn't wait to be asked, and with a finger to his lips, whispered, "Remember what we were talking about the other night, Myfanwy? Making the opposite case?"

The warmth that lit Myfanwy's face didn't last long; she frowned questioningly.

Taid anticipated her enquiry again.

"Sorry, Myfanwy, I'm still not going to tell you."

Evidently, whatever the scheme, Myfanwy's approval of its end was overwhelmed by fear of the means. Taid's friendly, slightly wicked smile shrivelled in the face of her impatient response.

"Please, Taid, stop playing around, will you? I'm worried enough about you, but there's more to it than that. I mean, Peter is only a child, and… "

"OK, OK, Myfanwy, fair enough," interrupted Taid, "We're going for a ride up to the lake," and he nodded towards Arenig Fawr, "Now, are you happy?"

Myfanwy eyed him, her antennae clearly on full alert. Her pose was taut and eyes restless. She was obviously thinking at breakneck speed, and she seemed to be on the verge of speaking. Perhaps the prospect of making the opposite case to Peter proved irresistible, for in the end she just pursed her lips, nodded and waved briefly as she turned towards the farmhouse. Taid glanced at Peter, raised his eyebrows and they shared a conspiratorial smile. What a huge relief it was that he hadn't been pressed to tell her more: to tell her that he was going to climb with Peter to the north shoulder of Arenig Fawr; show him his little red dragon tattoo; sit on the spot where he and his special friend had gazed at their valley countless times, and let the wonder of it all wash over them; tell him the tale of the fork that had split their special friendship; relate Wyn Williams's visit and the news he'd brought of this special friend named Edward Jones; describe the circumstances under which Edward's granddaughter had not been brought up in Welsh; explain that if this could have happened in Edward's family, then it could happen to anyone; and conclude that the decline of the Welsh language should not be carelessly blamed on south Walians, but attributed mainly to circumstances beyond their control. Yes, it was a great relief that she hadn't pressed, but grief was soon to follow.

After two hours and a quarter, and still no sign of Peter and Taid, Myfanwy could stand it no longer. She'd had a funny feeling about it all from the start, and now to make matters worse, dark clouds had gathered and the wind had shifted. She should have pressed Taid further because she'd had a feeling then that he wasn't telling all. She'd wanted him to put Peter right, of course, but how on earth was he going to do it? It was important that someone should make the opposite case, but what knowledge in particular did Taid have of south Walians? What made him so confident that he held the key? Regardless, she should have stopped him from going. She should have done this and she shouldn't have done that, but now she was in no doubt what to do. As unpleasant was the prospect, she decided to enrol her husband's support, for she had a growing sense that she'd need assistance. She hurriedly gathered a hat and raincoat, and quickly found Edgar in a field just behind the farmhouse. To her relief, he said he might as well walk the fields below the trail and check on the sheep down there, and meet her up at the lake, all right? Of course it was all right! It couldn't be better... but for the circumstances. She hurried and scurried up the trail, her mind tightly wound, her eyes to the ground for fear of losing her balance. Consequently, she didn't notice the rain on Arenig Fawr, nor the gorse and heather now coming together in colour, nor even Peter's head bobbing erratically over the brow in the distance.

"Mam! Mam, quick!"

Peter's words were garbled in the wind. Myfanwy waved as she started running, desperately craning her elegant neck to hear and predictably, stumbling.

"Quick, Mam! Taid isn't very well. Quick!"

She knew it! But at least Peter was all right.

"He's not moving at all, Mam," from Peter as his mother hugged him, "And he's talking rubbish. It really scared me, because he didn't seem too bad when I left him."

"What d'you mean, you left him?"

Myfanwy's tone bore the tiniest edge, but enough to alarm poor Peter.

"I… I didn't want to leave him, Mam, but he insisted that I climb to the shoulder, and… "

"What? In this weather?"

"No, no, it was fine then, Mam. He kept on asking me to climb to the shoulder, and let the wonder of it all wash over me. That's what he kept on saying to me, Mam, 'Let the wonder of it all wash over you'. The funny thing was that on the way down, I didn't see him till the last minute. That gave me a… "

"So where is Taid then? Where is he, Peter?"

That edge again: faint as before, but he faltered in reply.

"He's a little bit… higher than… the lake, Mam."

"Above the lake? What's he doing… ?"

"He's not far above the lake, Mam, and I came to get you as fast as I could."

She realised to her shame that he was close to tears. She relented, and drew him warmly towards her again.

"I know you did, Peter bach. You know something, I better stop talking or we'll never get to Taid. Hold my hand, all right, and lead me to him," and off they set towards the brow, Myfanwy breathing heavily. At the lake, they were met by rain.

"Up there, Mam. Can you see him? He's not much above the lake, is he? Crikey! There's Dad! That's a bit of luck, isn't it, Mam?"

Her heart sank. It upset her to hear him talking about Edgar with warmth, and as always when she reacted like that, she became upset with herself as well. How could she one minute feel so much love and so much resentment the next? It wasn't fair at all. Edgar was running now, and soon she saw him lift Taid in his arms. By the time Myfanwy and Peter approached the cart, Taid had already been laid in it, and was being wrapped by Edgar in as many sacks as he could find. Suddenly, Peter ran ahead of his mother, and after picking up Taid's stick, helped his dad tuck the sacks around him. That simple gesture could so easily have derailed Myfanwy. Not this time though, for the threat was thrown aside by the combined forces of breathlessness, relief at Peter's safety and urgent concern for Taid.

"Poor Taid!" Myfanwy thought, as she leant over him, "What's he trying to say? Sounds like mumbo jumbo to me, too, and he's shaking like a leaf, poor dab."

She clambered on the cart and consoled Taid as she laid her raincoat over him.

"Come on, Edgar, let's go now, and pass me your cap, will you? Peter, please come up here and hold Taid's hand. That'll help keep him warm, see."

The horse and cart broke into their staccato gait. Myfanwy lay on her side in the cart, snuggling up to Taid, gently rubbing one of his hands, while Peter was consumed with the responsibility of warming the other. Naturally, they all realised the rain had stopped, except for Taid, perhaps, but none noticed the upper slopes of Arenig Fawr break out of the clouds for a few magnificent moments. Again, Taid may have been the exception, for why otherwise would he have mumbled:

"Farewell Arenig Fawr,

You've meant so much to me,

Please impart to Peter here

A love of country free of fear

And devoid of bigotry."

Well, no one will really know if this is what he mumbled. Myfanwy was right at his side, and to her 'twas mumbo jumbo.

Myfanwy made a point of telling Nain what had happened gently, but it seemed to make no difference. The old lady was devastated, and retreated to the fireplace in the kitchen to cry quietly. Myfanwy pitied her, envied her and then pitied her again. For a change, she badly missed Rhiannon, who was at a meeting somewhere to do with the chapel. Myfanwy hurried upstairs ahead of Edgar, who once again had Taid in his arms. Catching her nemesis in an act of such kindness unsettled her, but fortunately, thoughts of poor Nain intervened.

"Poor thing! She's so upset. It must be nice though, to feel like that about... oh, God! I need to let Enid know, don't I?"

While Edgar laid Taid on his bed, she hurried downstairs, and in an urgent whisper instructed Peter to fetch his Anti Enid.

"And if you happen to see Rhiannon, tell her as well. All right?"

A little later, as she tended to Taid, she heard the horse and cart in action once again. Another act of kindness, unsettling as before, for Edgar was off to a farm halfway to Bala, from where he could speak to the doctor on their brand new phone.

"But I'm afraid there's not much even the doctor can do by now."

Taid breathed laboriously in fitful slumber. She gazed sadly at him and found herself wondering if he'd had the chance to make the opposite case. In response, her mind disconcertingly focused on life at the farmhouse without him. She'd considered the prospect vaguely several times before, but this vision was vivid. It depicted a life without a fulcrum, and without balance, especially for the boy. Perhaps Nain wept not for Taid, after all.

A little later, a tearful Enid knelt at Taid's bedside. At the same time, downstairs, Myfanwy tried to console a quietly sobbing Nain. Casually, she glanced outside and noticed Peter pacing without purpose in the farmyard. She felt sick to her stomach when it struck her that he, as much as anyone, might need consoling. In a rush, she imagined his distress and isolation at finding Taid slumped on a desolate slope; his guilt, possibly, at having left him alone at the lake; and grief now, surely, at the thought of losing a real friend for the first time in his life. She was ashamed of her neglect and hurried to redress it. She offered a hand, which he took willingly and led him to the gate at the far end of the farmyard, where they sat on a bench that Taid had built. The warmth of the sun's glow magically defused her grief. She offered Peter a block of Turkish Delight. The treat enhanced their intimacy. She took his hand again and said, "I'm sorry, Peter, that I haven't made much fuss of you since we got home. You must have had such a fright when you came across Taid on the ground, aye?"

Peter flattened his lips, shrugged his shoulders and said nothing.

"I should have stopped him going, shouldn't I, but he should have known better, mind you. It wasn't fair of him to put you in that position."

Myfanwy was curious as to whether Taid had managed to make his case to Peter, but decided wisely not to pursue the matter. She slid forward on the bench, put both her arms around one of his, squeezed it affectionately and hugged him. They sat there, silent, in the sun. Myfanwy felt some peace.

"Mam, Taid showed me his little red dragon."

Myfanwy's heart leapt. So the dragon was part of the ploy? She should have thought of that, but then what? She curbed her curiosity again, and without shifting, simply asked him, "Did you like it?"

"Oh, it was brilliant, Mam."

So wrapped up was Myfanwy in her mission that she never

considered alighting on the sentimental story that underlay the dragon.

"So, did Taid say anything, Peter?" casually.

"Nothing special, Mam. You see, we were going to climb the shoulder together, but he felt funny after getting off the cart. That's when he showed me the dragon."

"Don't tell me he took his shirt off up there by the lake," said Myfanwy, still clutching Peter's arm.

"Yes, almost. He had no strength though, Mam, so when he said that I should climb the shoulder on my own, I refused, but he went on and on about it. He kept on telling me that it was important for me to feel the wonder of it all wash over me. Remember I told you that, Mam?"

Myfanwy nodded.

"When I agreed to go, he perked up a bit and said that when I'd come down again, he'd tell me a story."

"Was the story, whatever it was, going to be part of his ploy as well?" Myfanwy wondered. Regardless, he'd been thwarted. It was certain now that Taid had missed his chance to make the opposite case! It was obvious that he'd never got round to it. Myfanwy was utterly frustrated, but felt for Peter, nevertheless. She couldn't help but admire his sensitivity, his enormous capacity for emotion. Kindly, she encouraged him.

"What was it like up there, Peter?"

"Oh, it was great. There were all these rooks gliding and diving below me. I could have stayed there all day, Mam, but honestly, I wasn't there that long. I can't understand why Taid tried to come after me. He must have been worried, I suppose, but I didn't stay long, Mam. I promise I didn't."

At moments like these, frustration inevitably fares poorly against affection and protection on the maternal scale. Myfanwy held her position close to Peter and squeezed his arm reassuringly as she spoke.

"Peter! Don't be silly, now. I believe you... I really do. In any case, you could see that Taid wasn't thinking straight which is why he was coming to look for you, it was only because he wasn't thinking straight. You didn't do anything wrong, Peter, and I'm very proud of you."

For months now, Myfanwy's energies had been channelled towards surpressing anger and living with resentment. That she was capable of a simple, sincere, loving remark came as such a relief that she choked on her emotions. They were further inflated by the genuine grief that she felt at that moment for Taid. It all became too much; Myfanwy began to sob quietly.

"I've tried so hard to be brave... and just look... "

Her tears tumbled, but she managed to splutter, "Let me stay here for a bit, all right?"

Her sobbing soon subsided, and while her thoughts stayed with Taid, they switched disconcertingly from his fight for life to his failiure to make the opposite case.

"Am I making too much of this?" she wavered, "Am I overestimating Edgar's influence over Peter? No, no, and in any case, if I'm going to go overboard on an issue, this one's as good as any. Edgar's attitude towards south Walians is so typical of him; narrow-minded, uninformed and worse, ungenerous, and I don't want Peter to grow up to be like that! No, you stick with it, Myfanwy. So what was Taid up to then? What knowledge is he privy to that gave him such confidence regarding this business?"

She'd love to take up where Taid had left off, if only she knew his ploy. There was the dragon, of course, and Arenig Fawr's north shoulder. From these two clues, she deduced that Taid's childhood friend Edward was probably involved, but she couldn't take the plot another step further. She would never have heard of Wyn Williams's story. She would ask Enid! Yes, of course, that's what she'd do, but she'd be disappointed, because

Enid hadn't heard it either. She did wonder whether Rhiannon and Nain could point her in the right direction, but Rhiannon wasn't friendly and Nain was far too sad. There was another who certainly could, but it never occurred to Myfanwy to ask him, even when he interrupted her thoughts, as she sat on the bench that Taid had built, with Peter at her side.

"Hello, Doctor," she said warmly as she rose to meet him, still holding Peter's arm, "Thank you so much for coming. Taid isn't at all well, you know."

The doctor had awakened Taid from his slumber. At the time, Myfanwy had wondered whether that had been kind, but now that Taid had brightened up a bit and babbled as before, she'd changed her mind. He still spoke mumbo jumbo mostly, but there were a few discernable words. "bake" or "wake", then "wake him" were the ones he repeated most. As he jabbered, the doctor held his hand.

"He is squeezing my hand every now and then," he said with a wistful smile, and then, "Myfanwy, would you do me a favour? I'd like to have a little drink while I'm here with my friend. I've got a flask of whisky in my pocket, but would you get me a glass of water, please?"

He smiled again, playfully this time, disarming Myfanwy's expression of mild surprise. As soon as she'd left, the doctor lent forward towards Taid and said quite firmly, "Take?" and then, "Take him?"

Taid repeated the doctor's words, and strained pitifully several times in attempts to complete the phrase, but to no avail. Myfanwy was heard returning, already at the foot of the stairs, and the next time Taid said, "Take him," the doctor continued with, "Under your wing?"

Myfanwy was taken aback by the change in Taid. He'd stopped babbling and seemed so peaceful.

"What happened?" she asked with alarm.

"Nothing, Myfanwy. He's still breathing, but more peacefully. Just before you came back now, he squeezed my hand for longer than before, more urgently even, and then he seemed to relax. He must have had a happy thought, I suppose."

The doctor drank most of the water and then doubled up what was left with whisky from his flask. He settled back in his chair, holding Taid's hand once again.

"I'm going to leave you alone with him, Doctor," Myfanwy said, nodding knowingly.

"No, no, stay! It's all right," but she left anyway, which was a pity because who knows what revelations might have leaked in such an intimate setting. How surprising would it have been had 'Take him under your wing' been brought up, and inevitably placed in historical perspective? The doctor would surely then have reminisced freely about politics, Wyn Williams and all.

As he prepared to leave the farmhouse, the doctor dropped in on Nain in the kitchen. He reminded her gently of many of the good times that she and Taid had shared, but a little later in the farmyard, he was much more direct with Myfanwy.

"Myfanwy, I'm sorry but I really don't expect Taid to last the night. He doesn't seem to be in much pain, but if things change… what I mean is that if it seems to you that he's suffering… you've got to come and get me. I know it's a long way, but I'm serious. You know that, don't you Myfanwy?"

Myfanwy nodded gravely. The doctor shook her hand and surprised her when he said, "I noticed you hugging Peter earlier. You know, Taid thinks he's great. He loves to talk about his Peter. My Peter, he calls him. You should be really proud of your son, Myfanwy, but not too proud, I hope, to turn to me if you need any help… or advice, perhaps."

These words unnerved Myfanwy. She couldn't be sure how

much he knew of her domestic difficulties. As a result, rather than gratitude, her reaction reflected confusion and shame.

"Oh, Myfanwy, don't be defensive, please," continued the doctor, "I offered to help only because I thought that's what Taid would have wanted me to do. Come on, now. Come up to the road with me and I'll show you my new car. Come on. Be a sport!"

"No, no, I don't think so. I think I should get home to Taid, and Nain."

What a pity! Myfanwy had retreated twice, and this time from a situation that may have held even more promise of intimacy than the first.

Taid was buried in the same grave as Geraint. The weather was wet but did not dampen the community's desire to pay its respects. Although Taid had not been as active in the chapel as some, he was universally liked and considered to be wise, so his funeral attracted the faithful and agnostic alike. There had been talk of Edgar and Myfanwy singing "Ave Maria", but Myfanwy couldn't bring herself to do that, not even for Taid. A few of those present felt the need to pay tribute to the deceased. The first made reference, rather slyly it was later felt, to the fact that but for the speaker's father, Joseph Jones, Elfed Evans would have held the honour of having been the youngest deacon in the chapel's history. The next recalled Elfed Evans's success not only as a farmer, but as a family man as well. The last but one speaker stirred things up rather when he said that he liked Elfed because he was one of the few deeply religious men he'd met in the valley who was neither pious nor pompous. Then came the doctor.

"Elfed was a close friend, as you know, and I think I knew him well enough to be qualified to tell you that after family and religion, three things... well, two of them were people, actually… stand out as being the most important in his life. First was Edward Jones, his dear boyhood friend, who migrated to south Wales when they were both nineteen, I think. The second was Wyn Williams of Bala, his midlife mentor, and the third, throughout his life, was Arenig Fawr. So I don't feel too badly for Elfed, because even though Edward is far away, his antecedents couldn't be closer by; Wyn Williams is no more than a few miles down river, and of course from his resting place, Elfed will be free to admire the north shoulder of Arenig Fawr whenever he likes. No, I don't feel badly for him. None of us should, because if I know Elfed, I'm sure he's not complaining."

Myfanwy listened to it all, but heard little. Nain was sobbing next to her, and anyway, she herself was far too upset to concentrate. What a pity! The doctor unwittingly had given her another opening. What a pity, indeed.

One's a pity, two's a pity, three's a pity… gone!

Forty

H E WAS ACCUSTOMED to coasting through life, so naturally, this bout of the blahs distressed him. He'd have bet his life that in the event of her death, he'd have felt a sense of relief. As it was, he, as well as the other two, felt as troubled over this loss as they all had when Dacu had died. So the blahs stalked him as he walked without his characteristic bounce, downhill towards the bungalow.

Once there, Jon Devereux, surprisingly unalert, almost failed to notice faces in the window. When he did, he froze and was startlingly reminded by the two sad, freckled faces of the four that had filled the same window on the morning of the march of the century, the morning of the day on which Dacu had passed away. Four faces then, now two, symbolic of why he felt blah and blue.

It was hard to believe that nearly five months had passed since Dacu had died, and now Mamgu was dead as well; dead and buried as they say, buried earlier today. At least she hadn't suffered in death as she had in life. She'd appeared perfectly fine last Saturday night, but the following morning, she'd failed to wake up. A terrible shock to them all, of course, but still, he'd thought that his main reaction would have been relief. After all, Mamgu had been the bane of his life. He knew in his heart he wouldn't miss her one jot, but his mind wouldn't settle at that. It went beyond: to worrying about Jane, whom he knew would harbour regrets. Since Dacu's death, Mamgu had been surprisingly persistent in reaching out to her daughter, but Jane had resisted: she'd found it hard to switch on the spot. She'd begun to respond though, and would have come round with time, without doubt, but time alas had now run out.

Jon worried about David as well. He'd grown so much since Dacu's death, the youngster…

"Wait a minute!" said Jon to himself, "It strikes me all of a sudden that quite a few things seem to have changed since Dacu's death! Funny I hadn't thought of it like that before."

In any case, David had grown much closer to Mamgu since Dacu had passed away. A lot of it had to do with their Welsh lessons, of course, but there seemed to be more to it than that. Since Dacu's death, they'd always seemed to stick up for each other, somehow.

"No question about it," thought Jon dreamily at the window, "Poor David's been hit the hardest of all."

Jon had another worry as well. While Mamgu was alive, he'd run his life around her shadow. Dacu and Jane had agreed that it probably would be best. Naturally, this arrangement had limited his freedom, but also freed him from certain responsibilities. He'd done his significant bit to support them all, but in pursuing his peripheral role, he'd never truly got involved in the domestic thick of things. Now she was dead, all that would change at a stroke. Overnight, he'd undoubtedly become the head of their family, and if that wasn't enough of a challenge, Jane was pregnant as well.

"This business of worrying doesn't suit me at all," he thought as he snapped from his reverie,

"Still, it'll pass before long," but in the meantime, a bout of the blahs embroiled him.

David lay on his back in bed, his head propped up by pillows. It was late, but still light, and the white of the sheets seemed luminous. The top one, drawn up under his chin, partly framed a round, freckled, slightly fretful face. It still didn't make sense to David that Mamgu had died. She hadn't even been ill! Mami had tried to explain to him that Mamgu had had a sad life, and that sadness can wear people out without warning. He sighed. It had been a long day, and sad, and filled with people too. He'd felt that he'd had to be on his toes, not just at the funeral, but during the preparations and the tea party afterwards as well. So he'd looked forward to being alone. Oh, no! Someone was knocking on his door. Mami, probably. Blue eyes became alert, and fair, curly hair was ruffled.

"Come in."

"Is it alright if I sit down for a minute, David?"

He nodded and smiled a warmer welcome than was felt.

"It's just that you seem so sad, David. I know you miss Mamgu, but I was thinking that perhaps you wanted to get something else off your chest."

David dropped his gaze and shrugged his shoulders, giving himself time to decide that he had better be on his toes again. Strangely, Mami said nothing more, piquing his curiosity. He raised his blue eyes reluctantly to find in hers an appeal for understanding. Her freckles appeared slightly raised, cloaking her pretty face in mystery and sadness. Suddenly, he felt badly not being warm to her, but there were no two ways about it, she'd really let him down. Poor Mamgu had gone out of her way to be nice to her, and Mami hadn't behaved at all as he'd expected. He couldn't help feeling hurt because Mamgu had done it all for him. He's the one who'd begged Mamgu to give Mami a chance, and look what had happened. He'd felt so sorry for Mamgu then, and so disappointed in Mami. Yet now, he felt very silly sulking like this. But he'd have to be careful what he told her: Mami would certainly be upset if she knew all the stuff that Dacu had told him on the day he died, particularly the bit about Mamgu being jealous of her. He couldn't mention that, but come to think of it, there was one thing Mami could probably help him with. As wise was his decision to engage his mother, David still couldn't shake his disappointment in her.

What had bothered him the most was that as far as he could see, his mother had shown little remorse over her behaviour towards Mamgu. His immature mind had jumped to the conclusion that his mother really hadn't cared, either about Mamgu or, by association, about him.

"Well, Mami," he began, with an innocence and calm that belied his inner conflict, "Mamgu isn't here any more, so… "

"Oh, I know, David bach. It's all so sudden."

His mother looked so pretty, so warm, that for a moment he had the feeling that she was going to say all those nice things about Mamgu that he wished she would. She didn't, and he managed to hide his disappointment.

"What shall I do about my Welsh lessons?"

She appeared to be taken aback and didn't answer immediately, but when she did, it was his turn to be surprised.

"Well, of course, your lessons. We mustn't forget about them, must we? By the way, David, I've been wanting to say something to you for a while, but I was afraid I'd upset Mamgu, I suppose. I've no idea what made you ask her to give you Welsh lessons, but whether you know it or not, it was a brilliant idea."

It struck David that his mother looked prettier and warmer than ever.

"Mamgu, poor dab, was never able to forgive herself for not bringing me up in Welsh, even though it wasn't her fault at all; so when you suggested taking Welsh lessons, in a way you were giving her a second chance. Whatever gave you the idea?"

She smiled so affectionately as she placed her hands on his shoulders. David never got round to answering her question, because he was preoccupied with what she'd just said. So Mami knew some of his secrets! That was a shock!

"And you know what I think, David? It was no accident that about the same time, Mamgu started going out of her way to be nice to me."

He shouldn't tell her, should he, that it was he who had begged Mamgu to be nice to her?

"But you know, David, I couldn't be nice back to her. When someone's been mean to you for years, you get used to distancing yourself from them. Both Dadi and I went through that with Mamgu, so it wasn't easy for either of us to change on the spot. You can understand that, can't you? Anyway, things were beginning to get better, but then... I'll never be able to forgive myself for not being able to give more back, even though I know it wasn't... "

David could tell she was going to cry, long before she burst into tears, so his embrace was immediate. So was the wave of relief that swept away any remnants of hurt, disappointment or doubt that, despite her earlier confidences, had stubbornly held out. So she really had cared all along!

"Oh, David bach," in between sobs and sighs, "It means so much more than you can imagine. You see, I had noticed that you'd become a bit distant. I wondered if you were jealous of the new baby, but I suppose I knew it was something to do with Mamgu, but there again, I didn't want to say anything that might upset her. Anyway, it doesn't matter anymore, does it? You are my friend, and that's the most important thing in the world to me."

Once again, her sobbing got out of control, and earned her a bigger hug. She was reconfirmed as David's heroine, a mother and a mentor as well. Her views once more were of value. When she'd recovered, she returned to David's question.

"Now, about those Welsh lessons. What do you want to do, David? It's up to you, really, isn't it? If you think you want to carry on, I'm sure we could find someone to help you, someone from Mamgu's chapel for example. What d'you think?"

He hung on his mentor's every word.

"I don't know, Mami. Do you think I have enough time for the lessons?"

No word was forthcoming from his mentor yet, so he continued.

"Remember Mamgu complaining that they were always a rush? She did think I was doing well, but she often said I'd do much better if I broke a leg."

"Thank goodness you didn't do that, but… "

The oracle was poised to pronounce, and the petitioner most receptive to her perfectly practical recommendation.

"Look, David, if you're not sure, my suggestion is that you take a break from the lessons. It seems to me that you've got enough on your plate as it is, and anyway, if you find that you miss them you can always start again, can't you?"

That was that! Well, nearly anyway, because despite his mentor's blessing, David still wasn't quite sure what Dacu would think of him if the Welsh lessons were given up. They hadn't been Dacu's idea, but a few things had been said on that ridge on the day that he'd died which had given David pause, and would until tomorrow!

Over time, David's homework would become more demanding, his choir practices more frequent, his woodworking more satisfying, and his cricket and football with his father more fun. Too busy and happy to miss anything, Welsh lessons for him as an issue would soon be dead; to be honest, even if he'd persisted, it would have been an uphill struggle. Where would he have been encouraged by the spoken word in Welsh? Certainly not at home, and rarely at school. Admittedly, his choir sang songs in Welsh, but very few, for it was based at an English chapel which Jane attended… now and then.

"Good night, David. I love you."

The following day, still bothered by the blahs, Jon opened the batting for Tonypandy Cricket Club against Ferndale. A few had questioned the propriety of him performing in public on the day after Mamgu's funeral, but in the end, dubious logic had wondrously won the day. Who in his neighbourhood, it was argued, could Jon possibly offend, when the game was being played away? Actually what clinched it was the skipper's offer to allow David to go along with the team; not an insignificant gesture, in light of the fact that the whole side, two reserves, an umpire and a scorer had long been dreading being stuffed into Ifor Williams's little, red bread van. It wasn't far from one Rhondda to the other, but no one was heard to complain when on the way back, David persuaded his father to get out of the van right at the high point of the road between the two valleys.

"You take my bag, all right, Ieuan?" said Jon to the driver, who was Ifor's only son and a nice man, but was on the team, 'twas a well-known fact, only because of the van, "We'll find our own way back," followed by, "What's going on then, David?"

It was still quite close to the longest day of the year, and the sky was very clear; the evening light was bright, even at half past eight. No coal-black clouds congregated in the west, as they had on the day of Dacu's death.

"Can we go up there quickly, Dadi?" asked David, pointing vaguely up the ridge. Jon was nonplussed, but he agreed. He supposed he'd know soon enough what lay behind it all, so he followed closely behind his son. David took the same path as he had five months earlier, skirting the ridge on its eastern side, before abruptly turning left for the precipice.

"David! What a spot! How d'you know about this?"

As before, the same array of valleys to the north like fingers on a massive glove, and fold upon fold of Welshlands to the west. As before, breathtaking, but this time, richer in shade and shadow, less grey and more grand.

"Dacu and I sat here just before he died."

"So that's what's going on!" thought Jon. To him it made sense that David, while grieving for his Mamgu, would miss his Dacu as well. Jon was touched by his son's sensitivity. He chose to say nothing.

"This is where he showed me his dragon. You remember the story, don't you, Dadi?"

Jon smiled and nodded.

"I'd like a tattoo like that one day, Dadi. Is that all right?"

The same complacency again from Jon.

"Dadi, I'm not going to take Welsh lessons for a while. Did Mami tell you?"

Jon should have known from his son's slightly darkened freckles that there was more to this jaunt than met the eye.

"No, but I think it's fine if you take a break."

"You do?"

"Yes, of course! What's on your mind, David?"

"Well, when I was up here with Dacu, he said that people had spoken Welsh on this spot for the last twenty-five hundred years. Just imagine!"

Jon suddenly wished that Jane was there to deal with this difficult drift in the conversation. As ever, when in danger of being dragged out of his depth, he blocked with a very straight bat.

"So?"

"Come on, Dadi, you know what I mean."

Skittled, stumped, whatever! Still, forced into philosophy, he fared surprisingly well.

"Things change, David bach. They're changing all the time. I mean, what language did people speak up here before the Welsh turned up, aye? And a thousand years from now, who knows what… "

"But I am Welsh, Dadi, so don't you think it's right for me to be able to speak Welsh?"

"Look, David, I think you're missing the point a bit. I can't speak Welsh either. I wasn't even born here, but no one feels more Welsh than me, and it's how you feel that counts, don't you think?"

"I… I suppose so."

Then, Jon played a shot that Jane would have blessed. Dacu was invoked and David was stroked, and his mind put completely at rest.

"You know, David, I wouldn't be surprised if Dacu's up there somewhere listening to all this, and I bet you he's dying to tell you something. I think he would say that if you learn Welsh one day, then that would be great, but he would also say that even more important than being able to speak Welsh is that you feel Welsh, and enjoy that feeling, and be proud of it… every day."

David made no riposte to that. He just gazed thoughtfully down into the valley of the Rhondda Fawr in shadow, betraying no emotion. Jon wished he knew if David was convinced.

"I'm beginning to feel cold, Dadi. Can we go now?"

When they set off in single file, David wore a cricket sweater that dangled down to his knees. Once at the road, he took Jon's hand. To a father, that was answer enough, but the freckles had confirmed it anyway.

Martha Mowbray had been buried on the very same day as Elfed Evans. Mamgu to one family and Taid to another had died but a day apart. It wasn't surprising perhaps that Mamgu, divisive in life, should be survived by harmony, while the opposite would be the case for Taid: not surprising, and yet, ironic. Jon soon got over his bout of the blahs. With warmth re-established between his wife and son, the three prepared in common cause for the arrival of the little one. No common cause, alas, to encourage those up north.

Forty-one

"TAKE HIM... "
"... under your wing?" and a long squeeze from an otherwise limp hand had confirmed it. He'd been in no doubt of Taid's dying request.

"Take him under your wing."

The doctor only wished that he could, as he stood in his study reshaping a few flies that he'd fished with earlier in the day. Two and a half years had elapsed since he'd coaxed this final, faltering phrase from his friend. Not at all unheeded, but still unfulfilled, it had evolved in the doctor's mind from a request into a running reprimand. In a way, he'd only himself to blame. After all, it was he who'd originally floated the phrase by offering the identical advice to Taid with respect to Edgar. Of course, it had been to no avail and by now it looked as if he too would fail, in his case with respect to Peter.

"Take him under your wing."

So at Taid's death, there'd been no doubt about the message, but much about the motive. Taid had referred to the tensions in the farmhouse, but as far as the doctor had known, they were well contained, and Peter unaffected by them. He'd been unaware of Edgar's recent more active role and the resentment it had fanned in Myfanwy. Taid's request though, unreasonable as it had seemed on the surface, had resonated with him regardless. The familiar phrase had precedence, and had implied that there was more to Peter's position than had met the eye.

"Take him under your wing."

So moved by Taid to duty, the doctor had felt bound to consult his wife. She, childless, had responded encouragingly.

She'd thought a protégé would be most appropriate, especially now that the doctor was nearing retirement.

"It's never too late to nurture," had been her timely turn of phrase.

So the commitment had been made with an enthusiasm that unfortunately had proved difficult to sustain. The doctor had had no qualms about circumventing Edgar, but he'd judged Myfanwy's cooperation to be essential; so he'd taken every opportunity to remind her of the offer he'd made on the day that Taid had died.

"Don't be too proud, now," he'd chided her, "I'd love to help Peter in any way I can, for Taid's sake, you understand," but his overtures had been consistently rejected. As a result, he'd settled for the time being for following Peter from a distance. He'd taken to attending concerts and plays at Peter's primary school, and so delighted were the teachers that none had thought of questioning his motives. Soon enough though, this peripheral patronage had proven unsatisfactory and frustrating. Without encouragement, he'd have probably packed the project in. Then Nain, poor thing, had passed away, a mere six months after Taid. The doctor had gone to her funeral, and that's where Enid had spilt the beans which would marry him to his commitment for good.

"Hello, Doctor bach," her banter had begun, "This is all very sad, isn't it?" and then after a while she'd carried on about such topics as pregnant girls with tiny girths, and recent births and breaches.

"May I talk to you about something personal, Doctor?" she'd then asked, glancing furtively around the vestry, where mourners tucked into their tea, "It's about Myfanwy, actually."

At that, the doctor had done some glancing of his own.

"Oh, Myfanwy. What's the matter?"

"Well, I'm very worried about her. She'd be really upset if

she knew I was telling you this, so let me know if you see her coming…"

Enid's opening intimacies alone had so disarmed the doctor that he'd chipped in with his own. He'd long contemplated enrolling Enid as a conduit to Myfanwy, so in the vestry in the valley he'd ventured.

"Oh, there's no chance of her joining us, Enid. She'll want to keep clear of me, don't worry."

"What d'you mean by that, Doctor?"

When he'd told her the story of Taid's dying request and Myfanwy's reluctance to cooperate, she'd moved closer, and continued.

"So poor Taid had seen it coming, aye? It's so obvious now, but I never realised how much would change at the farmhouse after he died. To begin with, I would never have guessed that Edgar would have moved back there for good. Mind you, Myfanwy still sleeps on her own upstairs, but the situation is driving her mad, Doctor. I'd been hoping that you could help, but if you say Myfanwy won't warm to you… funny she hadn't mentioned this to me."

"Enid fach, I'd love to help, but she won't open up to me."

The doctor had half-turned to put his cup of tea down, and to his surprise and mild consternation had caught Myfanwy staring at him across the room. In fact, she'd stubbornly held his gaze until another mourner had distracted her attention.

"It's nothing personal, Doctor. She just hates the thought of people knowing how she feels. More than anything, she's determined that Peter doesn't get caught up in the hatred she feels for his father. Still, Myfanwy can bottle up her feelings only for so long before they explode. What d'you suppose goes through Peter's mind when he regularly sees her flying off the handle? Doctor, I'm afraid he's beginning to behave the same way himself. He's still a nice boy, but the sooner you take him under your wing, the better."

To the doctor, Enid's disturbing revelations had not only at last fully explained Taid's dying request, but had also added urgency to it.

"Where's Myfanwy gone?" he'd asked himself. She'd moved from where she'd held his stare, and her disappearance had disturbed him. Enid had carried on talking by the time he'd recovered his poise.

"Somehow, Doctor, you've got to help Peter before he grows up to be bigoted like his father, and temperamental like his mother for that matter. You've got to do it, if only for me, because I think the world of the boy, you know."

"Enid, I'll do all I can, but you need to talk to Myfanwy and... Oh, God! She's coming up right behind you, Enid! Hello, Myfanwy. This is a sad occasion, isn't it?"

"Yes it is, Doctor, very sad indeed," and turning to Enid, she'd commented amiably, "You two seem to have a lot to talk about?"

"Well, you know... medical bits and pieces."

Her friend's face had hardened in a flash. She virtually spat at Enid.

"Don't give me that nonsense, Enid. What kind of fool d'you take me for? And to think I thought I could depend on you. As you just said, Doctor, it's a very sad day... indeed."

The doctor had been on the point of attempting to placate her, when she'd turned away abruptly and continued mixing with mourners as if nothing at all had happened. She hadn't made a scene, but she'd certainly made her point. Enid had had to accept that the doctor would have little success in counselling Myfanwy, while he had resigned himself to continuing in a peripheral role with respect to Myfanwy's son. A year and a half on, Peter had graduated from the primary school to the grammar school, and in his extracurricular repertoire, concerts and plays had been complemented by soccer matches and cross-country meets. The doctor had attended them all. With the aid of a friend on the staff at school, he'd followed Peter's academic progress as well, and had been pleased. Each time he'd met Myfanwy on the street, he'd casually hinted at his continuing interest in her son. She'd not responded, and he'd not pressed. Her indifference had not surprised, for Enid had kept him abreast of Myfanwy's thinking. As time had ticked by, he'd often felt frustrated, but since Nain's funeral, he'd known he'd never give up on his goal. In his failiure so far to comply with Taid's wish, this conviction had been a reassurance, but by the same token, the request, while unfulfilled, had become a running reprimand.

"Take him under your wing," his dying friend had said.

The doctor only wished that he could, as he stood in his study reshaping a few flies that he'd fished with earlier in the day. The coal fire crackled unusually angrily, but still comforted on a cold and windy winter's afternoon. It was already nearly dark, it wasn't far off the shortest day of the year, and it was a Sunday. The doctor checked his watch and craned his head towards the window. He'd like to take his puppy, a Wheaten called Walter, for a walk, but couldn't tell if it had stopped raining. He took a few steps forward and screwed up his face against the pane. The rain had at last waned, but his relief was short-lived. As he backed away, he did a violent double take. A female figure stumbled unsteadily into view along a path that led away from the surgery door. She was dressed inappropriately for rain. The doctor resolved to go to her aid, for her demeanour distressed him, but at that moment, she turned clumsily to reveal a familiar face.

"Oh, my God! Delilah! Where are you? I need your help... quickly!"

While appealing to his wife, he pulled on wellington boots

and grabbed two raincoats before rushing outside to the path where Myfanwy dithered.

"Myfanwy fach, what's happening?" as he carefully wrapped the coats around her shoulders.

She shivered, and seemed dazed as she gazed at the doctor.

"Doctor? What are you doing here?" she stuttered, and then stared at him vacantly.

"What d'you… well, this is where I live, isn't it?"

She seemed to focus then, and burst into tears before leaning into the doctor's arms. In between sobs she whispered, "Take him under your wing, Doctor."

The doctor froze for a second. It shocked him momentarily that Myfanwy was aware of Taid's request. He quickly deduced that it had to have been Enid and overcame the distraction. To the reprise of the phrase that would have been music to his ears under less worrying circumstances, the doctor ushered Myfanwy gently into the house. By the time they'd reached the doorway, Delilah was there to assist.

Half an hour later, Myfanwy had been comforted and bathed, and now was asleep in Delilah's warmed guest bed. A mild sedative had done the trick, and as she rested, the doctor watched over her.

"Take him under your wing, Doctor," she'd whispered. Naturally, he was very, very pleased and allowed himself to relax at the prospect, until he began to fret over why she'd changed her mind. He pondered the possibilities until Delilah, graceful as always, appeared on the landing and tiptoed towards the room.

"Enid's here," she whispered, "You go down. I'll stay with Myfanwy. Come on! And by the way, I've shut Walter up."

Walter, their soft-coated Wheaten terrier puppy; at one end, docked, and forelocked to the full at the other. He was a dear, and indeed adored, but when disobedient was not exempt from expulsion to the washroom.

Enid sat in an armchair, her eyes moist, her lips drawn and she was slowly shaking her head. The doctor let her whimper for a while.

"Enid fach, don't worry now. I'm sure she's going to be fine. She'll wake up a much stronger person, you'll see, and I have a feeling she'll want to get a lot off her chest."

According to Enid's tearful account, a despondent Myfanwy had left her earlier in the afternoon and headed homeward. Most concerned she'd been a little later to be informed by a neighbour that Myfanwy had been spotted walking in the rain in the opposite direction. Enid had followed but failed to find her. Though now relieved, Enid remained shaken. The doctor suggested that she at least see for herself that her friend was comfortable, and while she did, he prepared Welsh rarebit and a pot of tea, and considered how dreadful might have been the drama that had driven Myfanwy to near madness.

Over tea that refreshed and rarebit that revived, Enid was informed by the doctor, smiling knowingly, of Myfanwy's reference to Taid's parting phrase. Her only response was to grin confidently and shrug her shoulders as if to say, "Well, you did ask me to try and help you with Myfanwy... "

She was much more forthcoming when asked about her friend's confused behaviour.

"It's nothing more than mental and emotional fatigue, Doctor. You've probably heard, haven't you, that since Nain passed away, Rhiannon and Edgar have more or less cut Myfanwy off from anything to do with the business side of the farm; to think that Rhiannon had mellowed so much over the years, but sadly all that was reversed when Geraint died. D'you know, she's even forbidden Myfanwy to pick up the post! All this, of course, makes it even harder for Myfanwy to tolerate Edgar, but what makes it so much worse is having to stomach Peter being bombarded by his father's bigotry, which gets more extreme by the month. Myfanwy's just worn out, Doctor. There's no more to it than that."

Enid reminded the doctor of how Edgar had inexplicably started attending chapel after Peter's birth. Then out of the blue, just after Nain's funeral, he'd become an evangelist, and peppered his political speeches with religious views. Though fundamentally a pacifist, he'd then decided to support the fascists in the Spanish Civil War, predictably haranguing the "commies" in south Wales in the process. More recently, because of the tension mounting between Germany and Britain – or England as he insisted – he'd pinned his fascism to that fellow Hitler, espousing the line, "My enemy's enemy is my friend."

"Peter's at many of these meetings," continued Enid, "And it's driving Myfanwy mad. What's really worrying her is that Edgar is now urging his followers to disrupt English… English, mind you… to disrupt English military installations anywhere in Wales, and listen to this, Doctor: Myfanwy told me today that last Wednesday evening, her mad husband went on a "mission" himself… mission, honestly… and took Peter with him. Now what d'you think of that, Doctor?"

His face had paled in an instant.

"How did Myfanwy find out?" he stuttered.

"She forced it out of Peter, but don't worry Doctor, nothing happened that night. The mission had to be aborted. Those were the very words that Peter used. Can you believe it? The mission had to be aborted! He's only eleven, poor dab. In any case, nothing bad came out of it, except that Myfanwy was tipped over the edge."

The uneasy silence that ensued was Delilah's to disarm. Appearing at the doorway to the doctor's right, she remarked with mild amusement, "What's the matter, love? Don't tell me you've seen that ghost again."

From the little she knew of Delilah, Enid liked her a lot.

Still attractive at sixty and strikingly tall, her hair was as fair as Walter's and woven in a bun. Delilah! What a name, and what a connotation, but no Philistine, no voluptuous temptress she. This Delilah was if anything understated, but still naturally elegant, which had led many, including Enid, to mistakenly assume she was proper. So Delilah's levity at that sombre moment shook Enid and rubbed her the wrong way. Enid feared that the doctor too may be offended, especially when he replied without facing his wife, "You know that stork we've been waiting for all these years, Delilah? Well, I think it's just arrived."

Enid was predisposed to sense resentment in these words, and felt her instincts were confirmed by the wetness that welled in Delilah's eyes, but she'd read it so woefully wrong. Little indeed she knew of the doctor's wife, and even less of her marriage. With obvious pleasure, and far from proper, Delilah approached her husband from behind, and placing her arms over his shoulders, held his hands which were limp in his lap.

"I'm so happy for you, love," was all she said. To compound Enid's shame and isolation, the doctor turned and kissed his wife's damp cheek.

"Thanks, Delilah, but from what Enid just told me, I may have bitten off more than I can chew."

"Don't worry, love," she reassured, "From what I hear, he sounds like a lovely boy."

Enid, eager to make amends and rejoin the fold, chipped in with, "I've told you that before, haven't I, Doctor? Despite everything, he's still a nice boy. It's amazing, really."

The two ladies followed the doctor's gaze towards the ceiling.

"Mr Elfed Evans," he pronounced grandly, "I hope you're happy now. Take him under your wing! I'm sure that's what you meant to say, anyway, but it would be nice to have confirmation. Any little sign would do. I'll tell you what! Make Delilah kiss me… " and he must have, on the spot, because she did, happily without bothering Enid one bit.

Thus was the doctor set on a course, which as a preliminary, took him and his car up the Tryweryn that stormy evening. Enid was dropped off at home, and Peter and Rhiannon, across the valley, were informed of Myfanwy's condition and reassured regarding her recovery. The next morning, as expected, Myfanwy awoke refreshed and almost whole. She duly repeated Enid's story, and after apologising at length for not having done so earlier, literally begged the doctor to take Peter under his wing. All that was needed now was Peter's cooperation. Peter's cooperation! This the doctor had never taken lightly, but suddenly and irrationally it assumed the standing of a stumbling block. Myfanwy though was all confidence, which would soon be put to the test, for they would meet Peter at the station that afternoon. The doctor saw no reason why she shouldn't go home with her son on the train after school. He was optimistic that Myfanwy would be a stronger, more secure person now, relieved at revealing the past and more confident of the future with him as a confidante.

"Hello, Peter! You remember Doctor, don't you?" Peter, blue-eyed and wide-mouthed, nodded warmly enough, and shook the proffered hand. So far, so good, and the doctor relaxed a little.

"Now listen to me carefully, would you, Peter? I'd like you to get to know Doctor better; to spend some time with him, OK? I think it would be good for you to be away from the valley a bit more. Don't you find it quiet at home?"

Peter shrugged his shoulders and half turned towards the train that had shunted into the station. This was discouraging for the doctor who, after all, had doubted the outcome, but the mother knew her son. Peter had inevitably been tarnished by his father's ingrained anger, and following his mother's example, had been prone of late to emotional outbursts, but despite everything, Peter was still a nice boy, as Enid had put it. Above all, he'd retained his childhood gift of naturally giving pleasure.

"Excuse me, Doctor. You were Taid's friend, weren't you? I miss Taid. Do you?"

The element of surprise, the sentimental reference to Taid and admiration for the boy's sensitivity and timing, taken together, almost proved too much for the doctor. He choked on this emotional cocktail, and barely managed, "Yes! I do a lot."

"So, when we get together, we can talk about Taid then, can we?"

Immense relief was added to the pot, and the effect was overwhelming. The doctor could only grit his teeth, nod briefly and wave hesitantly, before turning and leaving the station with as light a heart and step as he could remember.

Forty-two

ENERGISED BEYOND REASON by the outcome of their meeting on that Monday, the doctor had wasted no further time in taking Peter under his wing. It took but till Wednesday for the two to meet. At the end of the school day, Peter didn't hurry to the doctor's house. In fact he'd chosen a long way round. He stopped, and took his time to tie a bootlace.

"I feel funny about this."

Again he stopped to tie the other.

"I suppose I'd feel better if Mam had told Dad."

Despite kicking his heels, as well as all the kickable stones along the way, he arrived at the house much sooner than he'd have liked. He was surprised to be met by a lady with long fair hair, very tall and pretty, who'd been waiting outside to greet him. For a moment his funny feelings were forgotten, as shyness overcame him in her presence. Peter had never imagined the doctor with a wife, but if he had, he was sure she'd have been a lovely lady; a lady, as it happened, who smiled so warmly that he noticed, and who asked him to call her Delilah. While they waited for the doctor to finish his work, Delilah spoilt him. She poured him pop after pop and plied him with wonderful Welsh cakes. She asked him about his various activities at school, always so warmly that gradually his answers began to flow. He relaxed with Delilah, and Walter the Wheaten didn't hurt matters either. Peter's broad smile was infectious again and his blue eyes had regained their sparkle. In between exchanges, he glanced around the living room, self-consciously at first.

"Gosh, it's posh here," he mused, "They must be rich. She's posh as well, I suppose, but she couldn't be nicer, and she's so pretty too. Come to think of it, she treats me just like Anti Enid does."

Time flew as they chatted. The phone rang. He wasn't used to that. Delilah stood, tall and elegant. She drew her long fair hair away from her face and answered the phone in Welsh, but immediately changed to English.

"Oh! That's a posh English accent, if ever I heard one, but I don't care. I like her, anyway."

Back to chatting like chums, and before Peter knew it, the man of the house arrived. To his surprise and disappointment, Peter suddenly felt almost as uneasy as before, as if he were starting the process all over again. Yet, Delilah smiled as warmly as ever and the doctor couldn't have been more eager to please. So for the second time, and happily less gradually than the first, his unease lifted, defused by their courting and attentiveness. Flattery, friendship and food, in combination, had seduced yet another eleven-year-old. Homeward bound, the thrill of the ride in the doctor's convertible, racing-green MG was icing on the cake. It was a dark night, but dry. Peter was mesmerised, in thrall of the throaty engine. The convertible's constant wind noise, though curtailing conversation, added to the excitement.

"Shall we do this again then, Peter?" shouted the doctor, as they swung off the road towards the farmyard.

Had it not been so dark, Peter's expression would have been answer enough.

And so began a series of meetings at Doctor and Delilah's house. Each time, Peter was waylaid by Walter the Wheaten, thoroughly spoilt by Delilah, served a sumptuous high tea and engaged in conversation in the lounge that he found so posh; each time it seemed, the doctor said something in a provocative tone. It upset Peter to think that the doctor may be trying to catch him out, and he would have withdrawn into himself often had not Delilah's warm and encouraging smile consistently convinced him that she was on his side.

For example, during the second visit, out of the blue the doctor had said, "Don't you find it a bit odd, Peter, that you all speak Welsh during breaks at school, but the classes are held in English?"

Then the following week: "I wonder why Enid never got married? It's strange, isn't it, Delilah? I'm sure she'd have made a wonderful wife."

At another time, while lauding Taid: "But who'd have thought of Taid as someone who had a tattoo?"

Silence followed that. For once, the warmth fled Delilah's face as she glanced quizzically at her husband. Peter shifted uneasily and started to speak, but wavered, until Delilah, all warmth again, resumed her cheerleading role.

"Well, what I was about to say was that Taid showed me his little red dragon. He showed me on the... on the day he died."

Delilah personified sympathy and the doctor too seemed moved, though not enough to stifle his next remark.

"I am glad to hear that. So poor old Taid didn't take it to the grave with him, after all."

Peter was confused. Once again, the doctor had said something in a provocative tone that made no sense at all. This time, Peter said nothing despite Delilah's encouraging glances.

At home, later that night, the cadence of two steps was all it took for Peter to identify the person who'd started to climb the stairs.

"Mam has changed so much over the last few weeks," he thought, "All of a sudden, she's standing up to Dad."

Then, quietly, "Mam, I'd like to ask you something."

Tonight, Myfanwy carried a candle. She set it down on an empty chair, and there it flared and flickered.

"Doctor said something odd tonight, Mam. See, I told them that Taid had shown me his tattoo... "

"That's right! On the day that he died, wasn't it? I remember now... but how terrible!"

"What's terrible, Mam?"

"Well, that I didn't explain it to you. You know, tell you the story behind it. I suppose I had a lot on my mind, but still that's no excuse. Funny isn't it that neither of us has mentioned it since?"

So she told him the story of two local boys and the fork that clove their laughter, and the bond that bound them while they lived and would, they hoped, thereafter. This simple, poignant tale hit close to home and diverted Peter, but soon he returned to his original question.

"I still don't understand, Mam, what the doctor meant when he said he was glad that Taid hadn't taken the tattoo to the grave with him. He seems to say these funny things now and then."

"Oh, Peter bach, he's just keeping you on your toes, that's all. Anyway, remember me saying just now that Taid and Edward Jones had agreed that they'd try and keep the tattoo as a tradition in... "

"Oh, I get it now, Mam. Because Taid showed me his tattoo, Doctor was saying that I'm more likely to get one and carry on the tradition. Then it wouldn't end with Taid, right? So, I should get a tattoo, then, shouldn't I? Perhaps Dad could take me. What d'you think, Mam?"

Even in the absence of candlelight, Peter surely would have sensed his mother's dismay.

"I don't think that would be a good idea, Peter. Believe it or not, your dad has a tattoo as well. Why do you think you haven't seen it? He's ashamed of it, that's why: the thought of his tattoo makes him angry because he feels he was forced into it. You see, your dad and Taid didn't have much time for each other, so I don't think your dad will go out of his way to help you do anything that would have pleased Taid, especially when it's to do with the tattoo. It's up to you, mind, but I'd speak to Doctor about it, if I were you."

Now it was Peter's turn to betray dismay. He knew full well that Mam didn't get along with Dad, but it looked as if Taid hadn't either. It had hurt to hear that. He hoped like mad she wouldn't want a hug. That might be hard at the moment.

"OK, Mam," he whispered, "Good night."

"Good night, Peter," and soon his room was deprived of light; literally dumped into darkness.

Shortly after came his first meeting without Delilah. After supper, she'd had to leave unexpectedly to give a hand to a grieving friend, and Walter went along for company. Her reassuring aura absent, Peter felt noticeably less comfortable and found himself on guard. The topic that evening was Myfanwy, and Doctor spoke in glowing terms that well could have led to complacency, but deprived of Delilah, how could Peter relax? He found himself unable not to anticipate a provocative remark, apparently designed by Doctor to keep him on his toes.

"Well, I'm on my toes, all right," he thought.

"Do you wonder, Peter, why your Mam never sings in public any more?"

Peter shrugged his shoulders and shook his head with reasonable assurance, while continuing to mull the matter.

"The last time I heard her," continued Doctor, "was at a concert with your dad; three years ago, I think it was. You were there too. Remember? Anyway, your mam was amazing. She even put your dad in the shade, and that's not easy to do, is it?"

Peter remembered it, all right. It was the first time he'd

really heard his dad sing, and nothing could have been more amazing than that. So he was surprised that Doctor had spoken the way he did: surprised, and on guard again.

"Your dad's a born performer, isn't he?"

A compliment possibly, but Peter couldn't help feeling it was part of a set-up. Suddenly, he wished more than ever that Delilah was at hand.

"Give him a platform and he's a different person, isn't he, Peter?"

Peter nodded warily. This was no fun. He felt trapped, and he hoped he was ready for whatever was coming.

"It must be nice to have a famous father, a father who's recognised as he's walking in the street. You've got to give it to him, he's articulate. He's got the gift, all right, but… "

The predictable, inevitable "but". Peter braced himself.

"… But don't you think it's a pity that he feels so strongly about everything? Don't you think, Peter, that a little grey here and there is a good thing?"

Peter couldn't have been better prepared, but still the anger welled, as it invariably did when his dad's views were challenged. He didn't know why, but he was terribly touchy about these things. Somehow though, being prepared gave him an edge in containing his anger. There, in his high-backed chair, he forced himself to concentrate on controlling it, but he was disconcerted by Doctor's gaze. He felt very alone, and wished so much that Delilah was there. Perhaps it was the thought of her that helped him over the hump.

"Dad says that some people feel strongly, and other people don't. He's one of the ones that do, that's all."

There! He'd done it! He'd remained calm, and to his huge relief, Doctor merely nodded thoughtfully and dropped the subject. The crisis was over, for now anyway.

Peter wallowed in the warmth of Delilah's attention. Doctor even, seemed mellower than usual, and Walter? Well, docked or not, the Wheaten's wagging suggested he'd waited all week for Peter's visit. Delilah had just outdone herself with an extra large, extra special mixed grill. As a matter of fact, Delilah was always outdoing herself for him; like Anti Enid, really, but there was a difference. There was no denying he liked Anti Enid a lot, but Delilah excited him. He wouldn't admit to this, but he loved to look at her and he loved the way she touched him so perfectly naturally at the slightest excuse. She waved at him now from across the room.

"I've been thinking quite a bit, Peter," abruptly from Doctor, "about our conversation last week. You remember don't you, when I said that it was a pity that your dad felt so strongly about everything?"

Oh, no! This wasn't fair, at all. One moment unvexed, and the next, under threat. Peter had been wallowing and wasn't prepared for this.

"I remember exactly what you said about it then, but still, if someone like your father wants to be taken seriously, it seems to me they've got to show good judgement, as well as have conviction."

Peter felt panic rising through his anger. He didn't know where to turn; he didn't know what to do. He'd appeal to Delilah, but she'd half-turned to face the doctor. To his disappointment, he gained no consolation from her expression of incredulity, and that's what tipped him over the edge.

"You see, Peter, I could probably agree with your dad on many things, but it's hard to when I hear him being so extreme on some others. Take this business about south Walians, for example. I... "

"Why can't you leave my dad alone?" Peter whined frantically, vibrating his fists in the air.

"Oh, Peter bach, come on now. I… "

"All you posh people hate him," and with that, he shoved his chair along the floor behind him and burst into tears as he ran headlong for the hallway. Once there, he slammed the door, and the house literally shook.

In shock, Delilah turned to her husband.

"Did you have to be so harsh, love?"

The doctor, the perpetrator, seemed taken aback as well.

"Well, maybe I was a bit too hard, but sooner or later we'd have had to confront this failing of his. You go and console him, Delilah, and I'll stay in the background for a while."

Not even Delilah was up to this. Her attempt at a hug in the hallway was violently rejected.

"Don't touch me," in an extraordinary fury.

"But Peter bach, I didn't say anything to… "

"But you didn't say anything against him," in a whine still angry, but now tinged with woe, "I should have listened to my dad. I should never have come here in the first place."

Less angry perhaps, but just as distressed, he disappeared through the door into darkness.

Delilah looked distraught. It was Doctor's turn to hug.

"Delilah! Listen to me now. I'm certain he trusts us, all right? So I've no doubt he'll want to come back and see us sometime soon. I think I better get the car now and make sure he gets home alright."

Two days later at lunchtime, Peter called at Doctor's house. Walter's welcome was overwhelming, as if he appreciated the significance of the visit. Delilah was so relieved and delighted, and touched too when told that he'd come hoping that he could apologise to her while she was on her own. She assured him no apology was necessary, but he insisted on saying his piece. He'd been mean and rude to her, her of all people. He felt terrible about the way he'd behaved, but it seemed he just couldn't help it sometimes. He was very sorry. Delilah choked on these confessions. Inevitably, they hugged, and then broad smiles of mutual relief.

"Does Doctor come home for lunch?"

"Yes. He should be here in a few minutes.

Peter admitted that apologising to him wouldn't be half as easy.

"Oh, Peter, come on now! He'd do anything for you. He thinks of you as his son."

Delilah had attributed to her husband emotions and sentiments that were identical to hers.

"I know," she continued jovially, "Let's practise. I'll pretend to be Doctor. Now, you tell me how awfully sorry you are for calling me posh and so on and so forth," and she clapped her hands and laughed and laughed, and she could tell that Peter felt better. When Doctor arrived, and had received his heartfelt apology, they all felt better still. As Peter left for school, Delilah suggested that he return for supper that evening. After all, this was a very special day, and surely his mam wouldn't mind an exception, here and there? Couldn't a friend tell his mam he'd be late? For their own slightly different reasons, the trio had little difficulty agreeing to this. Delilah walked with Peter to the road, and as she watched him, jaunty and boyish, on his journey back to school, she felt connected and content. Delilah had wanted children, but for years and years now she hadn't dwelt on it; and yet, when she'd first felt a bond with Peter, her joy had been tinged with regret... but no longer. These days, the dull echoes of her childless past were overwhelmed by the pleasure she was certain she saw in her future.

Later that evening, Delilah couldn't tell whether Peter was aware of the subtle shift in the balance of their relationship.

During the afternoon, Doctor had agreed that she should as delicately as possible assume a greater role. She supposed this change might account for Peter's contentment now, but more likely it was due to the fact that he was under constant reassurance, from Doctor as well as herself. They'd agreed on that too, for Peter was about to face a few facts.

Doctor began gently. He reassured Peter that he was far too nice a lad to live for long with his, shall we say, tendency. He was advised, in the meantime, to be alert to his emotions in obvious situations, and when caught unprepared like the other night, to grit his teeth and fight for control.

"You'll be fine, Peter. Don't worry about it. Delilah and I are very proud of you."

Peter's concentration and good spirits during Doctor's dissertation encouraged Delilah to take up the running. She brought him gently down to earth.

"Doctor's right, Peter. You'll grow out of it soon, but it probably will happen again, though. Now, if it does, it'll be so important for you to get it off your chest as soon as you can. I just want to say that Doctor and I will always be here for you, always available to talk. D'you understand?"

She cocked her head enquiringly at Peter, and his smile was answer enough. She beckoned him to sit next to her, and he did, endearingly shyly. She placed her arm around his shoulders, nudged him closer and asked Doctor, "D'you have anything else to say to Peter, love?"

A perfectly natural cue to a well-rehearsed conclusion.

"Well, perhaps just one more thing, Peter. You'll look back on your childhood and chuckle at your uh... childish... outbursts. They won't have any lasting consequences. However, some things do, you know. If you're caught breaking the law, for example, it'll be a black mark against you forever. If you're caught damaging government property with your dad..."

Delilah felt Peter stiffen, so she firmed her embrace and took his hand.

"… With your dad or with anyone else, that black mark will handicap you for the rest of your life. It's terrific that you feel strongly about things. Delilah and I wouldn't want you to be any other way, but we'd like you to promise, wouldn't we dear, that however strongly you feel about something, you'll never break the law of the land. Will you promise?"

Peter's cheek was pecked by Delilah. She immediately wished she'd withheld to see if he'd have nodded without it.

"Your dad will be upset about that, won't he?"

More nodding, and more emphatic this time.

"Well, I don't know," continued Doctor, "Perhaps you could tell him that you can't save the language if you spend your life in jail. How does that sound, d'you think?"

There must have been something about it that pleased, because Peter beamed a big one.

For the next eighteen months, Peter's life at the farm was subject to two distinct influences: regular, healthy support from his mam and Anti Enid, and periodic indoctrination in their extreme views from his father and, occasionally, Rhiannon. She was in a position to influence him generally, but was discouraged by Peter, who often found her too contentious for comfort. Layered on these was increasing contact with Doctor and Delilah, who saw their role as building on the one, and tempering the other. Boosted by Delilah's overt, but still sensible, affection, Peter became more self-assured, and inspired by Doctor's touch and simple dedication to his patients, he became set on becoming a doctor himself. So Peter flourished, and gave his patrons pleasure. As a sign of their only concern, they measured his material progress in terms of not only levels of achievement but also frequency of flare-ups. Happily, the former soared and the latter dipped, but not to zero.

Doctor and Delilah had become Peter's alter-parents, to unqualified approval from all, but for the parents themselves. Not surprisingly, Edgar resented the doctor's interference and aired his feelings, but was reluctant to follow up on them. These days, he knew only too well that Myfanwy would create one holy hell, and also, fair play to him, he recognised that Peter was thriving. Myfanwy's position was more complicated. As the promoter of Peter's renaissance, she had only herself to blame for the nagging void she now carried, a void once filled by her son before the shift of a slice of his love to Delilah. Enid as well suffered similar symptoms, and therefore was a natural, sympathetic source of comfort to Myfanwy. Oddly, Myfanwy's loss was not held against Doctor, for after all, she admired and respected him; nor against Delilah, for wasn't she Doctor's wife? Still, someone had to be held accountable. Who better than Edgar to be cast as the devil? While it was true that she, Myfanwy, had been the medium for Peter's drift, her husband's insensitivity was at the root of it. Her anger towards him was as deep-seated as ever, but no longer did it consume her. Since her breakdown, and her ensuing alliance with Doctor, her emotions had been more stable, and of course it also helped that Peter was set fair. So she was happier, much happier than before, and as the price to be paid for that, Delilah was just about acceptable.

For eighteen months, this pattern prevailed within Peter's support group, but by July 1939, its dynamics were changing. War clouds had darkened to the point of justifying conscription in the United Kingdom. As a result, patriotism in Wales mushroomed, but in general rallied not to the Red Dragon but to the Union Jack of the British Empire. Edgar was marginalised by these developments, to the point that he no longer spoke in public and abandoned his designs on disrupting government projects. After all, his views, which once had been tolerated as crankish, could now easily be construed as subversive, and worse, his activism as treason.

Doctor and Delilah were heartened by this. On the tantrum scale, Peter, though better, was not yet completely cured. They were confident now though that Edgar's retrenchment would tip the scales their way, reinforcing another development which could only be favourable. Doctor had retired, and was already spending much more time with Peter. He'd sold his practice to a young doctor who seemed keen to cooperate in nurturing Peter's enthusiasm for the profession. Doctor had more time to think, as well... more time to think about Taid. During that late summer, while Hitler and Stalin plotted the partition of Poland, Doctor often thought of his friend. Clearly, he'd followed Taid's directive, but was he doing well? He would appreciate confirmation that Taid was pleased.

"To show your approval, Taid, make Delilah kiss me."

Funny really, but that never failed when Taid's approval was invoked out loud.

Forty-three

D AVID HAD JUST turned thirteen. He was aware for his age and taller than average. Yet, the highlight of his day, especially during the long summer holidays, remained the ritual stroll, often with his mother and little sister Doris, to meet his father walking home from work. On a Thursday in July, then, three freckled faces, two topped with fair curly hair, crossed the bridge below their bungalow and followed the river towards Tonypandy. As usual, meeting his father made David feel content, and as if that wasn't enough, on this day there would be a surprise as well.

"Well, David," started Jon, casting a guilty glance at his wife, "I did manage to get the day off tomorrow."

David's face lit up, but then suddenly was shadowed with doubt.

"Dadi… are you sure that it'll be… "

"Of course it'll be OK You've talked about this for months, so don't get cold feet now. There's nothing to it. Trust me!"

Completely reassured it seemed, David bumped shoulders with his father, and beamed.

"So we'll do it tomorrow, then. All right?"

"Hey, what's going on? What are you two up to, eh?" exclaimed Jane, clearly in the dark, "Can Doris and me come too?"

"Sorry Jane. This one's just for us boys."

David tried his very best to go along with his father's jest, but didn't feel comfortable about his mother being left out in the cold. He glanced back and forth from Jon to Jane, betraying his discomfort. So touched was she by his concern that she abandoned what had been fake indignation, and hugging her son, endorsed their mysterious venture.

"I was just joking, David. I love to see you having fun with your father, but we'll have a good time too, won't we Doris?"

Doris skipped excitedly, her round face and smiling, blue eyes completing an appearance that was the spitting image of her brother's.

"But I'd still like to know what they're up to, wouldn't you, Doris?"

Jon had been told that the establishment they sought in Cardiff didn't open till ten. Regardless, they had decided they might as well catch an early train, so that by half past eight, they'd already had their tea and toast in a cafe close to Cardiff station. Then they browsed the city centre, their shoulders brushed by thousands who rushed to be at work on time. David, in particular, was in awe of an ambience which seemed worlds apart from the one he was used to.

"Look, Dadi! There's Cardiff Arms Park."

Cardiff Arms Park! The home of Welsh rugby, and a name that rolled as readily off Antipodean lips as it did off those all over south Wales. Father and son, side by side, stood reverently, it seemed, at the entrance to this shrine.

"Dadi, I'd love to see Wales beat England in there."

"It doesn't look as if that's going to happen very soon, unless the Welsh pull their socks up."

David seemed to grow an inch at that.

"See, Dadi! That proves it!"

"Proves what, David bach?"

"That you don't care who wins."

"Hold your horses, young man."

"Well, you are English, Dadi, so why should you want Wales to win?"

David smiled warmly as he spoke in a jocular tone that seemed at odds with his persistence.

"My word! Where did all this come from, then?"

David shrugged his shoulders with a slight swagger, and completely devoid of malice as before, continued to challenge his father.

"Well, before you moved to Llwynypia, who did you support when England played Wales at rugby?"

"Shows how clever you are, Mr David Devereux," countered Jon, raising his voice a little, "Rugby league was my... "

He stopped suddenly in mid-sentence. Either prodded by good sense or disarmed perhaps by David's gentle smile, he lightened, and slapping his son with affection on his shoulder, adopted his friendly banter.

"So, how long have you lived in Wales, David?"

David burst out laughing, knowing full well what was coming next.

"I think you've got me there, Dadi."

"Come on, David! Enough of that stuff. Let's see what that chap over there's got to say for himself," and they crossed the road to the Angel Hotel, where a middle-aged man balanced effortlessly on a particularly tall log while lecturing a small but growing audience. His right fist pumped with each point, and for further emphasis, off came his flat cap revealing a head as bald as a billiard ball. This was July 1939, and he spoke of a war that was merely waiting in the wings. He spoke of its inevitability following the foolishness of that treaty with Poland, which sadly had been questioned by only a few, including, he claimed, Lloyd George, fair play. He spoke of the necessity nevertheless to resist the Nazis at all cost, for should they prevail, workingmen of the world would be neutered. He spoke of the glorious decades of remarkable progress for the Labour movement which the Nazis would reverse in a flash, and he spoke of the irrelevance of petty nationalism at a critical time such as this. He spoke and he spoke and he spoke.

"Dadi," whispered David, out of the blue, "who would you fight for if England and Wales were at war with each other? Would you fight for Wales?"

David spoke as before, with a gentle smile and generous manner. Jon responded in kind.

"David bach, you're being a bit ridiculous now."

"No, I mean it, Dadi. Which side would you fight on? Would you fight for Wales?"

Jon nudged his son a few steps away from the group, which was becoming livelier, and spoke now above a whisper.

"We'll never go to war with England."

David hesitated, perhaps aware that his father's use of "we" was tantamount to an affirmative answer. Yet, he had a point to make, so he persisted, and his banter assumed a more pointed tone.

"Well, we've done it in the past, Dadi."

"Yes, but in those days, David, they treated us like dirt, didn't they? We were second-class citizens in our own country, so we had reason to go to war."

We, we, we and us, us, us! Affirmative answers galore, but there was more to come from David.

"Dadi?"

"Yeees, David?" from Jon, continuing in good humour, "What now hath my son up his sleeve?"

"Well, if it's a reason you want, what if the English made us fight this war for them, the war that chap over there's talking about. What if they made the Welsh fight the war while they just stayed at home playing cricket, or something? What if they did that?"

Jon exhaled deeply, shook his head slowly and then scratched it.

"Where on earth is this stuff coming from?"

"But what if they did that, Dadi? What if they made us fight this war for them?"

David's insistent tone was attracting the attention of a few in the group.

"Come on, David bach, let's go, before you get both of us into trouble," and off he went hotfoot, followed by his son.

"But Dadi, wait! That's exactly what the English are going to do, if there is a war. See, I heard another chap like the one back there, talking in the square yesterday. He was saying that the unemployment we've suffered in south Wales has been a deliberate English tactic... those were his very words, Dadi... so that when a war comes, we Welsh will have nothing better to do than fight. He said that it should be obvious to everyone that this is what the English have been doing: making sure we're so poor that we'll have no choice but to fight in a war."

Jon reverted to shaking his head, but this time in amazement at his son's understanding and eloquence. With pride he smiled, as did David with pleasure at his father's approval.

"See! I've got you there, haven't I, Dadi?"

Jon agreed half-heartedly, and then teased his son with, "You're a right little Welsh nationalist."

"No, no, I'm not, Dadi; just Welsh, that's all."

Smiles all round, and then Jon, tongue in cheek, "How do you know you're Welsh, by the way?"

"Just as you've always told me, Dadi. I know it because I feel it, right?"

"Quite right, David bach."

They bumped shoulders to cement their camaraderie.

"But you still haven't answered my question, Dadi."

"Oh! You're a little devil! I'd be very surprised if we weren't both on the same side, wouldn't you?"

One more bump of the shoulders and, "Right then, David. Let's go and put a smile on your Dacu's face up there in heaven, shall we?"

Jane huffed and puffed and panted as she crossed the bridge. She could see her bungalow now, halfway up the hill, but she'd pushed herself too hard and had to take a breather. She'd been so keen to be home before the boys and greet them, and yet she'd lingered too long with a group of old friends from the bakery. She'd even known on which train they'd most likely come home, and still she'd lingered. Then, she'd rushed homewards, carrying Doris the best she could, yet fearing that her hurrying was bound to be in vain. She approached the bungalow and fumbled in her pockets for her key.

"Everything seems awfully quiet," she thought, "Surely, I'd be aware of something through the windows if there was somebody at home? Perhaps they're not here, after all. They're on the next train, I bet you!"

She was still fumbling when the door sprang open, revealing Jon and David, stripped to their waists.

"Welcome home, ladies," said Jon gaily.

"Oh, Jon!" from Jane, "Where are your shirts?"

David's response was to turn to his right very, very slowly and thrust his left shoulder towards his mother before racing away to the kitchen. Jane gasped, and gasped again as Jon ran through the same routine.

"Oh, Jon! Not you as well!"

"What's the matter, Mami?" asked Doris, with a mixture of amusement and alarm.

"Come back here, boys," said Jane, shaking her head in disbelief, "Come and show Doris."

David and Jon backpedalled to the door, twitching their left shoulders and the little red dragons tattooed thereon.

"Oh, they're pretty, Mami. Can I have one?"

Before Jane could react, David tactfully intervened, "You can share mine, Doris. What d'you think about that?"

Then he knelt, and she felt it, her face aglow with pleasure. They trooped into the kitchen, where Jon asked gently, "Jane? I never saw Dacu's little red dragon. Did you?"

"Oh, yes, now and then. I even washed his back a few times while he was still underground. But he didn't go on about the dragon much. He told me the story behind it, but I hadn't heard a thing about keeping some tradition going until David told me after Dacu died. If you ask me, it's a bit silly, really."

"Are you upset at me then, Mami?"

"No, no! Well, maybe a little bit perhaps, but only because you didn't tell me."

"Oh, Mami, I'm sorry, but how could I have told you? I was afraid that you wouldn't be willing."

"David, it's all right," but not all right enough for David, obviously, for he continued, "I know that Dacu didn't ask me point blank to get a dragon, but you know, even though he was in pain and everything, he made a point of telling me that he and his friend had agreed to try and keep the tradition going in their families. So it seemed important that... "

"David, it's all right. I can understand why you didn't tell me. And as for the tattoo itself, I must admit I did get a shock just now, but because Dacu had one, then... but why on earth did you do it, Jon?"

"Because David is a sissy. He wouldn't do it without watching me doing it first. Noooo! I'm just joking. I did it to prove once and for all to my son that I am Welsh. You see, I know he feels Welsh, but even though I feel just as Welsh as him, I can understand how he can't be sure of that. However, now that he's got his red dragon and I've got mine as well, I have a feeling that'll do the trick. What d'you think, David?"

David confirmed his father's feeling simply by bumping shoulders.

The day had been long and busy, and from its early beginning to end, the family had conducted their affairs in English. Not a word of Welsh had they spoken to each other. Yet they all went to bed that evening thoroughly comfortable with their Welshness.

Later, David lay in bed, wide-awake. His fingers felt for the dragon. Funny, he couldn't feel a thing. Then he wondered how Dacu felt, somewhere up there in heaven with a smile on his face.

"That was Dadi's phrase, wasn't it?"

At that moment, he felt wonderfully close to both his Dadi and Dacu. He felt wonderfully close to someone else, as well, someone he'd never met; someone with a shoulder with a dragon like his; someone made from a similar piece of cloth to his; someone indeed who may not even exist, but regardless, someone he knew he'd instinctively take to should they meet. It was an exciting prospect.

Someone knocked on his door. It would be Mami, more than likely.

"David?"

"Yes, Mami?"

"I want to tell you something."

"You can come in," and she did, and sat on his bed, a dark grey figure in the dusk.

"I want to tell you how sorry I am for saying that this business about the dragon is silly. I hadn't really thought about it, to tell you the truth, but I've been talking to Dadi, and he's put me straight. I am a bit late joining the party, I know, but it's so exciting, David, to think that there's probably someone else walking around with a dragon just like yours, and even more exciting to think that you may actually meet that person one day. Don't you think that's exciting, David?"

"Yes, Mami. As a matter of fact, I do," and he sat up in bed and placed his hand on hers.

"I just wanted to say that, that's all. Good night, David."

"Good night, Mami."

His mother was remarkable. She really had the knack of reading his mind. Perhaps there was nothing more to it than they thought so much alike. Come to think of it, he felt wonderfully close to her as well.

Forty-four

DOCTOR STOOD ALONE at the summit of Arenig Fach. Weather threatened from the west, and where clouds had earlier scudded by, they now strove to bond, and some already brooded right above him. Across the valley, Arenig Fawr's north ridge seemed unconcerned, stepping confidently towards the cloud cover before surrendering to it just below the summit. Doctor, on the other hand, fidgeted with his high collar, flipped his hood forward and hurried off the top. He stopped briefly at a point where the path fell off more steeply. There, he surveyed both valleys and the village far to the left, before picturing Peter's family's farmhouse which was hidden by a little hill. Peter bach!

"Thanks, Taid," he whispered, "Not content just to do so in life, in death you've blessed me as well."

Doctor descended with care, and thought of how lucky he was to lead such a full life in retirement. He'd always loved to fly-fish, and was fortunate to be one of the few to have been favoured with extensive fishing privileges on the Tryweryn and the Dee. He hiked a lot now as well, although he'd left it till his fifties to get started. Taid had been a catalyst on that occasion as well. Doctor thought back to that day, when to his dismay, a quarter of a mile uphill had nearly killed him. That was the day when he'd met Elfed and Geraint at one of the most special spots on earth, and had played apologist for Edgar; and when taken aback by breathlessness, had realised he'd better get fit, or else! Around Bala, what better way to do that than to hike? Many had been surprised, however, when Delilah had become his partner trekking those moors, and screes and tors and ridges. They'd had difficulty reconciling her natural elegance with stamina, but Doctor had known better. He'd known her at school, long, long before she'd assumed the trappings of a country doctor's wife. Today though, Doctor was alone, and he hurried again towards his car as it began to rain.

Around these outdoor activities, he fulfilled the few medical responsibilities he'd assumed as a favour to the new doctor. He served as a locum, for example, and because the surgery physically remained in an annex to his house, he often helped out with emergencies. So, fishing, hiking and doctoring, and overlaying them all, his role as an alter-parent. Peter bach!

"I can't believe how he's changed Delilah's life," mused the doctor on the mountain, "I really thought that she'd got over her disappointment long ago, but seeing the joy that came with the boy, it makes me doubt that she had."

For a couple in their early sixties, this shot of youth had been wonderful, but with wonder had come worries, not the least of which was the lad still lost his temper; not often any more, but nevertheless, Doctor had to admit to disappointment. The lovely boy was well on his way to becoming a lovely man, but occasionally and inexplicably he lost it. Surprisingly, this trait so far hadn't tarnished his standing at school, but Doctor knew it was only a matter of time. In a general sense, Peter had been weaned by now from his dad, but his Welshness still mattered deeply to him, and at its core lay the language; unfortunately, in line with Rhiannon and Edgar's thinking, those "so-called" Welsh men and women who'd "betrayed" it had become his bête noir, and these days, it seemed to Doctor, supplied the flashpoints for those few flare-ups.

"It's stuck in his gullet," fretted the doctor, "And no logic, not even Delilah's, seems able to dislodge it."

And then there was the worry, as ever, of Edgar, even though, thanks to a revitalised Myfanwy, his influence over his son had waned. Obviously, Edgar's life-long fixation with "those traitors who'd betrayed my language" hadn't helped Doctor's cause with Peter; nor had his most recent stand, which to Doctor and Delilah's horror had resonated with his son. Doctor mulled the matter on the lower slopes of Arenig Fach. It felt like a lifetime, but it had only been two weeks ago, on the morning of the last day of Peter's summer term, when Edgar had declared to Myfanwy, "No son of mine will be caught dead in an English university, and that's all there is to it!"

It was the summer of 1941 and Peter would soon turn fifteen. In another year, he was expected to matriculate at the grammar school for boys, and Doctor had quietly been grooming him for a place at Liverpool University to study medicine; when the time came, he and Delilah would foot the bill, of course. So Edgar's declaration couldn't have been more unwelcome, and that hadn't been all. According to Myfanwy, Edgar had then distinctly raised his voice to make his next point.

"In fact, I think it's foolish for him to go to college at all, because he's safer on the farm, isn't he? The main thing is he won't get called up to join the army while he's working here. I know most of my neighbours won't approve of this attitude, but I don't care: there's only one thing I can think of that's worse than fighting for those bloody English, and that's going to jail for refusing to do so."

Articulate as ever, he'd prepared the ground perfectly for his final demand.

"And if he's not going to college, there's no point him staying on at school, is there? So you go and tell them at school, Myfanwy, that he won't be back next year. It's the last day of term, so… " and off he'd paced with a cap in hand and crook in the other.

Doctor vividly remembered his stomach churning at the news. As a matter of fact, Myfanwy had chosen not to tell Peter the whole story. To him, she'd confined his father's demands to the bit about the English University. She'd reasoned that Edgar would soon get over his outburst, but he hadn't, and the following Monday he had visited the headmaster personally and demanded the removal of his son from the roster for the following term. To make matters worse, Peter had sided with his father when he'd heard the full story, because he didn't want to fight for the "bloody English" either. It was touch and go for days. Doctor had frantically sought a compromise; eventually, he and Delilah had prevailed with Peter. They had sensed from his reactions that he would seem to have no qualms taking advantage of one form of English institution while adamantly refusing to serve another. So they'd conceded on the issue of not fighting for the English, as Peter insisted on putting it. They'd agreed that it made sense for him to work on the farm till the war was over, but surely at that point, he might reconsider university, or perhaps one of the professions? So, just in case, didn't it make sense to stay at school, get his matric and spend that extra year in the sixth form? Of course it did! What did he have to lose? Myfanwy, though, had been advised by Doctor to take a different tack with Edgar.

"Don't mention university to him, Myfanwy. I'd play up the matric bit and the year in the sixth form, if I were you. Tell him Peter might want to be an auctioneer or be articled to an accountant or something like that, so doesn't it make sense to get his matric? What does he have to lose? That kind of thing, OK?"

The ploy seemed to have worked, but who knew at the time if the crisis had been permanently averted; at least it had been postponed. Doctor had heard the good news just two days ago, and had immediately arranged to pick up Peter after the hike today. This would be the first step in resuming normal relations. Peter would spend the night at their home, as he had done once a week throughout the last school year.

The clouds had congregated in earnest by now, and visibility shrank as the car literally nosed up the hill, away from the farmyard to the Bala road.

"So, you're OK, Peter?"

Peter nodded, and smiled warmly. He'd sprouted in his early teens and his face had become less chubby, further exaggerating his widish mouth.

"You're sure you've sorted everything out with your dad, now?"

A more emphatic nodding this time. Doctor took a deep breath: there was something he needed to say.

"There's another guest for dinner, Peter."

Doctor wished that Peter's head had turned just a little less sharply.

"Remember me telling you about my friend who's well up in the department of medicine at Liverpool?"

He was sure he sensed a softening then.

"Well, he just happened to drop by this morning. He's visiting a relative in Bala, and as he seemed interested in you, I asked him to have an early dinner with us. That's all right, isn't it?"

Peter beamed as only Peter could. What a huge relief it was, because even though Doctor thought he'd read things right, his confidence had been dented where Peter was concerned.

"I mean, we've got nothing to lose, right?"

Peter shook his head deliberately. The road climbed briefly, and then leveled off. Little of their lovely land was in view as Doctor drove cautiously past one of the most special spots on earth, where once he'd vowed to get fit, or else!

Despite a world at war, the next two years were exceedingly happy ones for Doctor and Delilah. Put plainly, it was a time when they reaped the most reward for the commitment they'd made to Peter. No doubt, to have heard their feelings expressed in such terms would have horrified them. As they saw it, they were simply fortunate to be able to take pleasure in his company and pride in his accomplishments at school, and there were plenty of both to savour. Peter now stayed at their home for two nights each week, and as his school was just up the road, to follow and support his exploits there couldn't have been more convenient. At no time in the past had their lives been more intertwined. So despite a world at war, Doctor and Delilah would look back on Peter's last two years at school as halcyon days.

A soft–coated Wheaten sat absolutely still as his master fished in the Tryweryn. Walter's obedience lessons had clearly paid off. It was the Thursday morning of Peter's last week at school – July 1943 – and in between casts, Doctor reviewed the great day they'd had on Saturday. Delilah and he had taken Peter to Chester. It was a celebration of Peter's school days, and they'd treated him royally: a posh lunch, with white wine; a row on the river; and a dragon, a little red dragon tattoo in exactly the same spot as Taid's. A tradition had been perpetuated, not reluctantly as in Edgar's, but proudly. As Walter watched the water rippling by, Doctor continued to reflect on Peter's achievements. He had to admit to disappointment that Peter hadn't developed as a soccer player. The skills were there, he laid them bare, and what quickness off the mark, but Peter lacked the stomach for physical contact in the park. Rather, his forte now lay in the arts, where poetry was his speciality, Welsh-language poetry. With Doctor's encouragement, he'd become a dabhand at the traditional metres, in which rhymes and alliterations in conjunction with strict correspondence of consonants had already tickled Welsh ears and moved their minds for millennia. When Peter read his poetry in public, as he often did, his signature introduction was striking.

"This one's for Henry VIII," he'd say, "More than likely

caged in hell, and as evil as the Devil himself; son of a Welsh father, and yet the scourge of our nation. This couplet's aimed at him."

Live long our lovely language,
Foil his aim, you'll roil his rage.

'Twas gall, but the hall was hooked. Just as Doctor was Peter's mentor in poetry, so Delilah was in debate. Never had she doubted his mastery of the facts, but honestly, the first few contests had been almost too much to bear. Each time, her heart had settled in her mouth for fear of Peter flying off the handle. After all, in that arena his views and prejudices would regularly and vigorously be challenged. To her huge relief though, Delilah had soon found that she could hang her hat on what Doctor and she had sensed all along: that Peter never lost his temper whenever he was on guard, and he steeled himself on those occasions. She'd wondered if others could see it. Oh, how she'd loved him for exposing himself like that, for literally throwing himself into the lion's den, and how she'd admired him for his concentration. Love and admiration, tinged with one regret.

"In person he's naturally witty, but in these debates, the world doesn't see him at his best. He's so caught up in himself, poor dab, that his humour can't break through."

She'd regretted that, and had loved him all the more for it.

Actually, Doctor was surprised at the taming of Peter's temper, for at times he'd begun to fear the worse. There was little doubt that the credit for the improvement lay largely with Delilah. There had been no diminution in Peter's passion for all that was Welsh, but somehow Delilah had managed to soften his stances and polish them in part. Yet, there lingered a shadow of a language line, a pale of prejudice. Grouped inside the pale were those who could speak Welsh, and outside, those who couldn't, and well beyond it, those who should but didn't.

Meanwhile, Walter watched as Doctor fished and reminisced.

The war in Europe was won! Doctor wasn't sure if the word "won" was appropriate, but at least it was over. On that day, Delilah and he sat among a small group at a poetry reading given by Peter. None of the poems addressed the war, and the timing was coincidental. However, Peter had omitted his signature couplet with comments lambasting Henry VIII.

Doctor thought, "He's not just getting better, but wiser as well."

He was so pleased at the intellectual vigour that Peter had displayed over the two years since he'd left school. He'd worried that his protégé might have atrophied in the relative isolation of Tryweryn. Even more pleasing was Peter's clean sheet on the tantrum front. Unaware of any single incident that may have been responsible for this, Doctor just assumed that Peter had grown out of it. For months though, he'd held his breath, braced for a breakdown. What a relief now to realise that Peter had come to grips with his weakness, and presumably, as part of the same process, had softened his stance on south Walians.

Doctor turned to face Delilah. She was almost seventy, but still very striking, with surprisingly little grey in the hair. He could understand why the boy had always been attached to her. On occasion, Doctor had felt left out of things, but he hadn't minded, and in any case, he'd get his day in the sun soon enough. Now that the war was over, it was almost time to prepare Peter for med school again, and that duty would naturally fall to him. Of course, they hadn't bargained for national service. That too could be avoided by staying on at the farm, but Doctor was convinced now that Peter was determined to study medicine, even if it meant serving in the army… the English army, as he put it… for eighteen months.

"That boy has a touch of ruthlessness," thought Doctor, "Not a bad thing, and neither is the facility to bypass principle for personal gain… now and then, anyway. Of course, his dad will be livid, but he'll learn to live with it."

Not an unreasonable supposition, Edgar's intolerant nature notwithstanding. After all, he was a leading light at the chapel by now, a respected man of God, with a reputation to protect. How many of his congregation would approve of a stand, principled or otherwise, that would deprive his son of the best possible education.

"Yes, Edgar will learn to live with it."

Not often was Doctor wrong when it came to judgement calls like that.

For the next twelve months, Peter worked on the farm on weekdays, studying only sporadically so as not to rouse his dad's suspicion. Then, on weekends, he crammed under Doctor's supervision. After a year of this routine, he took a test at Liverpool University. Three days later, Doctor's friend, who must have been very high up indeed, phoned with his congratulations. Peter had been accepted on the understanding that he'd complete his national service first. On the morning of the 21st of June, 1946, Peter broke the news to his dad. The twin blows were too much. All he said was, "Get out of my house," and he never spoke a word to his son again. Soon afterwards, Myfanwy and Peter were alone in the farmyard.

"He's a bad person, Peter. You know that I've gone out of my way not to badmouth your dad, but I'll tell you now that I'd give anything to see the back of him. I'd much rather live with Anti Enid, but of course I can't leave him. They'd shun me around here if I did, what with him being such a big wheel at the chapel and all. They'd make my life not worth living."

Peter grimaced sympathetically, and nodded.

"Take him at his word, Peter, and leave. It's the best thing for you, anyway. Doctor and Delilah will be delighted to take you in. I'll hate to see you go, but at least I'll have the consolation now of openly hating your father for it."

Peter hugged his Mam and spoke slowly.

"Mam, I understand how you feel, believe me, but don't you think it would be best to keep this within the family. It won't reflect well on any of us if the truth comes out."

He moved away slightly so that he could look her in the eye.

"Look, Mam, no one will guess what has happened if we keep it quiet. Most people will think it perfectly natural, under the circumstances, for me to move to Bala and live with Doctor. I really do understand your frustration, Mam, and how badly you must want to let off steam, but you won't look good doing it. Anyway, you've got Anti Enid. You can get it off your chest with her. Hey, Mam, how about going over to see her now? I've got plenty of time."

With such understanding, Peter mellowed his mother. However, he succeeded only because her love for him matched the hate she felt for his dad, but of these strong feelings, the good would in the future at times succumb to the bad.

Early one morning in late July, Peter took the train to Wrexham for his national service medical. Doctor had assumed that the process would take days, so he was shocked when Peter returned that evening. Walter, as usual, went bezerk in the hallway, while Doctor and Delilah were unusually restrained by curiosity.

"What happened?"

Peter's expression revealed nothing.

"Peter! What happened?"

"They couldn't find my heart… "

Doctor burst out laughing.

"… And when they did, they didn't know what to make of it."

"So what did you say?"

"Me? Nothing, of course. They're the experts, aren't they?"

"So you didn't tell them that you've known for years?"

"Known what?" impatiently from Delilah.

"You didn't know? Well, no… that's right… I probably didn't tell you, because it's not that… "

"Well, what is it?"

"His heart's on the right side rather than the left! There's nothing wrong with that, and we've known about it for a few years, but I haven't thought anything of it since, or obviously you'd have heard. So Peter, what did they say in the end?"

"Well, because they didn't know what to make of it, they sent me home and told me to go to college."

All three could see the humour in that, and shared it.

The following day, Myfanwy visited. Doctor informed her that Peter would leave for Liverpool in a month, and didn't she think it would be a good thing for him to take a holiday between now and then, and did she have any ideas?

"Well, I do have a sister in Borth-y-gest, and she would love to have him."

Doctor glanced at Peter, but there was no reaction.

"And of course, Mavis lives in Llanelli."

Llanelli, in south Wales!

"She's always writing and wondering whether Peter will ever come and stay."

Again Doctor glanced at Peter, and this time their eyes met.

"Hmm! Llanelli. Now that sounds interesting. Don't you think so, Peter?"

Perhaps he was weighing Doctor's intent, because he didn't say yes, but there was no dissent.

Forty-five

H E'D ONLY BEEN gone a day, but he missed Delilah already. Most would find that at least faintly ridiculous, for after all, she was old enough to be his grandmother, but it felt perfectly natural to Peter. In fact, had he not been so preoccupied since his arrival, he'd have missed her even sooner.

Peter had been met at Llanelli station the previous afternoon by the whole family; Anti Mavis and Uncle Dai, their nineteen-year-old daughter Delyth, and Daniel who was twelve. Peter was immediately struck by resemblances. Delyth, like her mother, was effusive, a bit fussy and plain, while Daniel's mouth was just like his dad's, slightly lopsided and shaded with humour. Their welcome couldn't have been warmer. He'd felt relaxed on the way to their home in the car, but once there, Anti Mavis hadn't allowed him a moment to think, nor a chance to miss Delilah. Most of the evening, he'd been too busy deflecting his aunt's enquiries. She'd been nice enough, but definitely aggressive, he thought, in winkling out every little nuance of their lives in Tryweryn. Though born and raised in Borth-y-gest, Mavis had taken to the people down south and had assumed their lack of reserve, and their warmth as well, for that matter. So she liked to chat and be in the know. What Peter had considered intrusive was to her natural curiosity within a family. He just wasn't used to the ways of the South, that's all, and for hours had persisted in parrying what he had perceived as prying. Delyth had probed as well, but to Peter's relief with much less success than her mother. Daniel couldn't have cared less, but he too had contributed to Peter's discomfort by practising the same tune incessantly on the piano in the adjoining parlour; "Sosban Fach" it was called, they'd told him.

And of course, there'd been Uncle Dai. He could hardly speak a word of Welsh, but amazingly the other three had carried on in it as if he did. Now, that had been a tricky one for Peter to reconcile with his preconception of the south. An enigma indeed was Uncle Dai. Still, he must have understood most of what had been said, because he'd laughed a lot, and he must have sensed that Peter had felt somewhat under siege, because several times he'd teasingly encouraged him, only then to turn around and quip, in English of course, that his money was still on his wife.

"You're putting up a good fight, boyo, but she'll wear you out in the end, you'll see."

The Peter of old, especially on the defensive, would surely have bridled at Uncle Dai's banter. Here was a south Walian who to Peter had epitomised the worst in Welsh society, a compatriot who clearly could have spoken the language but didn't; yet anger hadn't welled as it might, due in part to Delilah's moderating influence and his own maturing self-control, but there was something else in the air as well. That Uncle Dai was essentially allowing the others their Welsh had thrown Peter. It had made no sense to him that an accessory to national shame could exhibit such tolerance. So yes, Uncle Dai certainly was an enigma, and of course his prediction regarding the good fight, boyo, had inevitably come true. Peter may have laughed gaily as he'd thrown in the towel, but actually, Anti Mavis's pressure had still bothered him, and his submission had hurt quite a bit.

"I'm sure Mam has told her most of the stuff that's going on at home" was his rationalisation.

So in the end, he'd spilled the domestic beans, but not without salvaging some pride. When it came to his dad, he'd been stubbornly even-handed, too much so for Anti Mavis's liking, he'd sensed with satisfaction; and while details of Doctor had been freely divulged, much about Delilah he'd skillfully managed to keep to himself, and that had helped his wounded pride as well.

Worn out by his aunt's tenacity, he'd flopped into bed that night.

The next morning, from their parlour, he admired the view of the Loughor Estuary and the Gower Peninsula beyond. The others had just left on foot for chapel. The ladies had been so disappointed that Peter had declined to join them and had pressed the best they could, but he'd held his ground, insisting only that he was tired. He'd blamed it on the sea air, but in truth, he'd wanted some time to himself.

"Why can't all women be just like Delilah?" he'd sighed.

She was quick without being showy, pretty without being flashy and firm in her views without being pushy. He'd only been there a day, and he missed her already. All morning he'd wondered what on earth he would do for the next three weeks. Delyth had no such qualms. She knew exactly what she was going to do. She looked forward to it too, as she'd told him over breakfast.

"I can't wait for Greda to come back to work. It's been no fun… "

"Who's Greta?"

"Oh, sorry! She's Dadi's bookkeeper, and she works here in the house; by the way, it's not Greta, it's Greda with a 'd'. It's softer isn't it, and nicer too, I think. Anyway, she's been on holiday for a fortnight, and it's been no fun around here without her, but she'll be back tomorrow… " and at the prospect, her face had lit up, and was almost pretty.

"Then two weeks today, Daniel and I are going to stay with Uncle Jimmy. He's Dadi's brother, you know. I love being on his farm. Pembrokeshire is so lovely, and I like my cousins a lot as well. So, we'll be there for ten days, and soon after that, I go to nursing school in Swansea."

Now that she wasn't hounding him, Peter quite liked Delyth. She'd continued warmly, "And what are you going to do for the next three weeks, Peter?"

An innocent question, but it had taken Peter aback. She hadn't been reading his mind, had she? He'd shrugged his shoulders and smiled, and now, as he gazed dreamily at the estuary, he reviewed their conversation.

"So it's Greda, aye? Now, how could anyone come up with a name like that?"

You'd be surprised, Peter bach.

When Peter met Greda on Monday, 'twas with feelings that leapt from his heart. Though her hair not fair but auburn, he still thought she resembled Delilah. In looks, darker but prettier: her mouth better-defined, her eyes a shade deeper and her cheekbones much higher, he noted, and though not as tall, still lithe and pleasingly shapely. In demeanour, he would find her by day's end to be as sensitive and sensible and quick as Delilah, and as gentle in expressing her views, as well. Ironically, while often reminded of Delilah this way, he would manage not to miss her anymore.

Peter talked little to Greda that day. On her first day back, she was naturally occupied with duties, and Delyth of course, who was convinced that Greda had suffered a fortnight's neglect, and was in need of compensation. Effusively, she smothered her friend with affection, effectively excluding Peter from most conversations. Fortunately, for the time, enchantment sufficed for him. Many, smitten as he was, would have desperately sought the other's attention, but Peter for now was content to observe. To that end, rather than walk to the beach as he'd intended, reasonably plausible reasons were found for lounging around the house; and others, perhaps less so, for visiting the office where Greda worked and Delyth dawdled. As hard as it was, he was careful not to overdo it, not to show his hand so to speak, because the last thing he wanted was Uncle Dai teasing him again.

So, while in Greda's graceful presence on that Monday, Peter mostly noticed; noticed everything about her with wonder and warmth: her high forehead, softened by strands of hair that never failed to flop; her blue eyes set deeply under delicate, darkish eyebrows; her long nose and finely drawn lips. Perfection was his verdict. Her smiles were generally restrained, yet soft and expressive, but when full, revealed such lovely teeth that he wondered why she wouldn't smile that way more often. Her one flaw, a little, pale diagonal scar on her left upper lip, perversely enhanced her allure. Her long fingers, which regularly flicked the locks from her brow, particularly caught his eye, and it was as much as he could do not to follow them each time to their natural resting place just above her knees. He'd feel terrible if she caught him looking at her knees, although they were lovely too.

And how thoughtful and gentle she was with his cousin. As many qualities as Delyth had in common with her mother... warmth, gregariousness and enthusiasm, for example... there was one she lacked. Unlike Anti Mavis, Delyth often spoke without forethought, and then came across as insensitive and unwise, as she did a few times on that Monday. On those occasions, she was ever so politely and kindly corrected by Greda, and to Peter's surprise, far from being offended, Delyth actually seemed to appreciate her friend's suggestions.

"How does Greda do it?" he wondered, "She seems amazingly self-assured. Whatever would she see in me?" and stirred by this lapse in selflessness, his better instincts surfaced.

"Peter! What is this nonsense? Aren't you getting this the

wrong way round, worrying about what she might think of you?"

He became vaguely aware of Delyth greeting her father in the adjoining kitchen. He listened lazily, until he was totally distracted by a furrowing of Greda's brow, and the sad reflection he felt sure was expressed by her half-open, still pretty mouth.

"What was that about," he thought, "For a moment, she seemed sad," and then he wondered whether she might not need some comfort after all. As hard as he tried to be selfless, for the very first time he allowed himself to wish for a sign, any little sign that showed that she liked him. It was only a slightly selfish thought; not enough to make him feel guilty.

So for much of Monday he'd merely observed, and most of that night while waiting for sleep, he thought of all he'd noticed, in perfect peace but for a few moments of fretting over a sign that might not materialise. To his credit though, he was handling his emotions well so far, particularly in light of his inexperience. Excepting Delilah, and of course his love for her was different, on only one previous occasion had he presumed he was in the least bit in love. Eleri was a farm girl who lived further down the valley. She was but one of several girls he'd been equally close to in chapel and school. As to why he picked her, he supposed he'd been lonely, and really, had only latched onto Eleri for her politics, which had matched his in tone and intensity. No surprise then that his most vivid recollection of the affair was not of her, but of his Mam, openly devilish in intent, just wondering that's all, how dear Delilah was dealing with it. In any case, within months the relationship had fizzled, and now at last, he understood why.

By Wednesday, when still no sign was forthcoming, Peter's enchantment was gradually yielding to growing insecurity. Late afternoon in the office, Greda pored over columns of numbers and Delyth knitted. For the umpteenth time, Peter noticed his favourite fingers flicking locks from his favourite brow. He left briefly, to return with a book which he would have read, had his mind not wandered and succumbed to daydreams instead.

"I think you'd enjoy Mynydd Sylen," said Greda softly without raising her head from the ledger. There was no reply, prompting her, and Delyth too, to straighten their backs and glance at Peter in surprise.

"Peter?"

"Yes?… oh! Were you talking to me?" and in the face of those features he loved so well, he suddenly felt so foolish.

"I was saying that I think you'd enjoy Mynydd Sylen. You know the railway down the road? Well, it goes to Horeb, and the mountain isn't far from there at all."

He didn't feel he was stretching for that elusive sign, when he wondered and wondered why she'd said that, so completely out of the blue. And in light of his growing frustration, he knew that sooner or later he'd have to take a chance.

"You live near Horeb, don't you Greda? D'you like to walk? I mean, would you like to walk up the mountain with me?"

There! He couldn't believe he'd forced himself to say it, but what if she wouldn't…?

"Well, yes! Why not? That's a lovely idea. I could meet you in Horeb, couldn't I?" and she gave him the smile with the lovely teeth, and the lovely eyes and lovely chin, and the lovely knees and lovely skin; now, there was a sign for you!

"We could do it tomorrow, actually… "

Peter sullied the beauty of the moment with the thought that not many would have handled this better than him.

"… It's one of my days off, and I haven't… "

"Hey! What about me then? I'd like to go up Mynydd Sylen as well," from Delyth, as if divinely appointed to prick Peter's pride; and be immediately assisted by Greda, who begged her friend to join them on their walk, with an enthusiasm that Peter had assumed was reserved for him. Suddenly, his emotions all at sea, he almost dismissed Greda's sign. He'd have totally devalued the moment had his better instincts not come to the surface again.

"Come on, Peter! What are you doing, wasting your time flirting with self-satisfaction, when you've been handed the opportunity to delight in her, to love her. For goodness sake, let her be the object of an unselfish love. Peter, Peter, Peter!"

And it did the trick. There and then, he decided that he would really try to consider everything in relation to her well-being, and in the process, relegate himself to it. He was sufficiently wise to know that the road to heaven is paved with disappointments, but his compass was set right at least. With a bit of luck, no longer would his emotions be wound around his ego. Nor would they be programmed by expectations of her, for if true to his ideal, there'd be none. Within this paradigm, even rejection could be seen in a positive light. Amazingly, he felt securer and more serene.

As Delyth bowed her head and returned to her knitting, Greda smiled secretively at Peter. It wasn't easy not to wallow in that smile, nor in the wicked wink that followed. He had to calm himself as a wave of warmth suffused him. Out of the blue, Greda's eyes reminded him of Delilah, but he didn't miss her.

On the Saturday, he decided to dress more smartly than usual, and was reading in the office when Greda came to work. She was late, so he'd been waiting a while, but no wait was too long for the warmth of her smile, and the sight of her beautiful face; in any case, he had an important question to ask.

"Hello, Peter. My bus was late again, and because I was rushing, I stepped in a puddle, so my sandals are soaking now. You look very nice."

He could have said the same of her, with her shoulder-length auburn hair drawn in a ponytail, revealing the delicate curve of her neck and highlighting her brilliant bone structure. As she bent forward to undo her sandals, her blouse crept well up her back, exposing a swathe of spine, and her toes, like her fingers, were unusually long, he noticed. Her head bounced back up, and she turned to Peter with a carefree smile, but her face froze, presumably because his was so serious, and the eyes that held hers so intense. Her brow furrowed till he broke the tension with a shy smile, which she returned. They held each other's gaze till she blushed, and then she lowered her head.

"So at last she knows my feelings," he thought, dreamily admiring the nape of her neck, "And I think I know hers as well."

"Greda," he said softly, "We could do the walk tomorrow, if you're free."

He referred to the walk planned for last Thursday, which they'd cancelled because of the rain.

"Oh, Peter! I can't, I'm so sorry."

That she too, moments ago, had experienced the onset of intimacy was surely confirmed by the caring and concerned tone in her voice.

"I've arranged to be with my mother tomorrow, I'm sorry…"

She needn't be sorry. She needn't apologise for enabling him to trust her and to believe her to be honest and fair.

"… And next Thursday and Friday as well, but I could do it next Sunday."

Talk about grounds for self-satisfaction, but echoing her transparency, he immediately reminded her that Delyth would have left for Pembrokeshire by then.

"Oh that's right," she gasped, and thought for a moment, "She'd be upset… Oh, hello, Mr Davies", over her shoulder at Uncle Dai, and then quickly in earnest to Peter, "But I really can't change my plans for tomorrow."

He understood perfectly why she felt the need to say it again, but he wished she hadn't in front of Uncle Dai, who justified Peter's misgivings by provocatively raising his eyebrows at him several times, before huddling with Greda at the table.

Uncle Dai was a generous man, but he loved to tease, and it wasn't long after Greda had gone that he began to taunt Peter.

"So you fancy her, aye?"

"Oh Uncle Dai, don't be silly," dismissively.

"Well, I heard what she said, Peter. Sounds to me as if someone fancies somebody," in a mocking falsetto voice.

"She's just company for me, Uncle Dai, that's all. I hardly know anyone else here, do I?"

"Pretty good-looking company, wouldn't you say, Peter, so you can't blame me for... "

"Why," Peter wondered, "do I have to put up with this?"

Better if he'd ridden it out than abruptly changing direction, especially in light of the subject that came to mind.

"Uncle Dai, why didn't you bother with Welsh?"

"That's a pretty bold change of tack! However, being that you asked, I didn't think it was important. I didn't think it was important then and I don't think it's important now. There's no more to it than that, Peter bach."

For the first time in months, anger welled in Peter's breast, though he'd only himself to blame. Actually, he'd managed to control these flare-ups quite easily for a while now, but with Greda in the picture, he preferred not to take any chances. He reverted to a technique that had worked infallibly recently, and for the second time in their conversation, he abruptly changed the subject, and as before, to one that came naturally to mind.

"Uncle Dai, I shouldn't have avoided your question. I admit I do like Greda, or fancy her, if you like. I mean, why wouldn't

I fancy her. Everyone else does, I'm sure. Does she have a boyfriend, d'you think?"

His candour disarmed Uncle Dai.

"I haven't got a clue… "

Uncle Dai loved to tease, but got no kicks from delving.

"… But I bet I know someone who does. I'll have a word with her, if you like."

Peter of course had first-hand experience of Anti Mavis's predilection to probe, but he doubted that she'd know much about Greda's love life. He expected to learn little more from her than he had from Uncle Dai, but he wasn't to know that Anti Mavis had access to an insider. Had he, the thought that soon one word from her could affect the rest of his life would have been unsettling, to say the least, even for one who'd prepared himself to accept rejection in a positive light.

"Peter? Your Uncle Dai asked me to… "

"Yes, he said he would."

"Don't hang your heart on her, Peter bach."

What on earth was she on about? How could she be so matter of fact on a subject so dear to him? And yet, she'd spoken with an authority that was disconcerting.

"I know she's beautiful and has a lovely nature and all that, but mind my words, Peter bach, she'll break your heart."

He was verging on anger, when suddenly her opinions and predictions were replaced by facts.

"I know you don't want to hear this, Peter, but listen now. Greda's had many boyfriends, which comes as no surprise, right? But d'you know what, she left them all, and in each case after only a matter of weeks or months. What does that tell you?"

Whereas tentative his response to her opinions, firm was his mind in challenging her facts.

"That's not that unusual, Anti Mavis. She's just feeling her way, and learning from her mistakes, don't you think?"

He needn't have asked because even before he'd finished, he'd read on her face that's not what she thought at all.

"Peter, I'm sorry, but she just doesn't trust men, and when you don't trust them, it's hard to grow to like them, isn't it?"

Surely an opinion, spoken as if fact, was Peter's assessment of that.

"You see Peter, I'm her mother's friend."

Deflated, he reflected, and elected to listen.

"I've known her mother for ages, but it's only in the last few years that we've become friends. We never used to see that much of each other, but since her mother's death about a year ago, we've become much closer; and now, of course, you know how we found Greda."

Now her source had been satisfactorily established, he wished Anti Mavis would move along and expand on the information itself.

"Anti Mavis, you said that Greda didn't trust… "

"Listen, Peter. Greda's first boyfriend was a huge mistake. He treated her badly, but she was infatuated with him… first love and all that; so she stuck with him, until he struck her on the mouth. I'm sure you've noticed the little scar on her upper lip? Well, that was him. Bad luck, I suppose, but it's no surprise, is it, that she can't trust men after that. She's attracted to them, but can't trust them, so her affairs don't last that long."

Though Peter had no basis for not believing what she'd said, his heart had to have its say.

"I can't believe it, Anti Mavis. I know I'm young, and perhaps naive, but to me she seems perfectly well adjusted: the opposite of the way you've described her."

"It all goes to show, doesn't it, Peter? Please keep this to yourself. I've only told you so that you can take care of yourself."

"I know, I know, Anti Mavis, and don't think I'm not thankful, but after all that, does she have a boyfriend or not?"

Anti Mavis's chin slumped, her eyes shut and her head shook in exasperation.

"Oh, Peter! Why did I bother? You still want to know, even after all that? OK! Let me put it to you this way. A month ago, my answer would have been "yes". Now, that says it all, doesn't it?"

She couldn't have fired a more telling shot to end the conversation, but Peter, predetermined not to be derailed, fell back on a standard defense: the past was history, and a mystery, all right, but theirs was the future, inevitably bright; and supporting this romantic optimism was the confidence of one to whom rejection held no fear. And yet, so surprising were his aunt's assertions, that he wouldn't have been human not to wonder, just a little, now and then; and so he did, as he walked for miles on the morning of each of the next seven days; as he smiled at Greda, and she in turn returned the smile with a warmth that belied what he'd heard; as he inadvertently touched her hand and couldn't tell if she felt the thrill as well; and as he accidentally brushed against her body, and allowed himself to dwell on it. So yes, he did wonder, but just a little, now and then, until the following Sunday, when walking along the railway to meet her, he wondered a little more, and wondered again, but not so frequently as to blind himself to nature's distractions: blackberries ripe, hazelnuts not, a blackbird so clean and a robin so mean, intent on defending its plot.

"Past the reservoir," she'd said, "and when you see the brickworks on your left, you'll know you're almost there. And watch out for the trains, though there may not be one that morning."

There hadn't, leaving the countryside in peace to reclaim the derelict brickworks. He guessed the time to be quarter to ten when he saw her, tall and willowy in the distance. She waved at him gaily, and yet, his wondering resumed with a vengeance. He was really surprised that she'd brought a friend, but he shouldn't be, should he, had he given an ounce of credence to one word that Anti Mavis had said. Disappointed, he withdrew into himself, but "Wait," said his better nature, "you're losing the plot again, Peter. It's her well-being, remember? If she's more comfortable with a friend, then allow it. You can still admire her, and love her."

By the time he was close enough to Greda to greet her, he'd no need to put on a brave face. He'd already adjusted positively while some distance away, but more to the point, as he had neared, he'd realised with relief that the friend was far too smartly dressed for walking up Mynydd Sylen.

"Peter, this is Sally. She's my only Baptist friend," and she cocked her head playfully at the chapel behind her, where groups were gossiping in their Sunday best.

God! Greda was so beautiful: her blue, blue eyes, her auburn hair, her long, long fingers, her arms quite bare, all beautiful, and that little, little scar on her upper lip; and all her beauty loosely clad in the pastel shades of a sleeveless blouse and a summer skirt that stopped around her knees.

"Looks as if it's about time for you to go inside, Sally," and when her friend had turned to leave, Greda took Peter's hand and led him from the platform to the road. She'd taken his hand!

"You took my hand!"

Had he not subdued his ego, Peter would likely have been too self-conscious to have said something as silly and as honest as that. Greda smiled a little shyly, and as if to cover her slight awkwardness, moved closer to him and put both her arms through one of his. Peter couldn't believe it! The girl he fancied, as Uncle Dai had put it, was the most beautiful girl in the world, and here she was, arm in arm with him. He was cocooned in a cosy feeling, which cried out for a kiss, but he resisted, for he would prefer her to continue to set the tempo, and in any case, he'd promised himself to wait till Mynydd Sylen. Then, via two bridges, they walked under the railway and over the river.

"You took my hand!"

"Well, I like you, that's all."

Peter moved away slightly, and looked at her sceptically as if to say she'd have to do a bit better than that.

"I like you a lot, then," with a naughty smile.

His expression implied that that was better. Then, without prompting, and suddenly very serious, she said, "I like you because you make me feel good, and I trust you. I can't ask for more than that."

And that explained it all! That reconciled Anti Mavis's misgivings with his own quite contrary impressions. While in others, she'd not trusted, in him, she did. Peter left it at that, and as they climbed up the road away from the Lliedi valley, Greda told him of everyone who lived in every house they passed, and in every farm to be seen on the southern slopes of Sylen. As he listened lazily in total contentment, he played with her fingers, and then stopped, awaiting encouragement before playing with them again.

"Why do you trust me?"

"Well, I've been watching you, haven't I, and sizing you up for a fortnight, now. I wasn't quite as detached as you might have thought. And I've talked things over with my mother and father, too... mainly my mother, though. I told her everything about you that I could think of."

"What d'you mean? What kind of things?"

"Well, how gentle you are, and generous; and what you look like, and you come from near Bala, and... "

"Near Bala? Didn't you tell her that I live high up in the Tryweryn valley?"

"No! I didn't know that."

"Didn't I tell you?"

"No, but I wish you had. It sounds much more romantic than Bala!"

They were approaching Four Roads, and beyond the crossroads, trees were sparser and the landscape moorish.

"So Greda, it sounds as if you're close to your parents?"

"Well, yes, I suppose I am. I do value their advice, and on some things in particular."

That same, sad look again, a furrowing of her brow and her pretty mouth half-open, revealing the tips of her lovely teeth. He wanted to brush away that lock of hair so badly, but the intimacy would have led to a kiss he was sure, at a time that wasn't yet just right. In any case, she quickly assumed the initiative by moving closer and putting her arms in one of his again.

"Anti Mavis told me about your scar. It must have been frightening."

She turned towards him as if acknowledging his empathy. She was almost as tall as he was. Her eyes, sincere and sad, were on a level with his, and as for her lips, it was as much as he could do not to...

Quite unaffectedly, she confirmed Anti Mavis's story of her scar; and how later, she'd dated several boys and how none had lasted long; how she'd put trust on a pedestal and set her expectations high, and how no one had met them... and with a glance at Peter... until now! Her candour dispelled any vestiges of doubt; no longer would he wonder, not even a little, now and then.

"You can see the top from here. Look! Come on," and she ran ahead of him up the trail, seemingly ablaze, with her blouse and skirt and hair all shimmering in the sun. At the top she turned, her bare arms raised uninhibitedly above her head. Her little breasts heaved as she caught her breath. God! How wholesome she looked, and so happy. As he approached, she abruptly took his hand and dragged him excitedly in all directions, reciting the names of prominent spots, near and afar. Then, arm in arm, she led him slowly to the mountain's western end.

"See the water tank, and the semi-detached houses behind? That's where I live, in the one on the left, and that's my bedroom window, upstairs on the right. See? Funny to think that I'm usually down there looking up," and with that thought, her animated expression faded into seriousness as she turned towards him, and laid her long arms around his neck, her eyes on a level with his... this on the very spot where twenty years earlier, her mother had cajoled his father into singing "Calon Lân". Peter did what he'd been dying to do for hours: he ran his fingers very slowly along her bare arms, carefully brushed the lock off her forehead and held her face tenderly in his hands. He kissed Greda, his half-sister, gently at first, but then with increasing passion as each fed on the other's response. How magical, affectionate and sensuous their moment, and how cruelly unfair.

To witness her daughter's uninhibited enthusiasm for the boy was a joy for Dorothy: though Greda was tolerant in general, she hadn't been with boys... until this one. So, it would seem that the troubling legacy of Greda's disastrous first affair had at last been swept away. She could only wish that Donald and the others were there to see it too. It was still early days though, for Greda had only met him a fortnight ago, and to complicate things, he wasn't from Llanelli, but on holiday from Bala in north Wales. Dorothy's mind, once again, inevitably fixed on Edgar, another north Walian, another from Bala, who'd holidayed here. Of course, the circumstances were completely different, but the coincidence was eerily striking all the same. She dwelt on that until interrupted by Greda, who burst back into the kitchen, still glowing with excitement.

"Oh Mami," she said, hugging her mother extravagantly, "It was brilliant. The mountain was lovely, and so was Peter."

Over Greda's shoulder, Dorothy smiled at Millie's picture which hung above the mantelpiece.

"I never want to go up Mynydd Sylen again, though," Greda continued, "I just want to remember it the way it was today."

Dorothy's hug tightened. Mynydd Sylen! That rendered the coincidence more eerily striking still.

"We're going to the Gower on Friday," and suddenly very sadly, "and then he goes home the next day."

The Gower! With a sense of relief which for a moment struck her as irrational, Dorothy noted that the coincidence ended there. But the coincidence would be laid completely bare when later Dorothy would be made aware by Greda of a dragon. In the meantime, the young lady and her half brother would have one more day in the sun.

Forty-six

A WIDE, COMFORTABLE path follows the Gower Coast along the sea-cliff tops from Port Eynon to Rhosilli. Only when it drops off to traverse the occasional valley and scrambles back up again, does it narrow, and even then it is not especially demanding. From one of these dips, an elderly couple bobbed into view, leaning heavily on their walking sticks as they took each step. They looked the part in their heavy boots, multi-pocketed trousers and stylish hats. Once on level ground, they stopped to rest, and while his companion fumbled for her water bottle, the man glanced around casually. Various shades of summer colours intermingling on the cliff tops contrasted sharply with the consistent, cultivated greens just over the fence to his left. Beyond, but not very far, a prominent ridge seemed worlds apart from the stunning scene to his right. There, the Bristol Channel in hypnotic motion; on its far side to the east, north Devon looming surprisingly large; straight out to sea, Lundy barely visible; and accompanying the whole spectacle, the muffled might of waves breaking and battering below.

The man suddenly focused, and turning to his companion, pointed to another pair approaching in the distance. Within minutes, they were seen to be a young couple, and soon, as they passed, restrained greetings were exchanged.

"I do believe they were a brother and sister. Don't you agree, dear?" the elderly lady said in English, with a twang.

"Well, if they are, how do you account for the fact that they were holding hands until they got quite close to us… dear?"

"Good gosh, were they really? That's awfully strange. I could have sworn I saw a resemblance."

The gentleman shrugged his shoulders.

"All I can say," he commented, "is that he must be a jolly strong fellow to handle that enormous pack on his back."

Struck by the same thought, it seems, they stopped and turned together, to find that Peter and Greda were holding hands again. The elderly couple glanced at each other, but she chose not to acknowledge his smug smile, which simply said that he'd told her so. Instead her gaze returned to the young couple, and with a leap to the dark side of her imagination, she resolved the inconsistency. In her mind, a drama unfolded, which would inevitably end in tragedy. The only uncertainty lay in the degree of anguish. Her hope was that Fate, the grand director, would see fit to drop the curtain much sooner rather than later. Saddened by her thoughts, she surprised her companion by taking his hand.

The enormous backpack lay empty and to one side. Its contents had been laid on one half of a large, white cotton cloth. After passing the elderly couple, Peter and Greda had hiked hand in hand for half an hour, before branching down one of the steep, grassy chutes that linked the upper, gentle Gower Trail to the more rugged one that hugged the coastline more closely down below. Two-thirds of the way down, they'd found their spot and unpacked their picnic. Afterwards, they lay on their backs on the cotton cloth, side by side. It was a hot and slightly sultry day. Peter sat up slowly, took off his shirt and carefully lowered himself down again. His gentleness in this, and in general, pleased Greda, and prompted her to turn lazily on her side and finger the fine hair on his chest. Difficult to divine the Grand Director's motives at this point, but in Greda's mind, under the circumstances, passion would inevitably be frantic and likely unfulfilling. On their last day together, to her it seemed more appropriate to show restraint, respect and affection. Peter rolled over, to be asked by Greda quite casually the significance of the little red dragon tattooed on his shoulder. She hadn't expected his story, and was moved by the emotion he injected into it. When he'd finished, she kissed the dragon, and her lips lingered. Then, she rolled on her back again. Their hands touched, and for a few minutes she lay peacefully, relaxed and content in the heat of the sun. To her dismay, Peter's hand shifted and settled on her thigh. This wouldn't do... not today. Yet, she felt herself warming to it. She thought of how thrilling their intimacies on Mynydd Sylen had been. It was tempting, indeed, but she just knew that on their last day together, one step further would be a step too far. Wishing to be sensitive to his feelings as well as true to her own, she could think of nothing but be playful. Without warning, she pushed herself to her feet and ran downhill towards the lower trail, shouting as she went, "Come on, Peter, catch me if you can! See if you can catch me!"

He was slow to react to her getaway. He had an emotion to deal with first: a fleeting feeling of rejection. By the time he'd wrenched himself into the spirit of things and pulled his shirt on over his head, Greda had already reached the trail, and was following it towards a high grassy ridge to the right. Not quite knowing why, he left their picnic things strewn on the cloth and gave chase, but she was over the ridge, well before he got there. Peering over the top, Peter was taken aback. Rather than follow the grass to yet another, higher ridge, the trail veered sharply across a near vertical rockface, along a narrow ledge – thirty yards long was Peter's guess – and then widened into a scree field. To him, the ledge seemed frighteningly exposed, and yet halfway along it, Greda, grinning and clearly unconcerned, glanced nonchalantly over her shoulder, egging him on with waves of her hand. His unease, initially fanned by her foolhardiness, turned in on himself. In a twist that surprised and bothered him, he felt cornered, and he tensed. He wasn't sure that if alone, he'd have even considered the crossing, but now pride was pressuring as

Greda egged him on. Increasingly ill at ease, he felt himself being railroaded into assessing the situation. He focused shakily on two unlikely, flimsy, windswept trees that sprouted at an angle from the lip of the ledge. Surely... surely, he could reach the first one, couldn't he, and then maybe... oh! He wasn't at all convinced. Oh, God! Greda was on the move again, ratcheting the pressure another painful notch. Particularly at that moment, he shouldn't have looked down. Wide-eyed though, he slowly followed the rockface downwards, past bushes here and there that seemed to be hanging in mid-air; downwards and downwards, faster and faster to the foam below, where waves were breaking and incessantly battering. No, he shouldn't have looked, especially then. The wobbles set in and disappointed him. This was totally ridiculous! He didn't have to put himself through this, but there again was Greda, on the scree now, waving and egging him on. Oh, God! He steeled himself the best he could, and entered the ledge. Eyes ahead and leaning into the rockface, he inched his way towards the tree. He rushed a bit at the end, but he made it. That wasn't so bad, was it, and he gained further confidence when he noticed that Greda wasn't watching any more: she had turned to take on the scree. His breathing became somewhat easier, and the wobbles subsided. Onwards he ventured, inching as before, and was almost at the second tree when he slightly stubbed his foot. Without thinking, he looked down, and experienced a stab of vertigo. Rather than compose himself, he rushed, as before, to cover those last few yards.

The tree is just that little bit further away than he thought. Outstretched fingers merely manage to graze it. Momentum takes him over the edge. Instinctively, he grasps at the lip of the ledge. He fails to hold there, but still, it slows his fall; so rather than tumble out of control, his hands and feet scrape on the rock as he slides. Four feet into the fall, he brushes a bush and grasps it. There he hangs, his legs dangling. A split second later, he grasps another to his left. There's an obvious handhold a foot above. If only he could raise himself! The bush to the right rips off in his hand as he leverages on it. He swings wildly to his left, toeing and froing till settling, hanging again in mid-air. This frenetic sequence takes seconds. His moves are instinctive: he's had no time to think. When he does, he vividly pictures the void below… the void below… the void below. In a totally inexplicable change of perspective, he feels no fear of that void below. There's nothing he can do now anyway but hold on. His fate hangs on the whim of a bush. No, he feels no fear of that void below. He just hangs, and a surreal calmness washes over him, seduces him even. It would be so easy to succumb to the spell, but at the thought of her, he yells, "Greda! Greda!"

Greda stops on the scree. She turns carefreely, intending to tease her friend. Instead, she's bewildered. He can't have turned back: he hasn't had time! Greda's already scrambling back when she hears him yelling her name. Constantly reassuring Peter, she urgently shuffles along the ledge. At the tree, she anxiously peers over the edge. So focused had she been on her footwork, that she'd not actually imagined his predicament. She's aghast, sick to her stomach, but in no doubt of what needs to be done. With arms wrapped tightly around the tree, she lowers herself to him, not reassuring any longer, but systematically yelling for help… clearly and regularly. One of her ankles is loosely grasped. She flexes, and feels him adjusting his grip. He'll try and heave himself up, he says. She steels herself to the limit, and prepares for the strain. When it comes, she's distraught. She screams that she can't take it, just as the bush rips from the rock and crashes into his chest. Somehow, she survives that momentary extra pressure, and the couple stabilise, hanging in mid-air, she from the tree and he from her ankles. She resumes crying for help. Perhaps the elderly lady they'd met on the trail had no idea she was playing with fire when she pressed the grand director.

Even if she had, how could she be blamed, for who could have imagined it would come to this?

Greda's relief is short-lived. Even in equilibrium like this, she knows now she can't hold him for long. Her sense that he's not tiring yet is of little consolation. Her spirit sinks, yet she strives to be strong, but can't quell her fear. Her will wavers, but she vows that she'll never let on that she's weakening. Never! At the slightest inkling of that, he'd let go, she is sure. She supposes there is some merit in saving one of their lives, but how could she possibly confess that she couldn't hold him a second longer, knowing it to be a sentence of death; and even if deferred to the very last moment, how could she be sure there wasn't a moment more… for miracles do happen, don't they? In any case, it's all immaterial, for as he goes, so will she… and that's all there is to it. She can see no other way. A mild panic grips her, and debilitates. In her funk, Greda concedes that she'll have to let go in the end, but she'll never, never let on, and that resolution revives her, till her arms start trembling and her breathing becomes short and uneven. Rather than betray her distress though, she stops shouting for help. Emotion overcomes her, and she's dying to tell him so many things: that she's never been happier than when she is with him; that she loves him and that she's never truly loved before; but she's afraid he'd take her confessions as a sign that the end is near…and let go. She recites her mantra: she'll never let on, she'll never let on, she'll never…

… Oh, God! There's someone on the ridge!

"Peter! There's someone on the ridge! There's someone on the ridge, Peter!"

She can't believe it. Her relief is huge, and hugs her. Her spirit soars, and to a lesser degree, her strength as well. It seems the grand director's not yet ready to let the final curtain drop.

"Peter! He's coming to help us. Hang on, for a bit longer. Please!"

The young man has already crossed the grass, and is shuffling confidently along the ridge. As he nears, she's struck not by his fair and curly hair, nor his noticeably round face, but by his freckles, which appear slightly raised and exaggerate the urgency that's etched on his face.

David Devereux had walked for well over half an hour along the higher, more comfortable Gower trail towards Rhosilli. Recently demobbed and reunited with his family in Llwynypia, he was spending this week in Swansea at the home of an army mate. This day though was his alone, and the only constraint on his time was the last bus back to town from Port Eynon. He intended to return to the bus stop along the lower trail, and stood atop a chute, wondering whether to drop down it. He had time to go further, for certain, and rarely was the weather as wonderful as this. As he debated, a long way down the chute he spotted some whiteness, which piqued his curiosity and helped make up his mind. Tightening his backpack around the shoulders, he literally ran down the chute, so in a flash, the blur of whiteness zoomed into focus. He slid to a stop and considered retreating, rather than invade someone's privacy. He scanned the chute, and as hard as it was to believe, there was no one to be seen. He was still undecided, but the sea below was beckoning, so soon, on he ran past the large, white cotton cloth, where he was careful not to appear too interested. He might have missed the picnickers, and would hate to be thought of as a nosy parker.

Approaching the trail, David winds down to a walk, and is on the verge of veering left, when Peter's cry is heard. Though fairly faint, no doubt in David's mind of its urgency, but still thinks little of it, and turns right rather than left, more out of curiosity than concern. It's the plea from Greda that grabs his attention. It's her repeated urgent cry for help that eggs him on, as he races up to the grassy ridge. Good God! On the face of the cliff is a scene that's surreal, more akin to a film set than a shot from real life. He's shocked, and shaken at the sight of a life, maybe two, literally hanging on by a thread. One year in the war had inured him to death, but not it seems when faced with it here on a gorgeous day in the Gower. His military experience though has not been in vain, for acting under pressure still comes naturally. His pack is dropped on the ridge. He sprints down the grass to the ledge and shuffles across it to the second tree, all the while assessing his options.

"I'm very weak," he hears Greda whisper, "But Peter's still strong I think."

Instinctively accepting her judgement, he immediately kneels in front of the tree, and as he leans his torso into it, calls, "Are you strong, Peter? Can you hold on?"

"Yes," rather feebly, from what seemed like far below.

"Everything I'm going do now will be very, very slow, so shout if there's a problem, OK?"

"All right."

David steadies himself, flexes and strains as he lifts Greda slowly by the armpits. God! This is so much harder than expected. The angles are all wrong and his arms are wrung with tension. They begin to tremble. He's actually afraid he can't hold his position.

"I don't think I can pull this off," he worries to himself, "I should try it some other way, perhaps. No, no! There's no time for that. Just hold it for a second. Just hold it! Concentrate now. Focus on your breathing."

As he does, the tension lifts. Not by much, admittedly, but that tiny change makes such a huge difference.

"He must have found a handhold! That's it! There must be a handhold. I never thought of that!"

Encouraged now, he slowly, very slowly, raises Greda again. At the appropriate moment, he steadies himself, and between gasps for breath, says, "Now, put both your arms to one side of the tree, and then around my neck, and hold me as tight as you can, all right?"

Only when he's absolutely sure of her grip, does he quickly transfer his arms and wrap them tightly around her waist. In this position, he's much more confident. He's pretty sure it'll be all right now. Still partly leaning against the tree, he recovers his breath and gathers his strength, before flexing once again. With a sharp movement, he lifts his right knee, and now has his foot flat on the ground. He steadies again, before raising himself slowly to a standing position. Peter's head comes into view.

"Grasp the tree when you can, all right? D'you have it? Fantastic!"

David is hugely relieved, so he can well imagine how Greda feels, back from the ultimate brink. She slumps in his arms when her ankles are released, and thanks, sobs and shivers, all at once, as the reality of her predicament and reprieve sink in. David rushes to lay her down, snug with the rock face. No need for haste, as it happens, for Peter has pulled himself up by the tree. Yet, he too is emotionally drained; who wouldn't be, having been so close to the end that he felt no fear of the void below. As he embraces David, he, like Greda, shivers as he thanks profusely. Then, the lovers touch: they touch incessantly, as if they're both blind. They touch for reassurance, and to reconnect. They touch the one they feared they'd never touch again. In disbelief, and relief as well, they just touch, till David suggests they get off the ledge. He moves to support Greda, but she indicates unobtrusively that Peter's the one in need of assistance. Once on the grass, the lovers embrace, but they still shiver severely.

David is worried. He knows of post-traumatic stress, and feels some of the same himself, but theirs seems so extreme that something should be done to help them. From the picnic spot, he retrieves two sweaters and the large, white cotton cloth. They readily comply with his suggestion that they lie on the sheet, and wrap themselves in it. Peter seems shy under David's eye, but Greda's unrestrained; her passion's at a pitch quite at odds with her instincts at the picnic, half an hour before. For her, it seems, the miracle that brought them back from the brink has marginalised restraint. She smothers with kisses, she can't get her fill, and moistens with tears, confesses at will; she sobs that she's never been happier than when she is with him; she loves him, and she's never…

David is embarrassed. He diplomatically offers to pack their picnic stuff, and neither in the sheet demur, and nor does the grand director.

In a hollow by a headland on the higher Gower trail, lay Greda and Peter, side by side, hand in hand. The grass was coarse, and at any other time, she may have wished for the large, white cotton cloth, which was folded in Peter's backpack, but during those exquisite moments, she wished for nothing, not even that the moments may last forever: that's how exquisite they were.

David sat on the headland, removed from the other two. From where she lay, Greda could only see his fair and curly hair. She marvelled at the warmth she felt for one she knew little about: the three had hardly spoken since the rescue on the rock face. Greda saw nothing odd in this, for their reticence perfectly reflected her mood. After all, the three had shared a life-changing experience, and to Greda's way of thinking, a bond so sublime had been forged that words might well have weakened it. She presumed also that conversation would more likely have occurred had one of them felt inadequate regarding their role on the rockface. Peter, of course, would have been the obvious candidate, but that notion had been scotched by David, very early on. He'd praised Peter's physical strength and presence of mind as well. Peter had been assured that without his assistance at crucial moments, all would likely have been lost. So, as David had packed the enormous backpack and then carried it up the chute, little had been said. Approaching the top though, with David in the lead, Peter had asked Greda in a whisper whether she'd noticed the freckles, and particularly the way they'd changed colour. She'd put a finger to her lips, and nodded. A little later, she and Peter had mentioned briefly where they lived. It appeared that David would have reciprocated, but after saying that he was staying with a friend in Swansea, he'd been distracted by concern over the timing of his bus. In the end, they'd decided he'd time enough to spare. Then, there'd been silence again, as there was now, while Greda and Peter lay in a hollow set back from a headland, just over half an hour from Port Eynon.

Greda lay in a mental cocoon of blissful contentment. The ingredients were no secret: a slightly sultry, sunny summer's day, the feeling of complete relief that follows only extreme tension, pride in her own performance, the love she felt for Peter and optimism for their future together. How could she not interpret their unlikely survival as Fate's unqualified approval of their relationship? How could she not? She'd been sure that Peter loved her, and how could he now be in any doubt of her feelings, after the pitch of her passion earlier? As she lay alongside him, how could she wish for more? And she'd never seen Peter as relaxed before, so content with her here in the hollow. So perfect her inner peace, so much her mind at ease, that she hadn't given a thought to Peter's departure tomorrow. These were beautiful moments, indeed.

Greda noticed David getting to his feet, and turning towards them. Her reaction, out of respect, she supposed, was to sit up, and Peter followed. She was easing out of her mental cocoon, where she'd been suspended in a wonderful, cosy weightlessness for an eternity, it seemed. She would now notice things again, and thoughts would intrude: thoughts, at first so pleasing that the change would be barely perceptible. Still holding hands with Peter, and speaking in Welsh of course, she told him she couldn't be happier. He replied in kind. They squeezed hands and agreed again that these were the happiest and most peaceful moments of their lives so far, and perhaps forever would be. Perhaps? Far too soon, they'd find out there was no perhaps about it!

David had approached, but still stood well above them, lean and long-bodied, his eyes a striking blue. She presumed that he was about to suggest that they got going, but he surprised her. It seemed that David, as blissfully content and therefore as vulnerable as Greda to the sentimental, had been overcome by a love for his country.

"I do sometimes wish I could speak Welsh," he said in English, "But you know, I can't imagine anyone feeling more Welsh than I do at this beautiful moment."

Greda heard, but his assertion didn't really register. Perhaps her mind was resisting what it sensed could be an assault on its cosiness, and in any case, Greda was curiously distracted by David's freckles. They were a very light ginger now, and not raised at all. They sat comfortably, uncontentiously on his round, open, gentle face. Regardless, they'd diverted her attention, so the shift in the situation sank in only when Peter let go of her hand and she felt his body stiffen.

"I know you don't really mean that, David," from Peter, "The very fact that you said you wished you could speak Welsh means it's obvious you feel less Welsh than... me, for example."

A provocative remark with an edge was the last thing Greda would have expected from Peter. From her experience, it was completely out of character, and surely an aberration. On this hope she hung her hat, in her reluctance to concede that their blissful contentment was at risk. However, the reality would fast become irrefutable.

"Oh, come on!" from David, "you need to move with the times. You should be excited that even though I can't speak Welsh, I really feel Welsh. I feel as Welsh as you. I know it!"

Peter was on his feet, and looking up at David, vituperative in his reaction.

"How can you possibly say that? It's your sort that has let us down. I bet your grandparents spoke Welsh, and look at you now. I can tell you barely know a word. You've essentially joined the other side. If you ask me, you're a traitor."

As blissful contentment took off and crashed into the cliffs from whence it came, Greda continued to minimise the enormity of the situation. Rather than accept Peter's extreme change of mood at face value, she chose to focus on its irrationality, and in this way pretend that what she'd heard couldn't possibly be happening. With her head well and truly buried in the sand, she was rather too casual in her attempt to calm Peter. In return for underestimating the seriousness of this matter to him, she was shrugged to the ground roughly, and was asked angrily in Welsh, "Don't you understand? The lines are drawn. You're either with me or you're not, and as it seems you're not, you're as bad as he is!"

No amount of sand could insulate her now. Soon, she would dwell on the reality, and be devastated, but for the time being was distracted by the action around her. For a start, Peter grabbed his enormous backpack, and without another word, stormed away through the heather towards the gorse. She on the ground, and David on his mound, watched him recede in stunned silence. Then abruptly, David rushed to help her to her feet. She noticed his freckles were dark again, and as before, appeared slightly raised, veiling his gentle face and tingeing it in mystery. Embarrassed, she hurriedly whispered an apology for her friend's behaviour, before stumbling off after him, to be faced with reality, and with it, devastation.

She felt so alone, so low, and utterly let down by not only Peter but herself as well. Exhaustion weighed on her, but the fear of breaking down should she stop, kept her stumbling on in pursuit. How could she have made such a fool of herself? Instinctively distrustful of men, how could she have fallen for this? What on earth had made her think that this time would be any different? To herself, she posed these self-recriminatory questions, over and over and over again. Occasionally, she mustered the strength to challenge one of them.

"But wait a minute! This really was different! I've never been as happy, and even confessed my love," but each time, Peter's inexplicably absurd overreaction brought her back with a bump to the matter of trust, and again, "How could I have been so stupid?"

To make matters worse, she didn't seem to be catching up with Peter. Close to the point of giving up, she was reminded for some reason of their unlikely survival as an indication of Fate's approval of their future together. She was encouraged by the thought of Fate as her friend, without considering that friendship occasionally entails the hurting of one by the other. Greda had no inkling of the resemblance that had earlier struck the elderly lady, nor the tragedy she'd mystically foreseen. Greda had merely fallen head over heels into a love that was untenable; and of course, had no idea that Fate, as a friend, had put an end to it, and in line with the elderly lady's hopes, much sooner rather than later.

So the mere thought of Fate as a friend, gave Greda a flicker of hope, and rallied her will to pursue. Predictably perhaps, Peter picked up the pace as she neared, aggravating her breathlessness, as she begged him to explain what was happening between them. No acknowledgement at all as he strode ahead grimly. Eventually, she clasped his arm, and although rebuffed, not so roughly as to discourage her from persisting. She clasped again, and though Peter initially feigned rejection, he did this time turn to face her, albeit with exasperation.

"Why can't you just leave me alone," he snapped, "You think you're the only one upset?"

"I just need to try and understand why… "

He wheeled as if to leave, but instead, turned to face her again, this time with resignation. He admitted to appear to have behaved childishly, and couldn't expect her to understand the intensity of his reaction. At its root was his frustration with the persistent erosion of the usage of the Welsh language. He told her that at one time, and not that long ago, almost all Welsh people spoke their mother tongue, albeit under the English thumb. Then, it looked as if the chapels might have organised Welshmen to the point of achieving some form of independence, even. Though still depressed, Greda had eagerly heard his tale, and at this point began to feel that their relationship might be salvaged. She wondered if she, too, had overreacted. She was close to apologising for her casual intervention earlier, but Fate, her friend, saw no choice but an end to the affair.

Peter continued by reflecting sadly that it seemed for a while as if the Welsh had God on their side. That in itself gave her pause, and yet she pushed him to continue. He then went on about King Coal cropping up at the worst possible time, bringing in its wake more of the English. He asserted that if not for coal, most of the inhabitants of Wales would have remained Welsh-speaking. He became decidedly more strident as he complained that the worst thing though was the way Welsh speakers, once drawn to the coalfields, had given up on their language: one of the most beautiful and oldest in the world. So, while the English were bad enough, even worse were these traitors. Greda became disturbed by that edge in his voice again, and offended by his remarks, which applied to not only many of her friends and their families, but also to David, who just happened to have saved their lives. Inexplicably, again, Peter then warned her against saying a word, against touching him, against looking at him, even, and abruptly departed down the trail. What remnants of hope remained, were tossed to the breeze by Greda. Yet, had she not felt so cowed and exhausted, she might have reminded him how fine the line that divided those who'd strayed to coal from those who'd stayed at home; and how fine the line, therefore, that according to him had led some men to treason, and left others as purported custodians of the truth. As it was, she wished for nothing more than to flop to the ground in Gower, roll herself up into a protective ball and wash her hands of it all, but she needed to get back home, and that left her with little choice. She waited a while before following him laboriously, at a distance she deemed comfortable.

David crouched awkwardly within the gorse. Little needles appeared from nowhere and everywhere to jab at his slightest move. Unaffected by these, his heart reached out to Greda, but it, too, was hurt, by the thought it couldn't comfort her.

He'd had no choice but to follow them to be sure to catch his bus. Nor could he dawdle, so he'd inevitably stumbled upon them at the spot they'd stopped to talk. He'd understood little of their conversation, but judging from his freckles, which were in a state of constant levitation, he'd got a hint of the gist of it. He'd dared to peep only when he'd gathered that they were on the move. Yet, Greda remained, looking absolutely drained, and it pained him for a moment that he'd been the one to set this mess in motion. Yet, he philosophised that had he not done it today, then another would have done so sooner or later. So he dealt not with guilt, but rather sadness at Greda's grief, and regret that he couldn't comfort her. In Peter's absence, he would have rushed to reassure; and while conceding his confusion over its virulence, he would have assured her that he understood Peter's reaction, and that it reflected not at all on her. He would have begged her not to take it personally, for the forces behind it had been out of her control. After a while, she too moved, laboriously following Peter down the trail, leaving David to lick his own wounds. That the language had become divisive, he'd earlier understood, but still, to see it victimise, left him feeling far from good.

The tension in the van on the way home to Llanelli was unbearable. Throughout the journey, neither said a word. Peter was gripped in a pout, and Greda saw no point.

Very early the following morning, and appropriately, in the rain, he left on the train for Tryweryn.

So not only was She old and beautiful, but divisive as well, at times. In 1946, for every Welsh person who spoke Her, there were two that didn't, and of those who did, most could speak English as well. Naturally, the non Welsh-speaking majority didn't take kindly to those of Her adherents, who defined Welshness primarily in terms of Her. Yet, the minority could not be dismissed; in fact, activists within it could almost certainly be expected to grow increasingly vocal in support of Her, should the minority's numbers dwindle further. In other words, while She lived, consensus on the definition of Welshness could prove to be elusive. She could not help but be divisive, unless, that is, She magically flourished and reversed the numbers. Attributing responsibility for this sad state of affairs was a dangerous game; for to have harnessed in Her favour, the unprecedented rapid changes that had rocked the Welsh social landscape over the preceding century and a half would have taken exceptional vision and courage.

Forty-seven

L ATE INTO THE evening of her day on the Gower, Greda was eventually persuaded by her mother to tell all; well, all that came to mind, anyway. Donald was at choir practice for at least another hour and Dorothy had motioned her two other children to leave the living room. Much of the time, Greda sobbed and spluttered as she recalled her emotional rollercoaster. Distracted by distress, she obviously failed to notice her mother's odd reaction to the tale of Peter's tantrum. There was nothing surprising about Dorothy's incredulity and sympathy, but surely, had Greda been on the ball, she would have expected rather more of the latter.

Dorothy was shaken. She'd known that Peter, like Edgar, came from the Bala region, and had only been holidaying in Llanelli, but she hadn't taken the similarities that seriously. Now though, they'd been sharpened by Greda to a pitch that shook her. How strange that both men should have become unglued, and completely without warning, over issues to do with Welshness, and for both to storm from the scene! Yet, Dorothy continued to try to convince herself that it had to be a coincidence. It just had to be! She desperately willed it to be so, for the alternative was too disturbing. Better then had she not pursued the possibilities, but too much of her past had been touched upon for her not to do so.

As nonchalantly as possible, she asked, in the Welsh that they now spoke at home and had since her mother died, "So, where does he live near Bala, Greda?"

"I've already told you that, Mami," still sobbing.

"No, not that I remember, anyway."

"Somewhere high up in the Tryweryn valley."

Dorothy could only hope that Greda hadn't sensed her body stiffening. Another nail, this, in the coffin of coincidence, and not for much longer would she fly in the face of the facts.

"I'm surprised I didn't tell you, Mami, and by the way, did I mention that he had a tattoo?"

Not a sound or movement from Dorothy; amazing really, in view of the finality conveyed by this remark.

"Mami?"

"What? Oh, the tattoo. No, Greda, you hadn't told me."

"He said it was a family tradition, or something. Romantic, aye, but I really can't bear to think of it."

Nor could Dorothy, but the question had to be asked, although she knew the answer.

"What kind of tattoo was it?"

"A little dragon on his left shoulder blade, a red one. Unusual, don't you think, Mami?"

Sadly and silently, Dorothy couldn't agree more. So much for coincidence! A connection now seemed much the more convincing alternative. Silence ensued as Greda mourned with her head on her mother's lap, and Dorothy deliberated.

"This is all too close for comfort," she mused, "It's just as well they've broken up because I couldn't possibly let her carry on dating her half-brother. I don't know! I wish I didn't have to think of Edgar at all. So, what possessed me to name her after him? It must have been a moment of madness. Still, not many would make the connection between "Edgar" and "Greda", even if they knew there was one. Oh, dear! I just don't want Donald to have to deal with this business again; he was so brilliant at the time. As things stand, there's no question in people's minds who Greda's father is, and I'd like it to stay that way, for everyone's sake. Still, if they've broken up, I've nothing to worry about..." and so on and so forth.

Much later, she said, "I fancy going to town tomorrow, Greda. I might as well go in with you on the early bus, don't you think?"

"Oh, Mami, I don't want to take the chance of bumping into him, so I was thinking of catching the next bus, actually. I'll be late for work, I know, but… "

Dorothy interrupted, and feared that she'd done so rather too eagerly, but Greda gave no sign that she'd noticed.

"Darling, that's fine. That's a good idea."

So tomorrow, Dorothy would probe her friend Mavis Davies, who she was certain could complete the picture; she'd have to be on her toes, though, and give as little as possible away. Mavis dispensed information rather freely, but rarely for free, and on this delicate subject, the lowest price, even, would be unacceptably high. She wasn't that good a friend, was Mavis.

"Mrs Davies. I'm so sorry I'm late. I can't… "

Mavis Davies knew quite well why Greda would be late today of all days, and generously intervened to put her out of her misery.

"Good God, Greda fach, don't worry about it. I bet it was the bus again. In any case, you can be late as often as you like, as long as you bring your mother with you. How are you, Dorothy? And how's the family?"

"Very well thanks, Mavis. I'm a bit wet, mind you."

"Come on in! Let's dry out with a cup of tea, shall we?" and off they trooped to the kitchen, leaving Greda in her office, while Dorothy quietly and casually closed the adjoining door.

While tinkering with tea things, Mavis reflected on the fact that Dorothy never came to town on a Saturday morning… always in the afternoon; but here she was today, in the morning, and in the rain as well! And to top it all, she'd shut the door. Normally, Mavis Davies would have taken these surprises with suspicion, but today she confidently assumed they were linked to another, the most disturbing surprise of all: Peter's persistent depression since returning from the Gower. Regardless of these mental meanderings, she slipped effortlessly into small talk, between sips of steaming tea and bites of chocolate biscuits.

Suddenly, Dorothy glanced deliberately over her shoulder at the door, and leaning forward, quietly asked, "Mavis, what do you think happened between those two yesterday. Greda was very upset when she came home."

Mavis smiled to herself smugly.

"No idea, Dorothy fach. Obviously, I could tell there was something terribly wrong; they seemed to be getting along so well, too. They even look a bit like each other at times."

Mavis was surprised, and therefore alerted, by what seemed to be Dorothy's awkward demeanour in declining to comment on that.

"But surely Greda told you what happened?"

"Not really, Mavis. She seemed reluctant to talk about what went wrong between them."

Now wait a minute! This didn't ring true at all. Mavis had a pretty good idea that Greda told her mother everything. Beneath her bonhomie, and belying her boisterous enthusiasm, Mavis's mind went into overdrive. Her antennae came to life, intent on not missing a trick.

"Peter must have told you about their lucky escape, though, didn't he?" from Dorothy, furrowing slightly.

Mavis was taken completely by surprise. Such unpredictability on Dorothy's part was totally out of character, and strangely upsetting. This wasn't at all the Dorothy she knew. Her senses went on red alert.

"No, he didn't. What lucky escape?" as uncuriously as she possibly could.

Dorothy proceeded to entrance her friend with a nail-biting account of the incident: emphasising how very close they'd been to death; focusing on the logic, rather than love, that lay behind Greda's decision to die along with Peter; highlighting the immense relief at the sight of the knight in shining armour; and glorifying the heroics of the rescue itself.

"Good God!" from Mavis, "I've never heard anything like it in my life. Funny he didn't tell me."

Totally disarmed by Dorothy's tale, Mavis thought nothing of the next question.

"D'you think they'll see each other again, Mavis? I mean, how often does Peter visit you?"

"This was his first time, actually."

"So his parents don't come here either, then?"

"Well, not that often. I think they find it expensive. Myfanwy used to come every two or three years, but she hasn't been for ages. Edgar came once, a long time ago, just before Peter was born. He sang in a competition here, I remember."

In fact, Mavis remembered a whole lot more, and in particular, an unaccounted day in Edgar's life. The thought of intrigue instantly reprogrammed her antennae to red alert. Gosh, how easily she'd been lulled into talking. It was hard for her to believe though, that Dorothy's tale had been designed to distract her, but if her friend was indeed after something, she'd have to work a damn sight harder for it from now on.

"Hmm! I just wondered if they'd have a chance to patch it up, that's all. How are your children, by the way, Mavis? Where are they?"

This was infuriating. It was bad enough not to be sure whether anything was going on, but worse to realise that if there was, she'd been wrong footed at every turn.

"They're with their Uncle Jimmy for a while. They'll be home on Tuesday," she muttered matter-of-factly.

Mavis decided she'd like some time to herself, a moment to settle her mind.

"It's stopped raining, Mavis. Look! Let's go to the shops, shall we?"

What could she say? Had she ever been known not to jump at an invitation to shop? Damn it! Dorothy had done it again!

"Good idea, Dorothy fach," she said gallantly, and regaining her footing a fraction, "Give me ten minutes to change, yes?"

Pelting with rain, and prematurely dark, on her way home on the bus, upstairs; on the front seat next to Greda; on a downer. No joy from the moves employed while she toyed with Mavis. Certainly no joy now that it was clear her fears were fully justified. And there was worse. She foresaw herself dealing with a sorrow that gnawed; no fun in healing while feeling like a fraud.

"Greda! Hellooo! Greda? Are you feeling better tonight, darling?"

Her daughter kept looking straight ahead. The double-decker seemed to lurch perilously as it flew around a tight bend.

"No, Mami. I never want to see him again in my life."

The very same tack that Greda had taken all day; such terseness was troubling. Last night, in contrast, her daughter had told her everything. That was characteristic of their closeness, so reticence rang bells and cast suspicion on her daughter's assertion; and in any case, regardless of what Greda said about Peter, severing an obviously perfect connection at the very first fence made no sense at all. With relief and pleasure, she'd felt the force of her daughter's passion, had witnessed true love enlivening her face for the very first time, and day after day had heard excitement in her voice; as any mother would, she had rejoiced. Oh, yes, Greda's relationship with Peter was far too special not to resurface. She was sure of that, and picturing herself in the role of subverter, she was saddened, but she'd have no choice.

She imagined her anguish in dutifully supporting the victim of her subversion. To her dismay, she experienced it even then, when her arm was placed around her daughter's shoulder; to rub salt in the fresh wound, Greda snuggled closer, in apology, she assumed. No fun in healing while feeling like a fraud.

Forty-eight

"AND ACTUALLY, DELILAH, she reminds me a lot of you," and though his smile was noticeably sad, it was still characteristically broad.

Delilah was doubly pleased. For the previous ten minutes, Greda's beauty had been shyly but surely extolled by Peter, so naturally Delilah felt flattered, but more importantly, relieved as well at yet another sign that he'd snapped out of his depression. His priority on arriving from Llanelli the previous evening had been to admit ashamedly that he'd let them down again, that he'd flown off the handle, and as usual, when he'd least expected it. The rest of his fantastic story had to be dragged out in dribs and drabs, and then, he'd dried up. Attributing this at the time to tiredness, she and Doctor had only become concerned when his uncommunicative manner had persisted throughout today. Why, an hour ago, he'd begun to come round, she couldn't tell. Was it perhaps that time had played her proverbial role. She wondered too whether Walter had helped. The Wheaten had been a pal to Peter, loyally tagging alongside him all day, lapping against his legs as he dragged around the house, and napping on his lap as he sagged on the couch. Whatever the reason, he appeared to be on the mend: still sad and upset, but at last, it seemed, considering the consequences and how to make amends.

"And actually, Delilah, she reminds me a lot of you."

Doctor chose this moment to propose a dram of whisky. The traditional toast of "Iechyd da" brought the three together and warmed the mood, as the Scotch would soon do too. Walter though, taking no chances, still stuck close to his pal. The water of life loosened lips, and Peter's in particular. He described in vivid detail his duel with death on the cliff face. While freely acknowledging that his faintness of heart had instigated the incident, he dwelt mainly on that mystical space he met, which allowed him no fear of the void below.

"I was so serene, despite swinging on Greda's ankles while she hung onto a tree. I felt strong, but quite sure that Greda was weakening fast, and just as sure that she wouldn't tell me when she couldn't hang on any longer. What was amazing was that my serenity allowed me to focus on when I should let go of her; I was preparing to jump, so that she at least would live. Oh yes, heroic stuff. Fortunately, David turned up and took the hero off the hook, and what did the hero do then? Little that was heroic. I can remember every word that David said, and just as clearly, I remember my anger rising, and being unable to control it. Some hero, aye?"

He carried on, regretting having destroyed the amazing bond that had stemmed from their unique experience. He felt sick to his stomach over his treatment of David. If only they could meet again, he'd make sure he'd make amends. They could never agree on the language, but next time he'd be prepared, and David would be treated with respect. Alas, that opportunity was unlikely to arise, so all the more reason for atonement with Greda. Apart from that, their connection was far too precious to waste. He would write to her at Anti Mavis's place. That's what he'd do! He'd tell her of his love, his overwhelming love for her. He'd express his admiration and profound regret, and beg for forgiveness, and he'd promise of course that such a scene would never happen again. Then, he took a long, deep breath and looked in turn at Doctor, Delilah and Walter too, for their reactions.

Delilah had been mesmerised by the image of her darling dangling close to death. She shivered as she glanced at Doctor, but immediately steeled herself, for she sensed from his body language that his thoughts were no longer in sync with hers.

"Peter," from Doctor, avuncular, leaning forward with

elbows on knees, and hands clasped, "I want to stress that what I'm going to tell you is meant kindly, OK?"

She knew it! And she thought they'd agreed last night to go soft on the boy. Ominous were Doctor's words, as, it seemed, was their tone to a canine ear that cocked.

"I really don't think you should write that."

"OK! I won't promise it'll never happen again. I'll leave that bit out."

Peter had anticipated so confidently that he'd carried Delilah along. Both were deflated, consequently.

"No! No!" from Doctor, his hands in motion now, "I wasn't referring just to that bit. I don't think you should write the letter at all… "

Three faces were transfixed, two shocked and the other forelocked.

"… Until you've sorted out your little problem. I don't think it would be fair to get in touch with Greda, without knowing, and I mean really knowing, that you've overcome your demon."

"But Doctor, what more can I do? That's why I'm so upset. This lapse puts me back years, doesn't it?"

Delilah in a dilemma! Permanently protective of Peter, she found Doctor's directness disturbing, and yet she couldn't believe he'd pursue this line without some hope to follow.

"But you see, Peter, I don't think of you as having a temper. You're a lovely person, but somehow on this south Walian business your brain blows a fuse. There are other challenges in your life, but they don't throw you. I suggest again that you force yourself to look at this one issue in a different light."

Whither the breakthrough that Delilah had divined?

"But Doctor, what's the point of going on? I can't help the way I feel about these things. That's what makes me who I am."

"Peter, I wouldn't have been as forceful, especially tonight, if I hadn't thought I could help."

Delilah was finally reassured, and ashamed now that she'd doubted her husband.

"I'm filling in for Dr Lewis this weekend, and got called out of chapel this morning. Remember, Delilah? Well, the call was from Capel Celyn. Up there, I bumped into your mother. I hope you don't mind, Peter, but I repeated what you told us last night. Anyway, the point is that she then said something that I wish she'd told me years ago."

Doctor paused as if preparing for the punch line.

"I know this is unfair but rather than tell you now what she said, I'd prefer all of us to hike up the shoulder of Arenig Fawr tomorrow, if the weather's half decent. Telling you up there would have more of an impact, I think. Is that all right, Peter?"

A shrug of the shoulders was his only reaction. His mood again matched the darkness of his complexion. Delilah rose and sat next to him, and Walter snuggled a bit closer as well.

"By the way, your Mam says hello, Peter, and Anti Enid too. They said they're both looking forward to seeing you soon. Another thing your Mam said was that if you do hike up to the shoulder, don't forget to let the wonder of it all wash over you."

That Peter reacted to this was evident to Delilah even from where she sat at his side. She wished she hadn't moved now.

"Let the wonder of it all wash over you!"

It wasn't long before Peter lay in bed. His mind, lapped by this phrase, was lulled into a more restful mood. Relentless self-recrimination and doubt gave way to thoughts of Taid and reassuring chimes from childhood. He thought warmly of Anti Enid as well, and the fun they'd had on her postal rounds, but mainly he dwelt on Taid, his friend and intellectual mentor.

Taid it was who'd kept him curious and above all, kept him honest. Taid had been dependable too: forever his morale booster, and especially after a skirmish at school. Funny, but he'd never blown up while Taid was alive. Was that a coincidence, or not? Regardless, he began to feel drowsy as he pondered his affectionate feelings for Taid.

"Let the wonder of it all wash over you!"

It struck him that they were probably Taid's very last words, and spoken to him! Feelings of affection intensified, and even softened his understandable scepticism of tomorrow's project. He'd lived too long with his liability to be optimistic, but he fell asleep into a chink of light at the end of the tunnel.

They were at the lake by nine. Below, glimpses of the valley punched through patches in the morning haze, which was rapidly evaporating. Above, Arenig Fawr's north shoulder was clear, thank goodness, lit magnificently by the sun.

Peter had awakened to those same warm feelings for Taid on which he'd slipped off to sleep: Taid, who he'd thought the world of, on whose every word he'd hung, and at whose death, his life had taken a turn for the worse, far worse it seemed than anyone had realised it would back then.

The roof of the MG had been down out of necessity. Peter had been nicely distracted in his role as controller of Walter. Hopelessly confined behind the seats, they'd wrestled in earnest the whole way up from Bala. In contrast, in the front, Delilah serene, her long fair hair amazingly well behaved in no more than a pink muffler; and Doctor decked, as ever while driving, in his well-worn leather gloves. They'd parked not far beyond a familiar and lovely spot, where Taid had brought Peter face to face with his Welshness. As the four picked their way through marshland towards a false ridge, and then beyond to another, which actually contained the familiar lake, Doctor had repeated

Myfanwy's words from the day before. She'd told him of a fateful evening, just before Taid had died, when Peter had accompanied his father to a political meeting. There, Edgar had slated south Walians, and when a few in the audience had objected, they'd been ejected from the barn.

"D'you remember that meeting, Peter?"

He'd nodded, thoughtfully. Warm thoughts of Walter and Taid had vied with doubts that nothing would come of their venture today. Doctor had continued to paint the picture. It seemed that over tea on the day following the meeting, Rhiannon had vigorously seconded her son's opinions.

"I'm sure you remember that too. Well, the point your mother wanted to make to me was that had poor Taid not suffered one of his funny turns that very morning, she was sure he'd have countered Rhiannon's arguments there and then; he'd have put it all in perspective, and perhaps saved you a lot of grief, she said. In fact, just after the meal, Taid had told her that he knew exactly how to make the opposite case, and intended to do so as soon as he felt stronger; and that's what he was doing, Peter, when he brought you up here on the day that he died. Taid was making the opposite case."

At the lake, details of those few days came pouring back to Peter, as if Doctor had broken a dam; not only the controversial meeting, but equally vividly his confusion that night over his father's views about south Walians, and his firm intention to discuss them with Taid. The funny turn had put paid to that, and then the matter had slipped his mind. So that's what Taid had been up to on the day he died! And the story that he'd promised had all been part of making the opposite case. Poignantly, it struck him that to that end, Taid had knowingly risked his life that day. Sadness and the sentimental softened him, and made him receptive to stabs of optimism that stemmed from the sudden realisation that Doctor's case would rest on continuous invocations of Taid.

"Remember, Peter, how he said he felt unwell, and that you should go up to the shoulder on your own, and he'd tell you a story once you'd come down? Remember?"

Peter daren't respond for fear of upsetting emotions uneasily balanced around a lump in his throat.

"And this is probably where he stood when he told you to let the wonder of it all wash over you. Such a beautiful phrase. Let the wonder of it all wash over you. His very last words probably, and to think he said them to you!"

Peter's blue eyes were seen to glaze for an instant before he sat on a boulder with his head in his hands. Walter nuzzled his neck in puzzlement, and Delilah reacted typically by moving to his side, while Doctor kept composing variations on Taid, for the moment with his back turned to Peter, his face to the Berwyn and the sun.

"Oh, Peter," shaking his head, "If only he'd lived to tell you the story, he'd have probably spared you a lot of grief. See, your Mam knew what he was up to, and guessed the introduction, but then got stuck. The pity is that at the time she never thought of mentioning it to me, because I'm sure I knew exactly what Taid would have told you. Better late than never though. Let's hike up to the shoulder, all right? Come on, Walter!"

Peter and Delilah followed arm in arm, till the path narrowed.

High on the north shoulder of Arenig Fawr, they stood on a slight slope, shoulder to shoulder in such a way as to accentuate their differences in height: Delilah supreme at one end, Walter well below, with Peter and Doctor appropriately sandwiched. This pattern conveyed a lightness of mood, an impression confirmed by Walter's wheaten head wrapped in a shocking pink muffler. And a lightness there was, indeed. During the ascent, with the occasional waft of Delilah's perfume and Walter's constant attention, Peter had convinced himself that this therapy would do the trick. Doctor thought so, obviously, and much more importantly, so had another. In Taid's name, then, Peter had laid himself bare to enlightenment. So relieved was he, that once on the shoulder, he'd told Doctor and Delilah, at which she'd celebrated by wrapping her Walter in pink, and playfully arranging their positions. Doctor's reaction had been to milk the emotion of the moment with a reminder of the countless occasions Taid and his special friend Edward must have sat on this very spot, letting the wonder of it all wash over them. Doctor's hands had dramatised the vastness of the vista, but when then he'd come to the story, theatrics had been abruptly abandoned. Rather, now that Peter was receptive, he clinically reeled off the tale he felt sure that Taid would have told.

While four in a row nostalgically faced northwards, Peter was told of external events, completely out of Edward's control, that led to a fork in his friendship with Taid: of Edward's emigration to south Wales, but not before they'd bonded, in the form of little red dragons; of their vow to ensure that this tradition would be adopted by their descendants; of economic realities, once again beyond their control, that discouraged contact between the friends; of Wyn Williams, who years later brought news of Edward to Taid, his family and the circumstances under which Edward's granddaughter had not been brought up to speak Welsh; of the assertion that Edward couldn't possibly be blamed for that, nor could most south Walians in a variety of related situations; and the suggestion that if this could happen in Edward's family, then what family would be immune?

"So, Peter," Doctor concluded, "There may well be a young man living in south Wales, who's Edward's great-grandson. From the sound of things, it's unlikely that he speaks Welsh, but through no fault of his own, but because of circumstances out of his control. Now, if you met him, you wouldn't be justified in calling him a traitor, would you? Of course not, no more than you would be in blithely blaming the decline of the Welsh language on south Walians in general. Anyway, those are the things I think Taid would have told you had he lived to tell the tale."

Silence! Suddenly, Doctor, presumably perturbed by the lack of reaction, turned rather sharply to Peter, whose furrowed brow seemed to confirm Doctor's concern. It was misplaced though, for Peter, as he'd known he would, had long embraced Doctor's premise, and had moved on to scenes of himself with David and Greda on the Gower. As it happened, he'd been picturing David with his fair, curly hair, baby round face, light ginger freckles and all; he'd been picturing these features at the very moment that Doctor had hypothesised a great-grandson of Edward's living in south Wales.

"Well," Peter thought, "If that great-grandson exists, it's good to know that I won't be calling him a traitor... but wait! Oh, no! Please... please don't tell me I've done so already!"

What a preposterous notion! That's when Peter's brow had furrowed, and Doctor had become concerned.

"D'you know anything about Edward, Doctor? What did he look like?"

Relief registered on Doctor's face before he admitted that of course he'd never met Edward, but from Taid's description, he'd had fair hair...

"Was it curly?"

Doctor and Delilah started, and glanced at each other.

"I don't think so. Edward was quite tall, apparently, quite unlike Taid who was stocky..."

Peter began to relax, tuning out Doctor's response. Preposterous indeed was the notion.

"... Of course, Edward's defining feature was his light ginger freckles... "

Peter did a double take, which he knew Delilah had noticed.

"… which apparently turned darker whenever he was ill at ease. Quite a handicap, wouldn't you say?"

Peter would look back with amazement at the panache with which he parried this bolt from the blue.

"You know," he said, with what seemed to be genuine enthusiasm, "I'd like to go to the top. How about you? Great! Come on then, Walter! Let's show them the way, shall we? We'll see you two up there."

In the same vein, he playfully flipped the muffler from Walter's head and wrapped it on his own, with little effect, he noticed, on Delilah and her knowing gaze.

Peter was pensive in his shocking pink muffler as he sat on the summit, with his back to upper Tryweryn. In his meagre, mid-morning shadow, Walter snuggled and sheltered the best he could. Normally, Peter would have acknowledged the peaks and ridges around him, but he'd freckles on his mind, and a few other things as well. At Doctor and Delilah's approach, Walter stuck to Peter's shadow, while Peter was struck once again by Delilah's knowing gaze.

"She doesn't miss a trick, does Delilah," and he wasn't surprised when she politely asked, "Do you want to tell us what on your mind, Peter?"

He knew really that he was only delaying the inevitable when he chose not to discuss David's freckles, but instead another topic which had bothered him on the peak.

"Delilah, you're frighteningly perceptive," he responded, "I'm delighted with what's happened, and I really haven't thanked you properly, have I Doctor? Still, I can't help feeling like a chair that's lost a leg; as if, with my anger subdued, my Welshness is incomplete."

Doctor immediately glanced at Delilah, and with her tacit approval, countered with, "Whatever you wished for Wales, Peter, you'd have been incapable of achieving it before your change of heart today. You'd have been bogged down by the notion of our language as a litmus test for Welshness. Now that you've seen the light, you're that much more of a Welshman, in my opinion; not a three legged chair, at all. Actually, you now have the tolerance and wisdom to really make a difference."

Broad the smiles these words did bring,
He knew, though, one still knowing.

Later that day, he told her, as they strolled along the end of Bala Lake. She experienced twinges of conscience, for she'd undoubtedly been pushy, but no regrets, for the result was that now she could help him.

"You saw me doing a double take on Arenig," Peter chuckled, "and you've sensed what it's all about, haven't you? Yes, David too had freckles which darkened when he was uneasy, but the more I think about it, the more far-fetched it seems. It has to be a coincidence, don't you think?"

Delilah's intuition strongly suggested that while he said one thing, he was feeling another; he was rationalising, but understandably so.

"Yes, maybe so, but now, how would you feel if someone told you for a fact that David was Edward's great-grandson?"

Peter stopped, ran a hand through his hair while gazing up the lake, and sadly said, "Well, I'd feel terrible, naturally. I'd feel as if I'd kicked Taid in the teeth."

Delilah was ready now. She'd just wanted to make absolutely sure she was reading Peter right.

"OK, Peter. Let's assume that David is from Edward's line;

434

not only does he have those famous freckles, but a little red dragon as well. Now then, speaking of coincidences, don't you think the one on the Gower was in a class of its own, so much so that it smacks of the supernatural? I mean, just think about it! Not only did Edward's great-grandson save Taid's great-grandson's life, but also participated in a showdown that led to him, you that is, becoming whole. If I were Taid, floating up there somewhere, saddened by the flaw he saw in you and aware of the grave danger you were in, I'd be delighted with the outcome, wouldn't I?"

Peter said nothing. He turned again towards the lake. At its far end, Aran's twin peaks were packed in cloud.

"Taid's got to be very happy now, Peter," she continued, "He was a gentle and sensible man. Looking down on us all, he must have been saddened by the growing divide in Welsh society, and above all, that you were getting caught up in it. Imagine how pleased he must be now to see you and David singing to the same tune. In spirit, at least, you've completed a circle for him and his friend. So no, Peter bach, you haven't kicked him in the teeth at all, and I wouldn't be surprised if Taid, in a patriotic moment, thinks of your alignment, your alignment with David that is, as the first wave in the turning of a tide, which when full will break on three sides of a united and independent Wales. What do you think of that, Peter Morris Evans?"

Delilah wasn't surprised at his patronising smile.

"Dear Delilah," it seemed to say, "that's going a bit over the top, don't you think?"

Yet, intuitively she knew that he so longed to believe in Taid's intervention, there was little doubt that he would, which happily justified the pressure her knowing gazes had applied, for in her opinion, the more closely he could link his change of heart to Taid, the more lasting it would be.

"But I treated David so badly," he moaned, "I must have really hurt him."

"You'll put that right one day, Peter, I know you will, and imagine the joy when that's fulfilled; you'll have completed the circle in substance as in spirit. Now, we're all assuming of course that David's really related to Edward... aren't we?"

She'd thrown one final sideswipe to measure his conviction. His questioning, but soon confident smile, confirmed that nothing could now be said that would cast any doubt on the connection.

"But first things first, isn't Peter?"

She'd changed the mood, and he chuckled.

"Oh!" tossing his head, "You mean Greda. At least I know where to find her, but will she forgive me? Do you think she'll forgive me, Delilah?"

"Of course she will, Peter. You'll see," and flirtatiously taking his arm, continued, "Does she really remind you of me?"

Forty-nine

"DEAR GREDA,
Occasionally I can convince myself that you'll be pleased to hear from me, but most of the time I despair, so I'm resigned to hoping only that you'll not be offended by this letter."

He wrote in his immaculate Welsh. Knowing hers to be more colloquial, he had wondered whether in such a sensitive situation, it might have been safer to have written in English, but no! Their relationship had flourished in Welsh, and in Welsh he'd attempt to revive it.

"So much has happened in the short time since we parted. I've so much to tell you that I don't know where to start, but I'll try and write in some sort of order.

I know you'll remember me talking about Taid. When I was a boy, he was my mentor, but he died when I was eight. Looking back, I realise he was the one who kept me honest. He'd have loved you, I know it. He'd have loved your sincerity, good sense and sensitivity. In any case, I've thought a lot about Taid since I left Llanelli, and with Doctor and Delilah's help – you know who I mean, don't you? – with their help, I've reconnected with him. I remember so vividly going for a hike with Taid one day. At one point, he sent me on ahead, but when I got back, he'd collapsed, and that night he died. It seems he'd intended to tell me a story that day, which he was sure, absolutely sure apparently, would have enabled me to resist my father's extreme ideas about south Walians, but he died, and I grew up with a blind spot on those matters. To my shame, you encountered that blind spot on Friday, but now that I've heard what Taid would have told me that day, I know I've seen the light; my views are now on solid ground, there's no blind spot any longer. You've no idea how ashamed I feel for hurting so many people over this business: hurting Taid, who I know is watching up there somewhere, hurting David, and of course, you. How could I have hurt you, I ask myself? You, of all people! How could I have possibly lost my temper with you? You must have been so disappointed. Greda, the funny thing is that Doctor and Delilah don't think I have a temper at all. They don't think I'm like that, because it just doesn't fit my personality. Their opinion is that my brain for some reason has always blown a fuse on that particular subject; only on that, and now that I'm whole, as they put it... well, you know what I mean!

You will forgive me, won't you? I'm begging you to forgive me, Greda... "

Up to this point, Greda had read hurriedly, almost scanning the letter. Uncertain of what to expect, her high forehead had been furrowed and her pretty mouth half open. Her attitude changed though, at the word "forgive". She glanced shyly at Mavis Davies. Her smile, initially self-conscious, broke out into one of joy at Mavis's obvious enthusiasm.

"Well? Well?"

"It's from him, from Peter."

"I know that, but what does he say?"

"Mrs Davies?" self-consciously again, "I hope you won't be upset if I go to the office to read the rest of the letter. I feel a bit awkward with... "

"Greda! How stupid and insensitive of me! Of course you should be alone, but you will give a few tidbits away, won't you," she joked, as Greda retreated.

"... You will forgive me, won't you? I'm begging you to forgive me, Greda."

She'd wanted so badly to forgive him for days. To her credit, she'd been well aware that this yearning made her vulnerable to misjudgement, but no such thoughts constrained her now. Of course she'd forgive him. She'd done so already!

"If you can't, I'll understand but as I write, I'm hoping with every fibre in my body that you will."

Vividly, she imagined Peter sunk in uncertainty, able only to hope and wish, while she was awash with faith in their future. The contrast was wrenching. In a rush, emotion engulfed her faster than she could find her hankie. A teardrop splashed on the letter.

"And if you can forgive me, Greda, will you... "

The next word was smudged, wet with her tear, but she knew full well what it was.

"And if you can forgive me, Greda, will you love me as well? Will you love me now as you did before?"

She couldn't wait to write that of course she would. The rest of the letter was icing on the cake. Through a mist of tears of joy, she read of those features that he longed to see again: her high forehead, often furrowed, and the lock that flopped and as often was flicked, her unusually long toes, her beautifully long nose, and her eyebrows dark and delicate. She'd no idea he'd noticed so much. She learnt that he'd never forget how they touched incessantly, as if they were blind, in disbelief and relief as well, on the ledge just after the rescue. She was also told, in conclusion, that he couldn't possibly contemplate life without her.

"So now you know how I feel, Greda. Please reply soon – very soon?

Warmest wishes and much, much love,

Peter."

Greda didn't read it again, not then, anyway. She just stared at her ledger with a smile on her face, as she imagined him sitting on the chair by the door. That's how Mavis found her, fifteen minutes later.

"Well?"

Peter's lengthy letter elicited two responses, both short, and both in English. The first was sent by return of post.

"Dear Peter, I am so happy to receive your letter. I can't believe anyone can be so happy. I want to write down all my lovely thoughts, and I'd love to do it in Welsh, but I'll be quicker in English, and it's important you hear from me as soon as possible. Of course I forgive you, with all my happy heart. Of course I love you, as I've never loved before, and of course, I can't wait to be with you again, although I know I'm going to have to because you're going to Liverpool before long. It may even be in a few days.

What more can we ask for now than to be together? Absence couldn't possibly make my heart grow fonder.

Please write with your address in Liverpool. I'll pour my heart out to you then, and I promise to write at least a bit of it in Welsh!

You have made me the happiest little Welsh girl in the world.

All my love, Greda."

Dorothy's response was contingent on a piece of information, which she deftly elicited from Mavis Davies, but not till the following Saturday. The fact that Dorothy had known deep down what would come of Greda's affair, had not made the outcome any easier to bear. To make matters worse, there was no avoiding a response that was unsavoury. Somehow, Edgar would have to be pressured into revealing the truth to Peter, who then would have no option but to break with Greda. There were obvious risks to her plan and these, in particular, had worried her. To have shared with Donald would have lightened her mind, but she'd vowed not to trouble him till she had to. Still, by the Saturday, she was reasonably reconciled to her duplicitous role. Following predictable platitudes on Peter's humility and Greda's such good fortune, she asked of Mavis quite innocently, "So Peter spends a lot of time at the doctor's house then?"

"Oh! Didn't you know? He lives with the doctor and his wife Delilah now."

"You mean he's moved from... what's the name of the farm again?" and after being told by an unsuspecting Mavis, "Oh, yes, that's right. So he doesn't live at home any more? What happened?"

Dorothy duly gaped and gasped at the explanation, before switching the subject to Mavis's children, who as usual seemed to have had the time of their lives at Uncle Jimmy's.

After carefully printing the day, the date and "Llanelli", Dorothy wrote in English, "Dear Mr Evans, I need to talk to you as soon as possible. The matter is of the greatest urgency."

She would give nothing away because there was a risk that another might read the letter as well. "As far as I can see, the only safe way of doing this is for me to tell you in this letter where to meet me. Of course, I could come to Bala, but I'm confident that if I ask you to travel to Llanelli, you'll manage it somehow. You can meet me on the Saturday after next... that's almost two weeks from now... outside the town hall between ten and half past in the morning. There will be lots of people around, but you'll recognise me easily enough, I'm sure. Just in case something turns up to delay you, I'll be there between three and half past as well. Yours sincerely... "

She'd realised she was asking a lot. For that reason, she'd wondered whether to be blatantly threatening, but surely, twenty years after an illicit affair, a letter out of the blue would be threat enough.

Fifty

A NTI ENID, IN her mid-sixties yet her posture still impressive, emerged from the doorway of her cottage and tugged her postwoman's hat down firmly. She squinted out of habit towards the west, where the weather usually came from. Then, at a pace untypical of her, she ambled up the road to the bridge that crossed the busy, babbling Celyn. With elbows on the parapet and chin cupped in hands, she could have taken her cue from the rain clouds congregating threateningly beyond Arenig Fawr. Beware! Play safe, they seemed to say, but they counselled in vain, for conveniently preordained as her compass was the Celyn. It offered, as she'd known it would, brighter and more palatable advice.

"Be buoyant," its intricate patterns reiterated, as they'd done many times before, "be buoyant, be busy, enthusiastic and bold."

Enid hurried home, and donning her granny glasses, expertly steamed the letter open. Addressed to Mr Edgar Evans in block capitals, and postmarked Llanelli, this letter promised to be interesting, which is why she'd genuinely wondered whether to mind her own business. As she had on several similar previous occasions, she'd warned herself that this tampering might one day hoist on her a painful dilemma. And, after all, she no longer had an incentive to rifle through Edgar's mail. No information so gained would be used by her to embarrass him or Rhiannon: her craving for revenge had long been doused by Peter. So yes, she had genuinely wondered, but as before, force of habit, curiosity and the Celyn, conspired to carry the day.

She prodded her glasses up the bridge of her nose, and began to read. The letter was written in longhand, which she guessed to be a lady's. It took two short sentences for Enid to regret her decision. She sensed with a stab of apprehension that the letter she held in her slightly shaky hand could be ammunition for Myfanwy, should she wish to discredit Edgar, and there was little doubt that she did... and would, with almost certain undesirable consequences for Peter. What a pity that would be, particularly now that he was on top of the world, settled at university and reconciled to the girl from Llanelli; yet, how could she withhold the letter from her best friend? In the old days, Myfanwy would have seen the letter anyway, and may even have opened it, but since Rhiannon or Edgar had been collecting the post...Oh! Better that the letter had been left alone, but it was too late to turn back; Enid's dilemma would persist even if she read no further. By tampering, she'd become aware, and a painful decision was unavoidable. Enid read on.

Soon, she crossed the bridge on her postal round and roundly castigated the river Celyn. Dressed for wet weather, with her bag beneath a cloak, she appeared uncharacteristically shapeless. Her load, which today would have been light anyway, was that little bit lighter still. Enid had left her options open. Her decision had been deferred.

"But shouldn't I do what inflicts the least pain? Myfanwy would never know, but then, how could I ever look her in the eye again if I don't show her the letter? She's my best friend! I depend on her, but would I feel as close to her with this business always weighing on my mind? Now wait a minute! Surely you can convince yourself that by not showing her the letter, you'd be doing her a favour, saving her a lot of fuss and bother; and what's more, acting for the common good. You shouldn't show it to her. I mean, what if you do, and get caught? That would be terrible! What would Peter think of you then? No! I think it's best that I deliver it tomorrow without saying a word, but... but there again, she's my... "

For the next hour or so, in a very fine rain, she debated. This indecision surprised her. Earlier, she'd have wagered that her loyalty to Myfanwy would have prevailed by now, but annoyingly, she found herself increasingly persuaded by the opposite case. Thus, torn and tiring of the whole affair, she debated till she approached another bridge, the little one over Tryweryn, just below her family farm.

"Oh, dear!"

She noticed Edgar kneeling on the narrow bridge, hammering away, with his back to her.

"Ooooh, dear!"

Edgar had assiduously avoided her all his life, but contact was unavoidable here. She vowed to be strong and civil. As she approached, Edgar glanced at her, but then went back to work as if she wasn't there.

"How are you, Edgar?

No acknowledgement, no response.

"Not a very nice day, is it?"

Indifference once more. This rejection, though quite routine, recalled memories of an idyllic youth, ruined by his ruthless mother, followed by exile, which he'd openly condoned. At a stroke, she was delivered of her dilemma. Coincidentally, Myfanwy met her that day, some way beyond the bridge.

"Can you come over this afternoon, Myfanwy? I've got something to show you."

"What d'you think, Myfanwy?"

Rarely was silence the response in this relationship. Though Myfanwy had thoughts aplenty, they hadn't quite been organised yet.

"What d'you think?" more urgently.

"Well, there's obviously something going on, isn't there, something that this woman wants to keep quiet about."

"Are you sure it's a woman?" like a shot from Enid, who'd had all day to dissect the situation.

"Well, I think so, don't you?"

Myfanwy appeared distracted. Actually, she'd already decided on her course of action. What preoccupied her was how to present it to Enid.

"D'you have paper and pencil, Enid?"

Myfanwy recorded the times and the venue mentioned in the letter.

"I've a feeling that you won't like what I'm going to say next, but I think we should burn the letter."

Enid looked aghast, as predicted.

"What? Burn it? I can't do that, Myfanwy, not even for you. I don't mind you reading it, but I've got to deliver it: it's my duty."

Good intentions were cast aside as Myfanwy pounced instinctively.

"And it's your duty to open it as well, I suppose?"

The one was clearly embarrassed, and blushed, while the other was thoroughly ashamed, and rushed to comfort her dearest friend.

"I'm so sorry, Enid. That was inexcusable, especially when I know you're doing this for me, but I've got to take advantage of this opportunity. I've just got to."

Kindness and self-interest coalesced in Myfanwy's decision to let Enid set the pace. Slouching beside her friend, Enid took her arm, and waited.

"What d'you think you'll do, Myfanwy?"

Myfanwy straightened and returned to her chair.

"I'm going to go and meet her in Llanelli, Enid. I have to, which is why Edgar mustn't see the letter, because I don't want him to turn up there as well, do I?"

Myfanwy's tone balanced empathy for her friend with firmness and a dash of bravado. From Enid's pained expression, the former was of no consolation. Yet, to her credit, she countered rationally.

"But you'll have no idea who she is, Myfanwy, and she might even be a man!"

"Oh! It's a woman, all right, and I think she'll make herself obvious, don't you?"

"But she won't tell you anything, Myfanwy. Why should she?"

"I'll just have to take my chances. Look, Enid, I know you're upset that I want to burn the letter, but that's the only way this will work. I feel terrible putting you on the spot like this, but this is so important to me."

Uncharacteristic silence once more. Again she waited for Enid to nudge their conversation forward.

Eventually, "What will you do if this woman cooperates?"

"Enid! You know how I feel about Edgar. I want to be able to turn the screws on him, that's all."

Enid then aired her heart-felt concern.

"But if you hurt Edgar, you'll hurt Peter as well, and I wouldn't want that."

"Enid fach, Peter doesn't care about his father. After all, he kicked him out… "

"No, no! What I meant was that if you shamed Edgar, that shame would rub off on Peter as well."

"Oh, OK, I understand what you're saying now. Look, Enid, no one in this valley is as pious and self-righteous as Edgar is these days, so any kind of exposure would ruin his life around here. So if I can pin something on him, I'm sure he'd go quietly, which means that anything I learn about him will never get out, will it? So can we burn the letter now, Enid?"

"What if I get caught, Myfanwy? Have you thought of that?"

"How can you get caught, Enid, if the evidence is destroyed? Can you imagine the woman who wrote it making a fuss? Above all, she wants to keep this quiet. Anyway, I can always say that I opened the letter, can't I? How about that?"

Enid lent forward, her chin cupped in hands, her elbows on her knees. She shook her head in hopelessness, and sighed.

"I was afraid it would come to this, Myfanwy. I've always thought I'd do anything for you, but this bothers me, bothers me enough that I can't make myself agree to it... not even for you. And it doesn't help really that I know you won't do it without my blessing. I'm right there, aren't I?"

Myfanwy nodded in resignation. For the first time since her arrival, Enid smiled, wanly with her head to one side. To Myfanwy, it was a sad smile. She presumed it expressed some relief, but more than that, it expressed Enid's deep regret at her inability to accommodate her very best friend. It seemed to say, Myfanwy thought, that given a whiff of a lifeline, she'd grab it. Well, she'd give her a lifeline, all right. Kneeling dramatically at Enid's feet, and gazing relentlessly into her eyes, she outlined the future.

"Enid, you're my closest friend, so listen now. This is what's going to happen," and continuing in an affected formal tone, "I'm going to find out something shocking about our dear Edgar, and when he realises what a pickle he's in, he will agree to, and then, carry out my conditions in the following order. First, he will sign over a quarter share of the farm to you. It should be more of course, but we won't push it. Then, he will sell the farm, and you'll get your money. After that, he will leave me, and given his situation, that will mean leaving the region altogether. And finally, we, you and I, will have to decide whether to live together here in the valley or move to Bala, say. Now then, Anti Enid, what d'you think about that?"

Myfanwy couldn't tell. She'd known better than to expect her friend to jump for joy. Under the circumstances, manifestations of a change of heart would be tempered by pride; by the natural desire not to appear shameless, shallow and self-serving. Even allowing for this, though, her inscrutability was baffling. Myfanwy really couldn't tell, until Enid, out of the blue, quite casually said, "You'll meet Peter's girlfriend at Mavis's. That'll be nice."

Fifty-one

M AVIS DAVIES WAS beside herself. This morning's interruptions could not have been more untimely. Just when she'd known instinctively that she'd need to be on her toes, the world it seemed had sought to distract her: Greda, whose work was normally routine on Saturdays, had already consulted her twice; Daniel, who rarely whined, had gone on and on about missing his sister; and now, Dai was after her! Such diversions had inevitably interfered with her antennae, which were on full alert, as they had been off and on since Myfanwy had phoned a week ago yesterday.

Myfanwy's uncharacteristic stubbornness during that phone conversation had lent an edge to the excitement surrounding her visit.

"It'll be lovely to see you, Myfanwy, but why don't you wait a few weeks? You can spend part of the time with Dai and me in Tenby then."

"No, I'd prefer to come next weekend, really!"

"But what's the rush?"

"Well, I haven't been for such a long time, and now Peter's gone to Liverpool, I decided not to delay any longer; and to tell you the truth, I can't wait to meet Greda!"

"Well, come a bit earlier than Thursday, then, so you can spend some time with Delyth before she leaves for college."

"Oh, no, I can't Mavis fach. I don't want to stay that long," and so on and so forth. It hadn't been like her sister, at all. Myfanwy's responses, which she'd considered marginally plausible at best, had left her nursing a very strange feeling that something was going on.

On her arrival on Thursday evening, Myfanwy couldn't have been warmer, nor more forthcoming on any topic bar the one that had mattered the most to Mavis. On the question of the timing of her visit, Myfanwy had fudged again, in Mavis's opinion, and had failed to dispel the funny feeling.

Then, a diversion yesterday in the form of Greda. She'd not been well, so the bloom had been off her beauty. Mavis had felt sorry for her, lacking her usual zest, not looking her best for Myfanwy. Happily, she'd more than made up for this though, with her enthusiasm for Peter. Mavis had been pleased that the two had got along so well, and proud of having brought them together; a little bit miffed perhaps, that of Peter's recent letter, more had been read to Myfanwy than to her. Overall though, she'd had to admit that it had been a happy day. Myfanwy had behaved so naturally again as to belie Mavis's suspicions. She'd humoured Dai, and fussed over Daniel, which had gone a long way towards making up for the Delyth disappointment. Yet, Mavis's funny feelings had resurfaced on and off, and this morning, they'd been vindicated. It was Saturday now and Myfanwy suddenly had seemed on edge. She'd even been edgy with Greda, who'd seemed hurt by her abruptness. Without a doubt, there was something going on! Mavis had wanted so badly to have all her wits about her, but the interruptions had put paid to that, and now Dai wanted to go over their holiday arrangements, of all things! Mavis Davies was beside herself, her antennae quivering in frustration. As she began to deal with Dai, Myfanwy left the kitchen for the office, where Greda was heard to say, "Excuse me, Mrs Evans. I would have liked you to have met my parents."

Mavis had to be blunt. She pressed her hand on Dai's chest, and asked him in a whisper to hold on for a minute. Predictably, he was highly amused, and silently mocked her, but she didn't care; not much of a toll to pay for intelligence.

"As a matter of fact, my mother did come to town with me

on the bus this morning, but she had to hurry home after doing her shopping. I was really sorry about that. It would have been nice for you to have met one of my parents, at least."

"That's odd," thought Mavis, "Dorothy's never in town on a Saturday morning, except for that time three weeks ago, and I felt funny about that as well."

"Perhaps next time, Greda," from Myfanwy, clearly not encouraging the conversation.

As if nothing had happened, Mavis went back to dealing with Dai, who was still smiling. When Myfanwy returned, Mavis for once had all her wits about her.

"I think I'll go for a walk, Mavis"

"Oh! I thought we were going shopping together this morning."

"I know, Mavis, but somehow I don't feel like it. I just need some fresh air; a brisk walk, I think."

"OK, then. I'll come with you, and we can go shopping afterwards."

"No, not this morning Mavis. I'd be better going for a walk on my own. To be honest, I don't feel a hundred percent."

"And you don't act like it, either," was Mavis's sarcastic thought, "This is all really strange!"

"So what time can I expect you back then?"

"I'm not sure, Mavis, but I'll definitely be back for lunch."

"All right. Perhaps we can shop this afternoon. What d'you think?"

"Perhaps."

What was going on? She'd known all along there was something fishy about this visit!

The previous evening, wishful thinking had followed confusion, before Dorothy had reluctantly accepted reality.

As she'd walked through the door, arriving home from work, Greda had asked, "Where are the others, Mami?" but without awaiting a reply, had continued, "Would you like to meet Peter's mother?"

Having spent close to a fortnight thinking of nothing but meeting the father, Greda's question had come as a shock.

"What d'you mean, darling?"

"Well, Peter's mother's staying with Mrs Davies. I was hoping you might like to meet her."

Dorothy had concealed her confusion by turning to the radio, and needlessly tuning it. With her back to Greda, she'd bought herself breathing room with, "Did you like her?"

"Yes, I did a lot. She was very nice, and she seemed pleased to meet me, too."

Still fiddling, and facing the other away, Dorothy'd asked, "And what about the father? Did you like him as well?"

"He's not there, Mami.! Come on, now! You remember Mrs Davies saying that Peter's parents aren't on speaking terms."

"Of course! I'd forgotten that, but I suppose he could have come down and is staying somewhere else."

Dangerously close to revealing her hand, Dorothy had got away with a daughterly reprimand.

"Mami, don't be so ridiculous, will you!"

With reality sinking in, Dorothy had retreated to the scullery, where she'd considered the remaining alternatives. Could Edgar have possibly sent his wife as an emissary? No! That would be absurd in light of what Greda had just said. Equally far-fetched was the notion that her visit was a mere coincidence, and of course, if it were not, then somehow Mrs Evans must have become privy to the contents of the letter. In this way, Dorothy had reluctantly settled on the only plausible explanation.

"So there's no point going to Llanelli tomorrow, then," she'd reasoned with herself, "I can't discuss this business with her. But how will I ever get in touch with Edgar? The same will happen to the next letter as well. Oh, dear! Perhaps the time has come to open up to Donald, and together we'll decide how to tell Greda the truth."

She'd dwelt on this thought for a while.

"No! We can't tell her. She'd never forgive us. I'll just have to think of some other way of getting through to Edgar. Shouldn't I go to Llanelli tomorrow though, just in case I'm missing something. It could be a coincidence, I suppose."

From the scullery, she'd inquired of Greda, "So, what's she like?"

"I told you, Mami, she's very nice."

"No, no, what I meant was what does she look like?"

"Mami, why d'you… "

"You know! How tall is she? Is she taller than me, for example?"

"No. She's about the same as you, I suppose."

"What else struck you about her? Does she have dimples like Nell next door?"

"Don't be silly, Mami! She does have a long neck, though, and a pretty large, distinctive mouth. Peter does too, actually."

"Gosh, Greda, you don't miss a thing."

"Well, she is a striking lady, Mami."

Somewhat more composed by then, Dorothy had thought she'd better put her head round the door, and smile.

The town hall was grand and stately, grey and built of stone, set off by brilliant flowerbeds and lawns, all newly mown. All around were railings, and on the far side, the town's main bus station. On a Saturday morning, in particular, this area was abuzz. Buses, mostly double-decker, disgorged hundreds of shoppers from surrounding villages. Most veered across the road in front of the town hall on their way to the shops; some scurried, others were unhurried, but by ten o'clock, all had to beware of early shoppers lurching towards them or across their paths, most of them grotesquely laden, intent on catching their buses home.

Despite the disorientating tendencies of human anthills, Dorothy pinpointed Mrs Evans almost immediately. Greda had been spot-on, she reflected with relief, particularly with reference to the long neck. Dorothy, herself, had dressed deliberately unobtrusively. She'd downplayed her height with the flattest of shoes, tied her long blonde hair in a bun and concealed it with a muffler.

Mrs Evans, it seemed, was as keen as Dorothy not to appear to be party to a rendezvous. She patrolled the pavement on the opposite side to the town hall. From a distance, Dorothy watched her pacing the same thirty yards, back and fore, over and over, glancing around covertly and occasionally gazing across the road. There was a moment when Dorothy was struck by the unfairness of it all, but the thought was stalled with vigour. As to her own agenda, she was so certain of Edgar's absence that she barely bothered to seek him out. The moves that she'd planned would be nothing more than a charade, but nevertheless, she too paraded; she made herself do it, just in case! Three times during the next twenty minutes, she virtually brushed shoulders with Mrs Evans. On the third, frustration wrung the lady's face. Again, Dorothy felt herself empathising with her adversary, liking her even, this time, but it made no sense to make contact... did it?

Later, during the afternoon session that she'd specified in the letter, it rained lightly. Dorothy, dampish, witnessed with bewilderment Mrs Evans's frustration degenerating into desperation. She'd resorted to stopping people in the street, all of them women, it seemed, and most of them roughly her own age. Dorothy felt sad. What was it that drove Mrs Evans to this? Suddenly, Dorothy felt protective of her so as to very nearly dissuade herself from fulfilling a fancy of actually being one of those middle-aged ladies approached by Mrs Evans. Well, it was more than a fancy, really. She'd had an idea that perhaps a brief, clinical contact might lead to something more. So, unfairly forewarned, and therefore forearmed, she subjected herself to Mrs Evans's agitated question, but in the end, gave her no possible reason to believe that she was the one... before moving on, in a quandary.

Removed from the fray, at the front of the top of a double-decker bus, Dorothy set about sorting things out. She still had little doubt that it would be better if Greda were kept in the dark; not better by far, as before, mind you, but... still better. As for Mrs Evans, she'd liked the look of her, she had to admit, and certainly had been tempted to confide in her. Yet, if she had, another would be in the know, along with by now, Mavis Davies, more than likely. So, as her conduit, the candidate of choice remained Edgar. She'd have to come up with some other way of getting in touch with him, that's all... and soon, Dorothy fach... soon!

The roads in Cynheidre were dry. The rain had passed the village by. Goodness knows why, but this lifted Dorothy's spirits.

She'd thought they'd never leave. Thank goodness the weather had improved enough, at last, for Dai and Daniel to decide to go to Dafen and watch a cricket match. Ever since Myfanwy, damp and down in the mouth, had returned from town, Mavis had been willing their departure.

"How will Myfanwy take it all, I wonder?"

Unusually for her, Mavis wasn't sure how best to broach the matter, but how could a sherry be taken amiss?

"Come on! Have a little glass, Myfanwy. I've got a nice,

sweet one for you. And let's go into the parlour. The light there is lovely this time of day, and we can gaze at the Gower."

They stood in the bay window, sipping in silence.

"Look!" from Mavis, perhaps a shade too brightly, she feared, "A little cloud is about to cover the sun."

Myfanwy, morose, was unresponsive to Mavis's comment. As the parlour was cast in shadow, Mavis laid her hand lovingly on her sister's shoulder, and besought warmly, "Tell me what's the matter, Myfanwy fach."

Myfanwy moved away decisively, but not in anger, Mavis thought.

"Please don't patronise me, Mavis. I can look after myself, you know."

Although this was curt, Mavis took heart from it, as she would have from any reaction.

"Myfanwy, I know that, but put yourself in my position. It's been obvious for over a week that there's something going on, and now it's just as obvious that it's not going very well. What am I supposed to do? Ignore it? Pretend that everything is fine and dandy?"

Myfanwy mum, and deep in the dumps. All Mavis could do was hope that her sister's spirits would pick up a beat when she got to the meat of the matter.

"Look, Myfanwy! I think I can help you. I'm not sure what's going on, obviously, but unless I'm completely wet, I know a couple of things that might help you."

"Tell me, then," immediately, in a challenging tone.

"See, that's the problem. I don't think I should, without being more in the know myself."

"My same, sweet, dear old sister," sarcastically from Myfanwy.

"I know! You think I've got my nose in everybody's business, don't you, and I suppose there's something to that, but I have a feeling I may have to protect someone else in all this. My main allegiance is to you, but... "

Her sister was still, and stubbornly silent again.

"Look! How about this? I'll tell you one of the things I know, and after that, you decide whether to play along. Is that fair?"

At least Myfanwy shrugged her shoulders! Mavis noticed the sun on the verge of re-emerging, soon to revitalise the room, and felt strangely optimistic suddenly, that her revelation would have a similar effect on her sister's spirits.

"Well, I'm going to tell you, anyway," and Mavis recalled in detail a day in Edgar's life that had been unaccounted for. On that day, twenty years earlier, homeward bound, he'd mysteriously extended a day trip on the train into two. Myfanwy had downed the last of her sherry, and Mavis showily followed suit.

"Why didn't you tell me sooner?"

"Oh, Myfanwy, you hadn't been married for long, and I thought you had enough on your plate as it was. Since then... well, you know... these moments pass, don't they?"

Myfanwy nodded understandingly, and added ruefully, "In any case, it doesn't matter. I'd have had nothing to go on till now," before abruptly leaving the room, to return with a piece of paper which she thrust at Mavis.

"Obviously, this isn't the actual letter. That was burnt, but this is more or less what it said."

A frantic scan was followed by a drawn-out whistle. Waving the paper as a politician would, Mavis gave notice of a change in style. She put pussyfooting behind her, for the ice had been broken now.

"I know exactly who wrote this."

"Who?"

"Greda's mother, my friend Dorothy."

"How d'you know?"

A pause.

"You're not going to like this, Myfanwy, but I followed you both times today."

"Oh, Mavis! How could you do that to me? How could you be so devious?"

No pause to parry this.

"Now, hang on! You're being rather pious, if I may say so. People in glass houses tend not to throw stones, you know. Speaking of devious, does anyone else immediately come to mind?"

"OK! But how do you know it's her?"

"I saw Dorothy both times, Myfanwy, this morning and after lunch, and she seemed to me to be keeping an appointment. Why otherwise would she walk back and fore in front of the town hall? Tell me that! Mind you, she wasn't exactly advertising herself, but she'd found out from Greda, hadn't she, that it wasn't the father who'd come, but… "

No resistance, she noticed, as she took Myfanwy's arm.

"… She walked close by you several times, Myfanwy, and even spoke to you in the afternoon."

Gazing towards Gower, Myfanwy shook her head in shame.

"Don't tell me you saw me stopping all those… I panicked, I know. You see, I was so sure I'd connect with her one way or another, that… "

"Hey! Come on now!" facing Myfanwy, "Don't be so hard on yourself. You were a sitting duck, Myfanwy fach. In any case, the point is that I'm sure it was Dorothy who wrote the letter, but I can only guess why she did it."

Myfanwy disengaged, and turned in surprise towards Mavis.

"Oh, Mavis! I'm not naive, you know! Edgar is Greda's father, isn't he? The dates fit perfectly. That means that she's Peter's half sister, right?"

She stared triumphantly at Mavis, who then developed the hypothesis.

"You can imagine that if Dorothy had latched onto this... and why shouldn't she have... she'd have naturally wanted to put an end to the romance... "

"... So she wrote to Edgar," concluded Myfanwy, "Insisting on meeting him, so that she could put pressure on him to present Peter with the facts, who then would break the romance off. All this rather than disclose the truth to Greda... "

"... And perhaps even more to the point, Donald," added Mavis, "We're sitting on a tinder box, Myfanwy."

They stood in the bay window, still. Mavis realised that despite the mind-boggling implications of their discovery, they were smiling at each other sincerely for the first time this visit. Soon though, Myfanwy became serious again.

"I must meet her, Mavis."

"I know. You've got to be sure, haven't you?"

Myfanwy nodded emphatically.

"I'm assuming that Edgar's the point of all this! Am I right?"

Emphatic nodding again.

"What exactly d'you have in mind?"

Surprising Mavis with her earnestness, Myfanwy described her grand design. Such a daring vision was rewarded with another drawn-out whistle, a "good for you, Myfanwy", and a long embrace, during which Mavis asked, "How d'you think Peter will take it?"

"Oh, he won't care. He's got over his dad by now."

"And Enid?"

"Well, she'll be doubly delighted, of course. She'll get rid of a pain and gain a companion."

Myfanwy faced her sister, and made her point with passion.

"So you see, this business is important to me, but to get what I want, I've got to confront him with absolute authority. I've got… " and she drummed in every "got", "… I've got to know that Greda's mother confirms our story. I've got to know some details, too. Where they met, for example; where they spent their time; where they lay together, even… that would make his head spin, wouldn't it… and I've got to know that she's prepared to support my story in public. I've just got to know all these things. I've got to see her, Mavis."

Rather than express disappointment over Myfanwy's obtuseness in even thinking of asking for Dorothy's public support, Mavis softly suggested to her sister, "Let me talk to her, Myfanwy."

"No, no! It's important to me that… "

"Slow down, Myfanwy, will you," a little more firmly this time, "We're in this together, you know. This is just as important to me as to you. Now, Dorothy's one of my good friends. You know that! Don't you think it makes sense for me to talk to her. Come on! Let me do it… please!"

Myfanwy acquiesced, and consigned to a waiting game, cooled off, visibly.

"I'll go and see her tomorrow. I know for a fact that Donald is away all day on a choir trip, and he's taking Greda with him. Now, isn't that a bit of luck!"

As would be expected, Dorothy put up a ritual front. Once it was dropped, however, her willingness to cooperate, considering how much was at stake, amazed Mavis; that is, until Dorothy revealed that Donald had always been aware of the circumstances of Greda's conception. Even Mavis, keen as she always was to extract information, had the sensitivity not to pursue that tidbit.

"As a matter of fact," Dorothy continued, "I came close to confiding in Myfanwy yesterday. You see, I'm wondering more and more whether to get it all over and done with by opening up to Donald and together telling Greda the whole story. What do you think, Mavis?"

Mavis's vast experience in eliciting information didn't necessarily qualify her to pass judgement on its dispensation, but on this topic, she spoke from the heart.

"It is tricky," she replied, circumspectly, "I know Greda would have a terrible shock. She would, wouldn't she? And it could really harm her. It's so hard to be sure, of course, but I wouldn't take the risk of telling her. I believe you're on the right track as you are, Dorothy."

"What makes it even harder, though, is that Greda, as you know, Mavis, hasn't had the best of attitudes towards boys, but this affair has been different. It was a turning point in that respect. So an abrupt rejection by Peter would be a huge setback for her. It would vindicate her caution and nervousness in the past, wouldn't it?"

"Yes, I know, but isn't that something she'd be more likely to get over, given time? I still think you're doing the right thing by keeping her in the dark."

Once they'd agreed on that, Mavis candidly described Myfanwy's grand design, and laid out her requests, bar the one considered impractical. Rather than flog that dead horse, she emphasised how crucial it was to Myfanwy's credibility with Edgar that she be armed with intimate details that would shock him. Dorothy divulged them all... well, nearly all, anyway. Keen, it seemed, to show that her baby was not unwanted, Dorothy even admitted, without elaboration, to her conniving role in the affair. In return, she asked only that Mavis promise on her sister's behalf to convince Peter to call it off while withholding the truth from Greda, and throughout, keeping both their names out of the public domain. Thus, a bargain was struck.

On her way home on the bus, in a more detached mood, Mavis became concerned. How could she, so perfectly calmly, have spoken on behalf of a sister who sought her husband's scalp so badly that she could well view any bargain as one begging to be broken? For an uncomfortable few minutes, the excitement and satisfaction of being in the flow was seriously marred by regret, which she eventually suppressed, of necessity, for she was in too deep to turn back. And as sisters, they were in this together, weren't they, as she'd sincerely told Myfanwy only yesterday. So Mavis was committed, but Mavis was concerned.

As well she might have been, for Myfanwy was determined to redesign her life. Armed with much, she would confront her husband with more. As part of her pitch, she would assure him that Dorothy was prepared to vouch for her... and in public! Had Edgar called her bluff, would she have kept to her side of the bargain? As it happened, he would fold, despite predictable resistance to his plan from Rhiannon. To deflect his mother's focus, Edgar would initially reveal to her only his determination to leave the valley.

"Are you out of your mind, Edgar? Why this sudden decision to go?"

"It's personal, Mam. That's all I can tell you."

Rhiannon would be shocked to the core, and angry too at being kept in the dark.

"And who'll take care of the farm when you're gone?"

"It's the farm that upsets me the most Mam, because I suppose we'll have to sell it. You can't run it without me, and I wouldn't be surprised that when I'm gone, Myfanwy will move out as well."

"Don't tell me Myfanwy's behind all this."

"No, no, no! This has nothing to do with her."

With that lie, he would eventually gain his mother's compliance. Fortunately for Edgar, age had weakened her will for a fight: the Rhiannon of old would have been ruthless in defence of her farm and relentless in pursuit of the truth.

Later when told by Edgar that Enid would share in the proceeds of the sale, Rhiannon would dig her heels in again, and her interest in getting to the bottom of the affair would be rekindled; but it would be too late to matter. She would already have convinced herself that at her stage in life, leaving the farm might not be such a bad idea after all.

So in the end, Rhiannon would relent on Enid as well.

Remarkably, by Christmas, Myfanwy would achieve her ambitious ends. Rhiannon, however, wouldn't accept the thought of being the second member of her family to be hounded from the valley in a century. She would stay, and live within striking distance of the chapel. As a result, Myfanwy and Enid would find staying in the valley unattractive; they would move to Bala, where they'd see much more of Peter anyway.

So, Edgar would go quietly, as Myfanwy had predicted. It was Peter who would put up resistance.

Fifty-two

S HE WAS STILL sad. In reflection of her mood, her brow was furrowed and her mouth set half open. She was sitting on a ledge in the lotus position, recollecting a moment almost exactly eight weeks earlier, when she and Peter had touched at this very spot, touched incessantly as if they were blind. She turned to the lonesome tree and smiled faintly, as if it were a friend. Then, rocking forward and leaning on her hands, she peeped over the edge. The memory was too painful, so she retreated immediately. As she rocked backwards, she could swear that she saw, out of the corner of her eye, someone move on the ridge to her left, but there was no one there. She glanced at the ridge several times later, often surreptitiously, hoping to surprise whoever she thought she'd seen, but there was never anyone there. She felt cross with herself for experiencing disappointment. At that, she flicked the locks from her forehead, and felt very, very sad again.

Myfanwy had visited Peter at his lodgings in Liverpool on the Sunday after returning from Llanelli, intent it seemed, on telling him all that she'd learnt on her visit. Once only had she trucked with the truth, when omitting Anti Enid's role in the affair. At first, his face had betrayed confusion, then incredulity. Distress followed, at which point Myfanwy had taken his hands in hers, and paused. Later, the story told, Peter had stared at the one window in the room, his face frozen and expressionless. He'd suspected nothing, so this bolt had truly come from the blue. He'd been toppled from the top of the world, and felt crushed. Myfanwy's occasional clumsiness in attempting to console him had suggested that she'd been unprepared for this as well.

Eventually, without looking her in the eye, "Does this mean Mam what I think it does?"

Myfanwy had nodded slowly and emphatically, and then there'd been silence again, during which Peter, to his credit, had acknowledged other sadness in this incredible affair: foremost of course, Greda's likely devastation; then his father's surprising infidelity, the hurt his mother must feel over that; and finally, Greda's mother's extraordinary machinations. On these he'd dwelt, till his mind again had honed in on the hollow in his heart. Then suddenly he'd queried, "Mam, are you sure this is all true?"

"Yes, Peter bach. Anti Mavis spoke to Greda's mother herself. I'm so sorry about this, Peter, but I don't know what else I could have done. I had to tell you, didn't I?"

Magnanimous in distress even, Peter had embraced his mother; her mind had been eased, only to be disquieted immediately by an animated question.

"Even if Greda is my half-sister, why can't she be my wife?"

"Well, I should have thought that was obvious. For a start, it's illegal, and you couldn't have children."

"So what! Greda and I could easily agree on that. What other reasons are there, Mam?"

Peter's blue eyes and prominent mouth had come alive. Myfanwy had appeared perplexed by his recovery; no reason could she muster but, "It wouldn't seem right, that's why," with the emphasis on the "seem".

"Mam, that doesn't carry much weight with people in love, and it makes no sense that an external event, which was out of our control should dictate how Greda and I feel about each other."

Peter had stumbled on a lifeline, he'd clung to it and it had worked. For a further half an hour, he'd challenged his mother to refute his reasoning. This he'd done firmly, but sensitively as well. As she'd prepared to leave, Myfanwy's face reflected her frustration at Peter's reaction. Still, she'd left him with, "And as much as I hate to mention this again, Peter, please remember when you talk to Greda that I have promised her mother that you won't reveal the truth."

To Peter, on a high, that had made no sense at all.

While with his mother, Peter had looked forward to being on his own. However, she, as an ineffective adversary, had helped sustain his high. In her absence, his spirits had come off the boil, his mind had returned to basics. The injustice of it all had rankled.

"And everything was going so well. I was so happy with my studies, with Greda and myself. Now, along comes this bombshell. It's so unfair."

Yet, his lifeline had not deserted him; he'd remained sufficiently optimistic to write a letter of everlasting love. No inkling would Greda gather of his emotional rollercoaster.

"I'd prefer to tell her face to face when she visits me in a fortnight."

Later, lying in bed, he'd pictured his mother. He'd felt for her. This couldn't have been easy for her either, and then to be challenged by her child. He would apologise to her, for certain. Still, how could she expect him not to tell Greda the truth? Then, he'd fallen into a troubled sleep. At five in the morning, he'd awakened to a different and disturbing world. Disappointingly, the hollow had returned to his heart, and to his disbelief, hollow too had rung the reasoning that previously had sustained him. He'd found he could not so readily refute his mother's phrase, especially when he'd repeated it with the emphasis on the "right".

"It wouldn't seem right."

Overnight, his lifeline had frayed; he'd wondered how he

could have slept at all. His impotence in the face of that simple little phrase had confused him, and his inability to reverse this drift to doubt had deeply saddened him, even frightened him a bit. How could it be that his future with Greda, which yesterday had appeared manageable, today was slipping away? This further emotional twist had proved to be one too many. He'd felt trapped in his flat... and severely distressed again. So what could he do, but seek counsel and comfort from Doctor and Delilah. By nine, he was on a train to Bala.

Delilah had been shaken by Peter's arrival, while Walter had gone wild with excitement. As she'd anxiously trawled for an explanation for his visit, she'd hoped above all that Peter hadn't erupted again.

"Where's Doctor, Delilah?"

"He's on a trip, Peter. He'll be fishing the Teifi all week. I know he'll be sorry to miss you, but why are you here? What's happened?"

So to Delilah, his tale had been a relief of sorts. In the kitchen, he'd told it at the table over tea. Evidently, 'twas an enormous relief for him, for when it was over, he'd cried like a baby in her arms and had seemed reluctant to leave them.

So, comfort had come first; counselling would follow. In an attempt to further distract Peter, and to afford herself more time to think, Delilah had suggested a walk to the lake with Walter. There on a bench, shoulders hunched like two sorry-looking crows, they'd sat, while Walter had hounded the real McCoys. After a while, Delilah had moved close to him, and pulling him closer still, had said, "Look at the Aran, Peter: both peaks are as clear as can be. A month ago when we were here, they were shrouded in cloud, remember?"

Peter had glanced briefly at the far end of the lake and had reassumed his hunched pose.

"Peter," continued Delilah ardently, "Will you come to bed with me tonight? I've always wanted to sleep with you, you know. Doctor's away and Walter won't tell."

Delilah had felt Peter stiffen. After a moment's stillness, he'd pulled away and stared at her in horror. She'd stared back, poker-faced. She'd held his gaze, and then to her huge relief, his face had gradually relaxed into a knowing smile.

"I know what you're up to, Delilah."

Without changing her expression, she'd insisted, "Well, d'you want to sleep with me or not?"

Peter had shuffled his feet, waved his hands and shaken his head.

"Ok, ok, ok," he'd answered, "I'll play your game if I must. No, Delilah, I don't want to go to bed with you."

"Why not? Don't you love me enough?"

"Oh yes, I love you enough, Delilah, but it wouldn't seem right. In fact, it would be wrong."

At that invocation of his mother's phrase, his smile had broadened, and Delilah, unable to carry it off any longer, had smiled broadly as well. Spontaneously, they'd embraced and lingered. Then she'd called Walter, and holding Peter's hand, had taken the long route back to Bala, along the lake.

"I know my relationship with you isn't quite like Greda's," she'd continued, in earnest once again, "but there are parallels, aren't there?"

Delilah had introduced the notion of a correspondence between herself and Greda.

"For Greda, think Delilah," she'd seemed to be saying. Peter had nodded thoughtfully.

"We naturally impose constraints on ourselves in certain situations. I did with you and you have done with me. I'm an old woman," over Peter's protestations, "and convention constrained you. Your instincts too helped define the way you behaved with me, not to mention your moral code."

Here she'd stopped and smiled sympathetically at Peter.

"If Greda had been your cousin, say, and you'd grown up with her, you'd have loved her but you wouldn't have fancied her. Convention, instinct and possibly common sense would have constrained you: the same old built-in constraints again."

"But I didn't grow up with her, and I did fancy her," pleadingly from Peter.

"I know, I know, that's the tragedy, but don't you think by now that you have to work your way back to where you would have been if you had grown up with her, knowing that she was your half-sister. The same constraints will be leading you in that direction anyway, and if you fight them, they may make your life a misery. Doesn't that make sense to you?"

Thoughtfully he'd nodded again.

"And of course," she'd continued, "we haven't even mentioned the business of having babies."

Delilah had promised herself not to betray any sadness at that point, but judging from Peter's expression, she'd failed. In an attempt to divert attention, she'd asked, "And how do you feel by now, Peter."

With a sympathetic smile that said he'd read her mind, he'd replied, "Well, I don't feel confused anymore, or fearful. For that, I have you to thank, but I am sad. And you, Delilah?"

"Well, I'm sad too, but won't be for long. Thanks for asking, Peter."

And again they'd embraced. Then they'd walked in silence. Delilah had thought it wise to allow Peter to settle into his new-found state of mind.

Later, during lunch, Peter had sought her counsel again.

"Despite my mother's plea, I've got to tell Greda the truth, don't you think?"

"Of course you do. It'll be a shock to her, but skeletons in the cupboard never lead to good. Anyway it's important that she knows she didn't misjudge you, and if I'm not mistaken, she's going to be one of your best friends, Peter."

"But how can it work, Delilah, given the way we feel?"

"Constraints, Peter bach, constraints. They'll reassert themselves, and sooner than you think, especially if you don't fight them. I know the adjustment won't be easy, but be brave, Peter. Though constrained, you and Greda will be close, you'll see, just like you and me, and how could our relationship be better?"

Peter had smiled shyly. Delilah hadn't allowed him time to think before continuing to develop the correspondence between herself and Greda.

"You think she's kind, don't you? And generous and wise and trustworthy?" and with a naughty smile, "You did say that she reminded you of me! So why wouldn't you be the best of friends? Why wouldn't you love her just as you love me?"

Quiet had prevailed and Peter had pondered.

"Peter," Delilah had continued, "I was worried about you this morning, but don't you think you feel well enough now to go back to Liverpool this evening? There's a train at four." After a pause, he said, "Deliliah, I'm not sure how to break this to Greda: she'll be really hurt."

Delilah had leant towards him, sensing an opportunity to complete the correspondence.

"I think I can guess how she'll feel, so just imagine for a moment that I am her. I would have appreciated being given an inkling in advance of my visit, so that at least I'd be on my guard. Then, when told the facts, I would need to be completely reassured that my judgement with respect to you hadn't been awry. That won't be easy, Peter, constrained as you will be. Next, I'd need to be convinced that we would remain the closest of friends; and finally, and possibly the most difficult, it would be nice if you could create a distraction for me; to help take my mind off you. I've no idea what that could be, but it would be nice."

Alone in his compartment, Peter, though sad, had been in awe of both Delilah and the power of companionship. His visit had been invaluable; his only regret being that he'd had no time to apologise to his mother.

Greda had been sorely tempted to cancel her visit to Liverpool. Looking back, it was just as well that she'd already bought her ticket. Her mother's attitude towards the trip had been really unsettling. Making no bones about her disapproval, she'd disconcertingly shied away from justifying it. To make matters much worse, Peter's last two letters, while still friendly, had been inexplicably restrained. What could she have assumed but that he'd been preparing her for another rejection? Little had she known that Peter had been following Delilah's script, as he would on the afternoon of her arrival, with the result that she'd gone to bed terribly upset and desperately sad, but at least not questioning her own judgement. She'd left him early for her bed and breakfast, finding she couldn't bear to be in his presence. All she'd wanted was to be comforted by him and to comfort him in turn, for he too was clearly hurting. Restraining herself had been too painful; it was better to be alone, but not much. The foundations of her life had been fractured. How could she sleep when so confused regarding her relationships with mother, father and friend? Would she feel the same about her brothers? And would she seek out her real father? How could she sleep? Eventually, she'd taken the pill that Peter had given her.

The following day, Sunday, had been marginally better. She'd asked Peter that they not talk much, but just walk and be with each other. She'd reasoned that if active, she'd be less likely to be mired in her misfortune, and in turn be more likely to become comfortable with him again. So they'd walked down famous streets and along a famous river and past innumerable benches. As they'd left a tearoom, he'd taken her arm as she imagined a brother would. She'd almost not minded. Soon though, she'd had to stop, and ironically, smiling at Peter for the first time that day, had whispered, "I am so desperately sad."

He'd hugged her spontaneously. In that embrace it had been hard for Greda not to imagine that this would lead to a kiss. Foolishly, she'd allowed herself the fleeting hope that this was merely a bad dream. Reality had ensued, and so had a deepening despondency. Then she'd cried quietly. He'd held her till she'd settled down, and then they'd walked again. Looking at his feet, Peter had ventured, "I still love you, Greda, but I'm doing my very best to love you in a different way."

At that moment, she'd felt as sad as she had the night before: so sad for him, so sad for herself that this time too she'd wanted so much to be alone. Yet somehow, shame had scuppered her selfish instinct.

"Poor thing! He's still hurting so much," she'd whimpered to herself, "Can't you tell he's crying for help?"

So rather than retreat, she'd taken his arm firmly, and had felt a welcome, if momentary, warmth.

Over supper, she'd referred to one of his letters, and had asked him to describe again his change of heart about south Walians. At that, he'd come alive, describing the experience in sentimental detail.

"The sequence of events was, shall we say, spiritual," he'd concluded, "culminating in Taid becoming my mentor once again."

She'd felt a surprising warmth for Taid then, recalling that Peter had once written, "Taid would have loved you, Greda. I know it!"

That's when it had struck her that his Taid was hers as well:

another in a string of constraints, but for the first time she hadn't minded.

That night again, she'd fallen asleep with an aid.

The next morning, she'd met Peter before his first lecture.

"D'you think we'll be friends, Peter?"

"Oh, Greda! I'm banking on it. You're my sister. You'll be my best friend," with an emphasis on "best".

"But how can we be only friends?"

Parroting Delilah, he'd assured her that natural constraints would do the trick if they were allowed to. Greda had been sceptical, while conceding that he'd had a fortnight to think about these things.

"To tell you the truth, Greda, occasionally, at the thought of you as my sister, I feel blessed, and given time, I'm sure the same will happen to you."

As much as she'd have liked to believe him, she'd felt far from blessed when they'd parted. Still, despite her persistent confusion and sadness, her comfort level with Peter had picked up. On this she had tried to focus as she'd tramped the famous streets for hours.

At dinner, Peter had returned to the subject of Welshness. Greda had thought it odd, but hadn't minded. She'd have approved of any topic that energised him.

"Funnily enough," Peter had said, "Now that I've moderated my views, I find I'm even more fiercely Welsh than before. Ironic, isn't it?"

Pressing matters of the heart had preoccupied her mind for days, and yet, somehow, she'd found a space and felt happy for him. His guileless enthusiasm on the subject of his homeland had struck a chord. In fact, her own Welshness had touched her then, as it never had before. Her attempt to analyse this feeling had been interrupted.

"Thanks to you, Greda, I'm a new person. You know, don't

you, that you're the one who forced the catharsis. Mind you, I don't think I'll ever fully live down my atrocious behaviour on Gower, even though I think I've rebuilt my bridges with most people: Doctor and Delilah, certainly; Mam and Taid too; and, of course, most importantly with you. I hope I have, anyway?"

She'd nodded, smiling enigmatically, as she'd flicked a lock from her brow.

"Yes, I've made it up to everyone who matters, really, except for our friend, David. I still feel terrible about him."

Excepting recent, difficult days, Greda had thought of David fairly regularly, and always with warmth. At the mention of his name, she'd pictured him, as she'd done each time before, forlorn on the Gower, stunned by Peter's outburst. His round, gentle face tinged in mystery by some strange darkening of his freckles, and as before, her brow had furrowed in sympathy with them.

"Perhaps I'm conceited," Peter had continued, "but I really think I hurt him, permanently I mean. That's an awful thought, but I've a feeling he'd forgive me too, if only I could find him. We don't have a clue where he lives, do we?"

As Greda had shaken her head thoughtfully, it dawned on her that thanks to Peter, her mind had flown its shackles for a moment.

"Will you help me find him, Greda?"

"Me?"

"You did like him, didn't you?"

She'd thought that a funny question, especially in that context. What's more, she'd had the impression that Peter was not himself: suddenly he was pressing, as if playing a part.

"The thing is, Greda, he's not just any old 'him', you know. I've this conviction now that he's my blood brother. You remember my dragon, don't you? Well, I think he's got one too, and you know what that means, don't you. I can feel this connection in my bones. Find him for me, Greda, will you?"

She'd shrugged her shoulders slightly, and drawn her lips.

"Greda, come on now. The three of us are blood brothers and sisters, really, after our fantastic experience together. Wouldn't you like to get to know him better, as well?"

That's when she'd realised that there was more to this than met her eye. Though unaware of Delilah's script, she'd got the gist of it.

"He's unbelievable," she'd thought, "I know he's still hurting over me, so this gesture must be so hard for him. He'll do anything for me."

Though his ploy had been awkward and untimely, she'd loved him for it.

"Well? Would you?" he'd repeated.

She'd shrugged her shoulders again.

"You do like him, don't you?"

"Yes, I do like him, but… "

Again she'd pictured David's face, gentle, tinged in mystery, and again her brow had furrowed… noticeably.

"He'll go back to the ledge, I promise you, Greda. He may have been already, but I bet you he'll go again. Will you go there as well, Greda, and leave him a message, or something? Will you, please?"

She'd nodded, unsure if she'd meant to.

Early the following morning, at the station, he'd said, "It was my dragon that convinced your mother, wasn't it? I've always thought of it as my friend, so as sad as I am, I have to believe it's for the best that it protected us when it did."

The thought had hurt terribly, and she'd still felt all at sea, but she'd almost been inclined to begin to agree. A few minutes later, she'd waved her brother goodbye.

She was still very, very sad. Having glanced in vain at the ridge one last surreptitious time, she raised herself from the lotus position. She took her time selecting a sharp, light coloured stone. Then, on the steep rock that rose from the ledge, directly opposite her friend, the tree, she carefully scratched in capital letters, Cynheidre. She thought that should be message enough, if David ever returned to the ridge, as Peter had assured her that he would.

Soon after, she followed the route that the three of them had trod in virtual silence that was sublime. She didn't stop at the dip where she and Peter had lain. Rather, she carried on to the point on the headland where David had stood. There, she gazed in wonder at the seashore with its bays and heathered headlands. She pictured the coastline that defined her lovely country on three sides, and surprised herself when she wished it had been four. At that moment, she felt blessed. She recalled, with satisfaction, that Peter had assured her she would.

Names With Keys First

{h} stands for hard version of consonant

{ } stands for "rhymes with"

Black underline indicates emphasis

Elfed   El..ved{bed}

Rhiannon   Ri[we]..ann..on

Geraint   G{h}..er{hair}..ain{nine}..t

Myfanwy   Myf{love}..ann..oo-ee as dipthong

Taid   Tied

Nain   Nine

Dai   Di, which is short for Diana

Dacu   Da{pa}..c{h}..u{me}

Mamgu   Mam{ram}..g{h}..u{me}

Place Names With Keys First

{h} stands for hard version of consonant

{ } stands for "rhymes with"

Black underline indicates emphasis

[ ] stands for "English meaning"

Words with "LL" omitted because they're impossible to describe

Capel **Ce**lyn [Chapel Holly]   Cap..el{well} C{h} el in

Ar**en**ig Fawr[big]   Ar{far}..en{ten}..ig{dig} Vow..r

Tony**pan**dy   T..on..uh..pan..dee

Borth y Gest   Borth{forth}..uh..G{h}..est{haste}

Mynydd[mountain] **Sy**len   Myn{fun}..ydd{with} Sullen

Cyn**hei**dre   Cyn{tin}..hey..dre{there}

Afon[ri**ver**] Try**we**ryn   A{la}..von{con} Try{the}..weryn{bearin'}

Rhondda   Rhonda but with soft "th" for "d"

Cymru[**W**ales] Fydd[will be]   Cym{come}..ree Vydd{seethe}

Cwm[valley]   C{h}..wm{sum in sumac}

Pont[**bridge**] Fach[small]   Pont{font} Va{la}..ch which is the sound
in loch

Tongue Tied is just one of a whole range of publications from Y Lolfa. For a full list of books currently in print, send now for your free copy of our new full-colour catalogue. Or simply surf into our website

www.ylolfa.com

for secure on-line ordering.

TALYBONT CEREDIGION CYMRU SY24 5HE
e-mail ylolfa@ylolfa.com
website www.ylolfa.com
phone (01970) 832 304
fax 832 782